Me Before Lou

Jess Torres

Rendition Publishing, LLC

Ebook ISBN: 979-8-9902154-0-5
Print ISBN: 979-8-9902154-1-2

Contributions by Drew Torres
Edited by Michelle Kowalski
Cover designed by Rendition Publishing
Character illustration by BookedForever

Contents

For Burty & the Beasts

One

"They spray-painted my house."

"Well, it's not really *your* house."

"Hannah, I signed the offer. I explained to the lender exactly where every single dollar of mine has come from in the past five years. I wrote a big, fat earnest check so I can close in twenty-one days and let the bank take every penny left to my name. It's my house."

Hannah grimaces and turns to reexamine the glossy black outline marring the white siding. "At least it's anatomically correct."

"How so? Because they added little hairs?"

"That, and this part curves a bit to the left."

"That's what you think is most accurate?"

"How many men have you met with perfectly straight penises?"

"Can't say I've ever taken a level to a guy's member to verify."

"Oh, you'd know. The curvy ones do magic things."

I groan loudly.

"Come on," she says, nudging me. "Let's hit the smoothie stand like we planned. I'll even buy your drink since all your dollars are apparently tied up in this penis-painted house."

I clock her playfully in the shoulder, but she hardly flinches and prances back to the street.

"We can even hit the dog park," she adds.

"Without a dog?"

"We can pretend."

"We really don't need to do that. I haven't been there since—"

"I know. That's why we're going. You clearly need some soft, squishy, adorable little faces you can rub your nose in."

It's not the worst idea. In fact, a face full of fur and a whiff of puppy breath is the closest thing to a vacation I can afford right now, so I abandon my efforts to scrape the paint with my fingernails and follow her.

We cross the street and trek two blocks over to our go-to stand. San Francisco has a food truck or a drink cart or a pot shop on wheels on practically every corner, but this is the only place that doesn't charge fourteen dollars for an organic, sugar-free, added-protein kale smoothie.

Hannah nearly gags as I recite my order. "That can't possibly be good for you."

I eye the hot-pink drink complete with whipped cream an employee is pushing into her hands. "Ditto."

Hannah just shrugs and stuffs a dollar in a divided jar intended to capture tippers' votes for their favorite superhero. Dropping a bill on the left half signifies a vote in favor of Superman. The right half, a vote in favor of Captain America. I'm not surprised when she goes right.

"So you're ready to fully suburbanize, huh?" she asks.

"We only come to this neighborhood every weekend *pretending* like we live here," I admit. "Is it really so bad I'm making it official?"

"I think you'll miss the city life."

"I think I'll enjoy having a backyard that isn't a patch of cement and an overflowing dumpster. Besides, the city-folk charm is a little old these days."

Hannah and I round the corner and spot the dog park, a gated field bordered with maple trees and divided down the middle by dirt paths trampled into existence over years of hundreds of dogs playing chase.

"I'm not sure the opposite side of the bridge will get you away from 'city folk,'" Hannah says as she unlatches the gate for us to enter.

She's not wrong. There's a tall, thin woman strutting in a pair of white go-go boots as soon as we enter. She's wearing a fur coat—ironically, probably genuine—and has a sheet of blonde hair parted precisely down the middle that dusts cheekbones sharp enough to maim anyone who gets too close. If I had to take a guess, she owns the pretty Afghan hound who's smugly skirting a particularly friendly rottweiler trying to stick his nose where it doesn't belong.

"But look," I counter, skipping to catch up to Hannah as she cuts left, "there's a totally normal old couple. And they've got a golden retriever."

Hannah eyes the white-haired pair, the woman clinging to her husband's arm as a goofy, long-haired dog trots at their side, pilfered stick in his mouth.

"Sure, but for every adorable old couple, there's three guys like that."

She shamelessly jabs a finger toward a man lying on the ground. He's got a black beard that needs to be trimmed and a kitschy T-shirt covered in dried grass that fails to hide the print across the front: "Schnauzers are like potato chips. You can't have just one."

A trio of black, wiry-haired schnauzers pounce on him, one tugging his earlobe and another with a hold on his combat boots. The third bows down in play, barking like a broken police siren.

"At least they're happy," I say, though I'm not even convincing myself.

"Get a load of this chick," Hannah deflects, letting out a chirrupy laugh, and I begin to get the impression she only accompanied me to the dog park for the people-watching.

She drives an elbow into my ribs and I crumple, but not before I catch a glimpse of the woman running our direction. She's got ashy-brown hair, a color straight from blatantly Photoshopped images on a Pinterest board that only incredibly patient hairstylists even bother to replicate, and it's rippling in the wind like long, elegant ribbons.

But I'm not fixated on the hair for long—and neither is anyone else, surely. Her skin-tight, baby-pink shirt guarantees it, wine-red font scrawled atop a screen-printed image of something that looks like a plain wooden box.

Scratch that. It's got multiple rows with carved-out divots. It's a wine rack.

"'Eyes off my rack'?" Hannah bemoans, reading the print on the woman's shirt before I fully register it. She's done nothing to temper her voice, and it's loud enough a passing dog stops, yips at her, and then trots off.

"No, no! Please come back," the woman cries, a crease in her brow surely undoing months of Botox.

"Oh no," I mutter as the dog she's apparently chasing beelines our direction.

It's a bully breed—a mutt, probably—but there's pit bull or terrier in there somewhere. It's obvious in the jowls and the square head and the burly shoulders and the absolute power behind every gallop. His paws are big enough he nearly flattens a passing Yorkie, and he kicks up turf in his wake, flinging mud in his mom's direction and spraying grass like a bagless lawnmower.

"I'd run too if I were him," Hannah jokes, and I barely have time enough to shove my half-drunk smoothie into her hands before teeth and tongue and dripping drool are all over me.

I shriek, partly out of shock and then partly because he's not attacking me—not aggressively, at least. He's got his big nose pushed into my palm, sniffing and snorting, clearly scrounging for treats, but when he realizes I have none, he doesn't even care. He nuzzles harder, spreading lines of drool with every nudge and then butting his head against my leg.

"Lou?" I say, the name slipping out unexpectedly.

"No, no, mister," the woman warns again, and I wonder if she really thinks a beast this size has any concept of her gentle command. "That's very naughty of you. Very naughty, mister!"

She teeters to a halt in front of us, propping one hand on her hip and brushing loose locks over her shoulder, making her hair fall effortlessly back into place.

"You are *not* being a very good listener today," she chastises once more.

She tucks her stiletto-shaped nails under the dog's red collar, trying—and failing—to pull him back.

"It's really no problem," I start. "Honestly, it's fine. He's just—"

But she tugs harder, sticking her booty out as she does so, and I wonder if she's got a catchy little phrase on the back pockets saying, "no tailgating."

"You just get right over here," she demands, and then she spins on her heels (yes, *high* heels) and primly calls for assistance from someone running up behind her—someone who's got his eyes on me.

"Millie?"

"Steve?" I glance from him to the dog and back again. "Oh my god, this *is* Lou."

The dog fights the woman's grip, panting and whining, and it's then I recognize those big, brown eyes. He's older now—it's been at least a year—so he's grown into his oversize jowls and some of the puppy wrinkles around his eyes. He was thirty pounds when I saw him last, and now he's got to be well over eighty. The woman doesn't stand a chance at holding him back, and sure enough, he slips her grip and bounds for me once more.

I'm on the grass in another second, and Lou drives his snout right into my neck.

"Oh geez, sorry, Millie," Steve says, and he finally hauls Lou off me, clipping a red leash onto his collar.

"Cap!" Hannah yells, raising both smoothies in the air.

I almost forgot she was standing next to me, probably dancing around in glee as I got pummeled. Meanwhile, the dog-chasing woman threatens the integrity of her Botox again.

"Cap?"

"It's an old nickname," Steve blusters, and Lou bounds excitedly, clearly in attempt to escape capture once more.

"What are you doing here?" I ask.

"What are *you* doing here?" Steve counters—a fair question.

"Smoothies and people-watching. Duh," Hannah fills in, and then she drops to her knees and puts her face right in Lou's, holding our drinks to the side as he gladly switches targets and drags his tongue across her cheeks. "It really has been too long, my sweet little boy!"

I'd argue it's been exactly as long as I intended.

"Sorry, I'm being rude," I say, and I scramble to my feet, quickly wipe my dog-slobbered hands on my jeans, and reach out to greet the woman. "I'm Millie."

"I see," she responds, though she makes no attempt to shake my hand—which I can't really blame her.

"So sorry," Steve jumps in, and he slips his free arm around the woman's waist. "This is Persephone—Seph."

I retract my hand and nod politely, and the introduction is enough to coax Hannah back to her feet. She shoves my smoothie back into my hands and then wags a finger between Seph and Steve.

"Oh, so you're..."

"My girlfriend," Steve fills in quickly.

"Aye, aye, Cap!"

"You know it's not Cap, and never has been my ranking, right?" he says, a small frown tightening his lips.

"Oh, buddy. It's never had anything to do with your ranking."

Steve cocks his head and tries to keep his lips from quirking into a smile. It's a familiar look, and the way he puffs up his chest and stoically flexes his free arm like he's holding a shield only proves Hannah's point. The guy's the spitting image of a wholesome, all-American, baby-saving superhero.

"It's detective," Seph offers up, and just as easily as when we caught a glimpse of her cringey T-shirt, all eyes are back on her. She leans into Steve and flattens a long-fingered hand on his chest. "Detective Steve Rogers, San Francisco Police Department. Isn't that right, honey?"

Steve doesn't blush—he's always had that on lockdown—but I can tell it goes against every modest bone in his body for her to broadcast a fresh title like that.

"Just promoted?" I ask, hoping it comes across like I'm tossing him a safety ring in the pool and not an anchor.

He nods—though barely—and Hannah wastes no time clapping a hand on his shoulder.

"Well, I'll be damned! New job. Beautiful girlfriend. Who knew Millie breaking up with you would bring so much good fortune?"

Lou takes the opportunity to let out another chest-rattling bark, and I welcome the distraction, considering I'm two seconds from turning around, running the opposite direction, and never looking back.

Hannah has no filter, no shame, and no cool, and she cheers excitedly like she thinks the dog is endorsing her comment. Seph, on the other hand, has crossed her arms over her chest and looks as though she's considering chopping up Hannah and me and sprinkling us atop Lou's dinner. A two-for-one: nix the nuisance old friends and probably do the dog in at the same time.

"I am so sorry," I say through gritted teeth. "We really didn't mean—"

But Steve waves a hand to brush me off and I'm really not sure this conversation can get anymore awkward. I reach down to pat Lou—maybe because it's habit or maybe because it's a good distraction—and he enthusiastically headbutts my palm in return.

"He's clearly happy to see you," Steve says.

"He's clearly a happy boy," I deflect, and I try to give Seph a reassuring smile. She buys it, I think, and lets down her arms, revealing that wine-rack screen print again, and because I'm really not a jealous person and I'm trying desperately to act like an adult, I say, "So, Seph, you're a wine girl?"

Her brows pinch together. "A rosé sommelier, to be exact."

"Ha!" Hannah cackles, tossing her head back. The ponytail she regularly flaunts launches into full swing and her smoothie sloshes inside the cup. "You're a hoot, Seph."

Steve's stoic smile falters, and Seph stiffens.

"I'm not sure what's so humorous," she says. "I'm an expert in rosé. One of only a handful in the world. The top-performing salesperson in the Bay Area."

"Oh," Hannah says. Awkwardly.

I know exactly where her mind's at. There's no such thing as a rosé sommelier. Is there?

"It's a niche market," Steve informs us, reassuring his girlfriend with that steadying hand again. "She's earned multiple sales awards. Distributes all the way up and down the coast. In fact, she's looking to break her own record when we head up to Sonoma next weekend."

Seph puffs out her chest, and I'm drawn to the wine-red font again. I hadn't noticed before that it's glittery.

"Steve is the one who earned us the trip. Got a little bonus through work, but who am I not to tempt a few wine sellers with the latest blush?"

"Sounds...lovely," I say.

"Truly *unexpected*," Hannah adds.

"I think it's the one your mom likes, Millie," Steve pitches in, and I know he's just trying to be nice.

That's his fatal flaw: *being nice*. He has no idea it's causing his girlfriend to prickle and Hannah to choke down a snicker and me to consider calling over the schnauzer guy and pretend like we're an item just to make it perfectly clear I'm not hung up on Steve and he doesn't have to be nice to me.

We're exes. By choice. *My* choice.

"Anyway, it should be a great time," Steve goes on. "Well, assuming we find a sitter for this beast."

Steve kneads his knuckles into Lou's head and the dog practically melts at the affection, leaning up against Steve's leg and letting his drooly tongue loll. The dog idolizes Steve—he always has—and I've always known bringing Lou home from the pound was the right choice, even if it was the nail in the coffin.

"What happened to your sitter?" Hannah asks unabashedly.

Seph scoffs gently. "We never had one. We've interviewed six people and no one seems eager to take a bully."

"Grant can't do it?" I ask, not even sure why I'm offering up services for someone I also haven't talked to in the past year.

Steve shakes his head. "Grant's pulling extra hours this week. Volunteered for another task force to keep his name in the running for the next detective opening."

"Your patrol buddy didn't get the bump up with you?" Hannah jumps in, and Steve seems to flinch at the thought.

"There was only one opening last year."

"I'm surprised they didn't treat you two like a package deal."

"It was a close run," Steve insists, though his smile falters. "He'll get the next spot. Heck, I'm pretty sure he's the only reason the department's letting me take this time off while I've got an open case; they know they can call him up to help if they need it."

"Nonsense. You got this trip because you earned it," Seph says, pressing a palm to his chest delicately, and I can't help but notice his T-shirt tighten thanks to the giant uneasy breath he inhales.

"Listen, my sitter is nothing for you two to worry about. It was nice to see you both, but—"

"Why doesn't Millie do it?" Hannah cuts in, and Lou lurches back to all fours and lumbers our direction.

I toss her a deadly glare.

"That's really not necessary," Steve starts.

"Why not? She's the one who got the dog for you," Hannah reasons, and she drops back to her knees to accept another kiss from Lou before grabbing him by the chin and resorting to the infamous baby talk everyone uses with him. "Don't you want to hang out with your old mommy? I'll bet you do. Yes, you do."

"*Hannah*," I threaten, and I turn toward Seph to give her an apologetic look that will hopefully keep my corpse off the cutting board. "I don't think she really means—"

"Sure I do," Hannah confirms.

"I can't let you do that," Steve says.

"Honestly, I don't have the time," I lie.

"Fine," Hannah spouts, and she finally falls down to the grass, sitting cross-legged as Lou shamelessly climbs into her lap. "I'll do it. I'll dogsit."

"You don't have a car, and Steve lives across town," I remind her. Nicely. *So* nicely.

"That's okay. You can drop me off."

"Well, that settles that," Seph jumps in, and I wish I could jump in the bay.

"You want Hannah to dogsit?" I clarify.

Seph shrugs. "Why not?"

"Honey, you know I can find someone," Steve urges.

"You just did, and you didn't even have to try that hard."

"He never has," Hannah adds.

Steve grimaces automatically and tries to cover it up with one of those charming laughs only pretty-boy superheroes have.

"I put in a lot of effort in all I do," he murmurs.

"Oh, we know," Hannah teases. "Boyfriending, dog-parenting, criminal-catching—I see why you're getting free trips on the taxpayers' dime."

"It's not—"

"Steve, you're the cop so good, you don't even need a bad cop. Didn't you convince a hostage-taker to voluntarily walk into handcuffs by only sharing a story about second-grade recess and a Slinky?"

Steve fidgets, though he's still prudently containing his blush. "It was a little more involved than that."

"I'm pretty sure I heard the guy's accomplices did their time and then joined a monastery after being released," Hannah goes on as she scrubs Lou's neck, sending short, brown hairs into the air.

Steve lets out a slow breath. "That...is...accurate."

"See? The epitome of good cop," Hannah reiterates, eyeing Seph as if she's expecting the woman to be taking notes. "Hang onto this guy, will ya? Lord knows *she* didn't."

Seph doesn't look at me even as Hannah jerks a thumb my direction. Instead, she just cozies up to her real-life superhero once more and says, "Finders, keepers."

Two

"You're telling me I get to see my grandpuppy again?"

"Mom, no," I groan as I take the salad out of the fridge. "I'm not dogsitting. Hannah is."

"But it's two weeks," my mom goes on, and she sets a casserole on the counter and peels off her oven mitts. "Surely we can arrange at least one outing, right?"

I focus more intently on mixing the salad I know my mom has already mixed. It's the one concession she makes to eating healthy during our weekly Sunday night meals, though given it's typically served alongside some sort of gooey, cheese-filled, twice-baked pasta dish, the salad's impact on cholesterol and salt intake is negligible at best.

"I don't know. Maybe," I finally concede, not daring to look at her. "I don't want his new girlfriend to think I'm imposing."

"She didn't have a problem hiring your best friend to dogsit, now did she?"

I dig the salad prongs deeper into the spinach. "Hannah offered first."

"Interesting," my mom coos, and she dunks a serving spoon into the casserole and drops a portion onto a nearby plate. "So she wants you to get back together with Steve too?"

"Mom, *no*," I repeat.

"But, honey, with all that charisma and charm and chiseled muscle—"

"Excuse me?"

"Don't be so prude," she nips back. "You can't deny the man looks like he was sculpted by the hand of Michelangelo himself."

"Oh, I guarantee I can deny every single word that just came out of your mouth."

She just tsks loudly and drops another serving on the next plate, then pushes both across the counter toward me. "Don't give me so much salad this time, dear. I'm not a rabbit."

I oblige and give myself her extras, and we make our way to the back balcony. My mom lives in a small, though charmingly splashy, condo on the outskirts of the city. There certainly will be pros living closer to her once I escape downtown, including her building's indoor pool and sauna and the million-dollar view of the bay, but this endless prodding is not among them.

"Why didn't Steve ask Grant?" my mom asks, clearly still fishing. "I mean, that is *his* best friend."

"Lou is Steve's best friend," I correct, and my mom raises two hands in surrender. I settle into my chair and let out a sigh. "I did suggest it. Apparently, there's a few high-profile cases open right now, so all his extra hours are going to the department."

My mom perks up like a wolf who's just spotted its prey. "Do you mean the drug case?"

I don't answer right away because I don't want to admit I know exactly which "drug case" to which she's referring and already considered the likelihood that Steve's case or Grant's task force is related. It's been all over the news lately, and though I tune in regularly, I can guarantee my mom's actually got the tipline on speed dial. I wouldn't be surprised if she even called up every old contact she met through Steve to help name the new drug.

It was dubbed Puppy Love, after all, though I suppose I can be reasonably sure it earned the moniker because it produces a high that's somewhere between the extra-cuddly euphoria of MDMA and the mellow, laughter-inducing effects of marijuana. Like bringing a puppy home. Or, so they say. I'm not sure that was the dog-adoption experience I had.

Regardless, no one knows the long-term effects of the drug. It's so new and so unusual, the cops are simply trying to destroy any they find, but in reality, they've been chasing their tails just trying to figure out where it came from in the first place.

"I'm not sure what the cases are," I finally say, "but I guess Steve's running point on one of them. He made detective this year."

"Oh, joy! I always knew he'd get that promotion," my mom says, and she waves a sauce-covered fork in the air like she's one of those fifty-dollar fortune tellers down in Chinatown.

"Anyway," I go on, stabbing a piece of spinach, "twelve-hour work-days and twice-a-day dog walks aren't doable for Grant."

"Steve manages it."

"Steve has superpowers."

"I'm glad you finally see it."

I try not to grumble out loud. "I've always known it, just didn't care for it."

"For the life of me, I'll never understand why. I mean, dashing heroism aside, do you remember those *calves*?"

"Mom!"

"What? They were impossible to miss."

"I am somehow both mortified and relieved that's the body part you choose to comment on."

"Is there another part you'd like to discuss?"

"Please, no," I say, and I drop my fork back to the table intentionally. "Steve and I broke up. We're not getting back together. And you *have* to stop commenting on his body parts."

"It's not my fault he was made to grace the front page of a magazine."

I do grumble this time and shove a whole cherry tomato in my mouth, chomping deliberately to prove to my mother I have no interest in en-tertaining her charade.

"I just want you to be happy," she finally says, abandoning her silverware and leaning back. The setting sun tints her pale skin, and I know the glimmer in her eyes is genuine.

"I am happy. If you'll remember, I got my own promotion last year, I get some of the best clients at the firm, and I'm almost ready to go out on my own. I'm buying a house and I've got a nice car and I'm happy being alone."

My mom props her elbows on the table, folds her hands together, and then rests her chin on top. "But I thought Steve made you happy too."

I let out a measured breath, one I've learned from my therapist as a coping mechanism to deal with my overbearing mother who so often comes up during my monthly sessions.

"He was always so polite," she goes on unsolicited, "and he always did so many sweet things for you. I mean, fancy dinners and the nice house and, honey, he sent you roses at work every single week. Most women would *kill* to have a man like that."

"Mom, I don't even like roses."

"What kind of girl doesn't like roses?"

"*Me*," I say, driving home the point. "*I* don't like roses."

"How can you say that?"

I push my plate away, having completely lost my appetite, and fix my attention on the sunset. If I walked away from my offer on the house right now and surrendered the earnest money I already put down, I'd only be out a few thousand, right? I'd still have a cool thirty k to pack up my bags, hop the first flight to the middle of nowhere, and start my life all over—out from under my mother's thumb.

"Mom, Steve is a great guy, and *Persephone*"—I emphasize her full name to ensure she remembers my ex is happily paired off again—"is lucky to have him. He pulls out all the stops and does all the traditional grand gestures, and she seems like the kind of girl who likes that. But I'm not."

"You don't like being wooed?"

"I don't like excess. I never have. None of the things he did for me were ever about me. They were big and bold and flashy—things that pretty, wine-drinking girls love." I wince meekly, not exactly having meant to criticize Seph but not inclined to take it back either. "Mom, I wanted to go to the beach. I wanted to watch movies at home on the couch. I wanted to have a hobby with him—something we did just the two of us. I wanted something simple, not an entire parade around town."

"That's clearly the auditor in you," my mother says, and it's like she hasn't heard a single word I've been spouting, "and you definitely don't get that from me."

"I know you're not about to insult Dad."

"Oh, honey, of course not," she says, but I know the same argument she's been making since they divorced when I was ten is about to follow. "He was just always so calculated, planned everything we did down to the letter. Honey, he had a five-year plan for our five-year plan."

"I can't see what's wrong with that."

She sighs as I give her a playful smirk and then waves her hand through the air. "Don't you want adventure? Mystery? Intrigue?"

"I think you should see some of my clients' books. Intrigue by the spreadsheet-full."

"I don't know where I steered you wrong, dear."

"I think I'm doing just fine."

My mom grabs her fork again and picks at the remaining pieces of her salad—which is most of it. "Fine, I'll let this one go, but I am not going to pass up an opportunity to see my Louie Boy."

I lift my chin to eye her more intently. "You'll have to take that up with Hannah. I have no plans to see Lou or Steve or Seph, for that matter, ever again."

Three

"I'm not going in," I say, and I shove the gearshift into Park to emphasize my point.

"Steve knows you brought me here," Hannah argues.

"So what? It's only going to take five minutes, right? You go in, get the key, and leave. I can wait."

Hannah drops her hands into her lap. She's wearing a half dozen bracelets on both wrists, so it makes a ruckus, but I try not to get distracted. I'm sticking to my guns here.

"Please, Millie? What if I don't remember all the rules he gives me about Lou's bedtime or his food preferences or the kind of chocolate he's allowed to have?"

I curl my fingers into a fist, hold it against my lips briefly, and then try to drop the hand nonchalantly. "You do know dogs can't have *any* chocolate, right?"

"Like, at all?" she asks, and I'm afraid her bewildered frown is genuine. "Not even white chocolate? The greatest fraud of the chocolate world?"

"Tell me you're joking."

"Go inside with me."

I stifle the urge to grumble *no* again. It's everything to do with Steve and Seph and the fact that I really don't want to go inside the house where I once lived with him, but I love Lou more than I hate the awkwardness, and I can't stomach the thought of subjecting my pup to Hannah's ill-advised sitting practices, so I pull the key from the ignition.

"I knew you'd come around."

Hannah beams, and it takes everything in me not to chuck my keys at her.

"Millie! Hannah! Glad you made it," Steve calls, seconds after we knock on the door.

I expected something more like, *Millie, still breathing air today?* or *Hannah, you didn't forget you committed to two weeks of glorified babysitting?* But, apparently, Steve hasn't forgotten his virtuous ways.

He pulls open the front door, ushers us into his tri-level townhome, and even comes up with a pretty good reason for Seph being out of the house. According to him, every restaurant in the Bay Area wants to wine-and-dine her for an exclusive contract selling the specialty rosé she's known for, but I wonder if he just booked her a spa day that intentionally won't conclude until well after we're gone.

"Sorry, I'm only here because I drove Hannah," I say, but Steve waves a hand.

"It's no problem. I know Lou wouldn't have it any other way—"

I barely catch the end of Steve's sentence because Lou bounds toward me, all giant paws and drool-dripping jowls. I'd hate it except for the fact that I kind of love it. We hardly had a few months together after I brought him home, but he still treats me like the hero who saved him from certain doom at the local animal shelter.

"Oh my," Hannah says, leaping back and ducking behind me. "Is he always like this?"

"Eager?" I ask.

"Happy?" Steve suggests.

"Slobbery," Hannah corrects.

I laugh and grab Lou by the cheeks, rubbing him more aggressively so his jaw drops open and his tongue lolls out. "It means you're doing something right."

"Something rightfully nauseating," she says.

"You'll get used to it," Steve reassures her and pushes the door open wider. "Come on in. I think you'll see not much has changed, aside from a few updates downstairs."

I eke past the dog and try not to tally all the similarities and differences in my head, though it's not easy.

The front door opens into the living room, where the same L-shaped sectional is neatly poised, but it's got yellow and baby-blue pillows drowning the gray leather as if spring needs an entire color-coded welcome mat. I never changed the pillows myself, but apparently Seph is one of those seasonal decorators. There's even a framed portrait on the mantel, one of several professionally taken couples' photos of them, with tiny bumblebees glued above the words, "Honey, can you *bee*-lieve it's spring?"

The TV above the fireplace is—to no surprise—playing the five o'clock news, and I can still see at least part of the dining room on the other side of the wall. The table is set for two and has an arrangement of yellow roses in the center, and I'm beginning to think they actually eat meals there, like happily-ever-after couples at the end of Hallmark movies.

Steve and I didn't and weren't, for the record.

His kitchen, to the left, is still outfitted with the top-of-line range neither of us ever touched because he preferred fine dining, though the name-brand blender on the counter I inadvisably purchased during my *new-year-new-me* phase looks like it's finally getting some use—not by Steve, surely, but use, nonetheless.

"What is this?" Hannah asks, extricating herself from the fridge I hadn't realized she started raiding.

Her bag is back on the couch and she's got a four-pack of canned wine in her hands. I don't need Steve to explain exactly how they got there, but he does anyway.

"Ah, that's from one of Seph's clients. Help yourself if you're into it. She can't bring herself to drink the stuff."

Hannah frowns at the can, then glances sideways at me, and I know she's considering whether it's too soon to point out Seph basically sells watered-down grape juice in a bottle and canned wine couldn't possibly be worse.

I give her a warning headshake and then turn back to Steve. "You'll have to give Hannah the whole rundown on Lou. I'm sure it's all different these days."

"A few things, maybe. Though he's mostly the same goofy guy."

"Feed, water, walk, repeat, right?" Hannah guesses.

"Something like that," Steve says, and then he bends down and scoops up a rope toy from the floor.

Lou, who's been hanging at my side, bounds across the room to snag it. He clamps down on the rope and yanks with enough force to jerk Steve forward, and I wonder for the dozenth time if Hannah has any idea what she's gotten herself into.

"Listen, Hannah, I really appreciate you doing this," Steve says.

She pops open the can and wanders back toward us. "Easy peasy."

"It's a big deal," he goes on, grunting as Lou takes a couple more good pulls. "There aren't many people I trust with Lou."

"Oh god, and I make that list?" she retorts unabashedly.

"You both do."

I don't reply, even though Steve looks directly at me.

"It wasn't that I couldn't find a dogsitter; it was that I didn't like any of them. And even if Grant weren't busy—well, I think he's been going through something lately. He's been a little off, so I didn't want to push it by asking."

"Off?" Hannah asks, and suddenly she's paying attention, pulling her drink down and frowning deeply at Steve.

"It's not important, but this trip is...let's just say it's *very* important to Seph. She really wanted the time apart."

"Time apart?" Hannah repeats incredulously. "How's she going to get that if it's your trip?"

"Obviously, I don't mean time apart from me."

"He means time apart from Lou."

I don't mean to say it, but it slips out anyway. Steve glances down and pulls on the toy, eliciting a few playful growls from Lou, and then sighs.

"She's been so patient and she's trying so hard, but, well...he doesn't always listen to her, and I know he's not the easiest dog."

"But he is just a dog," I point out.

"Just the wrong dog for her."

"I don't understand," Hannah cuts in. "What am I missing?"

Steve sighs again. "She's allergic."

"Allergic?"

"To all dogs?" I ask.

"Specifically large, short-haired breeds," Steve says.

I eye Hannah skeptically because what the heck else am I supposed to do? That's a fictional ailment if I've ever heard one, and I want to grab Steve by the shoulders and shake him out of whatever fantasy he's living in.

"It's not what you think," Steve hurries on, and I have to school my features into something that doesn't explicitly reveal how bonkers I think his girlfriend is. "She's trying really hard, but he makes things difficult sometimes, and she—"

"Wait—she doesn't want to—"

Steve swings his gaze my direction, and he knows what I'm about to ask. He finally releases the rope, sending Lou in a momentum-fueled tumble. The dog rights himself, shakes the toy violently, and then tears off across the room, presumably to go find a suitable place to hide his recently acquired treasure.

"No, she doesn't want to"—he pauses to drop his voice to a whisper—"*get rid of him*, but he's not on her good side right now either."

"What did he do?" Hannah asks before I can respond.

"Besides completely ignoring any command she ever gives him?" he says with a guilty shrug. "He chewed one of her Louis Vuitton purses."

"Oh boy," I murmur.

"That's a little naughty," Hannah adds.

"That's a lot expensive," I tack on.

"I know. I bought it for her."

Hannah and I exchange a look, though hers is doe-eyed and mine is fiery.

He tried to do the same thing for me on multiple occasions, and I had to tell him every time I couldn't care less if the bag came from the queen of England's personal collection: I didn't need a several-thousand-dollar satchel. Hannah tried her hand a few times at bartering with me, saying she'd just relieve me of the burden if only I'd accept the dang gift.

"She loved that bag," Steve adds, as if he knows I'm condemning it to thrift-store hell in my mind. "And I...do love her."

I snap my jaw shut, and I guess Hannah does too, because there's a distinct crack of teeth next to me. She takes a swig of her drink to cover it up and then jumps off the couch, calling for Lou like she has no idea he's in the next room over, where I assume his kennel is still stored.

"I didn't realize you were serious," I say, though I hate myself for uttering the words.

I was the one who chose to leave. I was the one who despised indulgences. I was the one who said I didn't love him. Who am I to judge his newfound happiness?

"I think she's the one," Steve says, and it's his sincere voice, the one I don't usually consider part of his superhero-like extravagance. It's the one he uses on criminals, the one that apparently turns them into god-fearing disciples.

"I'm glad you found the right girl," I say, and it's not a lie.

Steve nods, and I get the impression he's been dreading telling me the news but is relieved I'm not going to lose my mind over it, that I'm not going to claim I regretted ever having left him.

For a while after the breakup I did think he assumed I would come crawling back. After all, what kind of nice guy in the modern-day feminist world gets the boot and doesn't end up the hero in the end?

I look at the floor. I glance back toward the news still playing in the background. I eye anything that isn't him because I can't find it in my heart to tell him all the nice-guy fluff never did it for me. I'm not the girl who swoons over an upside-down Spiderman kiss. I'm not the girl who helplessly falls into the arms of the Man of Steel. I'm just not *that* girl.

"I should show you the downstairs," Steve starts up again, and he's speaking loud enough Hannah can surely hear us from the other room.

"Do I want to know what you keep downstairs?" she asks, not missing a beat, and Lou follows her out because she's somehow acquired the rope toy and he's dead set on getting it back.

"You do," he says in return, oblivious that Hannah is trying to goad him. He holds out a hand to take the toy, which Lou is still trying to reach. "He's not allowed, though."

"Not allowed downstairs?" I clarify.

"It's Seph's space now," he explains, and he chucks the rope toy in the opposite direction, hard enough it hits the sliding glass door in the kitchen, and Lou barrels toward it. Once he has it in his mouth, violently shaking it again, Steve ushers us to the lower level. "I surprised her a couple months ago with a little remodel."

"I think 'little' is the wrong word," I say, partly under my breath, as we reach the bottom of the stairs.

I can barely remember how it was laid out before—which wall had the weight sets and which one was tacked with mirrors—because now there's an entire room within the room.

"It's a simple wine closet," Steve says—the second lie of modesty I've caught him in tonight.

We pass through a glass door and enter a chilled room that isn't just outfitted with the standard rows of wooden wine racks; it's fully styled to look like a real stone-walled cellar. There's also a slim, multi-level platform table perched along the far wall. On it are several glass decanters, each a more extravagant shape than the last, and they're accompanied by gold-plated plaques and etched-glass awards.

"So, Seph really wasn't kidding about her whole sommelier bit?" Hannah asks shamelessly, already clutching a goblet-shaped award and peeking inside like she expects it to fill magically.

"Nothing to kid about," Steve says.

"Come on, Steve. It's just us now."

He shrugs.

"She's an expert in *pink wine.*"

"All right, I know, I know," he says with a mild huff as he raises two hands in defense. "I was skeptical at first too, but those aren't even all her awards. And she has a whole specialty rack to show for it."

"She's got a rack, all right," Hannah murmurs, and I'm just quick enough to steal Steve's attention before he hears it.

"Are these it? The specialty pinks?"

I slap a hand on a nearby shelf while Hannah cackles quietly at what we both know is more insult than polite curiosity and then surrenders the award she's been fondling. She runs a hand along the row of bottles filled with various shades of pink-tinted wine, tapping each corked top as she goes.

"In all my life..." she whispers.

"They're valuable," Steve insists.

"Of course they are," Hannah agrees.

"Naturally," I add in.

Steve just pinches his mouth, like he wants to frown but can't fully accomplish it.

"The stuff you really want to see is over there," he concedes, nodding to the opposite side where several rows of reds are neatly organized by color of label apparently.

Hannah tosses me a devious glance, like she's figuring how many bottles could disappear without totally messing up the illogical arrangement. I'm guessing at least one of each shade but don't suggest it in an effort not to encourage her.

"Care to share what this little masterpiece is?" Hannah asks, moving on far too easily.

She waves a hand at a painting that's artfully perched on the table and leaning against the wall. I never did understand the trend *not* to hang expensive artwork and instead place it on unstable furniture, but I'm apparently in the minority.

The painting depicts a bunch of grapes that are a pale, dusty pink with brown vines coiling like springs around them. It's tasteful and pretty, I suppose, if not kind of pretentious for a clump of fruit.

"Oh, that little beauty. I had it commissioned for her," Steve explains, and it really is all humbleness. He's not bragging. "It was a gift for our half anniversary."

"Half anniversary?" Hannah demands, her eyes bulging, and I'm glad she said it because I wasn't sure I could hold that one in—which would make me a jerk, I'm pretty sure.

Steve just gives her a pointed look.

"Okay, fine. But what *is* it?"

He purses his lips and pushes out a breath. "They're rosé grapes."

Okay, I'm definitely a jerk. I can't restrain myself anymore, and I let out a loud, obnoxious laugh, and so does Hannah. Steve crosses his arms and shakes his head, but there's a noticeable twitch at the corner of his mouth.

"She does know rosé isn't a grape, right?" Hannah asks.

"She knows what rosé is, doesn't she?" I add.

"Of course she knows," Steve groans, but he yanks open the cellar door and—as politely as he can manage—tells us to get the heck out.

Hannah giggles all the way upstairs, and I try my best not to join in.

"I was going to tell you two to help yourself to the red wine while you're staying here, but if you're going to be mean—"

"I'm not staying," I jump in before I think better of it.

"She's just the driver, remember?" Hannah says.

Steve clears his throat. "Of course. Well, you know you're welcome if you change your mind."

I don't plan to, even though Lou seems to cast a vote in Steve's favor. He pounces out of the living room as we return, toy in his jaw but his cheeks pulled back in an unmistakable doggie grin. I scratch behind his ears and tell him he's a good boy, and Steve and Hannah take off toward the room where the kennel is.

He starts explaining how many scoops of food Lou gets, which is probably significantly more than it used to be, but I deliberately hang back in the living room and head for the couch. The less I know about Lou's care, the less Hannah can call on me for help.

Besides, I kind of miss this couch.

I sink into the cushions, much squishier than those on my stiff IKEA find, and Lou follows me because what dog doesn't love scratching up a down-filled sofa?

"Do you still like to watch the news?" I ask Lou, teetering on the edge of that baby voice everyone seems to have for him.

He plops down next to me and drops his toy between his front paws, then whines a little, which I take as a fervent *yes*.

News or not, he's a good couch buddy at the very least.

I snatch up the remote from the opposite cushion and turn the volume up a few notches. There's a clip playing of a slick-haired businessman being interviewed down on the pier with an industrial warehouse strategically framed in the background, and I recognize him and the pier immediately.

"I should have known," I mumble, scratching Lou's neck as I look between him and the TV. "Every rich guy's just *got* to salvage some rundown warehouse for his own pretentious art gallery, doesn't he?"

I shake my head as the clip rolls and billionaire boy spouts something about a grand opening. I seldom let money get in the way of my perception of people—a necessary trait of a good auditor—but some people simply have too dang much, and he's one of them.

It's probably been about four or five years now, but my firm was asked to audit this guy's books when he put in the offer to buy this entire stretch of abandoned warehouses and docks down at the pier. I wasn't assigned to the case, but I got a peek at his profits—and it almost made me sick.

It made me sicker still when he got the seal of approval. Books clean as a whistle.

"I guess if it's not him, it'll be someone else," I lament, turning toward Lou, and then that baby voice I forgot I was hiding slips out. "Does he look trustworthy, Louie Boy? Is he going to put his mega surplus of dollars to good use?"

"He *was* the one who started our favorite Thursday night market at the pier," Hannah pipes up and I startle, swinging my head over my shoulder to see her and Steve exit the back room.

"*Your* favorite Thursday night market," I correct.

"Oh, give the guy some credit. At least he's not selling drugs to children. Are you seeing this?"

Hannah signals to the TV, where the reporter has switched to a new topic. There's a stock photo on the screen of pills spilling out of a bottle, and I know it must be a story on Puppy Love even before she says it.

"Is it seriously going around schools now?" Hannah asks.

"Yeah, it's no joke," Steve pitches in, and I realize he's dropped his hands to the couch right behind my head. Lou perks up, licks his fingers, and then tries to lick my face.

"That's horrible," I say.

"And interesting," Hannah adds, and I turn to catch her closing in on Steve. "So you know the case? Does that mean you're working it? Tell us everything. We need all the details."

Steve rolls his eyes. "You know I'm not allowed to discuss open cases."

"So you *are* working it?"

"Hannah—"

"*That's* the big case you keep talking about, the reason you're so reluctant to run away for the weekend."

"It's two weeks, and it's a big deal."

"I knew it. The second you said Grant was acting off—"

"Wait a minute," Steve interrupts. "What makes you think his being *off* has anything to do with this case?"

"Same reason you can't stand to leave while it's still open: kids are involved."

Steve frowns at Hannah and then looks at me, but I don't dare comment. No one wants to see kids get tangled up in something like this, but as long as I've known Steve as a cop, he's had the hardest time working cases with minors, and though Grant's always been a bit less emotional, it's pretty clear he feels the same way too.

"What about this case?" Hannah says, breezing back to the TV, where another segment on fraudulent art sales has just started. "Looks like it's SFPD too."

"I can definitely say I'm not on *that* case. It's been active for probably two years. Even some of our most tenured detectives haven't been able to crack that one."

"It's just white-collar crime, isn't it?" Hannah challenges.

"It's never *just* white-collar crime, and these guys are good. They know exactly what they're doing and aren't even ashamed of it." Steve turns to the TV as another graphic pops up on the screen. "Look, that's the signature on all their fakes. Stamped on everything they do."

"They have a calling card and you still haven't caught them?" I ask.

Hannah lets out a short laugh. "Steve, I hate to break it to you, but I think you work with a bunch of tenured morons."

Lou barks, and I can't help but agree, though I change the subject anyway as Steve's generous disposition is finally waning.

"So, you've got Hannah up-to-speed on all things Lou?"

"I did my best," Steve replies, then looks at her. "Everything's going to be fine while we're gone, right?"

"Oh, please, Steve," she says with a flippant wave. "You can tell your little lady she's got nothing to worry about while you two are off on your fancy getaway."

"It really is important, Hannah, and if you don't think—"

"I'll be fine," she insists, and then she drops a hand over the couch and tentatively pats Lou on the head. "See?"

"It's not you I'm worried about."

Steve jerks his chin toward Lou and Hannah glances down too, but I'm already reaching for the dog, massaging my fingers into the loose skin around his neck and easily finding my baby voice again.

"You're an angel, Louie Boy, aren't you? You'd never give Hannah any trouble."

Four

I almost bail the next Saturday.

I consider making Hannah catch a bus or, heck, hiking her booty across town as punishment for volunteering me to be her chauffeur, but the weekend routes are sketchy and I'm not a monster.

My mom, on the other hand—all monster.

"You're at Steve's now?" she cries, her shrill voice rattling over the Bluetooth speaker and causing my car windows to shudder. "And he's there?"

"Well, he wasn't supposed to be," I groan, tossing a glare Hannah's direction.

"I'm just as surprised as you are. He said he'd be gone an hour ago."

I don't believe her for one minute, but I can't exactly pull away from the curb without drawing attention to us either.

He's been standing a few cars in front of us with the trunk of his Charger open, glancing right at a stack of pink suitcases, then back at the trunk, then back at the suitcases. One errant move on my part and I know he'll zero in on my familiar crossover and come rushing over, welcoming us back to his neighborhood and probably inviting us in for drinks or snacks or whatever it is good hosts are offering these days.

But a second later, Seph saunters down the front steps, and Steve quickly drops his hand from where he's been comically scratching his head and grants her a face-splitting smile. She beams back just as obnoxiously and drops another flower-patterned tote on the trio of suitcases, which Steve simply pats lovingly.

"Oh god, they're made for each other, aren't they?" Hannah says.

"Who?" my mom asks, again loud enough to make the car shake. "Steve and his new girlfriend?"

"Of course that's who," I say, since I tried really hard to nail that point home at our dinner last weekend. "Now, take it down a notch before he—"

"Too late," Hannah interrupts, and she practically squeals in delight when Steve glances over his shoulder and lays eyes on my car.

He perks up, an exaggerated grin like he's just spotted his favorite celebrity, and immediately heads our direction. I don't even have my window all the way down before he's spouting all sorts of *hellos* and *how are yous* and *Lou has no idea how great his day is about to be.*

"Is that Steve?" my mom asks. Quite unnecessarily.

"Goldie?" Steve says in return, and then he leans in through the window and affectionately nudges my shoulder. "Don't tell me you've got your big sis on the phone!"

Hannah giggles like a four-year-old and my mom practically purrs at the schmaltzy compliment. Meanwhile, I'd be okay if the universe strikes me down right where I sit. There isn't another person in the world who can get away with calling her anything but Marigold, but for some absurd reason, she's never felt the need to correct Steve.

Once Hannah contains herself, she joins in as the other two exchange exaggerated banter, and I wonder if I should just slip out of the car, turn myself over to Seph, and let her do her worst to me. Anything would be better than this.

"Steve?" Seph calls, and I realize I stand to be corrected as she trots up to the car next, tossing a fluffy feathered scarf over her shoulders. "Let the girls go inside, will you? Lou's going to tear the house apart if we leave him alone too long."

"Where are my manners?" Steve says with a laugh, but it's moot because he's got every last one on display.

He shares another laugh with my mom and offers to chat again soon like the two catch up for coffee every other weekend, and then he pulls open my car door. I reluctantly get out while he scoops an arm around Seph's waist and then gratuitously points Hannah and me toward the house, and what other choice do I have?

Steve: two. Me: zero.

***

"Honestly, I thought they'd never leave," Hannah says as she bounds straight for the refrigerator.

I'm still figuring out how the heck I got myself into this predicament when I had no intention of helping with Hannah's dogsitting scam and instead had a date with my favorite 1980s documentary.

It's sitting at home on a burned DVD (*not* my crime, by the way, though I did accept it without much objection). You see, the highly underrated film, which details the life and crimes of an incredibly clever stock trader, is packed full of malfeasance, superstition, and intrigue, all while underpinned by the heartfelt motive of helping inner-city kids earn an education. The ultimate amalgamation.

Only, the guy at the center of the film hates it.

After it was released, the stock trader himself bought up all the physical copies, and he routinely scrubs any pirated versions from the internet. But Hannah managed to get her hands on it once and gifted it to me for Christmas. I kept it at her house until Steve and I split, for obvious reasons.

"At least he bought us all the snacks," Hannah says, her hands already full with several blocks of cheese, a jar of olives, and a tray of assorted grapes, like one color simply isn't enough.

"He got *you* snacks. I'm going home."

"Please stay, Millie? I can't be in this giant house alone."

"You have Lou," I argue, and as if proving my point, he barrels between my legs and heads straight for the woman with the food.

He may have a soft spot for me, but I can't even dream of competing with cheese.

Hannah swerves to avoid his jaw, and half her goods go tumbling across the kitchen counter. I lunge to scoop up an errant wheel of brie rolling toward guaranteed demolition.

"See? I need you!" she cries, dropping her surviving items on the counter. "Both to catch this cheese and eat it."

"I don't eat cold cheese, remember? Bake it in lasagna, sprinkle it on pasta, or melt in a toasty sandwich—fine by me. But cold cardboard cubes aren't my jam. Honestly, do you even know me?"

"Oh, come on. Charcuterie boards are just adult Lunchables."

"Wouldn't know. Never had them."

"Then why are there four in the fridge? That's a weird thing to stock for someone who doesn't ask for them."

"Sounds just like Steve," I say, but I regret it as soon as it comes out.

I really don't want to badmouth him, and it's clear he went out of his way to buy goodies for Hannah while she stays here, but if either of them thinks this is what I want, they're mistaken. My therapist would tell me to say *no thank you* and move on, but I just can't help the feeling of an old wound splitting open.

"Don't go home. Watch your documentary here tonight," Hannah begs.

"Who says I was going home to watch a documentary?"

She just frowns.

"I can't watch a pirated film in the house of a career cop who can't even fathom taking pens from work."

"It'll be our little secret," Hannah says, waggling her brows at me and waving around a brick of gouda that Lou's glued to.

"If I go home to get the movie, I'm not coming back."

"Fine. What about the finance channel?"

"You hate that."

"I do, but if that'll make you stay..."

I lift my chin, eyeing her skeptically, and she doesn't flinch.

"Fine. But I'm going to need a lot of wine."

"That I can handle. Watch Lou—I'll get it."

Lou skids all the way across the hardwood floor, chasing after Hannah, and she barely gets the lower-floor door shut in time. He shoves his nose in the jamb, gives a disgruntled huff, and then sniffs every inch of the gap underneath.

I stride over to him and wedge a hand under his collar. It's like what I imagine pulling a bear off a garbage can might feel like, and I have to heave with all my strength just to get him to budge. When he finally relents, it's almost enough to send me tumbling backward, and I catch a glimpse of something else, something flashing near the ceiling.

"Steve's got cameras?"

I yell it at the top of my lungs because *what the hell?*

Meanwhile, Hannah bounds back through the door, a bottle of red in each hand, and she screws her face up in admonition.

"What's the problem with cameras?"

I jerk a finger toward the ceiling. "He can literally watch us."

"It's aimed at the front door," Hannah says, waving me off with a bottle and taking off toward the kitchen again, Lou and me trailing in her wake. "They're to catch people who are trying to break into the house, not people who are already here."

"You knew about them?"

"Of course. He told me while we were going over Lou's food schedule—which reminds me: Should I be feeding him right now?"

I sigh heavily and really do wonder if Hannah's kept anything else alive in her life besides herself.

"No, he eats dinner after we eat dinner. It was something we learned in puppy training."

Hannah scoffs and thumps both wine bottles to the counter. "This hound has had puppy training?"

"So most of the tricks didn't stick—it's not my fault."

Hannah laughs and Lou barks, but I'm pretty sure it's because he's got his eyes on the brie again as she begins to unpeel the wrapper and not because I'm right.

"As long as the cameras aren't in the bedroom or the bathroom, I don't care," Hannah goes on.

"Well, I do."

"You already agreed to stay."

"I know," I say with defeat, "so we're going up to the roof."

Hannah beams. "Twist my arm."

She finishes unwrapping the brie and then spots an engraved cutting board propped up on the counter behind an assortment of decorative glass jars. Judging by the pair of carved-out initials in the handle, I'm pretty sure the board is supposed to be ornamental, but if Steve's got eyes on the inside, then he can call up Hannah and tell her himself not to ruin it.

I don't even wince as she drops the wheel on top, pounds the knife through the cheese, and then drags the blade right across the soft wood.

As she finishes, I grab a box of crackers I find in the pantry and then a pair of wineglasses from an old hutch that belonged to Steve's mother. A few minutes later, Hannah and I make our way upstairs, arms laden.

Lou's hot on our heels, undoubtedly waiting for one of us to fumble the goods, and it's a pretty close call when Hannah is forced to wedge the olives under her armpit, balance the cutting board in one hand, and open the door to the rooftop patio with the other. But she somehow manages, and Lou gets distracted by a pair of birds anyway.

The private rooftop space might as well be a set at a film studio: it has slate-gray stone pavers; a dark-washed pergola draped with a string of globe lights; and magazine-worthy, low-profile furniture, all arranged neatly around an electric fireplace. Plus, it's got a view of the bay.

When I first moved in, I couldn't figure how Steve ever afforded this place on a cop's salary, and believe me, I ran numbers in my head for every possible scenario. It's an auditor's habit, really, to calculate extravagancies, but I always came up short and ultimately resorted to the highly inappropriate method of straight-up asking him, and by god, his good manners never failed.

I spent thirty minutes listening to him explain how he bought it as a fixer-upper and did a few "odds and ends" to clean up the place. My mom just about died when she realized my new boyfriend was not only handsome but also *handy*.

"Wine me," I say as Hannah drops down on the sofa.

I set out the glassware and she gladly pops the cork and pours us more than we need.

It's at least an hour later, when the sun is sinking into the horizon and Hannah's buzzing on two-and-a-half glasses, that she finally asks the question I know is coming: "Why didn't you want this? Honestly?"

I don't look at her and instead eye Lou's tail, which is about the only part of him I can see. He gave up begging for food and resorted to pouting on the other side of the couch when Hannah finally pushed back her makeshift charcuterie board she'd practically licked clean.

"I mean, the *house*, Millie. It's beautiful. And all the food and the wine. You could be living this life and not just watching it."

"I don't care about the house," I tell her, and it's the truth. "I'm buying my own, and it's small and it's cute and it's all I need."

Hannah shrugs and lifts her glass, sloshing the last swig of red wine. "I guess your house does have more penises."

I chuck a piece of cheese at her.

"Oh, come on. You know I'm right," she whines, unsticking the cube from her chest.

"About the house?"

"About your life with Steve."

I sigh again. "Why does everyone seem to have an opinion on my dating life? You're single too and no one gives you a hard time about it."

She lets out a laugh that showcases her wine-stained lips. "That's because I didn't break up with America's sweetheart."

"You and my mother ought to start a fan club."

"All right, all right," she says, leveraging herself up in her seat, and she places the wineglass she's since drained on the edge of the firepit. "Let's look at this from a different angle: If your idea of a dreamboat isn't cut abs and smoldering looks, then what is?"

"I don't know. I just..."

"You just what? Need two of them?"

I roll my eyes and finish my drink because we've never quite gotten this far in the dissection of my failed relationship and I need the liquid encouragement.

"All the things Steve did for me, like the roses and the fancy nights out and the big, extravagant gifts, they just didn't make me feel good. And then, that made me be a not-good person to Steve."

"What do you mean? He's never said anything bad about you."

"I know, and he never would—he's too dang nice—but it drove me crazy. I couldn't get through a day without him showering me in *stuff* and I felt guilty and grossly spoiled, and then he'd feel lousy for making me uncomfortable and he'd overcompensate and start the cycle all over again."

"He'd buy you more gifts?"

"And he'd be even nicer and even more thoughtful, and by the end, I was so mean. It wasn't fair to him. Gift-giving and taking care of people is just something he loves, and I knew he deserved someone who liked that too."

"I had no idea," Hannah says, and she leans forward and grabs the wine bottle to replenish our glasses.

I let her, but I don't drink, instead twisting the stem in my hands. "Do you want to know why I brought Lou home in the first place?"

"It wasn't because you love cleaning up drool and five-pound turds?"

"Not exactly," I say with a laugh. "Honestly, I did it because I kind of thought it would take some of the attention off me, and if that didn't work, then it made me feel better knowing I wasn't leaving him alone."

"What?" she cries, and I know it's genuine shock because I haven't admitted this to anyone before.

I shake my head, reminiscing. "It did make him happy—I'd never seen Steve that excited before—but he thought I did it because I wanted to get more serious."

"And you already knew you wanted out?"

"Does that make me a horrible person?"

"Oh no, honey," she coos, and she crawls forward on the couch to reach across the gap and give me an awkward, mid-air hug. "No one thinks you're horrible, and I'm convinced the charity case you brought home"—she tosses a thumb over her shoulder—"thinks you're his hero."

"Lou doesn't even—" But I stop mid-sentence and peel myself out of Hannah's grasp. "Where is Lou?"

"Right behind—*oh no*." Hannah practically climbs up the back of the couch and dramatically looks left and right for the dog who we thought was sleeping soundly. "Oh crap."

We look to the door at the same time. We'd wedged a doorstop in the jamb because Hannah always worries we'll lock ourselves out up here, but the block of wood is now sitting askew.

We bolt from our seats, Hannah reaching the stairs first, me scrambling after her. She's already frantically calling Lou's name and I'm mentally figuring how likely it is Lou might be politely waiting for the dinner we still owe him.

"Oh, thank goodness," Hannah cries as she reaches the main level first. "He's right here and he's—*Lou!*"

Clearly she heard him before she laid eyes on him. Rookie mistake.

I catch the ear-piercing bark and round the corner to see Hannah taking off full-steam across the living room, and it's definitely too late for me to tell her Lou absolutely adores the chase.

He bounds around the edge of the couch, barking playfully, and then skirts the ottoman and comes barreling back toward me. As he closes in, I realize he's got something slung around his neck, all wooden pieces and ripped canvas, and I wonder how the hell he can destroy furniture in the time it takes us to polish off a single bottle.

I lunge for him, but it's in vain. Lou dips left, drops to his forearms, and lets out another playful howl before racing into the kitchen. I scream for Hannah to take the right side of the island while I go left, but her momentum sends her sliding across the wood floor and Lou dodges past her like a soccer ball skipping under the arms of a goalie.

I scream Lou's name this time, and he replies with another cheerful bark and shakes his head left to right, the mangled frame of whatever he destroyed twisting around his neck.

"Grab his toy!" I yell, and Hannah scrambles on her hands and knees to swipe up the knotted rope Steve had been teasing him with last weekend.

I know we look crazed because Hannah squats downs and wags the rope, trying to tempt Lou, and I vault onto the arm of the couch ready to grab him from behind, but it works. He leaps toward her and I jump.

She lets him snag the toy while I grab him by the shoulders, and even as he violently whips the rope back and forth, Hannah yanks the material off his neck. She falls back onto her butt, collapsing in a heap, and I do too as I release Lou and let him streak off into the room where his kennel is.

"Holy crap," I say on a ragged breath.

"He's a beast," Hannah agrees, sitting back up, half laughing.

She stretches out the mangled wood and paper, trying to figure out which piece belongs where, and eventually squares up the corners so it almost resembles a wide, rectangular frame.

"What is it?" I ask.

She tilts her head, frowns, and then tosses a terrified look to her right, and I follow.

"No, no, no," I say.

"Oh my god, oh my god, *oh my god!*" she wails.

"He didn't—"

"He *did.*"

Hannah clutches the torn canvas to her chest, and I'm pretty sure it's as bad as I think. I don't waste another second, scrambling to my feet and racing toward the door leading downstairs—the door that shouldn't be open.

I'm on the last step, stomping over errant scraps of canvas and paper and pushing open the swinging door to the refrigerated cellar when I realize the painting that should be on the table is gone, and in the room instead, dripping with slobber and chewed into pieces, is a plastic cheese wrapper.

Five

"You know, I was wondering where the gouda went," Hannah says.

I don't respond, instead scooping up some dog food from the bucket in Lou's room and pouring it noisily into his bowl. He's already drooling and practically swallows the kibble whole like he hasn't just downed an entire brick of processed cheese.

I'm only feeding him because I know he's going to need all the help he can get to work that dairy through his system, and I'm not about to endure his body's attempts to expel all the human food in a very odorous way.

"I guess I forgot it while I was getting the wine," Hannah adds, and this time I do look at her.

"And you forgot the door too?"

"I was distracted with you up here hollering about cameras and stuff."

I wince. "Oh no. Do you think Steve's already seen what happened?"

"Like he watches the cameras twenty-four-seven?"

"I don't know!" I cry, on the verge of panicking.

Hannah swipes the scoop from my hand and drops it back into Lou's bucket, then ushers me back into the living room.

"I'm sure he hasn't bothered to look," Hannah says, and she drops onto the couch, patting the cushion next to her like I'm supposed to cuddle up and turn on my movie. "Like I said, the cameras are just in the entry and they're for emergencies only."

I don't believe that, but I flop down on the couch next to her anyway and cover my eyes. "How bad is it?"

"What? This?" Hannah says, her voice unusually chirpy, and I can hear her fumbling again with the scraps she's collected. "I mean, I guess you can tell there was a nibble here and a little tear there and—*oh yeah*—an entire dog head right through the middle *here*."

I look because there's no point in denying it. Hannah has her whole arm punched through the center of the painting and has also managed to squeeze her head through it and is smiling obnoxiously, looking like one of those caricatures you get at the fair.

The frame of the painting is split in two places and completely disconnected at one corner, and I'm pretty sure she's gathered at least four or five strips of canvas that will surely be impossible to piece back together because they're all filled with the same indistinguishable pink circles.

"It was an honest accident," Hannah says.

"It's *destroyed*."

Hannah pulls her head out of the canvas and eyes it thoughtfully. "You think Seph will notice if we tape it back together?"

I groan loudly and drop my head into my hands.

"Why don't I just call Steve and tell him what happen—"

"No!" The response is out of my mouth before I can stop it, and I find myself repeating it, like a mantra. "No, no. No, we can't tell Steve."

"Why not?"

"You saw how stressed out he was. This is an important trip and Seph already doesn't like Lou and she's gonna have it out for him."

Hannah leans sideways, stealing a glance at the dog as he licks his bowl clean. "It *was* his fault."

"Says the girl who left the cheese out and the door open."

Hannah sighs and drops the tattered painting onto the coffee table in front of us, and it's almost like it summons Lou. He lumbers over, sniffs the remnants of the art piece he so carelessly destroyed, and then looks at me and licks my hand. I swear his brown eyes expand two inches.

"Ugh, Lou," I whine, and I pat his head semi-affectionately before looking at Hannah again. "We can't tell Steve. We need to figure something else out. Do you have your computer?"

Hannah perks up. "Well, I wasn't going to watch my steamy movies on Steve's TV."

I don't indulge the attempt at humor, but she pops up from her seat anyway and goes to the kitchen to fetch her laptop out of her bag. She's back at my side with the second bottle of wine we've yet to get to, just as Lou is slinking his way onto the couch. Neither of us object.

"Check that scrap," I say, pointing toward a curled-up sliver that's fallen to the floor as I fire up her laptop. "I think I saw a name."

Hannah swipes it up. "It says, 'Jean-Luc Pompo.' Is that a name?"

"Oh boy. How pretentious is this guy?"

"Apparently pretentious enough to paint fake grapes and use two first names."

"I can't believe I'm doing this."

I open up the browser and type in the web address for a search engine, punch in the phrase in the search bar, and easily find his webpage. It's gaudy by every definition of the word, and I momentarily consider the feasibility of fleeing the country to avoid both interacting with this art snob and inevitably dropping a bomb in the middle of Steve and Seph's relationship.

One piece of what he's billing as "minimalistic art" pops up, but it just looks like a bunch of paperclips strung together and glued on canvas. Then, something resembling a four-year-old's drawing of his family floats onto the screen, and at least three other paintings spin and twirl and bounce into view, like the whole site was made by a fifth grader who figured out how to use transitions in PowerPoint.

It's capped off with a video of the man himself, and he launches into his spoken autobiography, which includes things like "born with a paintbrush in my hand" and "called into the work by the universe itself," and I wonder if he was just the product of a poor bet the universe lost.

"Art people," I murmur grimly.

"I was really hoping you just opened up a really bad porno and not this artist's website," Hannah says.

She's got her face screwed up in disgust, though Lou has dropped his thick head on her crossed legs and she's rubbing his temples passively.

I hurriedly punch the Pause button on the video and try to clear all the other pop-ups to find the site's main menu. It takes a few more clicks, and instead of the typical hamburger icon in the right corner, it's a feather. I'm not sure what that has to do with his art, but I click on it anyway and find his contact form. It appears on the screen as a bubble and pops animatedly when I type my name into the first field.

"Help me come up with some sort of compliment for this horrible painting," I say.

"Oh, I've got this. Tell him, 'the soft pink is like the blush of freshly swatted skin' or 'the coils of vine are tight like passion twisting between reunited lovers...'"

I look up at Hannah as her voice trails off. Her eyes are closed and one hand is in the air as if grasping oxygen like it's palpable, and I gag.

"How'd you come up with that?"

She blinks to awareness, drops her hand back to Lou's forehead, and then shrugs. "I had a particularly passionate elementary-school art teacher."

"And he spoke like that to a bunch of ten-year-olds?"

"We didn't know any better."

I stifle another urge to spew and type something half as raunchy. Then, I follow it up with a not-at-all-disguised plea for any duplicate of the painting he may have in his back collection, praying that even a print of the original is available.

"You really counting on him to reply?" Hannah asks.

"It's the only idea I have right now."

"Look up my old teacher while we wait. Maybe I can convince him into making a dupe."

"A dupe? You mean, a forgery?"

Hannah scoffs loud enough that Lou jerks his head off her lap. She pats him reassuringly, and he resituates himself.

"If anything's a dupe, it's the original," she says. "Steve was conned."

I don't argue what is clearly truth.

She gives me her former teacher's name—Neil Jorgensen—which sounds just as fraudulent as Jean-Luc Pompo, though there are significantly more people with the same first-and-last-name pairing. I have to dig through several social pages before she thinks she recognizes a shiny hairless head and argyle sweater.

"He doesn't look quite like I remember," she says, pouting her lips and cinching her brows. "On second thought, maybe we don't reach out."

"Good call. But maybe you're on the right track."

"How so?"

"What's the politically correct way to solicit an art forger?"

She sits up straighter and blinks at me slowly. "Are you serious?"

"What other option do we have? If the real artist doesn't reply...I mean, we *have* to replace this painting."

"Okay," Hannah says, though she doesn't sound exactly convinced. "What about 'art copycat'?"

I enter her suggestion into the search bar, and it returns a bunch of anime women with cat ears, a few actual cats, and an image of a cartoon cat pawing at the *Mona Lisa*.

"Give me something else."

She pauses the ear-scratching and frowns. "How about 'art impressionist'?"

"Try again. The internet seems to think we want to decorate our house with paintings by Van Gogh or Degas or Matisse."

"I'm surprised you even know their names."

"I'm just reading the top hits."

"I see. How about—"

"Wait," I interrupt as a desktop notification pops up. I didn't even think twice about using Hannah's email in the contact form, but I'm glad I did. "The artist replied."

Hannah sits up again, eliciting a grumble from his highness. Each of us pats Lou, and then I pop open the message and read.

"'Dearest art enthusiast'"—I pause just to frown deliberately at Hannah—"'I am profoundly delighted by your inquiry for a reproduction of one of my finest works, *Rosé Veritas*. The vision for this piece first manifested itself whilst I was foraging for inspiration atop the Italian Alps...'"

"Italian Alps? That *has* to be the last place in the world to make you think of rosé."

She's right, but I keep reading. "'It was during my counseled tour...'"

"He means 'guided'," Hannah translates.

"'...that I experienced the abject pleasure of a beautiful, pale-faced woman breathing life into a remarkably round sphere...'"

"Oh my god, is he talking about—"

"'Bubblegum: the finest shade of fuchsia, glistening and vibrant, and the most perfect contour of comestibles. Thus was born the delicate and somber orbs of eventual, fermented bliss.'"

"Rosé grapes," Hannah bemoans, her mouth slack with disgust. "He means *rosé grapes*."

I nod in agreement, but I've already scanned the next line, and it makes my gut churn. "He's not going to do it."

"What?"

I turn the computer around and shove it Hannah's direction. "'Mercury's in retrograde' or something. He says he can't 'metaphysically return to the creative space in which that masterpiece was birthed'."

I'm quoting the message even though she's reading the whole thing.

"I'm not even sure that's the right use of metaphysical," Hannah says.

"What are we going to do now?"

"Don't worry. I'm not going to let you ruin your ex-boyfriend's new girlfriend's record-breaking trip to Sonoma."

She pulls the laptop onto her knees, and I urge Lou my way, partly because she's abandoned him and partly because it's kind of calming to stroke his brindled fur while he softly snores. Hannah's fingers skip over the mousepad and keyboard, clearly navigating to a new page and then typing hurriedly. She's several minutes in when she finally turns the computer around.

"How's this?"

I recognize the site she's on immediately because it's destitute. Plain. Hardly enough HTML to make it functional.

"Craigslist?"

"I'm guessing this is where all the art forgers hide," she says, and I don't think I can argue it.

She's written a couple paragraphs discreetly inquiring for someone with "artistic leanings" to "re-create a treasured masterpiece." It reads more like she's errantly misplaced her late great-grandmother's favorite watercolor and simply needs a near-copy to place at her headstone.

I glance at Lou, who's settled deeper into my lap. A string of drool slips from his jowl and soaks into my pants.

"The things I do for love," I say.

Six

"Back in her natural habitat," Hannah crows as her head pops up above my cubicle wall. "How early did you get here?"

I roll my chair back and tug my blue-light-blocking glasses halfway down my nose. "Well, between the destruction on Saturday night and another uncomfortably probing dinner with my mom yesterday, I didn't exactly have time to catch up on work over the weekend."

Hannah scoffs, shaking her ginger pony back and forth. "Catch up? Since when do you even fall behind?"

"I needed to get ahead, then. I've got to take an hour out of my day today to meet with the realtor about the, uh, *hardwood* issue at my house."

"That'll take five minutes," she argues, and she swings around the corner and prances into my cubicle, situating herself against the short filing cabinet in the corner she regularly uses as her conversation stool. "I need you to put away your spreadsheets and your"—she glances at my desk and frowns—"printing calculator? How old is that thing? And *how* have I never seen it before?"

I shove the vintage 80s machine with spooled paper just out of her reach. I don't need her punching the buttons for that satisfying *click-clack* sound or fidgeting with the wire paper holder and jamming up the feed.

"Don't you have work to do?" I ask instead, and she shrugs.

"I'm a recruiter. I've got all the time in the world."

"How could I forget?"

Hannah actually headhunted me—that's how we met—and I do remember several anxiety-filled phone calls with my mom where I was stressing over every passing day that my potential employer did *not* call me back after what I felt was a stellar interview.

Now I know what she must have been up to.

"Besides, this is more important," she goes on as she pulls her phone out of her pocket. "We got a hit."

"A hit?"

Hannah beams at me and pushes the phone into my hands. "Apparently, they're called replication experts. Who knew?"

I glance at the screen where she's got an email pulled up. It's hardly two sentences long, but judging by the automatically generated subject line courtesy of the internet's most basic website, I know it's a reply to the Craigslist post.

"He said he's in," Hannah confirms. "All we have to do is text him to set up a meet and—"

"How do you know it's a guy?"

Hannah frowns at my interruption but taps the screen and spreads two fingers to zoom in on the signature line at the bottom of the message, where the writer left his calling card. Then, she eyes me deliberately and cocks a brow.

"That's what he's using as an email address?" I demand.

"I thought it was clever."

"You need to raise your standards," I say, and I roll just out of her reach as she moves to pinch my arm. I grab my phone, punch in the number our respondent offered up, and then return Hannah's cell.

"What are you doing?" she asks.

I swipe open a blank text message and type a quick note. "Setting up the meet."

She bounds to her feet. "Ooh! Where should we go? I saw this super cute new coffee shop we could hit up. Or"—she claps her hands together—"it'd be a great excuse to go to the pier. And there's that fancy bar we've always talked about visiting—"

"*We* are not going anywhere," I say, and Hannah shrivels like I've just funneled all the blood out of her body. "I'll meet the guy myself after work."

"Why can't I come?"

"*You* have a dog to take care of."

Hannah waves a hand in the air. "Oh, that's a non-issue. I'll just hire someone to go let him out."

"You're kidding me, right?"

"It's so easy," she says, and her pony goes swinging again as she pulls out her phone. "There's even an app for it. I just punch in the date and the address and—"

"You are *not* letting some stranger go take care of Lou."

"Why not?"

"Because it's Lou," I argue, though I'm not really sure what it means.

There's nothing wrong with hiring help for hounds stuck at home, but for some reason, it rubs me the wrong way. I'm pretty sure Steve vets every person who comes in contact with his pup, including full background check, social media review, and heck, probably a drive-by of their residence to make sure they're not a closet cat-lover strategically planning to wreak havoc on the competing domestic animal.

"You can't possibly think meeting some stranger from the internet alone is safe," Hannah argues.

"You were about to take this guy out on a date," I point out, but Hannah just grins innocently, so I finish the text and hit Send.

"What'd you say?"

I recite my message for her: "'SFPD on Bryant. Six pm. Tell me what you're wearing.'"

Hannah throws her head back and lets out a cackle that can surely be heard all the way across the office. "Are you secretly a serial killer?"

I scowl at her. "What would you have said?"

"Not, 'Hi, I plan to meet you at an inner-city precinct so I can immediately be carted to jail after flaying you like a fish.'"

"Oh come on, it's not that bad."

"He's going to block your number."

"He won't if he wants this job," I argue, and I'm monumentally relieved (and a little surprised) when my phone dings with an incoming text.

Hannah snatches my cell from my hands before I can even open the message, holding it just out of my reach as she reads the response: "'What kind of pervert asks what I'm wearing?'"

"That's not what he said."

"Oh, it is," she murmurs, and she returns the phone, clearly satisfied.

I type out a scathing reply, uttering every word out loud: "'What kind of lunatic replies to a Craigslist ad for an art forger?'"

He replies in another two seconds, and I give the phone to Hannah, completely unwilling to voice his response, which suggests my level of lunacy far outweighs his, since he's a *replicator* and I'm a *solicitor*.

Hannah types another message, and the phone dings again. "He says, 'Show me yours and I'll show you mine.'"

"What in tarnation?"

"Tarnation? *Tarnation*? Dear heavens, you need to get out. He means your outfit."

Hannah turns the phone toward me, showing the image that's popped up, and it's either a strangely symmetrical photo of square plots of land butting up against a blue river or a really zoomed-in picture of brown checkered flannel on dark jeans.

"Absolutely not—"

But the click of a fake shutter sounds, and Hannah is promptly swiping her fingers across the screen and tapping buttons that result in the unmistakable swoosh of a sent text message.

I snatch the phone back from her. "You sent him a picture of my *legs*!"

"You moved," Hannah says nonchalantly. "Cute tights, by the way."

I swallow, and it feels like I've just gulped down a box of loose staples. I'm wearing a wool skirt and sheer tights and the tiny square frame Hannah managed to capture includes the gap between my thighs. If he thought I was a solicitor before, then—

"Look," she says as the phone chimes again. "Mr. Replicator's got a sense of humor."

I don't want to see it, but I also can't look away. He's returned a photo of his lower half—fully clothed, thankfully—but it looks like he's lying on his side, one leg extended and the other bent at the knee in what everyone understands as the *draw-me-like-one-of-your-French-girls* pose.

"This is a bad idea," I say, all the humor in my voice gone. I push away Hannah's hand, jump out of my seat, and start pacing the narrow three feet of my cubicle. "If Steve knew we were even entertaining this idea..."

"He's not going to find out," Hannah says, resettling on the filing cabinet and crossing her arms. "That's the whole point. You said so yourself."

I brake and spin on my heels to face her. "You know we had rules, right?"

"I'm not really sure I want to know—"

"Don't meet strangers from the internet, for one. And, in the scenario where it is absolutely unavoidable, *never* tell them what you're wearing. It gives them the upper hand."

"I'm pretty sure this is a lower leg."

"*Hannah*," I whine, and she snickers in return.

"You're meeting at the police department, for crying out loud. Call Grant and have him go with you if you're so concerned. He'll be glad to help."

"I'm not calling my ex-boyfriend's partner."

"Ex-boyfriend's ex-partner, technically. But fine, meet the guy alone. He seems like a real stand-up citizen."

I wonder if there's any chance this office building has a pillow I can scream into, but I know my therapist would be very disappointed with me, so I inhale two deep breaths and plaster on a fake smile instead.

"I'll be fine. There will be plenty of other cops there, and no one who's even remotely shady would agree to meeting in a precinct parking lot, so—"

"Okay, so maybe he's remotely shady," Hannah interrupts, though she's looking at the phone again. "He says, 'No cops. Meet me at the Museum of Modern Art. The bench under the Cassius Marcellus Coolidge exhibit.'"

"Who the hell is Cassius Marcellus Coolidge?"

Hannah frowns, prods the screen several times, and then laughs. She turns the phone around, showing me an image search of what must be his most famous paintings.

"Oh my god," I say. "I'm meeting an insane person."

Seven

The exhibit is not hard to find, and neither is the bench.

It's in the center of the room, a back-to-back bench, and patrons are sitting on both sides. There's an older couple at one end leaning up against each other, the man nodding off on the woman's shoulder, and a pregnant mom at the other end chugging water as her toddler stamps up and down on the seat next to her. In the middle, a few solo visitors are staggered on either side.

One guy tilts his head up and eyes me. He's leaning forward, elbows on his knees, and his jeans seem to be the same shade as those in the picture, but there isn't a scrap of flannel in sight. He's wearing a crooked trucker hat with an embroidered rooster and four letters I can't quite make out and I'm terrified it says something technically accurate but socially rude.

"Steve is going to kill me," I say out loud.

I think it comes with the territory, both being a woman and having dated a cop, that there are rules pounded into my head about staying safe when I'm out alone or being vigilant about my surroundings. Beyond the whole never-meet-a-stranger-from-the-internet bit, there's the few other no-brainers Steve expressly enforced: don't offer to exchange money, don't ever get in the car with someone you don't know, and *never* tell a stranger where you live.

The guy sits up, and I grant him half a smile. I'm not breaking any other rules yet, but *oh hell.* He stretches his arms across the back of the bench, and I finally get a clear view of the loose tee he's wearing. There's a giant *T, K,* and the delta symbol. Underneath it, the phrase, "Tappa Kegga Day."

I think I finally understand the meaning of his email address.

"Lou, you're gonna owe me," I mumble, and I head toward the bench.

I've barely touched the seat before the guy slides over, cocks a brow, and grins.

"Finally," he says. "Been here an hour and just now get to experience a work of art."

"Nope." The word is out of my mouth and I'm off the seat before he can even move.

"Okay, okay, I'm sorry," he blusters, raising two hands. "I just wanted to see you smile."

I grind around on my heels. "Do you do this with everyone you meet here?"

"Just the pretty ones."

"You need help."

"Oh, come on."

"No. No, you know exactly why I'm here and this—this charade or whatever is not—"

The guy opens his mouth, probably to utter something else just as appalling, but a distant shout draws our attention.

It comes from a security guard, like one you see in the movies. He's got crisp black slacks and a gray shirt buttoned all the way up to his neck. There's a giant gold badge on his chest and he's wearing one of those stiff perishing caps with a visor that I'm pretty sure isn't standard issue but rather an after-market internet purchase.

"You're not supposed to be here!" he yells, one hand on his baton—because he's a rent-a-cop and this is a public museum—and the other reaching for a walkie-talkie on his belt. "Stay right there."

"Oh shit," the guy in front of me mutters. "Kiss for the road?"

"*Kiss for the road*? You have to be out of your—"

"Eh, maybe next time, then."

Before I can even explain how infinitesimally small the chances of a "next time" are, he's pulling down his hat, hiking up his baggy jeans, and taking off across the museum, dodging the mom and toddler at the far end and nearly clipping the corner of a sculpture in the next room.

I'm still equal parts confused and appalled, distracted by the chase as the security guard dashes after him, when another man near the center of the bench speaks up.

"I'm pleasantly surprised. That wasn't the worst pick-up line he's tried this afternoon."

"Come again?" I say, though I'm not even sure this man is talking to me. He's on the opposite side of the bench, his back to me, speaking out of the side of his mouth.

"Nope, he didn't try that one yet. *Thank god*. You'd think parking it under a painting of dogs playing cards would deter all the lunatics. Guess we aren't so lucky."

I blink a few times, eyeing the exhibit this man is staring at without really comprehending it.

"Some poor girl sat down and commented on the piece," he goes on, "and that nutcase had the nerve to try both a line offering to *poker* and then to *bury his bone*."

"Are you serious?"

"Don't worry. That girl was smart enough to bolt."

"What is wrong with men?" I growl, and that gets the stranger to turn all the way around.

"Hey, don't lump me in with that guy. I'm the one who called security to get his sleazy ass out of here."

"What a relief," I say sarcastically. "Chivalry isn't dead; it's just hiding under sunglasses and a ballcap."

The man bristles, but I can't make out any other reaction given the ultra-dark shades and the way his bulky Carhartt jacket is gathered around his neck. He huffs shortly, dips his chin, and then turns around in his seat. From the bench next to him, he pulls up a newspaper—and I do mean an old-fashioned, fresh-off-the-press periodical—and spreads it out noisily, crinkling the edges as he uses it to shield his face.

"I must have missed the moral compass on your scholastic leggings," he mumbles.

"That's because they're math symbols. And they're not leggings," I say, barely controlling the urge to snatch that paper out of his hands so he can look me in the eyes while he insults me, but I drop my chin to the patterned sheers just as it clicks. "Wait, are you..."

"Took you for a girl who could put two and two together."

"Your email was *VanBro* at gmail dot com," I say with a scoff, and that gets him to abandon the newspaper and turn around in his seat again.

"What was I supposed to use? *PicassOMG* was already taken, and *MakeThatMonet* felt pretentious."

"What is wrong with you?"

"It's not like I put sixty-nine or four-twenty in my username. I'm a professional."

"Right. A professional art forger."

"Art *replicator*," he corrects, but it's under his breath like it's a bad word. "Will you please just sit down and stop trying to tell the entire museum you think I'm into criminal activity?"

"Well, you sure as heck look like it in that getup."

"What's wrong with my—never mind." He yanks off his sunglasses, unzips his jacket, and throws his hands in the air. "Happy?"

Every response I try to conjure seems to turn to dust and drift away on an invisible puff of air. He's in the flannel I saw in the picture, and there's a whole lot more to it than the rivers and fields I saw earlier.

It's snug in a way it shouldn't be, pulled taut across his chest. He's got it neatly buttoned, save for the first few at the top, where it bares the hollow of his neck. It shifts like thick fleece, and let me tell you, a shirt's got no business looking as soft and warm as it does, like it was destined for pajama wear and not outdoor chores.

He breathes—a little huff of annoyance, I think—but I want him to do it again because it draws my attention up. Up to the lines of his jaw. The ridge of his cheekbones. The curt *v* of his brow. And *oh my*. The slight shimmer in his irises.

"Hey," he nips, "look *in* my eyes, not *at* my eyes. I'm trying to have a conversation with you."

I snap back to attention, and the frown he's been wearing jumps to my face. "What is that supposed to mean?"

"You know damn well what that means. I'm a human being, not some object for you to ogle."

"Oh, if you think—"

"I don't have to think it; it's written all over your pretty little face."

"I—you—what did you say about my face?"

"There. We're even," he says, turning back around in his seat and getting comfortable. "Now that *that's* out of the way, will you sit down and tell me exactly what you need?"

Eight

I stay on my side of the bench and sit back-to-back with him.

He doesn't object, and maybe it plays into this whole undercover look he's got going on for some reason, but it also happens to situate us much closer together than I'd have normally allowed.

We're so close I can smell him. And I'm realizing now that sounds possibly more insane than anything this stranger has done so far, but that scent is unmistakable. It's the smell of lumber or freshly shaved sawdust, and I get the sudden mental image of a flannelled lumberjack swinging an axe in the middle of the woods, and *oh my god*.

I primly cross one leg over the other and flip back my hair. This is San Francisco. He might favor plaid shirts and somehow carve wood in his free time, but he's not chopping trunks in the middle of Golden Gate Park.

"What is it that you do exactly?" I ask, bringing myself back to the conversation and hoping my question sounds casual and not completely ignorant.

"What is it exactly that you need?"

"You saw the post, and I'm the one asking questions here. How do I know you're actually an artist and not just someone trying to rip me off?"

"If it's an art degree or a website you want to see, you're not going to get that."

I turn in the seat to get a better look at him. "No *VanBro* dot com?"

He glances sideways at me but then turns forward again.

"I'm going to need you to prove you're an artist somehow," I try again.

"What do you suggest?" he asks, but I get the impression it's just him returning the sarcasm.

"Draw me something."

"I don't draw on command."

"Isn't that all an artist does?"

He turns in his seat again, setting that rigid look on me like he wants to pin my mouth shut and something in me inexplicably wonders if he'd use his mouth to do it.

"You're the one who needs me, not the other way around," he asserts, and I try to bring my wandering mind back. "I didn't give you a hard time about your sketchy ad. I showed up to help you. I picked an art museum—for which you'll need to reimburse me, by the way. And I've got paint on my clothes. I am who I say I am."

He peels the jacket back farther to reveal errant splatters of white and yellow and blue across the taut brown fabric of his shirt, and it kills the urge for me to blatantly deny his request for admission reimbursement.

"An art replicator?" I manage to say weakly, slowly bringing my eyes back to his.

"An art replicator."

"Fine. I need you to re-create a painting destroyed by a dog."

He settles in again, leans back casually, and situates both arms across the back of the bench. "What kind of painting?"

"I don't know. What types are there?"

"No—what's it a painting of? Who's the original artist?"

"Oh," I say, stalling, and I find myself fidgeting with the hem of my skirt. "It's a picture of fruit, by some guy named Jean-Luc Pompo."

He whips around in his seat again, and I wonder why either of us is still insisting on sitting on opposite sides when we're both going to leave here with whiplash.

"Jean-Luc Pompo?" he repeats, but he says the name with a thick French accent, opposed to the ignorant American one I've been using to pronounce the name. "How do you have a painting by that guy?"

"Well, it's not mine, and if you think that guy's special or something, you're gravely mistaken."

He lets out a short, booming laugh, and I nearly shiver at the sound.

"That guy's the worst thing that's happened to art since Lisa Frank school supplies. Your dog did you a favor."

"Not my dog," I correct too quickly.

"This just keeps getting better."

It takes me about ten minutes to explain how Lou nearly ate the thing for dinner because the nosy art replicator who stubbornly refuses to move to my side of the bench stops me about every two sentences to spout shock over the fact my best friend volunteered to dogsit for my ex and how I'd even entertain the idea of replacing his new girlfriend's prized possession.

"Let me guess: You're still hung up on the guy?"

"No," I answer flatly, "and that's a pretty rude question to ask someone you don't know."

He's watching me again, his eyes darting down to my mouth as I speak, like the shade of glossy pink on my lips is somehow more interesting than any of the world-renowned art pieces posted up every five feet in this museum.

"Forgive me," he says, but his voice is a strange mix of humor and curiosity. "Make it even. Ask me something rude."

I pull my best shrewd look because, surprisingly, nothing comes to mind. My entire head is wordless and mushy and feels as if someone's tipped me upside down and shaken me like a snow globe. Any would-be thoughts are useless, fluttering flakes.

"I have nothing," I finally say, and one of his brows twitches.

"Save it for later then. Let's see a picture of this painting."

The snow-globe feeling intensifies, as if I've just been slammed back down to the counter. "Picture?"

"I need to know what I'm trying to re-create here."

"I—well, I didn't think to take a picture," I admit, and it comes out exactly as embarrassing as it sounds.

"You don't have a picture? How am I supposed to paint something to look exactly like something else I've never seen before?"

"I didn't think—"

"Do you have any way to get a photo of it?"

"I mean, it's at the house still. I can go back and get you a picture of it."

"Didn't you say it's in a dozen pieces?"

"So?"

"Don't you need this done immediately?"

I press my hands flat to my wool skirt to avoid poking him in the chest because, yes I do, but no, I don't like the way he's pointing it out.

"Within the next two weeks would be ideal."

"Then I need to see it tonight. Come on, let's go."

I don't have time to react before he's rising to his feet, zipping up his jacket, and refolding the newspaper and stuffing it into his pocket like he plans to do the crossword later.

"We're not going anywhere," I say, still firmly planted on the bench.

He settles both hands in his pockets and tosses me a look that makes me cross my legs a little tighter.

"Listen, I don't even know how big this painting is or what kind of paint it requires or how long it's going to take me to build a frame that goes with it. If you need this done before your boyfriend gets back—"

"*Ex*-boyfriend," I correct, "and that's rude comment number two."

"Take a raincheck," he grumbles. "If there's any chance we're going to get this done, then I need to see the painting tonight."

I hold firm in my seat, but it's all for show. He's not necessarily wrong, and I am officially starting to panic. When it comes to making well-planned-out, calculated moves, I'm the girl for the job, but this off-the-cuff stuff—this brazen, risky, spontaneous behavior I've somehow picked up in the past two days—is so far out of my comfort zone, and I'm not sure how to reign it in.

"Hannah's going to be there," I blurt, as if some man who looks built to haul entire tree trunks across wooded mountainsides is scared by the presence of a second, skirt-wearing woman.

"The friend who volunteered to dogsit?"

"Her and the dog, and he doesn't like everyone he meets." A lie, but I need at least a little ammunition.

"I have a feeling this dog's got pretty good taste."

"Fine," I say, though I have no idea why I'm agreeing to this. "I'll give you the address and then—"

"I'll just go with you."

"Oh, no, no, no. I'm not letting you get in my car," I say, and I think it's the first logical thing that's come out of my mouth since I started brainstorming synonyms of *forgery*.

"Well, I don't have one."

"So take the bus."

"Not happening."

"Then neither is this," I snap back, and he shrugs casually.

"Fine. I'm out. Good luck finding someone else."

He ends the sentence with a short click of his tongue and turns away.

I watch him go, all sharp edges and arrogant strides, and it's not the loss of his artistic expertise that seems to spear me through the chest but the absence of a tingle in my core that's been feeding on the mystery and intrigue and fiery co-interest. It's an unfamiliar, hollow feeling in my gut that swells with every step he takes away from me.

"Wait," I call, and I'm on my feet just as his gait falters. "Will you tell me your name at least?"

He turns slowly, tilts his head down, and meets my gaze as I catch up.

"I can't get in a car with a stranger," I say, "so just tell me your name."

His eyes flick back and forth between mine, and I try not to look *at* them but *in* them because I've already been scolded once tonight.

"Fin," he says. "One *n,* not two."

I run my hands down my skirt and reach for one of the embroidered math symbols on my tights—a plus sign, I think.

"Millie. No *n*'s at all."

Nine

It's somehow both the longest and shortest drive of my life.

I'm panicking internally—because, *hello*, I just got in the car with a man I met half an hour ago—but he also doesn't try to engage in conversation, so I queue up a few of my favorite songs, he eyes the display as they cycle through, and neither of us says anything else.

There is a small throat-clearing grunt when a song by The Cure comes on, and I know it's one Hannah can't stand, but it's on my regular rotation and Fin aims his gaze out the window and leaves it at that.

"This is it," I say as I bring the car to a stop in front of Steve's townhouse.

There's a small patch of grass in the front, a narrow alley on the side where the trash and recycle bins are stored, and then several steps up to the front door.

Fin eyes it curiously. "What does this guy do?"

"Don't worry about it."

It's the politest answer for what I deem another rude question, but I try not to make a big deal about it either. The less this stranger knows, the better.

I can see there's a light on in the kitchen. I texted Hannah from the museum letting her know to expect us, so I hurry out of the car. I'm at the front door, hand on the knob, wondering for the last time if this is the dumbest decision I've ever made, when the front door goes flying open and Hannah comes screaming out.

"Hot! Hot, hot, oh my god—you're not supposed to be here yet!"

She's got panic written all over her face. Her cheeks are pink and her eyes are wide and I'm pretty sure she's got flour in her hair, but I'm also distracted by the oversize oven mitts she's wearing as she brandishes a cookie sheet with something that looks an awful lot like lumps of charcoal.

"Out of the way!" she screams again, but it doesn't matter.

Lou has figured out the front door is open, and out of the corner of my eye, I see him barrel toward us. His jowls ripple and his shoulders flex and he heads straight for Hannah's legs.

Back on my left side, Fin is shucking off his jacket and spreading it out between his arms for some reason, and I'm wondering if he really thinks Lou is going to charge him and latch on like a trained attack dog. It's funny—for just a second—because we could hardly manage to convince Lou not to lick every person he met let alone train him to maul bad guys.

"Lou, no!" I command anyway just as Hannah starts to crumple.

"Give me the tray," Fin demands, and a few blackened lumps pop in the air as she practically tosses it into Fin's coat-covered arms.

Meanwhile, I scramble for Lou's collar with one hand and Hannah's arm with the other, and all three of us end up in a tangled mass in the entryway just as Fin dodges the doggie pile and stomps back down the front steps.

"Seriously, Lou," I moan, and it earns me a slobbery kiss on the cheek.

"Did he just...?" Hannah starts, propping herself up on her elbows.

I manage to sit up cross-legged and we watch as Fin lifts the trash can lid with one hand and dumps whatever's on the tray into the garbage.

"Are those...?"

"Cookies," Hannah fills in.

"For what?"

"Our guest," she exclaims, and she yanks out an arm that's pinned under Lou's weight. "What else are you supposed to feed art forgers?"

"He's not—" But the words never quite make it out.

Lou perks up as he realizes belatedly there's a third person wandering his front yard. He lets out a bark, lurches back to all fours, and tramples down the steps.

There's really no point in me calling his name, trying to tell him to slow down, or begging him to *please* refrain from bringing a grown man to his knees, but it's all moot anyway. Fin willingly drops the coat and the empty cookie sheet in the grass and falls to his knees.

"Whoa, boy!" he says, but it's not the rough and gravelly voice he's been using with me. No, it's strangely soft and gentle and...babyish? "You must be Lou. You're a sweet pup, aren't you? A good dog for chewing that horrid painting."

"What the—" I start.

"Is he—" Hannah begins.

Lou thumps his front paws to Fin's chest while Fin dodges Lou's slobbery tongue, and then both are rolling around in the grass like they've known each other their whole lives.

"Your text said he was kind of rude and broody," Hannah says, eyeing me.

"He *was*. He was a totally different person before...before...*Lou*."

Hannah lets out a short laugh and gets to her feet. "Weren't we all?"

I get up too and don't argue the point, instead calling Lou back up to the house. He gives a few more playful nips to Fin, who's enthusiastically encouraging him, and then bounds up the steps. Fin climbs to his feet, grabs the tray and his coat, and follows.

"I think it's cool now," he says, handing the cookie sheet back to Hannah.

Her jaw is hanging open and her eyes are practically glistening as she takes the tray in an oven-mitted hand and then offers to take his coat in her other, like we're really entertaining this guy and not about to engage in a somewhat shady exchange of goods.

Fin doesn't have a problem accepting the offer, and after he surrenders his coat, he reaches for the buttons on one sleeve of his flannel.

"Let's see what we're working with here," he says as he steps over the threshold.

His confidence only exacerbates Hannah's awestruck look, and now I'm sliding right into that same offense, practically ogling Fin's forearm as he meticulously cuffs his sleeve. The curve of his muscle is lined with faded black ink that loops and swirls, all soft lines and strategic shading that somehow converge into the image of an animal, maybe. There are wings and a beak but also a not-very-birdlike tail and—

"Ahem," Fin grunts, jerking my attention away. "The painting?"

"Right," I say.

"It's over here," Hannah adds, and she nearly purrs as she spins on her heels and struts back into the house.

Fin follows us into the dining area where Hannah and I left the remains of the painting.

Honestly, we did try to piece it back together Saturday night after we'd posted the ad, but the only puzzles I'm good at are the mathematical kind, and by the time we'd even embarked on the effort, we were buzzed on wine and had inadvisably navigated to the Missed Connections section of Craigslist. Reading those made for a much more entertaining evening.

"What did you say this was a painting of?" Fin asks as he eyes the scraps of canvas and twisted frame.

"Fruit," I say weakly. "Technically, grapes."

"They're pink."

Hannah ditches her oven mitts and sidles up next to me. "She didn't tell you they're rosé grapes?"

"Rosé grapes? You do know—"

"We know," I say with a huff. "Now can you re-create the painting or not?"

Fin grunts, seemingly back in his gritty mood, and refocuses on the scraps. He rearranges a few, turns some upside down, fills in most of the giant hole in the middle of the canvas where Lou's head was, and then tries to flatten the twisted frame.

"The painting isn't going to be a problem," Fin finally says. "It's the frame."

I edge closer to the table. "You need a custom size or something? Doesn't Michaels do that?"

He lets out a short laugh, and I nip back at him.

"What?"

Fin picks up a four-inch piece of wood that completely snapped off and holds it up, hardly an inch from my nose. He runs a finger along the edge, and I have to force myself to pay attention to what he's pointing at and not the paint flecks that dot his skin.

"This is a custom carving," he says. "There are grapes and vines etched into the wood."

I pretend like this isn't the first time I'm noticing it. "Can't you just re-create that too?"

"What makes you think I could do that?"

"I don't know. I guess I assumed you..."

"Assumed what?"

"You know..."

"You assumed I work with wood?"

"Don't you?"

Fin narrows his eyes at me, and I'm almost brazen enough to prove I know he does, but Hannah jumps in instead.

"I don't think I need to know about the wood he works with."

Fin's only reply is a sideways glance at Hannah and then he refocuses on me. "I need to call a guy."

"Oh no. We're not getting anyone else involved in this," I say, finally regaining some sense.

"Do you want this done in two weeks or not?"

I falter because I'm beginning to wonder if this attitude of his is meant only for me. "You better not be screwing with me."

He takes that as permission, turns back to the painting, plucks a phone from his pocket, and dials. Meanwhile, Hannah drags me by the arm back into the kitchen where I finally take notice of the disaster that was cookie baking.

Spilled sugar crunches under my feet, and there's flour dusted on the refrigerator door handle and a split-open bag of chocolate chips on the counter. The dog-mom in me automatically scans the floor for errant pieces and is relieved to find none, though I realize Lou doesn't even care what goods are in the kitchen.

He's at the table, sitting next to Fin as Fin scratches him steadily behind the ears.

"Holy hell, you didn't tell me this guy was *cute*," Hannah chimes in, and it's not exactly under her breath.

I try to shush her and move farther into the kitchen. "What does that have to do with anything?"

"You think you can manage to wait until *after* this fiasco is over to hook up with him?"

"Can *you*?"

"Oh, I've got all I need," Hannah counters, and she waves a hand like *cute* never came out of her mouth.

"What is that supposed to mean?"

"City-dwelling lumberjack seems more your type."

"Don't get your hopes up. I'm not hooking up with a stranger I met on the internet."

"It's really not that crazy anymore," Hannah informs me, and she leans back against the counter, scoops up a handful of loose chocolate chips, and pops a couple in her mouth. "I mean, between dating apps and social media and Missed Connections, it's impossible to meet someone *not* on the internet."

"Missed Connections start off in person," I point out.

"But as *strangers*. It's basically the same thing."

I ignore the comment and move on. "He's still rude and broody."

"Oh, I think it's all for show."

"That?" I say, jerking a thumb backward, where I expect to find Fin growling to some unfortunate chum on the other end of the line. Only, he's not.

He's squatting down, holding the phone to his ear with one hand and shaking Lou's paw with the other. He pretends to greet the dog in silence, while listening to whoever is on the other end, and then switches to the opposite paw, shaking that one too.

I whirl back around and zero in on Hannah. "This is just a job. We're hiring him to paint us a picture, and then we're done."

"Maybe *we* are, but *you* don't need to be."

"There are no other goods to be exchanged here."

"Oh, honey, I'm not talking goods; I'm talking services."

I shake my head but can't utter another word, and Hannah just beams amusedly. She then pops the last of her chocolate chips in her mouth and skips back to the dining room. I've barely caught up when Fin ends his call, gets back to his feet, and leans against the table.

"So, let's hear it," Hannah says. "Can we pull off the greatest art heist of all time?"

"Not technically a heist," I correct dryly.

"Do you know what a heist is?" Fin asks at the same time.

Hannah seems to bubble with glee as she whips her head between the two of us. "Ah, so you're both a couple of rule-following experts, are you?"

"Not a rule," I say.

"Just a pretty basic definition," Fin adds.

Hannah tuts primly. "Am I even needed here?"

"Yes," I insist, eyeing her pointedly before looking back at Fin. "Can it be done or not?"

"It can be done," he says, and Lou lets out a sigh and slumps down to the floor as Fin abandons pettings to cross his arms over his chest. "I collect my fee up front, plus ten percent for incidental costs. Supplies are on you. The frame is extra. Cash only."

"Yeah no, we're not giving you cash up front."

"I don't even know how to get cash," Hannah pipes up. "Don't you take Venmo or something?"

"Cash only," he reiterates. "Those are the terms."

I eye Hannah warily. I've broken every single rule getting to this point except one: don't offer money to a stranger.

Yes, I knew there'd be an exchange of funds at some point but not before our forger proved his capability and certainly not in unverifiable bills. Electronic payments are at least partially recoverable if this guy really is just trying to scam us for a few bucks. Not to mention, Hannah is, as she admitted, illiterate in cash transactions—doesn't even have an ATM card because "debit is dirty"—so anything requiring real, live greenbacks would be coming straight from my account.

"What's it gonna be?" Fin asks, and I practically tremble.

"We're not giving you cash."

"Then I guess we're done here."

"Not yet."

Fin tightens his posture as he looks down at me. "I don't think there's much else for us to discuss."

"There is," I say, barely holding my voice steady. I glance at Hannah once more because I'm pretty sure what's about to come out of my mouth is verifiably insane. "Neither of us are giving you cash up front, but I will go with you."

Hannah gasps loud enough it causes Lou to jerk his chin up from the floor. Fin still poses stiffly, still leans against the table with his arms crossed, and I kind of wish my comment would have elicited at least some type of reaction, but he's virtually unbothered.

"You'll go with me where?" he asks.

"I don't know, to the paint store or whatever. Isn't that where you get supplies?"

Fin pinches his lips together, and the ridges of his cheeks sharpen.

"I'll pay for everything," I explain, "and I'll give you half your fee assuming you show up and at least know what kind of supplies to buy, but I'm not letting you walk out of here tonight with all my money."

I look to Hannah for reassurance, and she's grinning. It's strange, but I try not to linger on it and find Fin again. He pushes off from the table, drops his hands, and then shrugs.

"Fine. Paint store tomorrow at six."

"It's a date!" Hannah chimes, and now I know for certain what that grin is all about.

She bustles across the room to grab Fin's coat she dropped over the back of the couch and hands it to him as he heads toward the door. Lou trots after us, and Fin bends down to pat his head affectionately before reaching for the door handle.

He turns back just as he steps out. "I'll text you the address."

"Wait," Hannah says, "doesn't Millie need to take you home?"

I'm tempted to smack her because I sure as heck wasn't going to offer, but Fin just lets the corner of his mouth quirk up.

"Are you crazy?" he says. "I don't know either of you. No way I'm telling a couple of strangers I met on the internet where I live."

Ten

"There you are," Fin says, tossing a quick look over his shoulder before resuming his perusal of a shelf. "What happened to six p.m.?"

I grip my coat a little tighter around myself. "What happened to us going to Michaels?"

Fin makes a disgruntled noise but doesn't bother facing me. "We go where the paint is."

I don't reply right away, instead eyeing each end of the aisle, not-so-subtly ensuring there's an unblocked exit in both directions.

This place is tucked away in a back alley between a pay-by-the-hour motel and a laundromat. I had to park two blocks up the street and then squeeze through three far-too-narrow aisles before I found Fin hunched over, plucking up tubes of paint, inspecting them, and then putting them back.

"This is the only place that sells paint?" I ask.

Fin shoves a tube into my hands and then moves farther down the aisle. "This is the only place that sells the *right* paint."

I glance at the tube he gave me, a shade somewhat more red than pink but reminiscent of fake grapes, nonetheless. "Does it really matter?"

"It matters."

"Is it the type or the color?"

"Both."

"I see," I say, though it's a complete lie. "Don't you have paints at home you could just mix up?"

Fin drags in another breath and straightens up, turning to face me. "Who's the artist here?"

"To be fair, you still haven't proven you're an artist, and taking me to a shady craft store isn't going to do it."

Fin expels an exhausted-sounding sigh. "Mixing up colors is not the same thing. Replicating artwork takes skill and patience and the right supplies. You don't just combine old paint and hope for the best."

I open my mouth to tell him to save the excuses, but he shucks off his jacket and holds it out for me silently. I sling it over my shoulder—because what else am I supposed to do?—and he continues on.

"The shade of pink this Pompo guy used in that painting is one you can typically only get from an exclusive retailer in Santorini. They ship it over here to rich assholes who claim to be artists. Those guys use it for a dab, toss the tube, and then mark up the painting ten-fold. It's all part of how rich hobbyists corner the market."

My mouth is still open, but I don't plan to interrupt anymore, not with the way he speaks, the way he moves so effortlessly. He's rolled his sleeves again, more casually than he did the day before, and his brow is gently furrowed and his cheeks are charmingly pink. It's like he's a different version of himself, like he's just emerged from some alternate dimension, the same person physically but on a different trajectory emotionally.

"This place can usually get ahold of the half-used tubes, and they'll sell them at a reasonable price. That's what we're looking for. Be glad I'm not asking you to cover the cost to ship a new tube from overseas."

"Okay, but this place—"

"Is our best chance at making a believable replica," Fin finishes for me, and he jams an arm into the very back of a middle shelf. "The slightest inconsistency will ruin even the best look-alikes. Everything needs to be identical to the original: the shade or tint of paint, the spacing of brush hairs and angles of stroke, the amount of pressure applied. It's all *precise*."

"Okay, I get it. I was just saying you could have warned me we were coming here."

"How much warning do you need? I gave you the address."

I can't argue the point, and Fin pushes another tube into my hands, then continues down the aisle. We round the corner and emerge near the front of the store where we have a clear view of the main door—boarded up on one side—and a few of the locked display cases in the front. Fin ducks left and starts scouring some lower shelves that clearly hold all the used tubes.

"What's wrong with this place anyway?" he finally asks, more to the shelf than to me.

"It's nothing," I say, but Fin must sense me looking around the meagerly lit store, and he jerks his head upward, frowning.

"Are you concerned about being here?"

All I do is sigh, but apparently that's answer enough.

"Don't be so quick to judge a book by its cover," Fin says curtly, ducking his head again.

"I'm not. I do know this area."

"So do I."

"Great, so we're in agreement?"

"No, I don't think we are," Fin replies, and he moves again.

I don't follow. Instead, I plant my feet and cross my arms over my chest, a tube of paint still in each hand. All I want is for him to stop and acknowledge me for half a second. I don't need to be coddled or comforted for having ventured into this particular area of town, but a little *hey, appreciate you schlepping it over here* would be nice.

It doesn't take Fin long to notice my failure to cooperate, and when he swings his head back my direction, I swear the look on his face is equal parts annoyance and amusement. He straightens and his shoulders rise as he drags in a breath. Then, he shakes his head, expels the air forcefully, and marches right back to me.

"If you're going to insist on coming with me everywhere I go, then you're gonna have to keep up."

"If I'm going to follow you around everywhere you go, then you're gonna have to slow down."

"Slow down so you can criticize every place I take you?"

"No, slow down so you can acknowledge I'm a human being and not a walking ATM machine or a mobile grocery bag."

Fin's brows cinch together, almost like he's surprised I ever would have been led to think that way, and he glances down at the colors I'm still holding.

"Noted."

It's all he says, but it feels like so much more than a single word because he reaches out for me. I immediately think I should back away, curtly reject this near-stranger physically touching me, do just about anything except stand here and let his hand slide behind my back, but I don't.

He settles his fingers near the hem of my cropped jacket and extends his opposite arm, gesturing me down the aisle with obvious exaggeration. I'm almost tempted to giggle because he dips nearly low enough to constitute a bow as I move past him, but then he stops me another few feet away to resume his search for the perfect shade of pink and I grasp the first thought that might get things back on track.

"So, do you come here often?"

Fin lets out a short laugh. "Are you hitting on me now?"

"You'd be so lucky."

"I would," he says, and I barely register the comment before he's brushing past it and returning to the original subject. "I'm here a fair amount. It's where I tell the kids to come."

"Kids? What kids?"

The bell over the front door chimes just as soon as the question leaves my mouth, and Fin tosses his head over his shoulder. I follow his aim, not because I want to know what's going on at the front door, but because I want to know what's going on in his head. It's insanity, surely, because he turns back and grabs me again.

This time, Fin wraps a hand around both of my arms and physically switches places with me, positioning my back toward the door. "Stand here."

"For what?"

Fin just plucks up another tube from a nearby shelf and puts in my hand. "Tell me about your job."

"Excuse me, but I—"

"You said you're human. I assume you have a job."

"I do, but—"

That protest dies on my tongue too because Fin scoops up a quart-sized bottle of paint this time and shoves it toward my chest. I swing Fin's coat off my shoulder and tuck it under an arm, transfer all three tubes of paint I'm already holding to one hand, and then grab the bottle he's forcing on me with the other just as my phone starts buzzing.

"Oh, for crying out loud," I mutter, and I already know exactly who's calling.

It's a familiar jingle, one I programmed years ago to prevent a repeat incident where my picture nearly ends up on the face of a milk carton. It's another juggling act to free a hand for the phone, and I don't even get a greeting out before my mom is launching into her standard list of complaints.

"You know it's been four whole days you've been babysitting my grandpuppy—"

"I'm not the one babysitting—"

"—and I haven't seen him yet."

"Mom, I'm a little busy right now."

"Too busy to bring my Louie Boy over?"

"Yes! Well, no, not that—"

"Why are you keeping him from me?"

I finally concede with a sigh. "It's not intentional, Mom, okay? I'm sorry."

"Two weeks goes fast, you know," she blusters on.

I don't try replying and instead let her take off on a tangent, something about Hannah and Grant, though I don't catch it all. Meanwhile, Fin grabs me again, shifting me farther down the aisle and re-positioning my back toward the door, but this time he crouches, and I do react.

"What are you doing?" I demand, jerking backward into a display of spray paint as Fin sinks all the way to the floor.

"Hold still."

"Get up," I snip, but he doesn't budge. Instead, Fin's hands find my legs, and I squeal.

"Millie, what's wrong?" my mom asks over the phone.

"Nothing," I manage to say, though I wriggle in place.

Fin cinches my thighs, only a thin layer of tights between his warm fingers and my trembling skin, and I don't have the hands to bat his away, though that's not exactly the urge I'm getting either. Heat seems to emanate from the pads of his fingers and that tremble works its way all the way up my thighs and belly and into my chest.

"What are you doing?" I hiss again, and this time Fin ducks lower, his head inches from nuzzling right between my legs.

I stifle another squeal, and then he shifts right, peering around my hips. I follow his gaze to catch what he must be looking at: two men by the registers.

One is tall and thin, a dark beanie pulled almost low enough to cover his eyes, and the other is significantly shorter and wearing a scally cap like a cartoon villain.

I turn forward again, intending to ask if Fin knows them, but that's not the question that comes out of my mouth.

"Is this how you always get dressed?"

Fin has tugged his coat from where I've wedged it under one arm and haphazardly shoves his arms through the sleeves, still crouching low to the ground. He zips the coat, then reaches for the shelf behind me and starts sliding the spray paint cans around, and I'm pretty sure he's clearing a line of sight to the front door.

"Millie, what is going on?" my mom cries into the phone again.

"It's nothing."

"Are you with someone?"

"It's no one."

"No one?" Fin challenges, and I'm surprised he pauses whatever he's doing to look up at me. "Good to know."

I don't bother defending myself because, to my mom, he really is no one, and she pipes up again anyway.

"Are you with a man?" she demands, and I realize she can probably hear every word even more easily than Fin can.

"Mom, no."

"It sure sounds like it, dear."

"I don't need you to worry about it."

"Where are you?"

"Mom—"

"Honey, you know I can just look up your location if I want to."

I groan because it's a credible threat. "If you must know, I'm at an art store, okay? Down by my old place."

"By Steve's?"

"No, where I lived *before* that."

It's the kindest way I can say it without bringing Steve's name into the part of the conversation Fin can easily hear. He glances up at me for just a second but fusses with his jacket once more and then peeks through his makeshift peephole again.

"Oh, Millie," my mom crows, and I already know what's coming next. "I am really concerned this breakup has taken a greater toll on you than you admit, and—"

"I'm just fine."

"Millie, dear—"

"You know what, I *am* with a man. Is that what you want to hear?" I don't even give her the time to respond before I offer up way too much information. "I met him the other day and he's an artist and we're working on a project together, so I really should be going now because—"

"Oh, dear. Don't tell me you're posing naked for him."

"Mom!"

"Okay, okay. I don't need to know."

"That's not what I'm doing."

"It's not my business, dear. I'll leave you to it, but don't forget, I do expect to see Lou soon."

"Fine, but I'm hanging up now."

She mutters something else I ignore because I'm desperately trying to figure out what the heck Fin is still doing one sniff away from inhaling my skirt. As I end the call, he suddenly pops up, straightens out his jacket, and shrugs.

"Found the paint," he says.

"Where?"

"Here," he confirms, and he starts plucking up the tubes already in my arms.

"We've had it this whole time?"

"You couldn't tell?"

I stifle a growl and pocket my phone as he takes the rest of the items from me.

"We need paintbrushes now," he says.

"Paintbrushes? You don't already have paintbrushes?"

He tosses me a scathing look. "Precise, remember?"

I roll my eyes and then take one more look at the front door now that I'm not a skip away from hopping on Fin's shoulders. The bell jingles again as the door bounces shut, and the two men I saw earlier disappear around the corner.

"For the record," Fin says, reclaiming my attention, "you can tell your mom next time you talk to her that I don't normally paint my subjects nude."

Eleven

"Any chance you want to explain what that was all about?" I ask as we burst through the one good door of the art store.

Fin picked up at least a dozen brushes, an extra canvas, a few posters, and a set of something he said was special effects palette knives that looked more like medieval torture tools to me, but he didn't say much else.

"Did you really used to live over here?" he asks instead.

"Is that so hard to believe?"

He shrugs as we emerge from the alley onto an equally narrow side street that's accumulated about the same amount of trash and graffiti. Our feet crunch over broken glass that's probably been here for a few weeks now, judging by the plywood-covered window under which it's scattered.

"So, you know the dim sum place around the corner?" Fin goes on.

I shrug listlessly. "Should I?"

"It is the best you'll find."

"I guess I'll have to take your word for it. Wouldn't know what to compare it to."

Fin stops dead in his tracks, and I have to double back.

"What's the problem?"

"Have you ever had dim sum?"

"Would it bother you if I said I'm not even sure what that means?"

He makes a strange choking sound, and I realize that must be code for *yes*. He shakes his head, resumes his march, and I follow.

"Well, you can't respond like that and then give me no explanation."

"You want to know what's hard to believe? The fact that you've made it to"—he tosses me a broody frown and then looks forward again—"whatever age it is you are without having dim sum."

"I really hope you're not asking me how old I am."

"I'm not," he responds, and again it's all rough edges and throaty growls but I now recognize something softer under there. "Come on."

"Come on where?" I ask, and I have to skip to keep up with his long strides. "My car is three blocks in the opposite direction and—"

"Extend your parking. You need at least another hour."

"Is this your idea of slowing down?"

"That is what you asked for, isn't it?"

"Sure, but I didn't agree to—"

"In here," Fin interrupts, and he dodges right down another alley I definitely would not have explored when I lived over here.

I don't manage another word before he pushes open a black-painted door set into a brick wall that's not painted but somehow just as black. We're greeted with the jingle of a bell that sounds like it's been flattened against a wall repeatedly, the clapper making a dull thump against warped metal.

Fin doesn't wait for a reaction, doesn't seek agreement, and instead moves down a dark hallway that smells strangely toasty and sweet at the same time. It's on the tip of my tongue to protest again but given my track record is lacking and we round the corner into the dining area of a Chinese restaurant, I realize contention is no longer the first thought on my mind.

"You brought me to food?"

Fin glances back long enough to make sure I don't stumble down the pair of steps leading into the room and then gestures for me to slide into a booth along the near wall. A few words of polite denial attempt escape, but they get jumbled, and I realize saying *no* to this stranger is becoming increasingly more difficult.

"Don't look so shocked," he says, and his brows twitch a little as they scoot closer together. "It's seven thirty. I'm assuming you haven't eaten since lunch."

"Well, no, but this isn't part of the deal."

"Food is always part of the deal."

"I don't understand," I say, though it's feeble resistance.

"Sit."

I don't move.

Fin sighs heavily, drops into the other side of the booth, and pulls out a menu that's tucked behind the soy sauce. "Suit yourself. I'm starving."

I take one more second to consider the likelihood this guy is a murderer and finally file it away for good. If anything, I'll at least be properly fed before I meet my untimely demise.

I slide into the seat across from him, and I'm pretty sure he peeks one eye over the menu like he's pleased with himself, but I hurriedly hide behind mine because I think this qualifies as a date, and I have no idea how the heck I'm going to explain this to Hannah. Or my mom. Or Lou, for that matter, who could probably sniff this Chinese food all over me the second I'm within a ten-foot radius and know I've wandered way outside my comfort zone.

"You can look at the menu, but it might be better if I order for you," Fin says.

I want to assure him I'm more than capable of choosing a meal and feeding myself, but so far I've seen only three pictures and a lot of words I don't understand.

"What is it we're ordering?"

"Dumplings. I promise you're going to like them. It's just fried dough filled with pork or chicken or shrimp or"—he slaps his menu down to the table and narrows his eyes at me—"wait, are you vegetarian?"

I grant him a smile. "Meatless Mondays are about all I can handle."

He mumbles something that sounds like *thank god* under his breath, but I don't blame him. I make up for all the Fish Fridays and Lasagna Sundays with my weekly kale smoothies, and I call it good.

A server appears at the table a moment later, but she and Fin don't even talk. Instead, she drops a long piece of paper and miniature pencil to the table, and Fin starts marking lines. I think he's writing numbers or making check marks, and the woman is nodding her approval. Eventually, she plucks the pencil from Fin's hands, circles the items he's marked, and then takes off.

"Any chance you ordered me a water?" I ask.

The corner of Fin's mouth twitches upward. "Figured you'd prefer that over sake."

"Definitely," I reply, and the relief is genuine. "I'm a lightweight. Drunk on two sips. Won't get behind the wheel of a car after so much as sniffing booze."

Fin doesn't say anything, but I think I see that twitch again.

"So," I go on, "you never answered my question. What happened back at the store?"

"You never answered my question. Tell me about your job."

I purse my lips in disapproval, not because he's blatantly dodging the ask but because that's not a question. Still, I oblige him. "I have a job most people think is boring. I'm an auditor."

"I think 'boring' is the wrong word," Fin says, and there's definitely a hint of a smile behind that stiff look.

"Okay, so people hate me, but I love it. I like the math and the mystery and figuring out exactly how people are getting away with their crimes."

Fin grunts. "Tell me you don't work for the IRS."

"God no. Private company."

"Not a whole lot better."

"Well, I don't see you saving the world over here. You copy art for a living."

"How many times do I have to say it's called *replication*?"

"How many times do you think my clients call it *diversifying their income*?"

Fin lets out a low chuckle, and I secretly revel in the knowledge that I caused it. I ready myself to ask another question because suddenly I want him to fill the silence, but Fin drags a pair of saucers across the table instead. They've already got shredded ginger in them, delivered when the server was at the table, and he plucks up the soy sauce and drowns the yellow shavings.

"So, is this the end goal?" Fin asks, and I'm not sure what he means, so I deflect.

"You need to answer my question first."

"Your job," he says, ignoring me. "You want to be an auditor for life?"

"There's nothing wrong with being an auditor," I say because he's hit a sore spot, "and yes, if you have to know. Just not at this company."

"Then where at?"

I open my mouth but don't get a chance to answer. A different server appears and he's holding a small tray piled high with a spiralized green vegetable. It's drenched in a dark sauce and sprinkled with chili pepper seasoning.

"Cucumber," Fin explains.

As simple as it is, it's a beautiful appetizer—even more intriguing than many of the fancy twenty-dollar starters Steve liked so much, but I shake the comparison. Fin is already picking up the tray and pushing a heap onto a small plate in front of me. I reach for the silverware, unwind the napkin, and nearly *die*.

Chopsticks. *Freaking* chopsticks. It's the only thing wrapped up in the napkin, and I veer straight into panic mode. I'm willing to admit I'm not the most cultured girl, but hell if I want anyone to know I'm hopelessly incapable of maneuvering two sticks well enough to scoop up sticky rice.

I've read the online instructions. I've tried all the tutorials. I've watched the videos that say *hold the chopsticks like a pencil* and let me tell you—it's the greatest lie of all time. My digits simply don't deliver.

"So where's your dream gig?" Fin asks, steering us back to the discussion.

He's not looking at me, thankfully, and I choose to indulge his question so he doesn't take notice of me trying to stab the swirl of cucumber with my dull utensil.

"Home, ideally. I'm trying to buy a house, and the plan is to convert one of the rooms into an office and work for myself."

Fin nods and effortlessly shoves a spiral of cucumber into his mouth. He crunches while I stir mine around on the plate.

"So she's smart and pretty."

"She is?" I ask automatically. Absurdly.

Meanwhile, he somehow breaks a curve of vegetable with nothing but a quick flick of his wrist. "You'll make more money that way."

"Ideally, but..."

The words drift away as a third server appears, and I wonder how many people can possibly work at this hole-in-the-wall restaurant. This woman has a tray of steaming, puffy dumplings. They're doughy and delicious-looking, of course, but there's only four of them.

I wait until the server takes off. "Is this it?"

Fin scoots the tray toward me. "They bring it out as it's ready. There's plenty more coming."

"Right. Of course. Can you please tell me something about you? How did you get into painting?"

It's the first question that comes to my mind because I'm also trying to figure out how I'll scoop a tennis-ball-sized dumpling on my pair of chopsticks when I still haven't managed to get a piece of cucumber anywhere near my mouth.

"My grandmother," Fin answers unexpectedly, and I wonder if he's finally warming up to me or if it's just the food in his stomach.

He miraculously squeezes a dumpling between his prongs and shoves the whole thing into his mouth. I think he says something like *she kept me out of trouble*, but I can't be sure.

"She taught you?"

Fin nods, but that's about it, so I resurrect an earlier question.

"What did you mean when you said you tell the kids to go to that store?"

"Didn't mean anything by it," he says, but the way his jaw stills and his chest settles tells me it's not the whole truth.

"Did she work with a lot of kids?" I guess, stabbing a dumpling right down the middle and still failing to lift it off the plate.

Fin drops his chopsticks to the table and just looks at me. I'm holding mine but have made no further progress.

"Do *you* work with kids?" I try again, and again, he doesn't answer. "You're not going to elaborate?"

"Why should I?"

"I don't know, because I asked, and it's a nice thing to do."

"It's not important."

"So you do work with kids?"

"Why does it matter?"

"Are you scared to admit you're a good guy?"

Fin drops his chin and practically glares at me. "I'm *not* a good guy."

I've got little evidence to argue the point and even less opportunity because the first server returns brandishing another tray of dumplings. These ones are smaller—steamed, I think, instead of fried—and the tail of a shrimp is poking out of the top of each one. They look even more tantalizing than the first set, and I want to cry because I'm not sure I'll get a bite of anything.

"Can you please bring her a fork?" Fin asks suddenly, and the server stops and frowns, her dark brows angling tighter. Fin sighs, picks up his chopsticks, and situates them so one protrudes uselessly between his pinky and ring finger. "Two forks, actually."

"I'm perfectly fine," I say, embarrassed.

"I know. But that has nothing to do with the chopsticks you can't use."

I have to repeat the sentence in my head three times before I realize what's going on. "Are you hitting on me now?"

"Has anyone ever told you your face is perfectly symmetrical?" he goes on.

"Does everyone verify the relative linearity of body parts except me?"

"So, that's a *yes*?"

"That's a *what the heck does it even matter?*"

"It matters because it satisfies every creative rule. You're an artist's dream."

I urgently try not to let my cheeks flush because I'm pretty sure the splotchy shade would throw off whatever facial precision he thinks he sees.

"Fin, I don't know if you're being serious, but—"

"I'm just making an observation."

"Do you regularly observe face shapes?"

"Only when they stand out."

He's looking at me so intently I feel like he can read the panic-slash-curiosity-slash-confusion whirring through my head.

"You're not very good at receiving compliments, are you?" he asks.

"Can't say I'm regularly lavished in them."

"No wonder you dumped that boyfriend of yours."

"Do you have a filter?"

It's out of my mouth before I can stop it—ironically. Fin is not at all bothered, however, and he leans back in his seat just as the server reappears with two forks. He accepts them and sets one by his plate and offers me the other.

"Honestly, who could resist complimenting you every day when you look like that?"

"Honestly, who gave you permission to flirt with me?"

"Do you want me to ask permission?"

I yank the fork from his hand and choke down the surprising urge to whimper *no*. I'm certain his stubborn attitude and sly remarks should make me want to run the opposite direction, but I already know what's at that end of the spectrum and it's nice and civil and charming—and it also makes me want to vomit.

"Can we just keep this professional?" I ask, though I find myself stabbing a dumpling with inordinate force. Steam oozes from the hole I poked like an ominous warning.

"I will if you will."

I try not to take the bait. I try not to reach across the table and grab him by that paint-covered, sawdust-smelling shirt. I try not to admit my mind keeps wandering wildly off track and my body is buzzing and I'm dying to flirt back and—*holy hell*—more dumplings arrive.

Twelve

"Oh my, you two are moving awfully fast, aren't you?" Hannah says with an exaggerated gasp.

"What?"

My reply is automatic, and I turn back to find she and Lou have stopped in the middle of the aisle.

She drops his leash on the ground and reaches for a row of bins in the middle of a towering, orange-painted industrial shelving unit and pulls out a section of galvanized steel chain that clanks loudly at every link.

"Chains?" she asks, tugging harder. Then she whips her head around the aisle. "Ropes and tie-downs too? After one date?"

I roll my eyes and stomp toward her, yanking the chain from her hands. "It wasn't a date, and that's not what I need from this aisle."

Hannah smirks as I drop the clanking steel back into the bin, scoop up Lou's leash, and return that to her instead. He looks between us but doesn't react otherwise.

"Is that because your lumberjack already has the necessary tools?" Hannah goes on. "A whole room full of straps and ties and stretchy little bungee cords for those days when you're itching for a little wiggle room?"

"For god's sake, Hannah."

"What? You've never told me what you're into, and I know you can't be *that* vanilla."

"Yeah, well, there's a fine line between kink and ending up on the next episode of *Dateline*."

Hannah snickers as I turn on my heels and continue down the aisle, keeping well away from all the industrial-strength equipment that is in no way delicate enough nor clean enough for my brand of proclivities.

"So then, what are we at the hardware store for, if not, well, *hardware*?"

"This," I say, rounding the endcap of the aisle and plucking up a roll of yellow caution tape.

"Oh, do tell what you'll be using *that* for."

I roll my eyes again. "It's for the new house. The city said they don't clean graffiti off private property and I already agreed to waive inspection to buy the place, so the current owners won't do anything either."

"Are you cordoning off the area to turn it into a local art display?"

"Of course not. I'm painting over it. I just don't need anyone else smudging the wet paint or whatever while it dries."

Hannah frowns and looks down at Lou, who practically grins. "Your mommy is very thorough, isn't she, Louie Boy?"

"Not Lou's mommy," I correct, though I put on my best baby voice for Lou anyway and scratch him behind the ears. "Why do anything if you're not going to do it right?"

Hannah lets out another laugh, and Lou's thick tail smacks against her leg. He couldn't care less what I was saying; so long as it sounds like an infant on a recorded loop, he's in heaven.

"Speaking of doing things right," Hannah goes on as I set my sights on the next aisle over, "have you ever painted before?"

"I mean, I did my room when I was ten."

"What color?"

"Why does that matter?"

"Speaks to the legitimacy of the claim."

"Okay, Detective Hannah. I think you've been spending too much time talking to Steve."

Hannah cocks her head like she's about to politely refute but instead reverts to the original question. "Color."

"So the color didn't have a name," I admit.

"Why not?"

"Because I mixed three different leftover cans and made my own. Happy?"

Hannah trades her casual stroll for a proud strut, Lou still lumbering in her wake. "I take it you haven't painted the outside of a house either."

"It can't be that different, right?"

"I think I know someone who can give you a little insight."

"I'm not asking Fin."

"I wasn't suggesting that, but hey, since you're so eager to chat about the guy, let's dissect what's going on there. Details. Stat."

"Details? There are no details," I say, but it comes out a little throatier than I intend, so I hurry down the paint aisle to avoid her scrutinizing look.

Through a very strategic arrangement of meetings and deadlines and barely believable excuses, I've managed to dodge all of Hannah's covert attempts thus far to get me to crack on my trip to the art store and subsequent dinner with Fin, but my resolve is definitely waning.

Two more minutes with her walking around this hardware store and I'll probably be shouting the play-by-play from the top of the plywood stacks, and it's surely going to start with *something's going on and I don't know what it is.*

"So the trip to the art store last night..." Hannah prompts.

"Was just that. A trip to the art store."

She tsks quietly as I reach for the paint cans, and I don't look back at her. Instead, I try to calculate mentally how much paint is necessary to cover a six-foot penis, and for some reason the numbers don't line up in my head and they turn a little squiggly and words tumble out instead.

"Okay, so we went out to dinner afterward," I confess, and it's half panicky.

"Aha! I knew it. I knew there was something there. The way he was looking at you—oh, hold on." Hannah drops Lou's leash again like she doesn't understand the purpose of it, raises a finger at me, and then pulls out her cell phone. "It's Steve."

"Wait, the way he was looking at me? How was he looking at me?"

Hannah just smiles and picks up the call, and then the part of my brain that is supposed to maintain oxygen flow seems to seize up. I'm not sure if it's Hannah's casual and confusing observation about Fin or the fact that the last person I want to be aware of Fin and why I've even met the man is now on the line.

"Cap! How the heck are ya?" Hannah howls into the phone.

I hiss Hannah's name, but I'm not even sure which warning to issue first, so she just waves a dismissive hand at me and whirls around, leaving me to recollect Lou, manage both the caution tape and sample-size paint can I picked up, and not errantly disclose the fact that I'm still hanging out with Steve's dog and have managed to let said dog destroy his girlfriend's most prized possession in the few days he's been under our care.

Or, Hannah's care, technically.

"Absolutely," Hannah croons. "We have everything under control."

I hurry to catch up. "Not *we*. I'm not here. I'm not part of this!"

"Yeah, Lou and I are just at the hardware store. Did you know it's, like, one of the only places that still lets dogs in around here?"

Steve must launch into some complaint about the lack of canine-friendly locations because Hannah just tosses me a wily look and then heads straight for a display of outdoor furniture. She plops down in a swivel chair, and it takes about two seconds and one good tug for me to lose the battle against Lou, who is insistent he deserves to lounge on the very expensive-looking matching loveseat.

"*Lou*," I scold through gritted teeth, dumping my supplies and trying in vain to haul him down. "Lou, please—"

"Heavens, no! Lou has been a saint," Hannah banters on, and I drop the leash. It's a little alarming how convincing Hannah can be when she wants to. "He's been eating his dinner and going on his daily walks and he hasn't even asked for a later bedtime."

That must get a chuckle from Steve because Hannah beams proudly, like she's just earned a gold star in art class, though the smile wanes quicker than it should.

"He misses you too," she says, her forehead creasing unusually.

I pretend like I don't see Lou drooling on the sofa and take the chair next to Hannah, frowning at her.

"Cap, why did you really call? Is something wrong?"

She asks the question so casually it catches me by surprise. I don't want to be nosy—I don't need to know if his free trip to wine country is somehow going off the rails—but I'm human and I can't *not* be curious, right?

"Sure, sure, okay," Hannah goes on, and then she pulls the phone from her ear.

I see her hit the Mute button just before she turns the phone to speaker, and even though I know he can't hear me, I feel obligated to whisper.

"You can't put him on speaker in the middle of the store—"

But Hannah holds a finger to her lips, and I realize Steve has been talking.

"It's just work," he's saying. "This case feels different."

I quickly scan the aisles around us, checking for any potential eavesdroppers—aside from me, of course—and then lean in closer. I don't know how Hannah is so good at it, but that girl hardly needs to say a word to get people to share their deepest, darkest secrets.

"I joined Grant on a call last week," he goes on. "A kid trespassing. It was a minor offense, probably could have let him go with a warning, but when I went after him, he ran. So, I had to bring him in. I hardly had the back door to Grant's cruiser shut before he was confessing to drug distribution."

Hannah unmutes the phone. "Come on, Cap, you don't have to feel bad for being good at your job."

"It's not that. The thing was—he was clean. I searched him myself. No drugs on him, none of the usual signs of using, but he had inside knowledge on running this drug, and it's not even one of the usuals, it's—"

Steve catches himself, and I know he's finally realizing he's sharing way too much information about the case, but Hannah quickly jumps in.

"What's going to happen to him?"

Steve sighs. "They're bringing him up on every charge they can, even though the kid didn't even have a record before. I mean, when it was just trespassing, he was facing a fine, maybe some community service."

"And now?" Hannah prompts.

"Hard time."

I cover my mouth to hold back the gasp and then reach for Lou for a little reassurance. He nudges closer so I can scratch behind his ears more easily.

"I know it's my job to get criminals off the street, but this kid isn't one of them. He was just at the wrong place at the wrong time, and I don't believe for one second he could do this. We've been searching for connections to Puppy Love for months and haven't even come close."

"Puppy Love? *That's* the drug he confessed to distributing?" Hannah cuts in, and Steve finally reels it back.

"I'm sorry, I really shouldn't be discussing—"

"It's just me, Cap."

Steve lets out a short laugh. "And Millie, I presume?"

Hannah grimaces, like she feels a little bad she just got caught, but it's short-lived. "Can't get anything past Detective Steve Rogers, can we?"

He chuckles. "Listen, I really appreciate you letting me vent a bit, but I should get back to Seph. I just needed to know Lou was okay and something was going right back home."

"You have nothing to worry about here."

She's got her convincing voice back on, and I feel like I deserve to be roasted on a spit. After all, I'm still scrubbing the ears of the dog who has guaranteed everything is definitely *not* going right.

Thirteen

Okay, so one thing goes right: my mom gets her wish. Hannah and I agree to drag Lou out to see her at the Thursday night market on the pier. The locally run event features farm-to-market food vendors and grassroots social campaigners and borne-out-of-the-basement crafters—basically everything our ultra-liberal city salivates over.

I can't exactly complain because my (farm-to-blender) kale-smoothie cart is a resident vendor, but that also doesn't stop me from internally cringing when we find my mom at a wine booth that boasts "grain- and gluten-free" whites. As much as I would love to surmise loudly whether all wines meet both criteria without effort, I don't want the baby-faced, bowtie-wearing bartender to have a reason to inform me otherwise.

"Louie!" my mom cries as soon as she spots us.

It's loud enough to draw the attention of a few bystanders, but my mom doesn't care. She's already on the ground accepting slobbery kisses from the dog while Hannah's aggressively petting his rib cage just to rile him up.

I let the leash go because there's plenty of people with their hands on the dog and scout the row again. There are several wine booths on this stretch of sidewalk and judging by the bottles clanking around in the reusable bag my mom just abandoned, she's already made her rounds. Which means, she's been to Seph's booth.

Okay, so the brand (and thereby its booth) doesn't belong to Seph, but at the rate the woman is winning awards for peddling the pinks to local restaurants, she ought to have her name on a barrel or something.

The booth is at the end. I recognize the bottles of tinted pink liquid as dupes to some I saw in Seph's cellar, and one of them is peeking out of my mom's bag now. Steve mentioned it at the dog park (a warning, perhaps?), that my mom just so happens to enjoy the same pink imposter Seph sells. It shouldn't bother me, but I've got the sudden urge to topple a row of rosés like dominos.

Unfortunately, I think that'd only exacerbate my mom's argument that I am somehow unhappy and unfulfilled and greatly in need of un-ruining what she is convinced was my one and only chance at love.

I haven't shared with Hannah anything more about my suspiciously date-like Tuesday evening, let alone with my mom. In fact, I haven't even heard from Fin since he walked me to my car and told me to "stop wandering around bad parts of town." I, in turn, told him to get back to work, that paintings don't get made overnight, and it's been radio silence since.

For a minute, I thought—hoped?—that he wouldn't take my demand for professionalism so seriously, but apparently he's a man of his word and I'm still incapable of taking a chance on anything unusual and unsafe and...*un-Steve.*

"But why, Millie?" my mom cries in the same baby voice I've been using with Lou. She's holding him by the cheeks, nearly brushing her nose against his as she murmurs affections, and let me tell you—my mom never *once* did that to me as a kid. "Why don't you want this baby in your life?"

"Mom, I never said that. I just—"

"I know, I know. You and Steve aren't getting back together." The exasperation in her voice makes me want to shove my nose in *her* face and tell her to cool it. "It's fine. I don't care anymore. I have someone else in mind."

"What?" I exclaim.

"You do?" Hannah shrieks.

She scrambles back to her feet, whipping her head around left to right like my mom keeps potential suitors for her daughter on a leash.

"Oh, he's not right here," my mom says, rising to her feet also. "He's over there."

I follow her aim as she nods left. There's a crowd of people milling around another tent, this one bright yellow instead of the typical white, and several police officers are flanking either side of a wooden podium underneath. Their uniforms are crisp, their utility belts displayed prominently, and they pretend not to notice the handful of plainclothes cops standing nearby. Their acting is terrible, by the way, but I'd have spotted the undercover cops anyway—because I know one of them.

"Mom, no."

"What? He's handsome."

"I'm not dating my ex-boyfriend's partner!"

"Hold up," Hannah interjects.

Meanwhile, my mom vaults to her tiptoes, looking over the crowd. "Oh, goodness. Grant is here?"

"That's not who you're talking about?" I demand, and now Hannah's dancing on her toes too.

"Oh, honey, I didn't even see him over there. I'm talking about the man all those cops are clearly here for."

All three of us are on our tiptoes now, popping our heads up and down like a pack of gophers so we can see around the bubbling crowd. Lou even whines pitifully, apparently bothered the rest of us are interested in something that isn't him.

"Not the guy in the plaid button-down," I say, half bad joke, half terrified plea.

"Oh yes," my mom croons. "Isn't he just a tall drink of water?"

"Is he ever!" Hannah cries, all dramatic sighs. "Your mom's got great taste."

"I don't see a wedding band," my mom banters on, and it honestly amazes me she can be so oblivious.

"Mom, that's Vincent DeLobo. He's the one who owns this market and half the buildings on this pier."

"And that's a problem why?"

I don't acknowledge the question and instead reach down to pick up Lou's leash and what's left of my sanity. "We can go now."

My mom's already got a hand on my elbow, directing me into the growing crowd.

"Let's just see what he has to say. Besides, if you aren't going after him, I bet Hannah will."

"Oh, I have my eyes elsewhere," Hannah deflects, "but it sure doesn't hurt to satisfy a little curiosity. What do you think's under that cloth?"

I pop up on my tiptoes one more time. Next to DeLobo is a lumpy, rectangular shape draped in white, a trio of legs protruding from the bottom.

"I'll give you one guess," I say.

"A rare bird in a cage?" Hannah suggests.

"A pair of glass slippers?" my mom adds.

"I'll bet it's a lottery wheel to pick the lucky lady," Hannah throws in.

I nudge both of them on the shoulder and then point to the GRAND OPENING sign hanging above the tent that clearly neither noticed.

"He's unveiling the name of his new art gallery. I guarantee it's a cardboard sign that says *DeLobo's DeArt* or something ridiculous."

Hannah and my mom mutter disappointedly in unison but drag Lou and me deeper into the knot of attendees. Meanwhile, DeLobo nods congenially at a few onlookers as he moves behind the podium under the tent. Then, he clears his throat directly into the mic, and I swear the entire crowd swoons.

I don't know what it is. The guy is all right angles and starched shirts. He's not wearing a suit tonight, but I guarantee it goes against every fiber of his being. A hundred bucks says the guy's publicist just made him hit up J. Crew on his way home to play up the down-to-earth, middle-class look, and I guess it works on everyone except me.

"What an incredible turnout tonight," he starts.

Hannah's already got stars in her eyes. Her hands are clasped at her chest, and I'm pretty sure if I kick her in the back of the knees, she'd crumple in a useless heap.

My mom, too, is admiring the guy dreamily, like he isn't twenty years younger and surely incapable of handling household chores.

"When I made the decision several years ago to restore this once-bustling pier to its former glory, I had no idea I'd have so much enthusiastic support," DeLobo goes on, and I try to tune him out.

After seeing the guy on the news a couple days ago, I did some more digging and found a whole corner of the internet dedicated to his so-called community-building efforts. According to one generous article, the born-and-raised San Franciscan couldn't bear the sight of the pier he remembered so fondly as a child ceding to "disrepair and rampant criminal activity."

I have no doubt that line was used ten times in his proposal my company audited, but there was no way I could compare notes and not be promptly called into my boss's office.

"I'm here tonight to thank everyone who has contributed to the success of this effort," DeLobo continues, and I'm afraid I begin to experience the allure.

The more he talks, the more sedated the crowd becomes, and I begin to notice the rhythmic thrum of my heartbeat and the soft whoosh of my breath. It feels like he's gently luring oxygen from my lungs, and I have to make a conscious effort to hold it in.

"If not for the brave public servants in uniform standing here with me, we would not be able to gather tonight," he says, and his lips curve into a smile that clinches the attention of the crowd. He claps a hand to the shoulder of an officer standing next to him. "Our police force has been crucial in fighting crime on these very streets and restoring a sense of safety and security and—"

Big whine.

It comes from Lou, but I feel it in my gut too, a small spasm of unrest jerking me from my temporary hypnosis. I peel my gaze away from DeLobo—with much more effort than I care to admit—and find Lou tugging at the leash, chin up and eyes wet with a desperate plea.

"You have to go potty now?" It's a strained whisper—unnecessary because no one even notices us. "Fine, let's go. We're not missing anything anyway."

I try to tell my mom and Hannah we're taking off in search of grass, but they just wave at me like I'm a pesky mosquito, so Lou and I slip out of the crowd.

Though the open-air market is technically dog-friendly, locations in which said dogs can do their business are incredibly limited. I duck between a tent selling mushrooms by the pound and one for a local theater troupe promoting their upcoming performance of *The Vagina Monologues* and then cross to a square of vegetation that's definitely ornamental. I'm pretty sure DeLobo would have a heart attack if he knew his decorative landscaping was about to get an extra watering, but there's no way I can—or even want to—drag this beast somewhere else.

I politely give Lou a little privacy and glance back at the mob where a whirr of applause has erupted just as DeLobo finishes his speech. Several people skitter toward the platform he's standing on, and a pair of men slinking behind him seem to sink backward, like the last thing they want is the attention DeLobo is drawing.

I don't think they have much to be concerned about, to be fair. The taller one is barely skin and bones with a mop of reddish-brown hair and pockmarked cheeks. His friend, who hardly comes to his shoulders, has twice the weight and half the hair.

"I thought that was you," a voice says, startling Lou and me.

"*Grant*," I wheeze, swallowing my heart back down as I turn to find him approaching. "You of all people should know you're not supposed to sneak up on women like that."

"You're armed with an eighty-pound guard dog. What do you have to worry about?"

"You know Lou couldn't hurt a fly."

"I wouldn't be so sure about that," Grant mutters, and I realize Lou's at my side, hackles raised and teeth bared.

Grant lifts two hands in surrender and apologizes meekly, but even as I tug on Lou's leash to give him a warning, he doesn't budge.

"Ignore him. He's forgotten all his manners. What are you doing here?"

"Didn't you hear? I'm fighting crime and 'restoring a sense of safety and security' to a 'once-bustling pier,'" Grant quotes, and I cringe.

"Yeah, that's about where I tuned out."

"You and me both."

"Don't tell me you don't love all this back-slapping and do-gooding?"

"You mean brown-nosing and pocket-lining?"

"I'm glad I'm not the only one who sees it."

Grant gives me a resigned shrug. "I probably shouldn't complain too much about the guy. He is the one footing the bill for all the free trips."

"Free trips? Like the all-expenses-paid jaunt to Sonoma Steve's enjoying right now?"

"It's one of three that went out to the force."

"Isn't that bribery?"

"I think they're calling it a generous donation."

"I'm going to pretend I didn't hear that," I say, the auditor in me barely contained.

"Knew you'd like that one," he replies as he pockets his hands. "More importantly here, how the hell did Steve con you into dogsitting while he's gone? He didn't even ask me. Should I be offended?"

I offer a sympathetic smile. "He said you were busy. And Hannah volunteered."

"Which means you're also on the hook?"

"You know she's one of those no-car people," I point out, and he nods.

"I'm aware."

"Anyway," I go on, both of us turning to make our way back toward the tents, "I should be asking how Steve conned you out of that totally aboveboard trip to begin with."

"Not a con. Strategy."

"You're not into free wine?"

"When I could be here scouting how to get free tickets to this play?" Grant says, nodding toward the tent I passed earlier.

I laugh. "I don't think that's what you think it's about."

He doesn't reply, but it's probably because Hannah has fully claimed his—and everyone else's—attention. She's spotted us from across the dispersing crowd and is practically screaming Grant's name. Meanwhile, Lou acts like it's a crime she's got eyes for anyone except him and lets out a demanding bark, rearing up on his hind legs at the same time.

It takes effort from both Grant and me to keep him from launching himself at her chest when she approaches, my mom on her heels.

"I swear this goof is more jealous than any of my ex-boyfriends," Hannah jokes, and she gives Lou a few affectionate chin scratches before resituating her attention on Grant. "What happened to you?"

Grant frowns as she screws up her face in bemusement and gestures toward his legs. I hadn't noticed it earlier, but his jeans are speckled from the knee down on one leg and mid-shin to ankle on the other.

"Get a little too close to the water?" she guesses.

"Splashed by DeLobo's drool, more like," I add under my breath.

"You know I have day job, right?" Grant replies.

"Does it involve stomping in puddles?" my mom jumps in, and Hannah gives her a grin of approval.

"Okay," he says, holding his hands up. "I'll have you know I *am* a guest of honor here tonight, and I will not be treated like this."

"Next time you receive a key to the city, consider ditching the day clothes," Hannah teases in return, and I swear Grant is fighting back a genuine smile.

I'm pretty certain the two haven't seen each other since Steve and I split, but there's still an air of familiarity there, a palpable feeling of comfort. It's dangerously reminiscent of everything *before*. Way back when the guys were still partners, when Lou wasn't a babysitting gig, and when I wasn't running interference for my ex and his new beau.

"Well, we've got a little shopping to finish," I blurt.

"Do we?" Hannah challenges.

I give her my best smile, but I know she sees right through my excuse to cut this unintentional reunion short.

"Right. Shopping," Hannah reluctantly agrees before turning back to Grant. "Guess that means you've got time to hit the laundromat."

"For what?"

Hannah giggles. "Your pants. Remember?"

Grant drops his chin to his jeans once more and tries to pass off his confusion with a laugh, but I'm pretty sure there's a hint of red in his cheeks.

"Ignore her," I say. "She still has no filter."

Grant mumbles something I don't catch and then hurries to say his goodbyes, nodding at my mom and me, offering a pet to Lou that the dog flatly declines, and then waving awkwardly at Hannah, as if she might pounce on him if he gets too close.

It makes me wonder if in the last year he really has forgotten what she's like, forgotten her signature tease. Then again, I don't think it's possible. She's the kind of girl a guy doesn't forget.

"I don't know how Steve did it all those years," my mom chimes in when Grant's out of earshot. "That guy couldn't spot a clue if it was right under his nose."

I keep my assent to myself. It's hard to live in Steve's shadow. I know it. Grant knows it. But no one else really sees it. They tend to be blinded by all the brawn and the charisma and the helping-old-ladies-across-busy-streets.

I glance empathically in Grant's direction—even though it's moot—as he sidles up next to the pair who were flanking DeLobo earlier. Both seem to defer to Grant's presence, and I wonder if that's what he brings to the table: influence. It's not quite as charming and genuine as Steve's, but it's there. Hidden, I think, or just untapped.

"Hannah, do you know those guys?" I eventually ask, and she perks up on her tiptoes to get a better look.

"You mean Thing One and Thing Two?"

She cackles at her joke, and I guess it's funny because the two are dressed in nearly identical jeans and red shirts. The only Suess-like trait lacking is the hair standing on end because Thing One just flattened his again and Thing Two is a far cry from having enough to do that.

"Definitely not," Hannah finally answers, "but again, I'm with your mom: your sights should be on that DeLobo guy."

"Both of you need to cool it," I say, turning around to find Hannah and my mom ribbing each other. "I have no interest."

"Is that because of this other man you're seeing?" my mom asks, and I swear the asphalt crumbles under my feet.

"You told your mom about Fin?" Hannah practically screams.

"Fin?" my mom repeats. "That's the name of the artist you were posing for the other night?"

My heart skips into my throat, and the only thing I can think to do besides choke out a bunch of unconvincing lies is run, so I yank on Lou's leash and flee toward the first booth I can find.

"Wait just a minute!" Hannah calls. "You were *posing* for him?"

"I knew there was something there!" my mom adds.

"We're not discussing this," I manage to say, and I hurry around a row of booths to find someone selling grain-free vegan dog treats.

Now I'm pretty sure all of Lou's ancestors would be rolling over in their graves at the sight of molasses-dipped quinoa radish bites, but considering Lou's instincts led him to eating a painting this week, I don't think he or his predecessors get a say. Besides, I'm desperate for a distraction, and I know this will do it.

"Vegan dog treats? How progressive!" I chime, practically throwing myself at the woman working the table. "We're always looking for ways to lower our carbon paw print! Get it? *Paw* print? Where are the ingredients sourced from?"

The woman, who's wearing a patchwork apron and tie-dye bandana, gladly launches into what is obviously a well-rehearsed spiel, and I do my best to feign interest. After several eager barks from Lou, however, she crouches to the ground and starts feeding him instead, reciting all the ingredients of each treat before tossing them for him to catch. It'd be fine, her explaining nutritional value to a dog, if it didn't immediately bore my mom and Hannah to tears.

"So you're Fin's muse now?" Hannah starts up again.

"You didn't actually get naked for him, did you?" my mom asks.

"No, I'm not his muse and I did not get—*no!*"

"But you wanted to," Hannah jumps in, and it's not a question.

I groan loudly. "I didn't and I don't and I haven't even spoken to him since dinner."

"Dinner?" my mom wails, and I hate that I have to explain the whole dim sum night out again, but it's not like I have many other options.

The woman at the booth gladly settles onto the refinished wood pier with Lou, who's already collapsed and rolled over in demand of belly rubs, so I spend the next few minutes regurgitating every detail of Tuesday night.

"Anyway, after this week, I won't see him again," I finish.

"Ever?" my mom demands.

"I guess so."

"Why?"

"Because we only hired him for—"

I gasp at my stupidity, barely catching the admission on the tip of my tongue. Lou scrambles to his feet in response, like he's concerned I just screamed for help, and the woman feeding him rolls backward.

"You are not exchanging money with this man, are you?" my mom demands.

"Money? We would never do that. We know better!" Hannah cuts in.

As nice as it is that Hannah has finally returned to my side, she's jammed far too much enthusiasm into her dramatized surprise. She pats my mom on the shoulder, reassuring her like a child, and I know my mom doesn't believe a word coming out of her mouth.

I sheepishly turn back to the woman at the booth. She's back on her feet, brushing nonexistent dirt from her apron and clearing her throat pointedly, so I force a smile.

"What do I owe you?"

Fourteen

"Five hundred dollars?" I cry, not nearly enough restraint to keep it under my breath.

I pop up from my seat, looking over my cubicle wall for Hannah, but she's got her headset on and feet kicked up on her desk, clearly in the middle of a screening call with a candidate who's probably biting his nails and sweating through his T-shirt.

I drop back down and read the text message again. It came in a few minutes ago under an unlabeled number. No pleasantries. No *happy Friday* or *it's almost the weekend*. No, it was just a short message: "Need money for frame. Send now." Then a screenshot of a handwritten invoice.

Another peek over the wall and I find Hannah casually waving a hand as she surely explains when the candidate will receive a decision. She's going to tell them one week. It will probably take four.

I get up and head the opposite direction because I can't wait for her and this isn't a conversation I'm going to have over text message. It's also not one I'll have in the middle of the office. It's a rule that was drilled into me when I first started out in auditing: no matter what the numbers are—high, low, or completely made up—money is a private conversation, and considering I've already announced the debt to anyone within ten feet, I dip into the nearest closed-door focus room and shut the blinds before dialing.

Fin picks up before the first ring even finishes. "Yes?"

"Hi. Fin. Um. I'm, uh, returning your text."

"With a phone call? That's practically a sin these days."

"I'm trying to be professional here."

He chuckles. "You're killing it."

I don't know if it's the hint of laughter or the fact that I think he's teasing me, but the air I inhale in response feels like it solidifies, melts, and pools in the bottom of my lungs. I try another breath. In. Out. Strangely liquid-y.

"Are you actually demanding five hundred dollars from me?"

"It wasn't a demand so much as a charge for services rendered."

"And what additional services have you rendered?"

"I commissioned you that fancy frame," he replies, a little snippier now. "The one that's hand-carved and nearly impossible to replicate. The one that is necessary to replace if we're going to pull off this art swap undetected."

I manage a weird breath out. "You had to commission it?"

"Told you I couldn't do it myself. I had to pay someone to make it. You do remember this was part of the deal, right?"

"But it's five hundred *whole* dollars?"

"One thousand half dollars, if you prefer."

I imagine grabbing the collar of the Carhartt jacket he's probably wearing to impart my annoyance but immediately dial back the aggression. Never mind the fact it's impossible to throttle him through the phone, just thinking about touching him—aggressively or otherwise—spurs a familiar shudder. I remember his hands on my legs in the art store, the way he moved me like I belonged to him, and suddenly I discover an unmapped part of my psyche that really enjoys reliving the experience.

"Are you going to get me the cash or not?" Fin asks again, and I have to consciously stop pacing the room.

"We've been over this. I'm not just giving you cash."

"You still don't trust me?"

"No. No, I do not."

Fin clucks gently, and I think he's holding back another laugh. "My guy's already working on the frame. It will be done tomorrow. What do you want to do?"

"Can't I just pay him directly?"

"You could if you want to drive an hour and a half."

"What do you mean? Where is he? Have any of you art people heard of Venmo before?"

This time Fin does let out a laugh. "'You art people'? Is that what you think of me, Millie?"

I deliberately trap my breath in my mouth because I don't trust my lungs and I find it strangely confusing to hear my name coming out of his mouth so easily, so cavalierly.

"I think you're making this more difficult than it needs to be."

"Last I checked, I wasn't the one begging for an authentic replication of a one-of-a-kind painting and hand-carved frame just to keep my ex-boyfriend's new girlfriend happy."

"It's not about *her*," I retort. "It's about Lou."

"Ah," Fin hums in return, and it's chipper, almost like he's just won a bet he made against himself. "Has anyone told you that you might have a guilt problem?"

I don't respond. I can't. Because as much as I struggled with the nice and kind and thoughtful things Steve did for me, I brought on my own burdens too—namely, gifting someone a living, breathing creature to cushion some hurt feelings.

"What's your favorite road trip drink, Millie?" Fin asks, and again my name sounds so curious coming off his tongue.

"I haven't agreed to a road trip."

"You kind of did when you insisted on paying my guy directly. And now that I know you're driving that direction, you can give me a ride."

"What do you need a ride for? You didn't have a way of getting there yourself?"

"Of course not. I don't have a car, remember?"

He pauses a beat as I let out an audible scoff.

"Listen, we can do this one of two ways: you can go with me to pick up this frame and pay the man himself or we can scrap this whole thing now. Your call."

The logical part of me thinks it's time to call it quits, to give up the charade, to confess everything to Steve and go our separate ways. He's not a monster, and I'm pretty sure Seph isn't either. They'd work it out, and Lou would be fine.

But the other part of me doesn't even care about the painting anymore. The other part of me just wants to know if Fin is willing enough to consume my favorite road trip drink.

"How about I get the drinks and you get the snacks?" I suggest.

He lets out a short grunt. "And you thought I made this difficult."

"Are we going or not?"

"Wear something comfortable. Second dates are always more adventurous."

I try to remain impassive because I can hear the smile on his voice and I'm afraid it's not innocent. Then again, neither is the heat swelling in my core.

"Fine," I say, feigning indifference. "Give me your address."

"Oh, like hell."

"Excuse me?"

"Trust is a two-way street, *Millie*."

***

We agree to meet on neutral ground at the museum.

I tell Hannah where I'm going only because she threatens to sneak Lou into the back of my car as a built-in safety buddy. It's a fine line trying to justify that Fin is friendly enough to travel with but not so friendly that this could be considered an extension of our Tuesday night dinner.

Ultimately, I think she's most concerned with the hardship of her sitting commitment. Something about having to wrangle an animal the size of a small hippo on a neighborhood walk...*every day.*

I make my ritualistic trip to the smoothie cart on the way to the museum. I can see how it might be cruel forcing the guy surely raised on meat and potatoes to drink the same kale smoothie I prefer on my Saturday mornings, but said guy also derailed today's original plan to blot out the unfortunate graffiti on my future home, so I figure it's appropriate penance.

He's outside the main doors lounging on a bench when I arrive and wearing essentially the same outfit (disguise?) he was sporting when I first met him, though he's ditched the ballcap in favor of a beanie. One boot-clad foot is resting on his opposite knee and he works his jaw like he just popped a Dubble Bubble, watching me approach.

I squint through my sunglasses as if the daylight is enough to distract me from this new *look* he's got. Like he's eager but doesn't want to show it, maybe.

"You look like you're dressed for a hike through some backwoods dairy farm."

"That makes one of us," he retorts, and I suddenly feel woefully underdressed in my shorts, tee, and high-tops.

"Tell me that's not where we're going."

"For a picture frame?"

"I don't know," I say with a shrug. "Maybe your guy works out of some barn carving old fenceposts or repurposed cattle corrals."

"One day I'd like to know why *that's* your first thought."

"One day?"

"That's not where we're going," Fin deflects, but it makes me hesitate.

He's still fixed on me, his posture just as stiff as his coat, but that eager look doesn't seem to have anything to do with the fact that I'm his ride across town. It's more like I'm a puzzle he wants to put together. Or maybe a knot he wants to untie. A maze he wants to explore.

A curious tingle climbs my spine at the thought.

"By the way, I don't even know where to find a dairy farm around here," Fin speaks up. "In fact, I'm pretty sure the only thing they milk these days is almonds."

"Maybe ten years ago. You know it's all oat or hempseed now, right?"

"Is that what's in those abnormally green drinks you've got there?"

His eyes dart away for just a second, and I finally remember I'm still holding the smoothies, condensation dripping down my fingers.

"Dairy and dairy-alternative free, actually."

His lips quirk. "Naturally."

"I'm assuming you brought something to counteract any good these might do."

"Lucky guess."

I choose to give myself more credit than that, but Fin scoops up a paper bag perched next to him, moving on as if neither of us just noticed the air practically shiver. He unravels the top, shoves a hand inside, and starts pulling out the contents one by one.

"Peanut-butter-filled pretzels. Gummy worms. M&M's. Oh, and I guess we don't need these."

He produces a plastic snack baggie, waves it around once, and then drops it back inside, but it's enough for me to recognize.

"Are those dog treats?"

He shrugs. "Didn't know if Lou would be joining us. Couldn't let the hound go without."

"Even after everything he did to get us into this mess?" I ask automatically.

Fin drops all the candy back in the paper bag and rolls down the top. He then swipes one of the smoothies from my hands and clamps down on the straw, taking a long, dramatic swig. I can practically see the liquid sinking down his throat, but he doesn't grimace like I expect, just swallows it down and crooks a smile at me.

"Who said this was a mess?"

Fifteen

"Are you ever going to tell me what my exit is?" I ask at least twenty minutes later.

Fin has been staring straight ahead, holding his half-drunk smoothie on his right knee and open hand on his other, fingers tapping gently. I drive a midsize SUV, but it looks like a clown car with him filling the front seat, his head almost brushing the ceiling.

"When we get there," he answers cryptically.

"Just like you're going to tell me what *this* is?"

Fin swivels his head my direction as I wave a hand between us.

"I don't follow," he says simply, though I find myself fighting a shiver at the intense stare he offers me anyway.

I haven't forgotten the fact that he implied this is a *second* date, but I'm not about to broadcast that either.

"You said this wasn't a mess. So, what is it?"

"I already told you."

"I must have missed it."

"Your loss," he replies curtly, and I look back at the highway.

I'm in the right lane driving on cruise control because I can't get my brain to settle. I don't know where we're going. I don't know what this is. I'm not even sure if Fin likes, hates, or has an opinion whatsoever on the kale smoothie because he hasn't said a word.

I do think Fin wants me to drive faster, judging by the way he checks over his shoulder every few minutes, as if confirming the next lane over is clear, but I don't indulge him. If I have to suffer in silence, I kind of want him to as well.

"If I tell you where we're going, will you at least drive the speed limit?" he asks.

Bingo.

"It would certainly give me a reason to get out of the right lane," I say with a cheeky grin.

"We're going to Capitola Beach."

"Really?"

Fin cocks his head my direction again, but I'm sidetracked. There's a shiver of tension that skips down his neck, and I follow it until it causes his fingers to twitch. He ditched the Carhartt as soon as we got in the car, then rolled the sleeves of his flannel underneath, and I tried all this time not to ogle his exposed forearms, but I can't *not* look now.

The lines curl and coil all the way from his wrist to his elbow, the ridges of his muscles and sinewy veins causing the image to distort slightly.

I mask the urge for the tenth time to simply ask the man what kind of creature he's sporting there on his forearm. It's too predictable a question. Too elementary. And, it turns out, there's a more demanding voice in my head daring me just to touch it and find out for myself.

"Slug bug."

Fin says it with surprising naturalness, a mild hum under his breath, but it's the hand on my thigh that jerks me back to reality.

I'm not wearing tights—a rarity for me and the first time I've been bare-legged around Fin—and he's noticed. Or, he hasn't noticed, and that's why he thinks it's okay to palm my leg like a basketball.

"Wait—are we...?" I pause my question and glance left to catch a yellow Volkswagen Beetle whizzing by in the opposite direction. "We're playing driving games now?"

"Thought that was a given," Fin replies easily, then returns to drumming his thigh. "Now what's wrong with Capitola Beach?"

I'm still over here wrestling the bad influence in my head, still attempting to keep the car between the white lines, still trying to figure out how the heck I fell so far behind in whatever is going on here, but I accept the chance to change the subject because that seems simpler.

"It's just—that's the place with the colorful houses, right?"

"So you know it?"

"I've seen pictures."

Fin glances my way, but I keep my eyes on the road.

"How long have you lived here?" he asks.

I shrug. "Since I was ten."

"And you've never been?"

I start to retort, readying to say something rude about how the world's a pretty big place and just because I haven't been to one particular beach doesn't mean I'm poorly traveled, but I realize Fin's tone changed as he asked the question. He's not mocking me, I don't think, and I glance sideways to see him lift his drink to his lips.

He clamps down on the straw and sucks emphatically.

"You're pretty proud of yourself, aren't you?" I guess.

Fin drops the cup and smacks his lips. "First to show you dim sum. First to take you to Capitola. I'm pretty sure I'm knocking it out of the park."

"I bet you take *all* the girls here," I tease, and I'm not sure why I'm playing into this maybe-a-date, pretend-to-be-jealous thing, but it's happening.

"Only one other."

"Oh. Someone you were serious with?"

"A little nosy there, aren't ya?"

"I—I didn't mean to pry," I stammer ridiculously, but Fin cocks a smile.

"I brought my grandmother. Every summer. Before she died. Bet you feel like an ass now, don't you?"

A laugh I'm not expecting spills from my lungs, and I take a swing at his arm. My hand connects with his bicep, and I swear Fin's eyes bulge two sizes. Mine probably do too.

I gasp—mortified at my severe lapse in judgment—immediately retract my hand, jerk my head back to the road, and outright lie: "Slug bug."

He settles back in his seat, and I'm pretty sure I can feel him shaking his head, but he doesn't point out the fact there isn't a VW Bug a mile in any direction. He just takes another loud slurp of his smoothie and I keep my eyes on the asphalt whisking underneath the car.

"So, do you like it?" I ask abruptly.

Fin swallows and then thumps the cup on his knee. "About as much as you like these gummy worms I brought."

"Yeah, I'm sorry. Gummy things make me queasy, especially when I'm driving, but I—"

"Timeout," he says, and he lifts a hand in the air. "Try that sentence again."

"I'm sorry?" I repeat, a question now. "Gummy things—"

"No. Try it without the 'I'm sorry' part. I don't know you. You don't have to apologize to me."

"Oh," I say, and I'm not sure whether I should appreciate the reprieve or be offended he's taking us back to square one again, but I indulge him anyway. "Gummy things make me queasy, but the variety's nice, and you can't go wrong with pretzels and peanut butter and chocolate."

"Noted," he says, and he looks forward again, takes a short breath, then thumps a finger on the cup. "Liquefied grass doesn't jive with my insides either, but I guess *my doctor* would think the variety's nice."

"Noted," I say in return.

For a while, neither of us speaks. We just listen to the grind of the road underneath the car and the whirr of passing traffic, and it's surprisingly refreshing, considering we began this trip as merely two people headed in the same direction on a pseudo-second date. But there's no pressure, no obligation, no burden.

Car rides with Hannah, alternately, require a several-hour dissection of our corporate workweeks, and drives with my mom require me to maintain a defense sturdy enough to withstand a barrage of questions even the nosiest therapist wouldn't ask. Road trips back when I was with Steve—well, those didn't really happen. He preferred safe, predictable destinations within the 46.87 square miles the city has to offer. They were always fancy, of course, but they weren't me.

"Do you have an aversion to music as well as the greatest candy on earth?" Fin asks suddenly.

I smile because I didn't notice the silence, but I swipe up to unlock my phone, tap the music app, and hand it over to Fin. "Take your pick."

"Hold up," he says, and he's squinting at the screen that's popped up. "Do you have podcasts favorited? On your music app?"

"What's the problem with that?"

Fin scoffs quietly but taps one, and the familiar voices of the show hosts come to life.

"Oh, this is a good one. They're investigative journalists," I say, and I crank the volume. "Last week they covered an underground black market where criminals are supposedly exchanging antiquities to launder their money."

"You call that a good one?"

"*Wildly* fascinating, and a brilliant con to be honest. It's almost impossible to trace fraud in antiquity purchases because values fluctuate so much and"—I pause, catch the rising look of bewilderment on Fin's face, and redirect—"and I'm boring you. Just fast-forward. I'm sure this week is something totally different."

Fin purses his lips and slides the time bar, landing somewhere in the middle of the hosts' conversation, the woman speaking first.

"...and they're doing so little about it," she finishes.

"Well, how do you expect the cops to trace a drug that's used every day in vet clinics or wild-animal sanctuaries? It's easy to get, poorly monitored, and half the stuff is shipped overseas by the boatload," the male co-host fires back.

"You're telling me the cops can trace an entire distribution ring to some seventeen-year-old kid but don't know which boat the shipments are heading in and out on?" the woman argues.

The man laughs. "Surely they don't label the crates 'Puppy Love'."

I gasp and whip my head Fin's direction. "I know what this is! I've heard about it."

"You've heard about a street drug?" Fin challenges, scoffing slightly. "Where? From the five o'clock news?"

"Well, yes, but also—" I stop myself short.

I'm not supposed to know Steve is working the case, and I'm not sure I want to know if this teen the hosts are talking about is the same kid Steve mentioned on the phone the other day. He said his kid confessed to distribution—not ringleading—but with his success rate, it wouldn't surprise me if the original charge led to more.

"You can't trust what you hear on the news," Fin says, "and you sure as hell can't trust cops."

I jerk with surprise, but it's not at Fin's comment. I've heard it all before. Plenty of people have distrust in law enforcement, and plenty of them are right to feel that way. But the tone of Fin's voice, the way he says it, makes me hesitate with my typical defense.

The charm and humor that's been bubbling under the surface seems to have popped, and I swear Fin's skin is prickling up underneath his flannel, even though I can't see and don't dare touch.

"Do you want to talk about it?" I try instead, a line straight from my therapist's handbook.

Fin doesn't acknowledge me. He just sucks down the last of his drink, looks out the window, and says, "Slug bug."

It's unanimated this time and he doesn't reach out to touch me, and I think that's the worst part. My skin tingles with anticipation, so I brush a hand over my knee to still the unusual feeling that probably shouldn't be there and then change the subject.

"How do you know this frame guy? How do you know he's down here?"

Fin swings back my direction. "We 'art people' aren't so few and far between."

"Says the guy who's making me drive an hour and a half for a picture frame."

Fin's lips twitch and he reaches for the gummy worm bag, plucking up one and shoving it in his mouth with intention. I go for the pretzels and hope it helps to reestablish the air of civility we had going before the podcast tried to claim it.

"People talk," Fin goes on, chomping on the neon-green worm. "Word gets around. And framing isn't the only thing he does to pay the bills."

"What else would a professional framer do?"

Fin shrugs. "You'll see. By the way, our exit was two back."

Sixteen

Pulling into Capitola Beach is like scoring the double-yellow card in Candy Land and cruising down a lollipop lane of gumdrop houses.

The edge of the neighborhood is spotted with homes painted lemon yellow and businesses a fiery orange. Some have lime-colored awnings or flamingo-pink gutters, but the closer we trek down the could-be Rainbow Trail, the more eccentric the dwellings become, until every stucco-textured building is slathered a shade of neon.

"This is incredible," I hear myself say. "I'm not sure I knew half these colors existed."

Fin tilts his head toward the car window. "Yeah, it's okay, I guess."

I scowl at him. "Okay, *Lord Licorice.*"

"So you do have a taste for other non-chocolate candies?" he teases back, and the smile that draws his cheeks up tempts me to pinch them until they're bubblegum pink.

"Don't misinterpret knowledge for taste."

"Don't worry. You've proven that."

Fin says it so quickly and casually, it catches me by surprise. "Is that an insult?"

"I mean, you're still hanging out with me, so what do you think?"

I don't reply, and Fin looks away, jerking a thumb toward a parking lot bordering a row of old-timey houses-turned-inns.

"Park here."

"Does your framer also own a bed and breakfast?"

"That wouldn't even make sense," Fin responds, but I think there's a smile under all that gruffness.

I do as he instructs and bring the car to a stop, refocusing on a row of shops on the perpendicular street, one of them painted a shade of turquoise bolder than any piece of jewelry I've seen.

"Will we have time to see the rest of it?"

"That is the plan," Fin says, and he exits the car.

I'm not sure what plan he's referring to because, thus far, it seems like he hasn't mapped out a single decision. Meeting a Craigslist girl at the museum, worming his way into an invite to a stranger's house, agreeing to this questionable charade—they all screamed *future regret* to me, but he's made it clear that he just acts.

Boldly. Confidently. *Recklessly.*

It's different than what I'm used to.

I hurry to catch up and together we dip beneath a salmon-colored archway and down an alley next to the turquoise store. We barely fit shoulder-to-shoulder, the bordering walls smashed together unevenly as if constructed of Play-Doh, but above us are brick-framed windows, some spilling with green vining plants and others framed by purple or orange or yellow shutters.

"Over here," Fin says as we emerge on a sidewalk dotted with several more businesses, hanging signs that denote their services protruding above each doorway. "This one."

I follow his gaze, skipping a chocolatier and a perfume store, and then I see it: Probasco's Wigs and Frames.

"Don't tell me—"

But Fin tosses me a warning look and throws the front door open, a jangling bell announcing our arrival.

"You fake it, we frame it," a croaky voice squawks from the back of the store.

I want to *shriek* in glee because I've never been so dazzled in my life, but I slap a hand to my mouth and instead duck underneath what looks like a chandelier of wigs, colorful mops of silky hair fluttering in the breeze we just brought in from outside.

"Oh, it's you," the croaky voice grates again, and now I've got a face to picture every time I think of this absurd store.

The man is hardly five feet tall, and either it's poor business sense or incentive for his customers, but he has hardly a wisp of hair on his head, just two white tufts poking out above either ear. I'm pretty sure he has more hair on his eyebrows, but I don't stare long because—I'm not kidding—there's an entire damn wall of wigs behind him, and each one is artfully boxed by an intricate, presumably hand-carved, frame.

"Petey," Fin says, a strangely casual hum to his voice.

The man's wrinkled lips thin as he tugs at his apron, jostling a gold nametag that clearly says Pierre. "How many times have I told you?"

"Never enough," Fin says. "There's someone you should meet."

I'm too busy gawking at a section of toupees to protest when Fin casually rests a hand on my back. It's warm and solid and a little endearing, I think, but I'm hurrying to catch up to the introductions and offer a hand to Pierre.

He doesn't take it. Instead, his eyes pinch tightly and he huffs at Fin. "Who's she to you?"

Fin clears his throat, and I can feel a twitch in his fingertips. "She's Millie."

"Millie," Pierre repeats, and it feels like he's rolling my name around on his tongue. Tasting it, testing it. "I can presume that is short for a much more esteemed name, no?"

"I'm not sure esteemed is—"

"No?" Pierre cuts in. "You prefer Millie?"

"Millicent," I concede, and I toss a sideways glance at Fin, who has not yet relinquished his oddly comforting hold for some reason.

"Illustrious," Pierre says, though his eyes sharpen. "Can you believe this one prefers to be known by a fish extremity rather than his proper moniker?"

I swing my gaze toward Fin once again. "You've got a proper moniker?"

"It's irrelevant," Fin says with a huff, and he finally drops his hand. "Petey, we're here for the frame."

"Naturally," Pierre replies with the enthusiasm of a dried-up bug.

He whips his gaze away like he's snapping himself out of a trance, then whirls around, shoves his hands into his apron, and shuffles behind a counter.

"Wait here."

We do, neither of us daring to flinch, but as soon as we hear the distinct click of a door closing in the distance, we're both whipping around and clamoring to speak—or shriek?—at the same time.

"What on earth is your proper moniker?" I demand.

"You're telling me you prefer to go by Millicent?"

"Oh no—you first."

"Not a chance."

"I bet it's Finnegan, isn't it? No, Finward. Actually, Finwald. That's got to be the secret name you've been hiding from me."

"How many Finwalds do you know?" he asks, screwing up his face at me.

"Just one if that's your real name."

"It's not."

"Fine," I say with a haughty tsk, and I cross my arms dramatically and glance around the shop again. "Then answer me this: Are you bald under that hat?"

Fin grunts. "Pretty sure you just used up your raincheck for a rude question."

"Don't worry. I have *two*."

Fin shakes his head, and I'm certain he's trying to conceal a smile. I know it's under there—I know he's capable of it—and I'm so close to coaxing it out of him again. So close to seeing the way his cheeks flush and his eyes flicker and how that rigid line of his jaw softens.

But I don't. Because I'm pretty sure that'd be flirting, and I'm not flirting. Right?

"Well, then," I say, trying to maintain volume just above a whisper so Pierre doesn't overhear from the back room, "if you're not bald—and I'm not convinced you've got a full head of hair under there—then how the heck did you find a place like this? I mean wigs and frames—*come on.*"

"What's wrong with it?"

"Who comes up with this stuff?"

"I told you. We 'art people' do a lot to make ends meet."

"And this works? Headgear really floats the framing business? I'd be more liable to believe this was a front for the Capitola Cartel."

"Who says it isn't?"

I don't bite. Mostly because I don't want to think too hard about it. After all, I am enabling a criminal-adjacent creative by employing him under the table to fake a unique painting and I'm not sure that's a whole lot better.

Still, money—and whatever people do to make it—is a private conversation, so I take my scrutiny on the road and start inspecting the eclectic variety of ornate frames and borderline comical wigs accompanying them. Some look genuine, I think, but there's also a shelf of comb-over styles that belong in a cartoon strip and a pair of green wigs that were surely once part of an Oompa Loompa costume.

"What are you doing? Don't touch that," Fin says as I reach for a weave of pink ringlets.

I don't know what possesses me to do it. It was draped over the corner of a gold-painted frame. Now, it's a fist above my head.

"You don't think I can pull it off?"

"You're not supposed to try on the wigs."

"Oh?" I lower the hairpiece an inch. "What happens if I do?"

"Don't."

"Are you going to stop me?"

"Millie, I'm warning you—"

But whatever threat he's fashioning dissolves as I drop the wig on my crown.

I know I shouldn't be breaking the rules, especially as the surprisingly weighty piece sinks halfway down my forehead, but it riles Fin up exactly how I expect. The muscles in his neck tighten and shock brightens his eyes and it makes me want to fit every damn wig in this place on my head if it means he'll finally crack.

"Tell me pink isn't my color," I taunt.

"Millie, please."

"You love it, don't you?"

"Not the point."

"Come on, Finny, live a little."

I fluff the ends, and Fin swallows noticeably. I'm not sure if it's the nickname that just slipped out or something else entirely, but his Adam's apple rises upward and then plummets. Something in my chest does the same thing. A loose lung? An out-of-place kidney? My *heart*?

"Give me that," Fin finally nips, and he swipes for the wig.

I dodge his hand easily and bound for a Raggedy Ann wig I find on a faceless head.

"Let me see what you look like in red," I tease.

Fin snatches the wig out of the air as I toss it at him, and the warning in his eyes is equal parts terrifying and tempting. He carefully replaces the headpiece while I ditch the pink topper in favor of a short blue one with bangs and smash it over my hair, my dark-blonde locks spilling out underneath.

"*Millicent.*"

My full name leaves Fin's lips and it seems to charge the air between us. My mouth dries up, my insides squirm, and I damn-near *whimper*.

"Oh god."

"It's just Fin."

Just like that, every nerve in my body spurs up, and I swear I've never been more stirred in my life. I pinch my lips together, tug the blue wig down, and then tighten every muscle within my control before I can completely dissolve into a lusting, rule-breaking mess.

Fin takes the opportunity to swipe the blue strands right off my head, and I don't stop him. The farther he distances himself from me and the faster he stashes that criminal topper, the sooner I can breathe. The sooner I can pretend like I'm not downright shivering in his presence.

Only, he doesn't back away. Instead, he takes a step toward me.

I helplessly sink into a bookshelf of hair extensions and half-price frames and inhale a breath through my nose like I'll never get the chance at oxygen again.

With hardly space for a frameless photo between us, Fin slips his free hand under the brim of his beanie and slides it off his head. Underneath are waves of hair, flattened by a whole day beneath a hat, but silky-looking, nonetheless. He draws his fingers through the strands, loosening them, and then joins his other hand to stretch the wig and plop it directly on his head.

It's all wrong for his square face. The blue fringe falls far too short on his forehead and the cropped cut doesn't even make it to his jawline, but I lose track of my thoughts because he's smiling. It's a little mischievous and a lot spiteful and surprisingly captivating, and I feel my jaw slip open.

I want his lips on mine. I hardly even know the man, but I want to feel the heat of his breath, the taste of his tongue, the solid beat of his heart pounding in competition with mine as we both fight for control. I want him no matter how wrong it may be.

"Ahem."

Fin whirls around, and I feel like I've slipped on a wet rock. Pierre has emerged from the back room, a massive frame in his hands, but the disdain on his face demands all the attention.

"That's a two-hundred-dollar lace-front wig," he says.

Note to self: *they are real wigs.*

Fin pulls off the blue crop cut, crumpling it between his hands. "It's...sturdy."

A smirk ghosts across Pierre's lips. "As is your wallet, I presume."

Fin doesn't look back at me, but I see the tension slip down his shoulders, every muscle tightening as if someone's just wrung him like a wet towel.

"I probably owe you at least that, don't I, Petey?"

Pierre shows no response except for a slight twitch of his nose, like a rabbit, and Fin reaches for his back pocket and pulls out his wallet, fetching several bills.

I want to stop him. I want to reach for him and apologize for my reckless and expensive behavior. But I also don't want to undo what just happened. I want to hang on to that look in his eyes that says he wants me just as badly as I want him.

It's on the tip of my tongue to say so, to slow everything down and wind us back just a few seconds to recapture it, but Fin jerks his head my direction and speaks first.

"Millie owes you the rest."

Seventeen

"Fin, I'm so sorry," I say as the shop door closes behind us.

He's got the frame in one hand and blue wig in the other, marching down the sidewalk back the way we came. I'm skipping just to keep up.

"Didn't know you were so damn funny," he says, and it's sharp. Precise.

"I didn't know he'd be so serious."

"His name is Pierre Probasco. He sells wigs and picture frames. What did you expect?"

"I'm sorry, I—"

Fin stops cold and rounds on me. The frame I'm sure Pierre spent countless hours meticulously carving ends up resting on the top of Fin's boots, but I'm more focused on the vein pulsing in his forehead.

"Apologize to me one more time."

I do nothing but gulp.

"Good."

"Fin, I—"

"No," he cuts in again. "You are a goddamn delight, and he's got a stick up his ass."

"What?"

"You heard me," Fin says, and he snatches up the frame again and dodges down the salmon-colored alley.

My first inclination to spout some sort of retort evaporates just as quickly as it arrives, and I have to pick up the pace to a half run just to keep up. When we emerge at the other end of the alley and head for my car, I manage to spit out a different thought.

"I don't think I've ever been called, you know, *pleasant* a day in my life."

Fin crosses the lot and stops at the rear of my car.

"I didn't say you were pleasant. I said you were a goddamn delight. Now, is there a magic word for me to get this thing open?"

He frowns at the back of my car, and I clumsily fish out my keys and punch the button that sends the door upward.

I don't do or say anything else because I'm pretty sure there aren't words to describe the mess of feelings inside me. I'd compare it to a picture, but squiggly colors don't quite do it justice and musical mathematics don't even make sense. What's happening in my head is simultaneously confusing and mesmerizing and not at all what I should be experiencing with someone who's still partly *stranger*.

"What is this?" Fin asks just as he raises the frame to place it in the trunk.

I blink a few times to catch up. "Oh. That. You don't recognize painting supplies?"

"I know *what* they are. What are they *for*?"

"My house."

Fin frowns again, reaching for a foam paint roller cover that's been flopping around loose in the trunk since I bought the supplies. He then pokes through the grocery bag I've yet to unload, which still contains the caution tape, a few paintbrushes, and a metal pan. He opens his mouth as if to speak, but then shakes his head and slides the bag into the corner.

"We don't have time for this right now."

"Time for what?" I demand, but he doesn't reply, instead gently settling the frame against the back seat.

"She'll be safe here for a while," he says, and there's a hint of affection there as he gives the frame one last look before closing the trunk.

I didn't inspect it, not that I'd really know if the dupe job was authentic, but by the way Fin cradled it when Pierre handed it over and how he practically kisses the scrap of wood goodbye now makes me think it's probably pretty dang good.

"Come on," Fin says as he rounds the car. "We're losing daylight."

I forgo challenging him further because he's got a point. Nightfall is creeping in and the ocean breeze is bringing in a noticeable chill. I follow him across the lot and down the sidewalk, catching a few signs pointing us toward the beach.

As we get closer, the neighborhood colors seem to meld into one another, pinks bleeding into blues, reds into deep shades of violet, and when my feet sink into sugary-white sand, I wonder if I've slipped down Alice in Wonderland's rabbit hole. A row of candy-coated houses sprouts from the grainy shoreline, and under the glimmer of dusk, the colors seem to shift and soften into puddles of dewy jewel tones.

But it's not the beachfront properties or their accompanying lounge chairs and giant umbrellas that make this place the postcard-worthy destination it is. It's the sunset.

"Pacific peach," Fin says suddenly.

He seems uncharacteristically somber, so I dutifully tease him.

"That would mean a whole lot more to me if I had any idea what you were talking about."

Fin's eyes skip my direction briefly before refocusing on the sunset. "That's the closest color I can get to this."

"Closest color to what? Kumquat orange?"

Fin jerks his head my direction this time. "What is wrong with you?"

"A few minutes ago you were calling me a delight, so it sounds like I'm not the one with the problem."

He scrubs a hand over his jaw, and I know he's trying to wipe away a smile because I'm battling my own. When neither of us concedes, he goes on.

"It's more pink than orange, but more orange than pink."

"And peach is too suggestive on its own?"

"It's too warm," he corrects, and I'm a little surprised I don't get a joke in return. He waves a hand toward the sun dipping below the horizon. "This is a warm color that appears cool. It's rare."

I consider his assessment and watch the sun tick downward. I've seen plenty of beautiful sunsets back home and many over the ocean along other parts of the Pacific coastline, but there is something different here. Something I can't quite pinpoint.

We stand in silence, only the slosh of waves and the whirr of wind-blown sand stirring around us. The air is enough to elicit chills, but it doesn't. I'm perfectly still next to Fin, both of us staring at this elusive shade of not-quite-orange, and I feel strangely undisturbed. Perfectly settled. Uniquely at peace.

"Kum. Quat. Orange."

Fin says it quietly, and I have to scramble out of my mental swirl to recognize that humming sound as his laughter. He looks down at me, his eyes crinkling in the corners, and I realize I had no idea his smile could be so full and rich and downright enticing.

"You're making me hungry," I blurt, and it's not what I really want to say, but it's safe, judging by the straight look I get from Fin in return.

"There's a wine bar on the other side of the pier."

"I'm not sure that counts as food."

"It's grapes."

"Grapes à la *liquid*."

"I don't think you'll care after a glass or two."

"I need to be able to drive later. I need real food," I say with a laugh, reaching for his arm.

It's quick, unintentional, and he glances down where I've absently touched his jacket. I hurriedly take my hand back, but he doesn't even flinch.

"I guess it wouldn't be a date if we didn't eat," he says simply.

"I don't know about you, but I eat every day. It just makes it a typical Saturday."

"Does it now?"

"How do you know there's a wine bar over here anyway?"

"I'll tell you when we get there," he says, and I think it takes him a second to peel his gaze from mine, but he eventually succeeds and turns on his heels. "Let's go see what food we can find you first. Can't have you risking your schedule."

We make our way down the shore and toward the pier, which appears barely propped up on spindly wood posts. There are a few buildings at the end—one that I think is a bait shop and another that's surely a restaurant—but Fin doesn't seem drawn that direction, and neither am I.

Instead, it's a small, red, white, and blue truck parked in the lot on the beach's edge that catches our attention.

"Does that say British Bulldog?" I ask, squinting at what I think is a personified dog in a blue soldier's uniform painted on the side of the food truck.

"Do you think Lou will be mad if he finds out we've cavorted with the enemy?"

"If you don't tell him, I won't."

"Deal," Fin says, and we cross the lot to the truck.

Both of us order fish and chips, and we do end up walking another half-block to the wine bar. They don't serve food—as I rightfully presumed—so they let us bring our to-go boxes in and set us up at a table in the corner of a large patio.

I order a mocktail, and Fin copies me. It comes in a cute little champagne flute that looks dainty in Fin's hands, but he just picks his up and

swings it around as he automatically launches into the story of how he
and his grandmother found this place.

I listen intently, trying to capture all the tiny details of his life he
has yet to share with me—the softer parts, the sweeter memories, the
good-guy-under-the-rough-exterior pieces that have slowly begun to slip
out. It's not until the sun finally disappears and the string lights draped
between wrought-iron posts twinkle to life that I let myself remember
the rest of him. The rest of this relationship. The reason we're here.

"So, how's the painting coming?" I ask, breaking a piece of fish and
dunking it in my too-tiny ramekin of tartar sauce.

"That thing I'm working on for you?" he asks smugly, and that smile
is still there.

"You know you're not hourly, right?"

"I'm painfully aware."

I grin, amused, and soak up the rest of my sauce with another bite,
then wave it in the air. "So?"

"It's coming along," Fin says, and he dips three fries into his ketchup.
"Actually, it's almost done."

"Already?"

"Is that a problem?"

"No," I say quickly, suddenly unsure why his being nearly done with
the painting is so unsettling. "I guess I just assumed with all this talk
about painting being so precise, it would take a little longer."

He eats a chunk of fish sauceless. "It needs another day to dry and a
few more hours for me to polish up some details, but the frame was the
last big piece I needed."

"I see."

He drops his hands to the table, and I busy myself by aiming another
piece of fish for my empty pot of sauce—only, it's not empty any longer.
Fin has unlidded his and slid it across the table.

"Trade?" he asks, eyeing my untouched container of ketchup.

I push it his direction, still caught up in the fact that the main reason we have to be in each other's company will be irrelevant by Monday. Maybe Tuesday if I'm lucky.

I dunk my piece, chew, and swallow slowly before asking, "What will you do after this?"

He shrugs and grabs another handful of fries. "Another job, I suppose."

"Is this really how you make a living?"

I ask the question knowing it's rude, but Fin doesn't call me out on it. He doesn't make me cash in my last raincheck and instead just dusts his hands on a napkin and leans back in his chair.

He never put his beanie back on, so he runs his hands over his head, his fingers slipping easily through his hair, and suddenly I'm imagining how that might feel. How soft his strands are, how much he might like the sensation of my nails gliding across his scalp.

I drown the thought with the last of my drink and then lean back too.

"Yes," he finally answers. "I make and sell art for a living."

"Always fake art, though?"

"No art is fake."

"But it's a copycat, right? So it's technically fraudulent?"

Fin purses his lips, and his eyes narrow. "If I painted your face, the art would be an impression of it, a copy. Would you consider that fake?"

"Would you really consider painting me?"

Fin lets out a short laugh. "No."

"Why not?"

"Because I don't paint on demand. We've been over this."

"You know, I still haven't seen any of your work. How do I know I'm going to pick up this painting next week and it's not going to look like a five-year-old did it?"

"I'm telling you right now that's not what it looks like."

I open my mouth to retort again, but our server appears at the table, a bottle of red and two stemless wineglasses in her hands.

"It's your lucky night," she says, fluttering her lashes underneath wispy black bangs. "A regular customer of ours has sent you a little something."

She places the glasses on the table, and Fin and I exchange a look.

"We didn't order this," I say.

"That's why she said someone sent it," Fin cuts in, and then he looks back to the server. "Who was it?"

She nods to her left as she fetches a corkscrew from her apron.

An older man smiles at us from a table near the back of the patio. His shoulders are curved over and his clothes are draping off his thin frame. The man is probably in his nineties, hardly a string of hair left on his sun-weathered head, but he waves a hand gently.

"He used to dine with his wife here every Saturday night," the server informs us. "This table, this hour."

"Oh goodness, we can move," I jump in, but the server shakes her head quickly and peels off the foil.

"He was thrilled to see you here. He and his wife actually used to share fish and chips from the same food truck you went to." She laughs and winds the corkscrew down. "He ate the fries. She ate the fish."

"That's...sweet," I say, and I look over my shoulder to give him a soft smile in return.

"He wanted you two to have this bottle—one of their favorites. He said he thought another couple should enjoy it."

"Oh, we're not—"

"Thank you," Fin quickly interrupts, and by god, he's dripping charm. He even drops a hand on top of mine and squeezes my fingers, giving me a curt smile. "It *is* our lucky night."

The server beams proudly, clearly pleased she's the one who gets to deliver the gift, and finishes uncorking the bottle. She pours both glasses, tells us to enjoy, and disappears.

"How can you accept this?" I say to Fin while managing a smile just in case the old man is still looking.

"How can you not?" Fin picks up the glass, swirls it, and sniffs. "Oh, that's going to be good."

"Fin, that poor man thinks we're going to carry on his legacy or something."

"And you want to take that away from him?" Fin smiles exaggeratedly and lifts his glass toward the man behind me, and then nods for me to pick up mine. "Come on, he's clearly sad."

"I'm not drinking this."

"You don't have to. Just lift your glass."

"We're not even a couple."

"So?"

"This isn't right. We're misrepresenting the facts. We're—"

"Doing the exact same thing with this painting."

I grip the glass of undeserved wine. Fin's not wrong, and I don't feel all that guilty about that little falsehood either. Which is unusual. Unfamiliar. Curiously un-afflicting.

"This still doesn't make us a couple," I point out.

Fin lowers his glass slightly and fixes his eyes on me, all but sucking any other protest straight from my mouth. His brows twitch and the hint of a genuine smile seems to ghost across his lips.

"What do you say we just fake it?"

Eighteen

"There's a dinosaur in it," I say, swinging my glass through the air. "Any movie with a dinosaur deserves five stars."

"It's an eighties documentary; is the dino animatronic?" Fin demands.

"Well, no, it's a toy, but"—I laugh as Fin throws his hands up in the air—"it's supposed to ward off bears in the market!"

"The stock market?"

"Yes!" I cry, and I tilt my glass back once more to discover it's empty.

Fin leans forward, a crooked grin on his face, and plucks up the wine bottle, tilting it over my glass. Nothing comes out.

"Uh-oh," I say. "Did you do that?"

He pulls the bottle back, closes one eye to squint inside, and then returns it to the table. "I think *we* did that."

"I drank one glass because the old man was sad and I'm not good at pretending."

"I drank one glass to make your performance look halfway believable."

"Then what happened to the rest?"

"Must have been the dinosaur."

"Damn dinosaurs," I tease, and I lean back in my chair, crossing my legs delicately. "One day, I'm going to make you sit down and watch *Trader* with me. You'll see."

"Is that the same day you'll explain to me why dairy farms seem to be a foundational element of your everyday knowledge?"

I giggle, and the best response beyond that is a sloppy grin and a scrunched-up nose, but it does get Fin to laugh.

"Should we call this pinot pink?" he asks, sitting back in his chair and folding his large hands together.

"Call what pinot pink?"

"That blush you have."

I think I squirm under the heat of his stare. "Blush is pink. Pinot is red."

He shrugs. "I like the alliteration."

I'm pretty sure my blush deepens. It's useless to pretend it hasn't been there since the first sip of wine, but I didn't really notice the heat until now. I try to tame the look by pressing the back of my hand to my cheeks.

"Alliteration or not, it's wholly inaccurate. I'm flushed at best. Pick something else to comment on, art boy."

Fin smirks but doesn't push it further. "Fine. Why don't you tell me what you think you're painting at your house?"

"Oh, that," I say on a laugh. "I'm painting your penis."

Fin's brows arch, and I recognize the mistake two seconds too late.

"I mean—I'm painting *over* your penis. Crap—oh god—no. I'm painting over *penises*. Period. Just other penises."

I slap a hand to my burning cheeks as the words tumble out.

"Millicent," Fin coos, his voice dripping with amusement, "I'd like to think I'm pretty open-minded, but—"

"I'm painting. Over penises. On my house," I reiterate, deliberately spitting out each phrase one at a time. "It really has nothing to do with you, okay?"

"Please forgive me, but I do need to know more about this before I just say it's *okay*. What happened?"

I throw my hands up again. "Kids happened. Kids who have too much time on their hands and really great health teachers. They used the side of my house as a canvas for disturbingly accurate body parts."

"I see. This is the house you're trying to buy?"

"Yes. And I'd really love to close on it, you know, phallus-free."

"Understandable," Fin says, but there really is no air of mercy there.

"I guess it's a good thing I met you. Now I know a painter."

"That's very different paint."

"But you have the skill, right? How hard could it possibly be?"

"You tell me. I haven't seen the artwork yet."

Fin grins at me, and I just grin back. Far too widely. And for far too long. Until it finally hits me.

I toss my head back with an exaggerated laugh, and Fin joins in too, a rhythmic thrum to his laughter. I'd contain myself just to deny him the credit of landing a really bad joke, but that low vibration of his voice rattles me all the way to the bone.

And I *like* it.

I like *this*.

I like *Fin*.

"I need the restroom," I admit instead, pushing back from the table. Then, "Oh no."

As I stand, the world seems to wiggle under my feet. Fin jumps up too and reaches across the table to put a hand under my elbow, but he's really not that steady either.

"I'll walk you there," he offers.

"I don't think we're going to make it."

"I don't think we can stay here either."

I swivel around, a little more dramatically than intended, but the patio is abandoned. The old man is gone, the server nowhere to be found. I think someone turned off half the twinkle lights.

"Actually, we really should be getting home," I say.

"Probably not a great idea."

"It's the only idea," I say, but I stumble another step backward and Fin has to round the table and grab my arm. "Where is the car from here?"

"Millie, neither of us is driving."

I stop, the wobbly ground finally coming to a rest under my feet. I know without a doubt now that I'm drunk. I also know I agreed to the first glass of wine, but once it started, I don't remember ever asking to stop. In fact, as it all comes back to me, I realize I asked for the refill, and I'm pretty sure Fin tried politely to urge me otherwise but eventually gave in.

I blink a few times, pretending I'm not a sloppy mess, and smile at Fin. "Let's just walk toward the car, okay?"

He doesn't openly agree but doesn't object either. He grabs his coat from the back of his chair, and I'm glad to see a signed receipt on our table, though I know I wasn't the one who paid it. Together, we exit through the patio gate and wander toward the beach.

We don't speak as we retrace our steps, but it's not uncomfortable. The slosh of the waves and the forgiving grind of sand under our feet are rhythmic by themselves, and it makes me want to move a little closer to Fin.

Without asking, he drapes his Carhartt over my shoulders, and I let him. It's warm from where he must have been leaning against it, and it smells like fresh-cut lumber. It smells exactly like he did the first day we met in the museum.

I still don't know why. Every time I asked him a question tonight, he deflected, and we ended up talking more about me or my job or my interest in mathematical proofs than anything about him. Besides the fact he has—or *had*—a grandmother, I don't know anything about him.

"Was I a bad date tonight?" I ask, not sure exactly where the nerve comes from.

Fin's stride falters as he glances left. "Why would you ask that?"

"I'm afraid I pulled a Steve," I mumble, the words tumbling out faster than I can think. "I never asked what you wanted or where you wanted to go or whether you even like drinking wine on the beach and—"

"This was all my idea."

"Right."

The word seems to fizzle in the dark, and we continue our march toward the row of beachfront houses.

"He wasn't a bad guy," I go on, again blurting thoughts before they're fully formed.

Fin just keeps his pace.

"He was a gentleman and always kind and seemingly thoughtful, but I don't think he really understood me. He didn't know who I was or what I wanted. He just assumed I wanted the same things he did."

Fin still doesn't say anything, and we finally reach the sidewalk that leads us back to the lot where we parked.

"If he could have kept me on a shelf in his house, he would have been happy."

"And that would have killed you," Fin finally speaks up.

He stops walking, and I do too because I realize he's threaded an arm around me. I move to separate us, worried our closeness was an accident, but he keeps me locked in, and my chest comes to a rest against his. We're steps away from the parking lot, away from my car, but I'm looking up. Looking at Fin.

"You'd think I would have loved the stability," I say, trying to keep my mind on track.

"You are the auditor," Fin agrees.

"What if I don't want to be anymore?"

"You're thinking of a career change now?"

"No," I say, and I pull my head back so I can see his face more clearly. "What if I don't want to be so calculated? So predictable?"

"I'm not sure I follow."

"I can't drive us anywhere."

"That I'm well aware of."

"And we're parked outside a bed and breakfast."

"I don't think—"

"What's the problem? Am I not the kind of girl you'd take up to a room?"

Fin's jaw tightens, and I'm pretty sure he's holding in a ragged breath, but he doesn't make a sound. Instead, he breaks us apart, grabs my hand, and starts dragging me toward the front doors of the inn.

It doesn't take long—that, or I've completely lost any perception of time—before Fin has a room key. We walk down the building and find our room at the end but at the top of several flights of stairs. I manage the first set, partially stumble up the second, and Fin practically carries me up the third.

He slots the card in the reader and pushes the door open. There's a king-size bed. A green velvet sofa. A pure white bathroom with dazzling gold fixtures. But my mind's already scrapping for the next move.

I shrug Fin's coat off my shoulders and ditch it on the end of the bed. He locks the door and runs a hand through his hair. I teeter more dangerously on the edge of abandon, driving myself to within six inches of him. His hands easily find my waist, and I'm spinning, but that connection somehow feels natural. Grounding. Consequential.

I ignore a contradictory twitch in his fingers and look up. The room tilts slightly around us, but I focus on the sharp edge of Fin's jaw and the rough shade of beard and the effortless flow of his hair. I've never really understood the fascination with art, especially portraits, but as I drink in each feature, familiarizing myself with every line, it starts to make a little more sense.

I want to capture this look. I want to memorize his image. I want a mental picture I can turn to every day so I never forget this is where it started. This is where everything changed.

He's so close now I can feel his breath on my lips. I perk up on my toes. Reach for his face. Close my eyes.

"Millie, no."

It's a splatter of paint on my imagined canvas.

"We can't," he goes on, though his fingers still snag my hips. "I can't take advantage of you while you're—"

"I'm not—"

"You are. We both are."

"So what?"

Fin responds only by letting his hands fall away, and it's a sobering move. He puts a foot of distance between us, and I find myself looking around the room, desperately scouring for anything that will preserve this moment before it completely crumbles.

"Fine, you don't want to kiss me, then draw me. Prove to me you are who you say you are."

My name ghosts over Fin's lips, but I don't stand still long enough to feel it. Instead I cross the room, snatch up a pad of paper and pen perched neatly on the nightstand, and then push them into Fin's chest.

"Draw me. Paint me. Show me something here is real."

"No," he says, and it's dark and rough and thunderous.

I pull back, my eyes suddenly wet.

"I don't get it. You go on and on about art being so authentic. You turned this into a date. You drove all the way down here with me and you're in this room and I'm telling you what I want and—"

"This isn't how *I* want it."

I choke over the breath rushing from my lungs as I try to catch up to what he's saying.

"This isn't how I want our first kiss," he says simply, and his voice is so soft I almost can't hear him.

He turns away, ditching the pad and pen on a table by the door, and tension seems to flutter down his back as he goes. I know he's toned under these flannels he wears, but I think I can actually see the muscles rippling underneath the fabric, like he's trying so hard to hold back, like he's trying so hard not to call me out as the bomb who keeps blowing up relationships.

I breathe out the embarrassment and slump backward onto the bed. I'd run in the opposite direction but the only option is the bathroom, and I already know I can't fit through the tiny window along the top of the wall.

"Listen," he starts up again, turning around, "I'm sorry, I—"

"Save it."

"Can't I explain?"

"I don't think that's necessary."

"Millicent, please."

I close my eyes, let my head hit the pillow. "That's Millie to you, Mr. Honorable *Fin*-tentions."

Nineteen

"Housekeeping!"

I think it's a funny joke Hannah is playing on me. She's done it a couple times before, once when we were in Vegas and I was too hungover to know what day it was and once when I was laid up in bed with the post-breakup blues.

"Housekeeping!"

I also think Hannah is really toeing the line on what's PC. She's faking an accent and banging on the door.

I grab the nearest pillow and pull it over my head and then I hear a loud thump and a painful groan and it clearly belongs to a *man*.

I spring up in bed grabbing all the sheets as I go, pushing back my hair, and frantically searching the room to remind myself where the heck I am because I am definitely not at home.

"Housekeep—"

"Can you give us a minute?" my man-panion calls, almost a growl, and as my eyes adjust to the darkness and my head catches up to reality I realize that voice belongs to Fin and Fin is on the floor.

And, *oh god*, I spent the night with Fin.

He groans again as he rolls up to sitting and massages a hand over the back of his neck. He cocks his head left, then right, and then scrubs his face like he's trying to wipe away the tiredness, but all of it's irrelevant to me because he's shirtless. Indecent. One-hundred percent exposed.

Okay, technically fifty percent exposed.

His shoulders tighten and the muscles in his back seem to lengthen, baring every vertebrae from his tanned neck to the space between his shoulder blades and all the way south to his *boxers*.

I breathe a sigh of relief but dutifully glance down at my own southern regions anyway because a girl can never be too sure.

I'm fully clothed. Thank goodness.

"Oh good," he says, shifting my direction. "You're up."

"Did you...sleep on the couch?"

Fin swivels his head the other direction, where a blanket is thrown up on the back of the green velvet sofa and a nearly flattened pillow is crammed against one armrest.

"Sleep is a generous word."

"What time is it?" I deflect.

"Well, it was about six a.m. by the time I fell asleep, so"—he swipes up his phone from where it slid under the couch—"that makes it just before noon."

"Oh crap. I'm so sorry. I must have—"

"Hey, what did I say about that word?"

It catches me by surprise, that old gruffness back on his breath, and I have to take a second to recalibrate. Though he's got his knees up and his elbows resting casually on his kneecaps, there's some ease missing there, and I wonder how far back we slid overnight.

"Housekeep—"

"Yeah," Fin bellows at the back of the door. "We're gonna need, like, thirty. Can you please come back then?"

The woman on the other side of the door mumbles something, and Fin scrubs his face again before turning back to me. I tighten up my covers.

"I guess I fell asleep pretty quick."

"Out cold."

It's no surprise to me. I generally sleep pretty easily but add a little booze into the mix and I could snooze through an earthquake. In fact, I have.

"You really could have slept in the bed and I never would have noticed," I say instead.

"Yeah, I was not about to cozy up with you."

"It's a king-size bed."

"And you managed to take up every inch of it."

"Excuse me?"

Fin lets out a soft grunt. "You had the covers untucked and swirled around you in the first ten minutes and still managed to have a limb in every corner."

"I did *not.*"

"I've got proof."

I work my face into a dramatic scowl. "Did you photograph me while I was sleeping?"

Fin lets out a real, full laugh this time, and it echoes around the room. Though I'm prickly and edgy this morning, the sound seems to soften all the corners, and I have to hug the sheets tighter to my chest to flatten the resounding flutter.

Fin drops his knees and lumbers to his feet, animatedly stretching his stiff limbs as he goes, like I was the one who insisted the six-foot man curl up on the couch. He reaches for a few loose pieces of paper on the side table next to the sofa.

"This was about an hour after you fell asleep," Fin says, and he holds a page in the air with one hand.

It's clearly a page from the notepad I thrust at Fin last night, with the hotel logo printed at the top, but there are lines and dots and smudges. A dark figure shadowed on the cream paper. A head of hair, an arm stretched to the right, the other hand fisting a puddle of blankets.

"Did you—"

"And this one," Fin goes on, dropping the first page to reveal a second, "a couple hours after that. Notice your right foot way over here and your left hand in the opposite corner."

He points to each limb in turn, and I try to look away, to figure out what I'm actually seeing, but I feel like all the edges of the room vanish. The windows morph into solid wall and the door into useless panels. There is no right and no left, no up or down—just Fin, standing in front of me, holding a picture that he swore up and down he wouldn't draw.

"Oh, and there was one point," Fin adds, revealing a third drawing, "where your head ended up sideways and your feet were hanging off the other end."

"There aren't feet in that drawing," I say, though I'm not sure why I feel the need to point it out.

"I know. You looked cold. I covered them up."

"That really is me?"

"Told you I don't typically take my models nude."

"But you—"

"You ready for breakfast?" he asks suddenly, and he collects all three pages and stacks them neatly on the side table.

"Fin," I say, but nothing else follows.

If I remember correctly, I basically threw myself at the man last night. Then, I demanded he draw me. And when he wouldn't do either, I pouted like a toddler. And now I'm not even sure I can manage a car ride back to the city, let alone another entire outing where I have to stare at that face knowing he spent all night drawing mine.

"Why are you really doing this?"

I ask the question, though I'm not sure what compels me to demand it except some nagging voice in my head.

Fin just frowns at me at first, so I curl my knees up to my chest, still wrapped up in the sheets, trying not to think about Fin wrapping up my toes last night.

"Why did you agree to do this painting, to drive all the way down here for this frame? Why did you even respond to our ad?"

Fin stills, and his chest falls as he lets out a breath. My eyes flick downward before I can stop myself, but Fin turns away and snatches up his jeans draped over the other arm of the couch. He pulls them on, then finds his white T-shirt, shakes it out, shoves his arms in, and tugs it over his head.

"Honestly?" Fin asks, smoothing his ruffled hair. "I need the cash."

"For what?"

Fin reaches for his flannel next. He slips his tattooed arm through first, then his other, and tugs at the collar until the shirt rests comfortably on his shoulders. Starting at the third down, he slips each button through its slot.

"I mentor some kids in my free time," Fin says, and it's somber and sedate. "Mostly teens who don't have a stable home life and have gotten in some trouble. I set up some space in an old warehouse a few years ago and brought a bunch of art supplies and told them to meet me there every week.

"Most of them do," Fin goes on, fastening the last button, "and it keeps them busy at least one night a week, but one of my kids—he, uh, got into a bit of a situation."

"What does that mean?"

"He got picked up by the cops and needed someone to post bail."

"And he called you?"

Fin tugs at the bottom of his flannel, straightening it out, and then reaches for the blanket he abandoned on the couch, folding it neatly.

"His dad's already in jail and his mom works two jobs just to keep his younger siblings fed."

"That's sad to hear."

"He's a good kid," Fin goes on, and he sets the blanket on the couch and then fluffs up the pillow and lays it on top. "The bail wiped me out, and he needs a lawyer now."

I just nod this time. It's clearly not my place to say anymore, to offer any advice. I'm not even sure what I would say. It's a messed-up part of the system. Even Steve agrees. It always bothered him to arrest kids with no resources, and he usually went for the bigger fish anyway, but I knew it was a part of the job sometimes.

"So, food?" Fin asks, and his pitch has picked back up again, but I hesitate.

I'm surprised by his explanation, but I'm more surprised by the fact that I wish it were something else. A part of me thought he invited me here because he wanted to spend time with me. A part of me almost believed there was something more between us.

"I think we should get back," I say finally. "I'm supposed to go over to my mom's later, and she'll send out a search party if I don't show up on time."

"Sure," Fin says with a nod, and he scoops up his jacket from the chair by the front door. "I've got plenty of gummy worms left for a balanced breakfast anyway."

Twenty

"He mentors kids in his free time?" Hannah cries, and she sits up in her foldable lawn chair she's parked outside my soon-to-be house.

I managed to make it through my Sunday night dinner with my mom last night unscathed based solely on her redirected interest in setting me up with a surely untouchable billionaire. She spent thirty minutes alone raving about the grand opening of DeLobo's art gallery later this week, and I gladly went along with it.

Hannah, on the other hand, wasn't so oblivious and immediately badgered me for a play-by-play the second I walked into work this morning. I told her I'd spill on one condition: it would be over a stress-relieving paint session where I blotted out every penis I could find.

I wedge a metal prong under the lid of the paint can and pry it open.

"I guess so, but I'm not sure that really means anything."

"It clearly means he's a good guy," Hannah spouts. "Don't you agree, Lou?"

Lou perks up at the attention, and Hannah reaches over the side of her chair to pat his head. He seems right at home sprawled out on the grass next to her, a marked improvement from where things began last weekend.

"Good guy or not, we won't be seeing each other again after tomorrow."

"What's tomorrow?"

"The exchange," I say, and I peel back the paint can lid, white paint dripping back into the container. "He's bringing the replacement painting to the museum, and that'll be that."

"You're not going to ask him out?"

"Ask him out? Hannah, I demanded the guy kiss me and he said no."

"You were drunk! It was the polite thing to do."

I scoff loudly, haul up the paint can, and tip it over the metal tray. It's pretty the way it spreads and seeps into every corner, and I pull back the can and grab my roller. I don't know the first thing about painting—just whatever I saw on YouTube—but I also think it's got to be somewhat intuitive, right?

I push the roller down the incline and soak the polyester fibers in the puddle at the bottom. It's sticky and gloppy and heavy, and when I drag it back up, the roller doesn't even spin, just smears paint all over the place instead.

"My god, do you really need a lesson on how to paint?" Hannah bemoans, springing out of her seat.

She grabs the roller from me, squeegees half the liquid off along the edge of the tray, and then assertively runs the roller up and down the ribbed incline several times, distributing the paint.

"Here," she says, shoving it back in my hands and then waving at the side of the house. "Now, make long, slow strokes."

I peek at her sideways.

"Yes," she confirms, "this does double as sex advice because apparently you need help with both."

"I do not."

"Says the girl who sleeps with a man without sleeping with the man."

I just plop the roller against the wall. It glides easily across the side paneling, though tiny flecks of dirt and dust roll up into little raised bumps.

"I probably should have cleaned this thing before I started."

"I hope that's not how you start all your encounters of the night," Hannah teases.

She wiggles her brows at me when I toss her a well-deserved glare. Even Lou lifts his head from the grass, like he's deciding which stand-in mom to stand by. I don't give him the chance to choose his new favorite and return to my project, inspecting the shadow of manhood still showing beneath the layer of glistening paint.

"I'm not sure one layer is going to do it."

"Honey, one layer's never enough for a bulge like that."

***

I find myself sitting on that same bench under that same Coolidge painting on Tuesday after work, determinedly *not* thinking about anything except the art.

There's a bulletin board of kids' interpretations of the original next to it, which I hadn't noticed before. It seems some third-grade art class was tasked with replicating the painting, and there's a quote in the middle of the display: "Art is meant to disturb the comfortable and comfort the disturbed."

It's a little morbid for an elementary class, but I guess I kind of see it. There are dogs playing poker in this painting after all. Innocent canines propped up like puppets on chairs, engaging in notoriously human behavior. Egregious. Gluttonous. Piggish.

"If you're looking for a deeper meaning, you're never going to find it," a voice hums from behind me.

I whirl around in my seat to find Fin wearing his usual outfit and carrying a cardboard poster tube.

"It's just dogs playing poker," he goes on. "I'm pretty sure this art teacher thought it'd be amusing to see what kind of messed-up stuff the kids could come up with. Now this kid"—he rounds the bench and tosses a finger at a crayon drawing of helmet-wearing poodles and

Labradors playing cards while suspended in outer space—"he's going places."

"I don't get it," I say, ignoring his joke. "How do you know what's art and what isn't? I mean, why is this"—I wave at the famed Coolidge piece—"any better than this?" I finish by nodding toward the kids' work.

"Art is subjective," Fin says, and he slowly drops down on the bench next to me and stretches an arm across the back of the seat. "Its value is determined by human perception and human perception has no rules."

"So, basically, you don't have an answer."

"Would it be any fun if I did?"

I press my lips together and break eye contact. I'm not sure if this guy bathes in sawdust but that smell is back, making my chest thrum eagerly, and I fear I've picked up on some of Lou's habits. I want to sniff him. I want him to pet me when I do. I want him to tell me I'm a good girl and—

"I'm sorry about Saturday night," Fin says, and it catches me off guard.

"I thought you don't like that word."

"I don't, but it's necessary in this case."

I keep my gaze fixed on a gray bulldog wearing a studded collar and clutching a card between his toes.

"You were never a bad date," he says, but I still hear myself asking the question all over again.

"Do you know how to cover up a bunch of black penises?" I ask instead, swinging my gaze toward him.

He smacks the poster tube against his knee and struggles to contain a telltale twitch in his lips. "I hope you're talking about the artwork on your house."

"I am," I say, attempting to scowl but landing somewhere between a smirk and a frown. "They're gray now. And a little bumpy."

"That sounds like the last thing anyone wants."

"So, can you get rid of it?"

"With paint?"

"What else would you use?"

Fin pauses. "Are you already disappointed to know our current arrangement is coming to an end?"

"I'm not disappointed," I lie. "I just—need help, okay? I thought you could consult on the project if you don't have another job lined up."

Fin lifts his chin slowly and finally settles back into the bench, both of us staring straight ahead at the dogs once more.

"You know, Millie, you could just tell me you want to see me again."

"I think you're misunderstanding—"

"Am I?"

I whip my head his direction, and his brows are swinging upward. I want to tell him he's not wrong, that I can't unhear Hannah demanding why the heck I won't ask him out myself, that I've been practicing the question all day long. But I'm also the kind of girl who likes to know all the possible answers before putting herself out there, and I'm not sure I have Fin figured out yet.

"It's a yes-or-no question," I cut back.

"It's a painting-type and level-of-skill question."

"So?"

"I don't do exterior painting."

He says it curtly, and I want to melt right into the bench, but I don't. I pull my shoulders back a little tighter and hold my chin a little higher. He narrows his eyes at me but quickly drops them and instead slides the tube through his hands once more and plucks off the plastic lid.

"Do you want to see the final piece?"

I nod, even though I don't care that much about the painting any-more, and he tips over the tube and gently taps the bottom, curled-up paper sliding out easily. With a practiced touch, he unfurls it and spreads it between us.

The paper, at least two feet by three feet, uncurls and I can make out the green vines and the uniquely pink grapes, but there's a small, notepad-sized page laying on top, right in the middle. A familiar mess of black lines and dots is there, but it's been filled with color—watercolor by the looks of it—shades of pink and green and blue all bleeding into one another.

"I thought Pacific peach was hard to replicate," Fin says, his voice hardly a murmur. "But this was...something else. I'm still not sure it does you justice."

I reach for the page and run my fingers along the edge, the sharp line tugging at my skin. It's the drawing Fin made after my first hour asleep, one arm above my head and the other clinging to the covers. A pale blue drenches the sheets and the fabric sort of blends into the too-casual outfit I so carefully chose, and that gives way to curls of color where my hair spills over my shoulders.

I admire the work in silence for a moment, and when I look up at Fin again, the lines of his face seem unfamiliar. Softer. Like he's not the person I first met on this bench a week ago. This look is a whole other image of him I've yet to capture. His eyes dip, and he starts to roll up the watercolor within the larger grapes painting.

"I like you, Millie," he says candidly. "I don't need to consult on your project because I'd rather take you out on a real date."

"A what?"

"Well, I think this would be our third date technically," he points out, and I have to keep myself from so easily confirming it.

"You want that?"

"Do you?"

I hesitate, even though I know the answer, and the auditor in me speaks up first.

"How do I know this is right? How do I know my perception of what's happening here is not some"—I jerk a hand toward the kids' drawings—"misinterpretation."

"Well, Millie, does it feel right?"

I shrug because part of me wants to scream *yes* and the other part of me wants to put on the brakes because I've got to be out of my mind to agree to this.

"Name the time and place and I'll be there," he goes on.

"You don't drive."

"I'll have you know I'm more than capable of getting to a destination on my own."

"Is that so?" I challenge, and a short laugh follows. "Seems like you've been hard-pressed to find transportation all week."

"That was different. We were working. Now, will you go out with me or not?"

I cross my arms and lean back, eyeing him suspiciously. It's not a hard question to answer, but I'd really like him to think it is. In fact, I'd love to come up with some ridiculous, isolated location for him to meet me, but he was right—there really aren't many dairy farms nearby, and I'd feel a little bad if he had to hop a Greyhound just so I could get a laugh.

He lets out a deep gust of air and I'm pretty sure that's code for *hurry up and say yes.*

"Fine. The DeLobo gallery," I say finally, though I think it's my mother talking. She's in my head still demanding I try to win the billion-aire over and also hassling me about posing naked for Fin and everything is all jumbled.

Meanwhile, Fin's brows dip together. "Why on earth would you want to go there?"

"I don't know. It's art?"

Fin's frown tightens.

"The grand opening is on Thursday," I go on. "It's at the pier where the farmers market is. Everyone says it's supposed to be amazing."

Fin still holds back his response.

"I'm beginning to think you don't really like art."

"I like art just fine," he replies. "Just not everyone's art."

"Do you have a better idea, then?"

"I'll make you a deal," he concedes. "Bring Lou, and that's where we'll go."

"What do you want Lou for?"

"Obviously we need to keep him away from this replica," Fin says, waving the tube in the air. "No way am I going to paint pink grapes again."

I roll my eyes. "I can't bring a dog to an art gallery."

"Why not? It's partially outdoors, isn't it?"

"So you do know a little about the new place he's opening?"

Fin's resounding huff disrupts the rhythmic hum of other museum patrons quietly admiring famous works.

"Yes, I know about the gallery and I know about DeLobo and I do like art that's not my own."

"Good. Now, what happens if they don't let Lou inside?"

"You just let me worry about that," Fin says, and he even taps my leg once with the tube before grinning at me. "Do we have a deal?"

Twenty-One

"You'd better be on your best behavior, Lou."

He tilts his head and lets his tongue loll as I threaten him. There's no way he understands anything happening here, but I don't think he cares either.

I didn't even get the full offer to dogsit out of my mouth before Hannah was practically gushing her approval. She tried to convince me to keep him for the whole weekend, but I held firm on one unsanctioned outing because I'm pretty sure Steve would find it unusual, at the very least, that his ex-girlfriend is voluntarily carting his dog around on dates while he's out of town.

I leash up Lou before letting him out of the front seat of my car. There are significantly more people at the pier than a typical Thursday night. My mom said something about the grand opening having a hosted bar, so I'm sure that's drawn a whole crowd by itself. Of course, it could also be the local theater troupe, which is still peddling tickets for *The Vagina Monologues*. I consider buying a pair both to support the cause and to educate Grant in the female essence.

"Finally," a voice says behind me. "Been here an hour and just now get to experience a work of art."

"There will *never* be a day..." I begin, but my voice seems to vanish, flitting away on the air as I whirl around to find Fin. I know it's him and

I know he's teasing me and laughter even buds in my chest, but surprise ultimately wins out. "What happened to you?"

His chin jerks, his brows pinch together, and he rubs his hands down the front of his coat. "What do you mean?"

"You—" But I catch myself because I think Fin got dressed up for this date.

He's wearing a peacoat. It's dark blue with crisp black buttons and a turned-up collar, and I get the striking impression he just walked off a ship that's been sailing the Atlantic for a month. The look is both rugged and polished. Hungry and disenchanted. Wild and restrained.

And, apparently, I'm not the only one who likes it.

Fin squats for a nose-to-nose greeting from Lou, who's way too enthusiastically playing the part of the loyal dog left home to stand guard until his sailor dad's return.

"There is some truth to that pick-up line, though," Fin says suddenly, scratching Lou's chin once more before getting back to his feet. He slips a hand through his neatly coiffed hair, and I try not to stare.

"I'm not sure I follow."

Fin grins. "Mona Lisa's got nothing on Millie Lou."

"Oh, get out! My middle name isn't Lou."

"Lisa isn't her middle name either, but, come on, how else did this guy get his name?"

Fin rubs his knuckles between Lou's eyebrows, and the dog slumps against his leg in dazed bliss. I swear Lou is nothing but trouble in a four-legged furry outfit.

When I don't respond, Fin dips a hand inside his coat pocket and pulls out a square of fabric, bright red and folded up. It's enough to lure Lou back to his feet, and as Fin crouches again next to his new best friend, Lou aggressively sniffs the item.

"Got this for the hound," Fin says, unraveling the piece and tugging it over Lou's head.

"Is that a fake service-dog jacket?"

Fin secures a Velcro strap under Lou's bulky chest and then frowns. "Nowhere on this thing does it say he's a service dog."

"Then explain *this*," I demand, pointing at the patch that clearly says *Dog-in-Training*.

Fin takes a step back and cocks his head, eyeing Lou like he's inspecting his latest artwork. "That definitely says Lou is practicing to be a canine, so I'm really not sure how anyone can be confused."

"Where did you find this?"

"Millicent," Fin says, dropping his voice to a teasing growl, "you do know there's more to the internet than Craigslist, right?"

I just roll my eyes and tug on Lou's leash because I'm all out of comebacks and I'm also concerned the pinot-pink shade Fin so easily identified the other night is about to make an unwelcome reappearance.

Fin hums brightly like he's just beat me at Go Fish and then follows as I lead the way through the various tents on the pier, heading toward the gallery.

It's on the far end of the dock, built into a warehouse that's partially roofless. My mom told me what happened to it, but the only part I caught was her gushing over how DeLobo apparently "married destruction with creativity." Her words—or those of some starry-eyed reporter—not mine.

There's a bar outside and several cocktail tables dispersed through the waterfront area. Mingling guests dressed for a black-tie event are clinking glasses with each other and probably reciting entire sections of their résumés word-for-word. We narrowly skirt a pair who might as well be the poster couple for expensive galas, the woman draped in a fur scarf and the man actually sporting a monocle.

"I don't mean to be rude," Fin begins as we head for the doors, "but are these the kind of people you normally hang out with?"

I let out a short laugh. "I was about to ask you the same thing."

Fin reaches for the handle, the slightest grin on his face, and Lou barges between our feet as we go inside. I'm not surprised in the slightest when the woman working the front desk nearly vacates her high heels. Her lashes flutter and her cheeks puff up and her smile tightens as Lou lumbers toward the desk, tongue dripping with a fresh string of drool.

"Can I help you?" she asks curtly, and her eyes dart over Lou's red vest.

"Isn't this the DeLobo exhibit?" Fin asks, that shade of terseness I first witnessed the day we met returning.

"That would be Mr. Vincent DeLobo's art gallery, yes. The highly anticipated Pecora Hall. Are you intending to join us for the grand opening?"

"Wouldn't dream of missing it," Fin says, and I'm pretty sure it's all sarcasm.

I know he's not slighting my choice of venue for our date, but I do think he's not quite in his element anymore. When he sheds his peacoat—equally as reluctantly as the woman who's clearly obligated to take it—he reveals a gray, long-sleeved Henley. It's charming, though casual, and does more for showing him off than helping him blend in.

The fabric is taut over his chest and snug across his shoulders and arms, and the sleeves are rolled enough to put the tattoo I've yet to ask about on full display. I study it a second more as he runs a hand up his sternum, almost like he's trying to massage away the tightness, but he quickly reaches for my coat next.

I'm not in anything much fancier—just a short shift dress and sheer tights—but if I'm feeling a little underdressed, then I'm sure Fin is too.

I awkwardly transfer my car keys to my skirt pocket (having not brought a clutch because—*surprise!*—I don't own one) and surrender my coat. As the woman takes it from Fin, she drops another pointed look at Lou.

"He prefers not to check his coat," Fin says.

Her lips flatten into a perfectly straight line, and I utter a quick word of thanks before urging Fin away from the desk and toward the first room.

"Honestly, I had no idea this would be so fancy," I admit.

"You think they're serving caviar tonight? Duck confit? Hundred-year-old bottles of Scotch?"

"It's not *that* bad."

Fin cocks a brow at me and then swivels his head left as a server bustles by with a tray full of champagne flutes. He plucks off a pair, offers one to me, and smirks.

"Okay, so there's champagne," I concede. "Didn't know you'd be so hard to please."

"I have become accustomed to a certain lifestyle, you know. One of a humble starving artist."

"You hardly look starving."

"Have you been checking me out?"

"Oh, don't flatter yourself," I taunt, but there's no validity to my deflection.

I smirk right back at him, tilt back the champagne glass for a healthy swig, and then strut toward the first row of paintings pinned along the far wall, dragging Lou along with me.

Fin catches up to us in front of a series of abstract paintings, and we silently wander along the grouping. I spend most of my time reading the obscure titles printed on the tiny cards next to each image. The prices are there too, but the numbers are clearly too long to fit, each candidly abbreviated with decimals and a scary-looking *M* following it.

"Maybe this was a bad choice," I say, tugging Lou a little closer to me.

Fin reaches for the leash and swipes it from my hand. "Time with you is never a bad choice."

I swallow my breath and try to manage a short smile. It's a little weak and maybe a little scary, so I keep walking. We view a few more paintings in silence, then a short series of photography, and end up in another room with sculptures.

One of them looks like something raided from the dumpster behind a hardware store. There's wire stringing together scraps of wood—all of it spray-painted silver—and a row of nails in the bottom of something that looks an awful lot like the sole of a shoe.

"Honestly, what am I supposed to get out of this?"

I try to keep it under my breath, but Fin lets out a laugh that's practically a snort, and some woman drowning in a gaudy pashmina tosses a sour look our direction.

"What do you want to get out of it?" Fin counters, and he settles in next to me, leaning back slightly and pursing over the champagne glass he's holding in one hand as he fiddles with Lou's leash in the other.

"I don't know. I guess I thought art was supposed to speak to you or something."

"And this doesn't?"

I barely refrain from pointing out the artfully crumpled wad suspended by wire in the middle of the structure is actually an old candy wrapper. I didn't take Fin to be the pretentious art snob type, but I also don't want to smear his entire career.

"I guess it could be...interpreted as commentary on...litter?"

Fin makes another noise and tilts his head away from me.

"Oh, come on," I whine, "what do you get out of it?"

When he turns back, his cheeks seem to be a little rosier and he's pawing at his smile again, like he's trying to wipe it off. "Absolutely nothing. That's clearly garbage. Let's go."

He downs the rest of his champagne and I follow suit so he can take both glasses and return them to another passing server. We wind our way between other patrons and enter a third room, this one much darker than the previous two.

There's only one painting in this space, and it's easily four feet wide. It sits on the far wall, illuminated by a pair of overhead track lights, and a knot of people is gathered in front, softly muttering to each other.

We move closer, folding between a woman sipping daintily from her glass and a man standing with his hands behind his back, both squinting at the image. Lou wanders alongside us and settles between our legs, the heat of his doggie breath palpable through my tights.

I recognize the painting but not because I've seen this actual piece before. It's a depiction of this exact warehouse on this exact pier—only, from fifteen-some years ago. Though the building is fully intact, it's not polished or pretty. In fact, it's a little run-down, and the artist even took care to depict overflowing trash cans and seagulls picking at litter.

There are people in the painting too, tiny figures dotted along every wall. Some are standing and talking with each other. Others are cruising through on bikes or rollerblades. A few are lying down in a spot of sun, newspaper draped over their figures.

"I forgot that's what this place used to look like," I say, still staring straight ahead at the painting.

"Does this speak to you?" Fin asks.

I shrug. I want to have a good answer for him. I want to sound smart and cultured and experienced, but I also feel a little conflicted staring at this artistic interpretation of something that doesn't exist anymore.

"How about this?" Fin says, and he turns around and faces the opposite side of the room.

I follow, staring at the empty black walls. It's a huge room, space for dozens of other pieces of work, but it's precisely blank, just darkness plastered in every corner.

"There's no art over here," I say at the risk of sounding obtuse.

"There used to be."

I tilt my head toward him, but he doesn't look at me, just lets his gaze slink over the barren space.

"This warehouse used to be our meeting spot," Fin explains. "This room in particular was where we did a lot of painting. There's no windows, no light, no distractions. The kids could throw paint at every wall and still find a blank space to start over."

"The kids you mentored?"

"All I did was show up."

I drop my chin and reach for Lou's head, scratching him for the comfort. "DeLobo ran you out?"

Fin doesn't respond, but I take that as confirmation anyway.

"Art doesn't have to speak to you," Fin goes on. "It doesn't have to speak to anyone. But it should create a feeling. Even that ridiculous trash sculpture—I guarantee the artist who made it actually felt something when he did it."

"This room used to do that for the kids. It used to be alive. And now it's just three blank walls and a painting DeLobo thinks proves he's done something good here."

I glance toward the art in question and hear a few new viewers murmur something about how this place is monumentally improved over its previous look.

"I'm all for the art," Fin says, "but people like DeLobo come through and destroy entire communities of true artmakers just to put up something polished."

I don't reply. I'm not sure there's anything I could say, but I do want to know more. I want to hear him talk. I want to hear him share everything about this passion of his. I want to know what feeling his paintings give him.

But I don't ask because Lou barks.

I cringe as I crouch down to calm him, and it feels like this giant room shrinks to the size of a coffin. Whatever murmuring was happening behind us is now squarely focused *on* us, and I shudder with embarrassment when Lou barks again.

"Lou, no," I command and grab him by his jacket as he bulldozes into me. He wedges his big head under my arm and lets out another howl and a pathetic whine, so Fin drops to his knees too.

"Inside voice, Lou. Have you learned nothing in doggie training classes?" Fin jokes as he scratches Lou's head and then looks up at the staring crowd. "He's a B-minus student at best."

I don't laugh at his attempt to lighten the mood because Lou whines harder. He drops to his front legs, tries to bound forward playfully, and nearly topples me while he's at it. I try to get a finger under his collar while scouring the room for whatever he's after when I see someone waving a tray of hors d'oeuvres on toothpicks in the air.

"Bacon. Wrapped. Dates."

Fin looks at me. "You want a snack right now?"

"He does," I groan, tugging a little harder on Lou's collar.

Fin gets back to his feet, still flashing that charming smile at everyone. "He may be a B-minus student, but his sniffer earns all A's."

Fin waves over the server who's carelessly flaunting the food around, and I'm pretty sure Fin's about to scoop up a bunch for doggie treats when his hand freezes mid-air.

His gaze moves past the server, and I follow it. Two men are slinking through the crowd. One is tall, a beanie pulled nearly over his eyes, and the other a shorter, squatter man in that conspicuous bad-guy scally cap.

"Time to go," Fin says, and he's already stooping to pull me back to my feet.

He's got one hand on Lou's leash and the other on my elbow, pushing me through the crowd and back to the sculpture room before I get a word out.

"Fin, what is going on? Who are those men?"

"Keep up," Fin says as we round the silver garbage piece.

"Fin—"

"Coats, now," he demands, reaching the front desk in a few more strides.

The woman looks about as appalled as I feel, but she snatches the claim ticket from Fin's hand and disappears into the coat room. Meanwhile, Fin tosses another look over his shoulder and Lou, too, tugs toward the lingering smell of bacon.

"They were the ones at the art store," I say. "You know them."

"Not now," Fin urges, and he turns back to me, flashing a hard glance before anxiously tapping the counter.

The woman doesn't reappear, but the men do. I catch a glimpse of them as they slip out of the sculpture room. They're moving toward us stiffly, trying to wind between clusters of patrons, which have grown in number and size since we arrived.

Fin curses. "We don't have time to wait. We need to go."

"Go? Go where?" I ask, but Fin tugs me and Lou back out the front doors, coatless.

We round the corner, dip behind a tent selling dirt-covered potatoes and carrots, and then speed walk farther down the pier. His hand is in mine now, and I'm not sure when that happened, but there's no extricating my fingers either. He's got me cinched tight as his pace picks up, nearly to a run.

"Where are you parked?" he asks gruffly, and I tug back on his hand.

"Down the street, but I can't drive. I had that champagne."

"Let me, then."

"No. Why are we running? What is going on?"

This time Fin stops, rounding on me, though his head swivels as he scans the booths we've just run by. He doesn't have time to get a word out before Lou barks again. It's an eager yip and it's aimed at the vegan dog treat tent. The woman who had fussed over Lou last week is there, distributing a giant tub of treats into smaller pouches, and Lou knows exactly what they are.

"Give me your keys and take him," Fin says, handing over Lou's leash.

I accept it but not before Lou pounces excitedly. I'm growling out another pleading *no* when Fin grabs my hand again, almost painfully.

"Now, Millie."

"What?"

"*Run.*"

I see what he sees at the same time: both men bursting between two white tents and full-out sprinting toward us. I don't argue anymore, and I pull Lou with all my force, the three of us taking off down the street.

I know when the men reach the dog treat pop-up because the woman staffing it shrieks. Lou and I look back to see the pair snatching up handfuls of treat bags. For a second, I think Lou thinks this is a fun game, and he barks playfully, still running forward but looking over his shoulder for the goods.

"The keys!" Fin reminds me, and I fish them from my skirt pocket.

I'm handing them off to Fin as we round the corner and my SUV comes into view. He aims for the driver's door and I yank open the passenger side, both of us piling inside in a panting mess.

I call Lou, screaming for him to jump on my lap because there's no time for the back seat when we're being chased by the two henchmen from *101 Dalmatians*, but Lou's still got treats on his mind.

He looks back, yanking on his leash, and that's when I realize our mobile-treat guys are down to one. The shorter man is still running toward us, waving bags of dog cookies in the air, but the other is gone.

I scream for Lou again and so does Fin—who's still trying to shove the key in the ignition—but our cries drown under a revving engine. We glance up long enough to see a white van jump the curb. It screeches across the sidewalk, swerves into the grass, and then jerks to a halt. The side door slides open, and the one remaining henchman finally gives up the chase.

But then, all the treats go airborne.

The shorter man has started running back toward the van, which is apparently driven by his partner, and is dumping bags of goods as he goes, creating a crumbly cookie trail straight to the vehicle. By the time it finally registers with me why he'd be flinging biscuits all over the grass, Lou is already gone. He's galloping toward the van, tail wagging, ears flopping, and hungrily snapping up treats.

I scream. Fin curses. But he reaches across me and pulls the door shut.

"Lou, no!" I cry, scrapping for the handle, desperately trying to get out.

"Let him go," Fin growls, and he's reaching for me next, restraining my flailing arms.

In the second I jerk my attention toward Fin and back, it's too late. The door to the van is shut, both men are inside, and Lou is gone.

Twenty-Two

"Fin, stop the car!"

"Buckle up," he says in return, swinging my SUV around a corner without slowing down.

"They just kidnapped my dog!"

Tears are tracking down my face, and I've reached for the door handle twice now, both times resulting in Fin lunging across my lap to keep me in. My breath is coming in horrified sobs, and when I don't make an effort to do anything except smear my tears, Fin reaches for the belt and pulls it taut across my chest, clicking it into place.

"I'm calling the police," I announce, scrambling for my phone.

"You don't want to do that."

"I have to!"

"Lou is going to be fine."

"How can you say that? Those men just lured him into a murder van!"

"A what?"

I sob more hysterically. "A white van with no windows. Everyone knows those are *murder* vans!"

"Did you get that from the five o'clock news too?"

I deliver a glare steely enough to make Fin shrink an inch.

"You've got nothing to worry about," he tries again. "They're not even—"

"They *kidnapped* Lou."

"I know, but they don't want the dog."

"Then what do they want?"

Fin dodges my repeat glare and takes the next corner too quickly, causing the tires to screech against the asphalt. He then drags a hand through his hair.

"They want me."

"Oh, I gathered that," I snip in return, angrily swatting at the moisture slipping down my cheeks. "What do they want from you, genius?"

"I'm gonna guess money. Or a painting. Or both."

"You're going to *guess*?"

"Hard to tell. Haven't bothered to ask."

"Fin, this isn't funny."

"I know, but I need you to take a breath. You're all puffed up and I'm afraid to roll the window down."

I want to bite back, possibly also clock him over the head with the heaviest thing I can find in my car (the driver's manual?), but my chest does have the distinct tightness of an overfilled balloon. Aside from the few words I did manage, I don't think I've properly expelled even half the air from my lungs since Fin practically dragged me out of the gallery.

I pinch my tights, wishing these had some cute math-themed pattern to distract me, but no, I had to pick the plainest, most boring pair I own because I somehow planned a date at a billionaire's stuffy art gallery.

Fin cracks the window and a gust of cool air blows in.

"How about another breath?" he says.

"How about you tell me what's going on here?"

He refocuses on the road, finally returning to the speed limit.

"I met those guys working another side gig. I was trying to raise funds to buy a new space since that douchebag DeLobo snapped up mine and—"

"The warehouse?" I cut in, not entirely sure why I care about the details.

"Yes, I needed another place for us to meet."

"You know an abandoned warehouse is a horrible place for kids to be hanging out anyway, right?"

"I'm aware."

"Really?"

"*Painfully.*"

"What happened? What did you do?"

Fin sighs, taking another turn and falling in behind one of those tiny smart cars that shouldn't be allowed on the road.

"It never should have gone down like this, but I was doing a job for those guys and my kid, the one I told you about, got wind of it. He showed up where he shouldn't have been and that's how he got picked up by the cops."

"But I thought you said—"

"I know what I said. I didn't exactly want to admit it was my fault he got arrested."

"Oh my god."

"I screwed up, Millie, okay? I know that, but once he got pinched, there wasn't anything I could do, so when I saw the chance to get a little revenge on those assholes, I took it."

"What did you do to them?" I demand, though my voice trembles.

"They're not good guys if that's what you're worried about."

"It's not."

Fin white-knuckles the steering wheel. "I scammed them out of a few bucks."

"How many is a few?"

"Twenty-five thousand."

I clap a hand to my mouth, only one word slipping out. "How?"

"The only way I know how."

Fin doesn't look at me, but he doesn't need to. His jaw flexes with tension and his eyes flick back and forth anxiously, and it doesn't take long for me to put the pieces together.

"You sold them a fake, didn't you?"

"It was a replica. And it was a little more complicated than that."

Fin makes two more turns and then brings the car to a stop. Aside from the few times I nearly tumbled out of my seat, I wasn't paying much attention to the direction he was headed, but I know where we are. We've pulled up next to a narrow channel of water—notably, the only channel of water within this part of the city.

"I know these guys," Fin goes on, turning in his seat toward me. "I also know what they're capable of and who's really calling the shots here because it's not them. They're errand boys at best."

"Errand boys who kidnapped Lou."

"Lou is going to be just fine. Maybe have a few too many dog treats, but they won't hurt him."

"They shouldn't even have him. I never should have—"

"We will get him back," Fin interrupts, and he kills the engine. "Now, will you just come inside my house so we can come up with a plan?"

***

It turns out *house* is a pretty loose term.

"You live on Mission Creek?" I ask.

"Yeah, so?"

I take another step away from the safety of my vehicle, which we left parked along the bank, and mount a narrow footbridge that stretches between the riverbank and the lone dock on the channel. Fin offers me a hand as the weathered wood groans under my step. I don't take it because I'm still doing the math.

"I mean, *how*?"

"*How*, what?"

"How do you afford—"

His brows arch when I cut myself off, and his hand twitches, like he's considering rescinding his offer of help.

I huff. "Never mind."

"I should make you cash in your one remaining rude comment for that."

"You got my dog kidnapped. I think I deserve a freebie."

Fin doesn't argue, and he doesn't point out that Lou isn't technically my dog either, even though I've said it several times now. I'm not sure what that means—if he understands the attachment or if he just doesn't see the merits in debating pet ownership—so I just take the olive branch he extended me and let him help me onto the dock.

"It was my grandmother's place," he finally explains as we turn and walk down the row.

"So it's one of the originals?"

"I guess so, but it's why I can't just have all the kids over here. It's small."

"Sure, but it's got to be worth millions."

Fin levels a stern look at me, and I shrug. It's true.

The Mission Bay houseboats are a small chain of docked floating homes. They were relocated here back in the 1960s, which is surely when Fin's grandmother arrived, considering most people who live here have held on to their homes for generations.

I figured I'd go to my grave before getting an invite to Fin's home. Never mind getting to see one of these. They're something of a legend around the city.

The one we walk to makes a shed look roomy, especially in contrast to the other recently remodeled, multi-level houseboats. It's not poorly maintained—just timeworn and modest. Sun-bleached wooden siding, twice- or thrice-painted trim, a single gaslight lamp posted next to the narrow door. That's been converted to an electric bulb, and it blinks to life when Fin approaches.

"Do those men know where you live?" I ask as Fin fits his key in the lock.

"No, and I'd like to keep it that way, so will you get inside?"

I keep my feet planted firmly on the dock. "This doesn't mean I forgive you."

"I'm not asking for that."

Fin swings the door open wide. Under any other circumstance, I might consider my options—make a pro/con list, estimate potential gains and losses, et cetera—but I'm pretty sure I wouldn't be able to recognize the difference anymore. So, I step inside.

The tiny houseboat is washed in moonlight spilling in from the wood-framed glass roof. It's arranged like a typical studio apartment with a mini kitchen on the right wall and a living space on the left. There's a tasteful leather couch that must convert to a bed and a cute, refinished table that seats one. And at the far end, centered in front of a bank of windows, is an easel.

"It's not much," Fin says, but I shush him and cross the room.

There's a stretched canvas resting on the lip of the easel, and even before I reach it, I get the whiff of fresh paint. It's that wet, chemical smell, though it's sweeter than the gallon-can type, I think. Almost citrusy. And I realize the shade streaked across the textured base is familiar: more pink than orange but more orange than pink.

"Pacific peach," I whisper.

The front door clicks shut behind me, and Fin must drop my keys to the counter, metal rattling on cheap wood.

"I think I got pretty close this time," he says.

I think he perfected it.

The painting is incomplete, but it's striking. In it, the recognizable spindly legs of the Capitola Beach pier disappear into a rolling blue ocean. A patriotic-colored food truck is blurred in the background. Twinkly lights are dotted in the distance. And splashed above it all is a polished, peachy sky.

The houseboat rocks under my feet now, but I'm back on the beach, sand swirling, salty breeze blowing. I close my eyes and I can almost feel the heat in my cheeks, brought on by that flagrant shade of pinot pink. I swallow and I think I can taste the sweetness of the wine we shared.

"What are we going to do, Fin?" I finally ask. "How are we going to get Lou back?"

Fin flicks on a light. Synthetic gold drowns the room, effectively blacking out the surrounding windows, and I turn back to Fin. Turn back to the only tangible hope I've got left.

"We're going to give them what they want."

Twenty-Three

"Let me be the one to tell you—*no one* wants this," I say, waving a dismissive hand at Fin and sinking back into his couch.

He's wearing his Carhartt jacket, but it's zipped up to his neck, and he just pulled out a fake mustache from his pocket and stuck it to his upper lip.

"They know what you look like. Why do you need a disguise?"

"You don't like it?" Fin asks, and he wiggles his upper lip, causing the stiff hairs to poke the bottom of his nose.

"The *Super Troopers* look never really did it for me."

"Are you sure?" Fin taunts, venturing another step closer. "I could do some good work with this."

"Ugh, please, no," I growl, and I grab a throw pillow from the corner of the couch and hide behind it. "Take it off."

Fin lets out a short chuckle, but I don't hear the distinct sound of skin glue being peeled up. Instead, a paper bag rustles, and when I peek over the pillow again, I find Fin smirking under familiar blue fringe.

"Oh no. There is no way—"

"Why not?" he says, wrenching the wig onto his head.

"First off, it's a woman's wig. Secondly, it's neon blue. And if you really need a third reason, you can still see half your hair underneath."

Fin frowns and yanks on the ends, trying to straighten it, but his full head of hair seems intent on showcasing itself. He pulls off the wig, and

I toss the pillow aside and jump to my feet, snatching the topper from his hands.

"I was fixing it," he says.

"You clearly need help."

"Sure, but that has nothing to do with the wig."

I roll my eyes, spread my fingers inside the cap, and then give him a pointed look. "Duck."

Fin obeys, dropping to his knees in front of me, and I try not to notice the way his breath fans against my belly. Instead, I focus on sliding the netting over his head, taking care to tuck his strands under the edges.

"Is it always like this with you?" I ask absently.

"You mean, me on my knees begging for help?"

I tug the wig harder. "No. Are you always this secretive? Always in some disguise?"

"I think you've seen more of me than you realize."

He tries to lift his chin and look up at me, but I grab the crown of his head, forcing his line of sight back down.

"Hold still."

"Millie, can I tell you—"

"There," I cut in, pulling the ends once more and then dusting the bangs across his forehead.

I take a step back, but he doesn't stand up. He just looks at me, his eyes narrowing, and though I don't think I know him that well, I can see the conflict swirling there. I can see something fighting to be freed.

And maybe it's because I'm conflicted too. I have a feeling whatever he wants to say has nothing to do with Lou's rescue, and I'm afraid if I give him the chance to utter it, I'll want to hear it. I'll be hanging on every word and I'll forget I'm only here in this moment at Fin's house to bring my boy home.

"You look ridiculous," I finally spit out.

"Is it that bad?"

"It leaves me questioning your sanity."

"Good. That's what I'm going for."

I put another foot of distance between us and return to the couch, spending more time than explicitly necessary scooping up the pillow again and settling it back on my lap.

When I look up next, Fin has dragged out the lone chair at the kitchen table and is pulling open his laptop. He positions himself so his back is to the windows, nothing but darkness visible behind him.

"The disguise is so they can't screenshot my face and distribute the image anywhere," Fin says matter-of-factly, settling in front of the computer and adjusting the screen and built-in camera. "These guys aren't smart by any means, but no need to risk it."

"What's going to happen when you call them up?"

Fin glances my direction, but I can't tell if he's really looking at me thanks to the shades he just put on.

"Ideally? I make sure Lou is okay. I give them an offer they can't refuse. We all go home happy."

"You still have the twenty-five thousand dollars?"

"That's not even on the table."

"What else do you possibly think you can offer?"

Fin ducks, looking at the computer screen again. "Don't say a word while I'm on this call, okay? The last thing I need is for them to know you're still with me."

"Why wouldn't I be with you? Are they that dumb?"

Fin tosses me one more look and cocks a single brow. "Yes."

I resign myself to obedience and hold the pillow tighter to my chest. In lieu of a warm dog, it's comforting to squeeze. Meanwhile, Fin clicks through a few screens, then taps a couple keys, and the familiar chime of an outgoing web call sounds.

I'm inclined to believe Fin's opinion on the kidnappers—that they really aren't very smart—mostly because Fin has a direct line to them. Apparently, when he signed up for this side gig of his, they exchanged personal contact information. It's useful in this moment, so I haven't questioned him further on it, but I'm also not entirely convinced this won't go down like the close of a soap opera episode: someone lying, someone cheating, and someone revealing they aren't who they say they are.

The ringing finally ceases, and Fin straightens up in his seat, clears his throat, and brushes back a lock of blue hair.

"Well, well, well," a voice croons on the other end of the call, rattling through the computer speaker, "could that possibly be the elusive Van Bro?"

"*Van Bro?*" I mouth silently to Fin, who pops up just to scowl at me.

I guess I shouldn't be completely surprised the apparently in-demand art replicator doesn't go by his "proper moniker" with a couple of co-conspirators.

"Didn't take you two asshats for a dog-napper," Fin claps back, refocusing on the call.

"I didn't take you for a guy who likes playing dress—*argh!*"

The man's insult is dramatically cut short by an unmistakable, deep bark, and Fin chuckles.

"Careful. He bites."

"You've got five minutes, Van Bro."

"Show me the dog," Fin demands, his voice dipping another octave.

"Show me the piece," the man counters.

"You don't care about that piece."

"I'll tell you what we do and don't—*argh!* Hold still!"

Again, his comment drowns under Lou's howl, and I have to slap a hand over my mouth to keep quiet as Lou starts whining. I'm certain the dog is pulling on whatever leash they've got him on, and considering I can hear the second man in the background making a strangled plea, Lou's putting up quite the fight.

"Show me the hound," Fin demands again, and finally there's a resigned grunt on the other end of the line.

The speaker cracks with rustling sounds, and I can hear the distinct click of nails on hard floors and the heavy pant of a dog, and as the man surely moves his phone or computer closer to Lou, I can even make out the sloppy sound of Lou's jowls.

"Happy?" the man grunts back. "All in one piece. Now give us ours."

"You do know dogs need to be fed twice a day, right?" Fin asks instead. "They also need fresh water and have to go outside three, maybe four, times a day. Do you even have a shovel big enough to scoop his—"

"We know how to take care of a dog," the man argues, but even I can sense the trepidation on his voice. It's not a glamorous or easy job, after all.

"Let me make myself perfectly clear," Fin says, and the taunting tone he'd taken on earlier vanishes. "If *anything* happens to that dog—and I mean if so much as a single toenail is scuffed—I will personally hunt both of you down and shave you piece by piece into tiny little flakes that aren't fit to feed goldfish. Understand?"

There's a brief moment of silence on the other end of the call before the man speaks up again. "Get us what we want and no one has to get hurt."

"I'm not returning the original."

"You will if you know what's best. And, since you want to make this more difficult than it needs to be, you're going to get us the twenty-five thousand dollars we're out thanks to your little scam."

I'm not sure if it's obvious to the men on the other end of the call when Fin squirms, but it's obvious to me. His throat tightens, his Adam's apple bobs up and down, and even the muscles in his cheeks go taut. There's no hope in me seeing his eyes, but if I could, I'm certain there'd be unease there.

He tries to put on a stoic look anyway by pulling his shoulders back. "That's never going to happen."

"Then you're never going to get your furry friend back."

"I'll pay it."

I say it without hesitation, without even thinking, and Fin jerks his chin up. It's a warning glance, one that tells me not to say another word, but I'm not about to be silenced.

"I'll even make it thirty thousand. I just want Lou back. Tonight."

"Who do we have here?" the man on the other end croons again. "Would that be your little lady friend? Still got her around?"

Again, I resist the urge to point out there's no world in which I wouldn't be here with the only person capable of getting Lou back, but it's beside the point because Fin is pulling the laptop closer as if he thinks they'll be able to peek around the edge of the frame and see me.

"I need a minute," he says, and he clicks two keys and folds the lid halfway down.

I'm assuming the call's on mute because he rounds on me next.

"What the hell do you think you're doing?"

"What do you think *you're* doing? I need Lou back. I'll pay whatever they want for his return."

"Where would you even get that kind of money?"

"Is that really your concern?"

Fin jerks backward and frowns deeply. "Is that your down payment money? For your house?"

I shift uneasily, still clinging to the pillow. "Most of it, yes."

"Hell no."

"I don't think you really get a say here, Mr. Van Bro."

"You know I don't really go by that name, right?"

"I'm not sure I know anything. You could go by Fin and Tonic for all I know. Or Fin Can. Or Fin-derella. Maybe it's *Finnow.*"

"Finnow?" he says on a scoff, but I don't break.

"A play on minnow."

"That's a stretch."

"It's perfectly on the nose considering you're doing nothing but floundering around on this call. Now, I'm not letting Lou get hurt because you're too proud to take my money."

"Lou isn't going to get hurt," Fin says, but I cross my arms.

I wish I could believe him. I *want* to believe him, but I've never put my trust in anyone who's not explicitly on the "Nice" list or at the top of every honor roll.

Fin finally sits back in his seat and opens the laptop again, though he wags a finger at me first. "Don't offer any more money."

I consider offering to pay double, but I know that's exactly how some of my more ego-driven clients get themselves into trouble. Meanwhile, Fin unmutes the call and settles in front of the camera once more.

"This is between me and you. I'm not giving you the original back, but I'll let you keep the dupe and I'll even get you two more replicas."

The man snorts on the other end, and I'm hard-pressed not to do the same thing.

"Why the hell do we need more fakes when we could have the real thing?"

"They're different paintings. Two you don't have. Two you can't possibly get your hands on."

"What would we ever do with those?"

Fin shakes his head, and I'm pretty sure he's rolling his eyes behind his sunglasses.

"You guys truly are the dumbest criminals I've ever worked with. Do you have any idea the replica you're currently in possession of is one part of an incredibly rare three-piece collection?"

"So?"

"They may be worth twenty-five k apiece, but they're double that when sold as a set."

"That doesn't matter if they're not real."

"It does if all three originals are permanently off the market."

The pair on the other end fall silent for a moment, and I can almost imagine them slowly fitting the pieces together in their heads. They're giant, toddler-sized puzzle pieces, but they're somehow managing.

"Does that mean you have the other two originals?" they finally ask.

"Wasn't sure you'd ever get there," Fin taunts. "Now, I'll get you replicas of those two, and I guarantee no one will know the difference. You put the set on the underground art market, and they'll be gone in a day. Money straight in your pocket."

"And how do you know that?"

"Because this is what I do."

Both men cackle on the other end, and Lou whines nervously, but I have to quell shock. If I understand him correctly, I'm pretty sure Fin just admitted the con he used to get even with these guys—the one where he stole their real painting and gave them a fake to sell on the black market—wasn't his first or only.

"I'll make this even easier on you," Fin goes on, and he leans closer to the computer. "The dog's a beast, a pain in the ass to take care of. I'll line up a buyer tonight if you trade me the hound."

"Do you think we're stupid?" the man cuts back.

"I was just screwing with you earlier."

"We're not giving you anything until we have the two new pieces."

"You know I'm good for it," Fin tries again, but I can tell he's losing ground. "You can trust me. I'll have them to you in a week."

The man lets out another laugh and his voice drops to a dangerous purr. "You'll have them to us in forty-eight hours."

"I can't possibly—"

"Time's ticking," the man cuts in again. "Always a pleasure doing business with you, Van Bro."

Before Fin can utter another word, the call ends. He yanks off the sunglasses and looks for me. His mustache hasn't budged and neither has the wig, and there's a fresh rigidity to his features.

"We'll get him back. Two days, I promise," Fin says.

"Great. Now do you want to tell Hannah that?"

Twenty-Four

I t's the third time she's called, probably because I've been sending
her to voicemail, so I pluck up my phone, her name glowing on the
screen.

Fin sheds his coat and then crosses the room in two strides, taking the
phone from me, answering, and switching it over to speaker.

"Don't you have better things to do on your night off than call and
check up?"

"It's almost ten o'clock," Hannah cuts back, all sass, "and I wasn't
calling you. Where are Millie and Lou?"

"Right here," I jump in, though my voice is a little shaky. "I'm sorry,
we must have lost track of time."

"Oh," Hannah says, then, "*ohhhh.*"

I bite my tongue so as not to vehemently correct her thinking.

"So when should I expect Lou to come home? You know it's well past
his bedtime, right?"

"I'm surprised you even remember he has a bedtime."

It's not real or enforced in any way, but Lou does have a habit of
toddling up the stairs at nine thirty every night, regardless of who's
around or still awake. The idea of him being holed up in some unfamiliar
place without a giant king-size bed for him to commandeer makes the
guilt swell a little stronger.

"You know, I think we can give you another day or two off," I say instead. "He's already asleep anyway, so we'll let him rest, and I'll bring him back to you this weekend."

"This weekend? You're going to keep him tomorrow and Saturday night?"

"Sure!" I say, finally snatching the phone from Fin's open palm and trying to punch as much enthusiasm into the word as I can. "How about I pick you up Sunday, and you, me, and Lou can do dinner with my mom? It'll be our last night together before Steve is back anyway."

"Right," Hannah says, though there's skepticism in her voice. "You're not going to hold this over my head, are you?"

"Why would I?"

"Oh, I don't know," she hums sarcastically, "probably because you tried your damnedest not to let me take this gig in the first place."

"If it makes you feel better, Steve never even has to know I babysat a few days. We'll keep it between us."

She clucks gently like it's a tough decision to make. "I suppose that could work."

"Sunday it is. I'll see you then."

I don't wait for a reply and end the call.

Fin is silent, watching me with a look I don't quite recognize, but I can't help but get distracted by the mustache he's still sporting. I've never really liked the look before, but the longer he wears it...

"What?" he says with a little twitch of his lip.

I turn away. Mostly to hide the blush. "Take that ridiculous thing off."

***

"Here," Fin says, and he places a pillow and stack of bedsheets on the armrest of the couch.

He brought them out from what I presume is the bath-room-slash-linen closet-slash-mini laundry nook near the front of the houseboat and came out with these. They're bright white and smell like fresh linen, but I frown at him anyway.

"I'm not staying here."

"I'm not letting you go home when those morons are out there kid-napping dogs."

"Good thing I'm not a dog."

"You know what I mean. Apparently they'll kidnap anything that breathes."

"I really don't think—"

Fin returns my frown, but I'm pretty sure his is stonier.

"Listen, I have forty-eight hours to get these paintings done, and I'm telling you right now I can work a whole lot faster if I know you're not getting scooped up in murder vans. Now, will you get off the bed so I can make it?"

He gestures toward the couch I've returned to, and I get up, crossing my arms pointedly. When he shakes his head at me, I'm reminded of that day in Steve's house when he came to assess the grapes painting. That prickle of tension mixed with a little curiosity.

Fin removes each seat cushion and stacks them neatly to the side, then pulls out the bed. It unfolds in one tug, and Fin snatches up the clean sheets and starts spreading one out.

"Can you really get these paintings done that quickly?" I ask, and it seems some of the anger I've been holding onto slips away as I reach for a corner of the fitted sheet.

Fin hooks the opposite end around his side of the mattress. "I really only have one I need to make."

"How do you figure?"

He glances up, and when I give him a flippant look, he drops the sheet and dips a hand behind the couch. Out comes a canvas, one that's already streaked in color.

"This is a replica of the second painting in the set."

"You already have it done? Why?"

"Do I need an excuse to make art?"

I pinch my lips together because I kind of think he does. I think there's something to it, a reason this particular canvas was stuffed behind a couch and not propped on an easel or pinned to the wall, but I'm also not sure he'd tell me the truth if I pressed him. I'm not sure our two-way street of trust has been paved yet.

Fin turns the back of the painting toward me, appraising his work like he forgot he's so talented. It's a little smug, but I've come to realize that's just who Fin is: Confident. Bold. Perpetually impressed with himself.

I guess it's charming in its own way.

He tilts the piece, surely to get a better look, and I catch a dark squiggle of lines in the lower corner of the canvas. It's too uniform to be an errant smudge, and though it'll likely be hidden when the work is eventually framed, I'm pretty sure it's not supposed to be there. In fact, I think it's another egotistical expression of his, a distinguishable marking that can one day be used to prove his worth as a forger. And I'm pretty sure I've seen it before.

"It's pretty remarkable, isn't it?" Fin asks, suddenly flipping the painting.

"I guess I don't recognize the original work."

"Not surprising. You've gotta be an art snob to know it."

"And your criminal buddies are art snobs?"

"Of course not," Fin says with a scoff. "But their boss is."

Fin lowers the canvas, sets it on the nearby table, and then returns to the bed. He secures another corner of the sheet, and I do too.

"Do you think they'll hold up their end of the bargain?" I ask. "Will Lou be safe until then?"

"They found our weak spot, and they're exploiting it. They're dumb, but they're not dumb enough to risk the only advantage they have by sending us a message we don't need."

I nod as Fin tosses the top sheet toward me next. It flutters to a rest on the mattress, and we both reach for the bottom end first, tucking in the edges. Then, Fin grabs the blanket from the back of the couch and spreads that out, finishing the setup by tossing the pillow to my side.

"Where's yours?" I ask.

He nods toward the chair at the table, where he laid out a second pillow.

"You're not going to sleep sitting up in a wooden chair, are you?"

"I've done worse," he says, and then he heads to the easel at the far end of the room. "I need to get my base layers down tonight. You can go ahead and get some rest."

"Fin, that really is unnecessary."

"Last I checked, sleep is *definitely* necessary."

"Not that," I say with a scoff. "We don't need a repeat of the hotel. You can sleep in the bed."

"Oh, we wouldn't be sleeping if I joined you in that bed."

I gasp. Or, rather, I openly choke.

"Get your head out of the gutter," he spits out, turning back around to face me. "All I'm saying is you're kind of a bed hog."

"My mind is *not* in the gutter. And I'm not a bed hog either."

"Let's agree to disagree on that one."

Fin gives me a candid smirk and then returns to the easel and removes the unfinished painting of Capitola Beach. He leans it up against a window where there's another stack of blank canvases and grabs one of those instead.

It did cross my mind, the thought of us cozying up in a bed that I'm not even sure I'll fit in solo, but I also wonder if it's just the loneliness getting to me. Perhaps, the fact that I've lost Lou. Maybe it's the potent smell of sawdust or the damp chill that seems to seep up through the floorboards that tempts me to seek comfort. Maybe it's just the con man in Fin that's tricked me into thinking his warm skin against mine might be kind of nice.

"Fin, how many people have you scammed?"

I ask the question before I can convince myself otherwise. It's still stuck in the back of mind how he so easily duped these criminals and then so cavalierly admitted they weren't the only ones.

Fin stills for just a second and then clips the canvas into the frame.

"I told you when we met I'm not a good guy."

"Does that make you a bad guy?"

"It's not that simple."

I fidget with the hem of my dress—the sensible, practical, date-night dress I exhaustively fretted over because I wanted to send the right message. I wanted Fin to know that I was serious about this, about *us*, about not screwing up a chance to find the kind of person who gets me. And I'm talking *all* of me. The adventurous part, the homey part, the part of me that's all math proofs and profit margins.

"How much trouble are we in?" I ask. "How bad is this? Am I helping you to commit a crime?"

"You're not doing anything. I'm taking care of the problem and getting Lou back. No one else has to know."

"Did you scam me?"

Again, the question comes before I can choose sense, and Fin jerks his head over his shoulder, not unlike the day we sat back-to-back in the art museum. It somehow seems like it's been both seconds and days since we met, since we raced out of the gallery, since we fled back to Fin's secret little house on the water.

"Do you mean with the grapes painting? We both know it's fake."

"No, I mean with *me*. Our drive, the night at the beach, our date. Was any of it real?"

Fin lifts his chin slightly. "What do you think?"

I shake my head because I honestly don't know. A part of me wants to think it was real because a part of it *feels* like it was real, but this isn't some work of art plastered up on a wall that I can interpret however I like. There's got to be more to it than just mushy, unverifiable feelings. Right?

"Bathroom's by the front door," Fin finally says. "I left a few things out for you."

"Sure," I say, though I learn pretty quickly that by *few*, he means *a lot*.

I retreat to the bathroom without argument since all I've got is an ID, credit card, and tube of lip gloss to my name, and am pleasantly surprised to find a stack of goods on the sink. There's a towel, a washcloth, toothbrush and toothpaste, a tiny bottle of mouthwash, a mini flosser, and clothes. *His* clothes. His clothes that smell faintly like sawdust.

I hope he can't hear me take a giant whiff of the cotton T-shirt on top, but I simply can't resist. It's warm and potent and strangely comforting, and I seriously have no idea where it comes from. Wood-shaving bath? Lumber maze? Secret timberland hidey-hole?

It smells even better after I get out of the shower, the billowing steam apparently a natural woodsy-smell enhancer. I don the tee, cinch up a pair of gym shorts he also left me, and laugh a little bit at myself in the mirror.

The shorts might as well be parachute pants on me. They're long enough to reach my shins, and no matter how tight I pull the drawstring, they still slip over my hips.

"Do I look like I belong on the cover of *Sniffin' Glue*?" I ask, striding out of the bathroom a few minutes later.

Fin glances back, screwing up his face at me. "How do you know—oh. Uh. You did see I left shorts in there for you, right?"

I shrug. "They didn't fit."

"So, you're just wearing…"

"The T-shirt you also left out for me. Figured that's what it was for."

Fin just blinks. His shirt falls about mid-thigh on me and is big enough both Lou and I could probably fit inside, but it's far comfier than swimming in mesh.

"So, is this more *Sniffin' Glue*, or are we loyal to *Punk Rock Confidential*?"

Again, Fin blinks deliberately. "How do you—"

"How do *you*?" I counter, and I gesture toward the black-and-white screen print on the band tee I'm wearing. "You never told me you were into punk."

"You never asked."

"When should I have asked?"

"I recall us taking a pretty lengthy road trip recently. Would have been a great opportunity to discuss preferred music genres."

"Somehow I don't think you would have shared that little tidbit with me even if I did ask."

He shrugs. "We had other things to talk about."

"Did we?"

"You seemed pretty enthused by your podcast episode."

"Who wasn't?"

Fin cocks a single brow. I fight the sudden urge to giggle.

"Fin, there's always room between hallucinogenic drugs and underground antiquities markets for your interests too. Especially when they're legal and in good taste."

His eyes flick to the punk tee once more. "*Sniffin' Glue* is definitely the more meta reference. I think you could bring that magazine back from extinction."

"Good to know," I say with a triumphant hum.

Fin returns to his painting, but he doesn't drag the brush across the canvas right away. Instead, he pulls in a deep breath that ripples through the muscles under his shirt. I'm tempted to cross the room and meet him where he's at just so I can feel every flutter under his skin, but that'd probably be a step too far. Learning one new thing about him is a move in the right direction.

After a long and heady pause—one in which I'm pretty sure both Fin and I try our best not to move—he finally breaks and dabs the brush in a puddle of white, then streaks it across the canvas.

I take a slower, safer step toward the bed and sink into the mattress. Fin makes a few more streaks while I pull back the blanket and the sheet and crawl under. Then, with my head on the pillow and my arm underneath, I prop myself up enough to watch Fin work.

His movements are somehow both leisurely and precise. He makes a gentle stroke one direction and then a more staccato stroke the other way. The brush slides easily through paint, stretching and striping the color across the canvas, and after a while, it feels almost in sync with the slow movement of the houseboat under us.

I lie there and try not to let my mind wander. I try not to think about Lou and how he's probably scared and lonely. But I also try not to think any harder about Fin. About us. About every line we've already crossed and every line we've yet to eradicate.

Because I'm losing my self-control. I'm losing my restraint. And I'm pretty sure I'm losing the battle of *not* falling for the *not*-good guy.

Twenty-Five

S unrise comes a heck of a lot earlier on a glass-roofed houseboat than it ever did in any apartment I rented, but I wake up like I do every morning: splayed out and well-rested.

Only, there are decidedly more body parts in this bed than there should be.

One of my feet is hanging off the side of the mattress and the other is warm, still tucked under the covers, yet I'm pretty sure I see another set of toes. Similarly, both arms are stretched above my head and yet there's an entire hand spread across my stomach. I've got one cheek to the pillow and across from me there's a whole damn face.

I almost shriek.

But then, I'd wake Fin.

His jaw is slack, and his breath is coming in low, measured puffs. His eyes flick under his lids, but he doesn't stir beyond that. His face is six inches from mine, his long hair tousled on top, and it is, indeed, his hand on my stomach.

I watch my belly rise with a deep breath and his fingers twitch in response. His shirt still covers me like a dress but it doesn't make me feel any less vulnerable, and a buzz of thrill zips through my chest as his fingers twitch again.

I take one more quick glance at Fin, who can apparently sleep through a solar flare, and then I reach for his fingers. I plan to move them, to gently place his hand on the mattress instead of my rib cage, but my fingers don't exactly listen. Instead they find a line of his tattoo and start tracing.

I've stolen plenty of glances at this piece over the past two weeks, but I've never quite been able to put it all together. The linework is incredibly detailed, including a full image of an animal curving around his forearm. There are feathers etched into his skin, tiny pinpricks of ink detailing every barb, and then there are long swaths of shading forming the body of a predator with sharp claws and a bristly tail.

It's artwork in its own right because it does make me *feel*.

"That tickles."

I flinch at the comment, just a curt, dry remark from my left, and hurriedly retract my hand. Next to me, Fin hasn't even bothered to open his eyes.

"I didn't say stop," he mumbles, and this time I know it was him. I see his lips move.

"Your hand was on me."

He grumbles and rolls over, his hand sliding away as he moves. "Your stomach was under my hand."

"I see you decided not to sleep on the chair," I say, though it's barely audible.

"Wouldn't matter if I did. Pretty sure you could still kick me from across the room."

"I would not—"

But Fin grumbles again, and I finally realize my one warm foot isn't hanging out solo at the bottom of the bed. As feeling resurges in my limbs, I'm acutely aware my leg from the knee down is twisted around his.

"Oh, god, I'm sorr—"

"Don't say it."

He bends his knee, tightening his grip around my leg even as I try to pull away.

"You were restless this morning. I had to hold you down to keep you from falling off the bed."

I silence the whimper in my throat.

"Close your eyes," Fin says, still facing the other direction, his voice muffled in the pillow. "You'll get used to the light, but I need at least another hour."

***

I think we sleep for two.

When I peel my eyes open again, the sun is baking one of my uncovered arms and the bed is noticeably roomier, but it's the loud knock and dull smack that rattles me.

"Ah, shit, sorry," Fin mutters.

He's bending over in front of the cabinets picking up a lid from the floor, and I realize it belongs to a glass blender that must have banged against the cabinet door as he pulled it out. He thumps it down to the counter and then peels open the fridge next.

"It's impossible to sneak around this place," Fin says as he retrieves a few chilled items wrapped in produce bags. "Did you sleep okay?"

I mumble affirmation, then, "What are you doing?"

"I know it's not Saturday, but—"

"Oh, *crap.*"

I toss the sheets off my legs as soon as it hits me and scramble for my phone, which I left on the table. There's two missed calls and three text messages from Hannah, but when I pop open the thread, I discover the woman's a saint.

Apparently, she cruised by my desk this morning, found it empty, and sold some ridiculous story to my boss that I was tied up interviewing an entire roster of potential auditors. It had slipped Hannah's mind to put it on my calendar, she explained, and I'd come through at the last minute.

She did follow up the explanatory texts, however, with one explicitly stating she'd call the cops and report me missing if I didn't reply by noon, so I shoot off a quick *thank you* to confirm my continued existence.

I get nothing but an eggplant emoji in return.

"Everything okay?" Fin asks, and I almost forget he's behind me and I crawled out of his bed this morning and we're now playing some very strange game of house.

"Yeah, I just—work."

"Ah," Fin muses, and he rinses the lid he dropped under the faucet. "You've never played hooky before?"

"I have too," I lie.

"God, I've given you a lot of firsts."

"You'd be so lucky."

I'm pretty sure Fin chuckles, but I try not to let the rare sound stir up that dizzying buzz in my chest because I don't think I'll be able to tame it much longer. Instead, I dump my phone and seek refuge in the bathroom, forgoing my manners and jumping in the shower without permission.

I don't really need a second shower, but I've got to keep the problematic thoughts at bay somehow. Unfortunately, I'm hardly under the water a minute before it becomes obvious they're not going anywhere.

I'm forced to use his body wash, his shampoo, and even his face-wash-slash-aftershave, and every lather makes me smell like I just single-handedly axed a forest of trees and then bowled down the front door of my one-room cabin.

It's worse when I get out and realize he's laid out more Fin-scented clothes for me. There's a flannel on the sink and a pair of gray sweats next to them—sweet, even though we both know there's no way those pants have a chance of staying up.

I'm really not trying to tempt fate here. I don't need to be sexy and I don't need to tease the man when I have a miniscule amount of control myself, but I was a teen in the nineties, and I know I don't look good in JNCO jeans or gaucho pants. Baggy gray sweats will be no exception.

So, I choose the lesser of two evils.

When I exit the bathroom a few minutes later with nothing but his flannel on, I discover Fin isn't inside anymore. He's on the other side of the windows, unmoving except for the sway of the deck under his feet. It was too dark last night for me to notice the pair of Adirondack chairs, but they're perched at the corner, and there's a plastic table between them bearing two inordinately green drinks in matching mason jars.

"Do I want to know what that is?" I ask as I push through the side door.

Fin's eyes take a detour, completely bypassing the drinks I'm frowning at.

"Sweats didn't work either?"

"You mean the parachute sewn down the middle?"

"They're the smallest ones I have."

"Yeah, well, even *this* is barely functional," I say, and I tug at the collar of the flannel I'm wearing, which bares my entire shoulder.

Fin runs a hand through his hair and then opens his mouth as if to retort, but I think it gets lost somewhere on the way out.

"So, the drinks?" I prompt.

"Yeah. They're grass."

"And you made those in your kitchen blender?"

He clears his throat awkwardly and finally moves, though it's sluggish like he's peeling his feet out of wet cement. He reaches for one of the drinks and then shoves it toward me.

"It's your smoothie."

"*My* smoothie?"

"I tried to replicate it. It tastes like grass, so I think I'm pretty close."

"Are you trying to say this is a smoothie cart copycat? A refreshment *replication*, if you will?"

"*Millicent.* Will you just try it?"

I pinch my lips together, trying to keep a smile from breaking free. There's something provoking about the way my full name sounds on his voice, but I don't have panties on, so I shut that down as fast as I can and suck down a mouthful of the drink instead.

I catch the spice of ginger first, but it's mellowed out by plenty of spinach, a little banana, and a hint of citrus that just barely distinguishes it from the original.

"How did you manage to get this recipe?"

"I didn't," Fin says with a curt laugh, finally slipping back into his casually controlled persona. "That guy who runs the cart thinks he's got the market cornered, so he wouldn't so much as breathe a basic ingredient list."

"I guess he's got to keep the edge somehow."

"Do you have any idea how many ridiculous liquids people use in smoothies to avoid dairy?"

"I have a feeling you're going to tell me."

"Wish I could. Stopped at twenty."

I take another sip and laugh. "What did you finally land on?"

"Orange juice."

"Clever."

"I still don't think it's right, but I gave up when I got to the aisle with the hemp seed milk because I'm pretty sure it'd put me out of house and home."

"We can't have that, now can we?"

Fin shakes his head almost playfully and then grabs the other smoothie and drops down into his seat. I sink into my own, ignoring the streak of sunlight demanding my attention and facing him instead.

"What would you have used?" Fin asks, finishing with a slurp and hiding a grimace.

"I wouldn't have. I'd have just bought it from the cart."

"It's a good thing I didn't ask you then."

"Don't need my opinion muddling your process?"

"Nah. Just don't need to miss this view."

His eyes meet mine, and I know neither of us have given the sunrise a second glance.

Twenty-Six

"Honey, you're going to have to say that again."

"I didn't go to work today," I repeat, one arm crossed, the other propping up my phone, as I pace the deck without intention.

My mom lets out a curt laugh on the other end of the line. "I realized that when I showed up to your office for lunch and found your desk empty."

"Why didn't you just call me then?"

"Oh, honey, I would have," she breezes on, a trill in her voice, "but I figured Hannah might know where you were, so I just popped into her office instead."

I close my eyes and drag in a steadying breath. "Let me guess, you coerced her into telling you?"

"Is free lunch considered coercion these days?"

I sigh because *yes*. More than a few "free lunches" have gotten some of my clients into considerable financial and legal despair. They always claimed their off-the-books meet-ups were innocuous, but I came to realize even the most innocent gesture was just another con.

I guess I found a way to get past it, though. Both at work and outside it.

Fin is back inside where we've been for the past several hours—peacefully undisturbed until now. He needed to continue working on the painting but had no intention of letting me leave, so he parked me right at the kitchen table.

I ended up logging into my work account from Fin's computer just so I could answer a few emails and lend some credibility to Hannah's cover story, though I'm not sure my fraudulent interview notes will convince anyone. Every sentence or two, I missed a word or jumbled a phrase because—*hello*—handsome distraction just humming away five feet from me.

And he enjoyed every second of it—the painting part, not the distracting part. I don't think he even remembered I was in the room after a while. He seemed to sink entirely into his work, making long, sweeping strokes with his whole arm and then short, stippled flicks with only his wrist. Fluid motion and ease in every gesture. And eventually the tension in his shoulders simply melted into a blissful contentedness, like the world around him had washed away and he could just *be*.

Fin may have been blackmailed into forging the valuable works, but nothing about his effort was a hardship.

"Listen, honey, I'm glad you have a new friend," my mom goes on airily, and it's strange because it goes against every fiber of her being not to tease me about him being something more, "but I don't think you should be sacrificing your career for, you know, some boy."

I turn away from the windows and face the sinking sun. "It's one day."

"You know, if it were Steve, he never would have—"

"*Mom*, it's not Steve, and it won't be."

"Okay, okay, I'm sorry, honey. Why don't you tell me about this *Fin* then?" She says his name like it's a foreign word she's practicing, one to which she doesn't really know the meaning, so it's a bit hesitant and uncertain. "You said he's an artist, right?"

I glance back through the windows where Fin is eyeing his work critically. One brow has inched upward and his lips have pursed and I don't think he'd notice a passing bird if it flew right into this window.

"He is," I say easily.

"And he sells his work?"

"He does," I say, less easily.

"To galleries? Private buyers? Would I know it?"

"Mom, no—he's just, he does it on the side."

"Oh, okay, then. What does he actually do for a living?"

I sigh again because even though I can put up at least a few more lies against my mom than Hannah can, it will all eventually come tumbling out.

"He showed me last night where he used to run an art program for underserved kids," I say, latching on to the one piece of good-guy influence I can comfortably share.

"Oh, and he makes money this way?"

I roll my eyes, even though I know she can't see me. "Mom, I like him, okay? He's funny and charming and he remembers things about me. He cares about things I care about."

"Are you implying Steve didn't?"

"No, I'm *saying* Steve didn't."

My mom tuts disbelievingly, and I collapse into one of the chairs Fin and I abandoned earlier. It's only a quick thought, but I start to wish he were out here with me. I wish he were watching the colors of the setting sun melt and shift because I'm sure he'd have a name for every shade. I'm sure he'd want to share that with me.

"Mom, what do I like to do every Saturday morning?" I ask, diverting the conversation.

"What does this have to do with anything?"

"Just humor me, okay?"

She sighs this time, and it's drenched in exasperation. "You always drive out to the suburbs and go to that little smoothie cart on the corner. It's where you get that horrible green drink you love. You and Steve used to—"

"No, Steve and I didn't. Hannah, Lou, and I are the ones who went there. We'd get our drinks and then go to the dog park because Steve spent his Saturday mornings working cases off the clock."

"Well, honey, if you're trying to paint him in a bad light—"

"Fin had that smoothie once, absolutely hated it but drank it anyway, and then spent the entire past week trying to replicate it on his own. He made it for me this morning—"

"You spent the night with Fin? And Lou too?"

"Mom!"

"What, Millie? First, you don't show up to work—a job you love, by the way. Then, Hannah says you volunteered to dogsit out of the blue, and this is for your ex-boyfriend whom you insist is some detestable and inconsiderate person. And now, you won't tell me anything about this man you're spending all your time with. What am I supposed to think here?"

"Steve is not...detestable?" I say, more a question than statement because I'm not sure where the heck she got that word. "But yes, I did volunteer to watch Lou because Hannah hates it."

"Does she really, or is something else going on here?"

"I don't know what you mean."

"Let me talk to him."

I nearly choke. "You want to talk to Fin?"

"No, of course not. I want to talk to Lou."

I swallow my first reaction because panic springs up in my chest instead, and I whip around in my seat. Fin is still in front of the easel, a paintbrush clamped between his teeth, and he's scraping one of the palette knives he bought during our trip to the art store against the canvas. He doesn't look at me.

"Mom, he's a dog. You can't talk to him."

"He's my grand-dog," she corrects me boldly, "and I will not be denied an opportunity to remind him that he needs to keep his mother out of trouble."

"For the last time, I'm not Lou's mother, and you're not his grand-mother."

"Let me talk to him."

"Mom—"

"Now, Millie, or I will track your phone and march right over to this *Fin*'s house to come see my boy myself."

I jump up from my seat immediately because there's way too much plausibility to her threat. Back when I moved out, she insisted on me letting her track my phone, claiming she'd use it only in the event of a true emergency.

Since that fateful day when I finally gave in, she's employed the track-ing function to find me at Hannah's house after I forgot to call when we got back from a hike, another time at the front door of a one-night stand's apartment because I didn't text her back promptly at seven in the morning, and once in the health-food aisle at the grocery store because I apparently turned left when she went right.

"Just give me a second, will you?" I say, and without waiting for a response, I put the phone on mute and tug open the sliding glass door. "We have a problem."

Fin jerks his head right, his features still contorted in deep concentra-tion. "A problem?"

"My mom wants to talk to Lou."

"Okay, so let her—*oh shit.*"

He shakes his head like he's just walked into a brick wall. He drops his palette knife next to an open bottle of purple paint on the side table and then looks frantically around the room like he might find my kidnapped dog hiding under the table.

"She wants to *talk* to Lou?"

"Yes, like, I think she wants to hear him bark or whine or something."

"Is this normal?"

"Fin, please. She thinks something's up, and if I can't prove Lou is here, she's never going to let it go."

"Who told her he was here?"

"Hannah."

"How—"

"Fin, *please*," I try again. "I just need to appease her."

Fin finally drops the act and waves a hand at me. "Give me the phone."

"What? No."

"Do you want to appease her or not?"

I roll my eyes, but there really is no point in arguing, so I hand it over.

Fin takes the phone off mute and holds it to his ear. He smiles, pulls in a breath but stops abruptly, frowns, and pulls the phone back down, re-muting it.

"Uh, what is your last name?"

"Oh god," I groan, and I slap a hand to my forehead.

I'm not sure when in a new relationship you're supposed to learn someone's last name, but I'd think most experts would say it'd be a lot sooner than now.

"*Her* last name is Sullivan."

He narrows his eyes at me like a dozen questions have just popped into his mind, but he doesn't ask them, instead returning to the phone call.

"Ms. Sullivan, what a pleasure to finally speak with you."

I cringe when my mom's scandalized cry comes through the phone.

"You're not Lou."

"No, ma'am, I am not," Fin concedes, not even missing a beat as he turns the call over to speaker. "I simply couldn't deal with a coat of fur year-round. It's unbecoming for my figure."

"Excuse me, but I—what?"

Fin mutes her and crosses the room, setting the phone down on the table and reaching for his laptop. He pulls up a browser, navigates over to YouTube, and then slides the laptop toward me.

"Pick one," he says.

"You want to use a video?"

"Do you have a better idea?"

I groan because the only idea I could come up with was barking myself, and that wouldn't fool a toddler, let alone my annoyingly inquisitive mother.

Fin grabs the phone again, heads for the door, and unmutes her as he's going outside.

"Ms. Sullivan, have I told you about the day I met your daughter?"

As much as I would *love* Fin not to say another word about that story to my mother, I know it's a topic that will hold her attention for more than ten seconds and am willing to bet he's going to glaze over a few of the more incriminating details.

I return to the computer, click the search bar, and type in "bully bark." There are dozens of videos, and I watch a few, but most are kind of menacing. Loud, scary-sounding barks or deep growls, and as vocal as Lou is, it's not mean.

I revise the search terms to "goofy bully bark" and then "happy pit bull barking and whining" and find something kind of close.

Fin pops his head back in the house, my mom apparently muted once more.

"Let's hear it," he says, and I play the first video, but Fin grimaces. "That dog sounds like he just figured out he's riddled with fleas."

"I'm sorry there isn't a video of Lou himself on the internet," I grumble, but I queue up another. "How's this?"

Fin frowns at that one too. "Millie, the first rule of replication is not to use exactly what you see."

"What does that even mean?"

"Don't search for the thing itself; search for the feeling it creates."

I screw up my face in very aggressive skepticism, but Fin just waves at me again and dips back outside, returning to the call.

"If I didn't tell that punk with his disgraceful look and reprehensible pick-up lines to hit the road, I'm pretty sure your girl would have knocked him sideways..."

Fin's story trails off as he slides the door shut again, and I try not to linger on his comment, instead searching for "bulldog gets a new toy" and "bulldog at the dog park." It's the closest thing I can come up with that might satisfy Fin's cryptic suggestion, and after two more changes in the search terms, I finally strike gold.

I wave Fin back inside, and as he comes through the door, he's loudly commenting on how we've made it through two dates since our museum meet-cute and how "the rest is history."

My mom hums curiously into the phone, loud and clear as Fin puts her back on speaker.

"Well, I must say, Fin, I was a little apprehensive at first, but you seem...charming."

"Oh, it's not charm, Ms. Sullivan. It's the real thing."

Fin beams almost sadistically at me, and I roll my eyes because the guy's a professional forger, for crying out loud. He waves another hand at me, silently urging me to queue up the video, and I obey.

"Here's your grand-dog now," Fin crows, and he holds the phone near the laptop.

I silently beg for forgiveness, hit the play button, and then freeze.

An ad pops up. Full volume, loud background noises, distinguishable commentary. Coincidentally, it's a spot for the grand opening of the gallery at the pier, and Vincent DeLobo in all his fraudulent, strategically-dressed-down, jeans-and-polo look strolls into view.

"Crap, crap," I cry, scrambling to turn the video off or the volume down or anything that isn't going to give us away.

Fin cradles the phone to his ear again and backs away, letting out an unusual cackle.

"Lou, no!" he cries, and he actually bats around his legs like he's fending off an over-excited Lou. "Calm down, buddy, your grandma's on the phone. Just a second!"

Fin waves his arm at me to tell me to hurry up, but I'm trying to muzzle a laugh at Fin's exaggerated enactment while skipping the ad, and it's not working.

Fin laughs again—an entirely manufactured laugh—and pretends to run from Lou in pursuit, actually skirting around his painting, before speaking to my mom once more.

"You've got a wily one here, you know that?"

"Got it!" I say, part whisper in hopes my mom doesn't hear.

I pause the video once more until Fin can get over to the table, fake Lou still on his heels apparently. Fin swats the air once more, adding another *good boy* and *here's grandma* as I press Play.

The video rolls ad-free, and my mom goes berserk. She starts cooing to the recorded dog in her unmistakable baby voice, talking over the sound and praising him for being such a good boy. She spends a few lines reminding fake Lou to keep me out of trouble, as promised in her earlier threat, and I eventually fade the video out.

"Atta boy, Lou," Fin goes on, and he walks away from the laptop as I finally close the lid. "He's been enjoying his stay with us, but I'm sure he'll be happy to go home on Sunday night."

"I'm just glad he's got so many people who love him," my mom coos, and I get up and snatch the phone from Fin.

"I'm bringing him over for dinner, okay? You can say goodbye before he goes back to Steve's."

"I would like that."

"Hannah's coming too."

"I'd expect nothing less," she says, and then, "I'll make extra just in case Fin would like to join us as well."

I give Fin a sheepish glance but don't commit to anything and then say a quick goodbye and hang up. It takes a moment for the adrenaline in my veins to wane, and I lean against the side table with Fin's paints and brushes to steady myself.

Meanwhile, Fin cocks a brow at me. "An ad, Millie? You had an ad queued up?"

"It wasn't there for the past three videos I watched. It just popped up out of nowhere!"

He eases closer, humor tugging at his lips and amusement evident in his eyes. "Rookie mistake."

"Oh, and you do this all the time? Queue up videos to trick people?"

"No, but I have used YouTube before. I know the scam."

"Ads aren't a scam. They're business."

"Nice to see you're finally coming around to the idea."

"Okay," I say sarcastically and raise a hand toward his chest as he somehow closes another two inches between us. "Your job *is* a scam."

"I don't see how it's any different than what you asked me to do here."

"I had no choice. She never would have let it go."

Fin shrugs unconcernedly. "What search term did you use to find that video?"

I hesitate. It's partially because I'm not sure I can admit what I used but also because there isn't space between Fin and me anymore. One of his hands is resting behind me on the table and I think his chin is about to brush my forehead. I let out a breath and it fans against Fin's chest and rolls back toward me.

"Come on," he urges. "What did you use?"

I lick my lips. Nervously, I think. "I shouldn't say."

"It was bad, wasn't it?"

"It was horrible."

"But it worked."

"There was no way it wouldn't."

"I won't tell," he says, and the timbre of his voice rings pleasantly in the air.

I swallow. Roughly. "I searched 'dogs greeting their owners returning from duty.'"

Fin swallows a laugh, but I can see it in his eyes, that shimmer of amusement.

"God, I think I've ruined you."

I don't even blink before I reply. "I think I like it."

Twenty-Seven

I 'm not sure who moves first, but it doesn't really matter because our lips meet with fiery intention on both sides.

Heck, I'm pretty sure I could crawl right up Fin's body, latch my legs around his waist, and plant my boobs directly in his face without an ounce of shame, but I've at least got to *act* like a lady for a little bit.

Easier said than done, of course.

Fin goes straight for the back of my legs, hitching me up and onto the side table, and I shriek.

"Watch out! There's paint and brushes and *this.*"

I peel my lips from his, squirming to reach for whatever hard thing is jabbing my booty. Fin breaks away only long enough to snatch what turns out to be the used palette knife from my hand. He drops it to the floor and then moves in again.

I'm pretty certain there's now paint smeared on this flannel of his I'm wearing, but he doesn't seem to care. He moves his hips between my legs and scoots me up against a loose brush, a paper plate palette, a blue-stained rag, and that bottle of purple acrylic I know is open.

I blindly fumble for the lid, trying to snap it closed, but, my goodness, he's like a dog with a bone claiming me as his, and I don't want to stop him.

I've never felt more in control and out of hand at the same time. His fingers are on my hips, clinging to the flannel riding up my thighs, and

I'm drawing him closer, tempting him to take his kiss deeper, to make his touch more venturesome, to award me every bite of electricity I've been craving.

"Don't make me beg," I say through heavy breaths, and Fin's first response is a low growl directly in my mouth, one that rumbles all the way down my throat and spills into my chest.

He slides his hips tighter against me, and though I do take the opportunity to latch my legs around him, he balks. "I don't even know your last name."

I nip at his bottom lip and then suck it in before panting back. "I don't know yours either."

"It's not right," he says on a huff, though he's back to kissing me, back to teasing up the hem of the shirt.

"I like it like that."

"Millie—"

"Please—"

He bites my lip, and I moan with absolutely no restraint.

"Goddamn," he growls, and whatever discipline he has left evaporates.

The man slides his hands underneath the flannel and beneath my thighs, securing his fingers in my soft flesh as I cling tighter to him. Then, in one quick thrust, he pulls me up and off the table, swinging me around.

We're absurdly off balance. He's slinging me with uncontrolled momentum and I'm scrambling to hold on and it's a trainwreck of a dance across the room.

I think we bump into the easel, and I know my foot connects with the side table. A loud smack sounds behind us, and I'm pretty sure another paintbrush rolls onto the ground, but Fin just tightens his grip, kissing me harder.

"The painting," I say, barely managing the words between his aggressive movements. "Did we...? Is it...?"

He nips me harder. "It's fine. It's drying and, besides, you started this."

I can't argue it, and he keeps moving. We skirt the kitchen table, his hip accidentally clips the end of the countertops, and then we're pivoting toward the couch. We go over the armrest—I have no idea why when the rest of the bed is a much larger target—but his knees hit the side of the couch and we topple onto the mattress, a flailing, wild mess.

It knocks the wind out of me, him falling on top, and I let out a strangled cry that's half shriek of surprise and half incredibly awkward grunt.

"Oh god, Millie, I'm sorry."

The breath floods my lungs again as Fin rolls off me, and if I let him, I'm pretty sure he'd tumble right off the bed, but I snag him by the shirt as he goes, tethering us together like a drawstring pulled taut.

"What did we say about that word, *Fin*-diana Jones?"

He lets out a low chuckle. "You're not getting any closer to guessing my name."

"Don't worry. I'm not trying that hard."

***

It's dark when we finally peel ourselves apart.

Fin comes back from the bathroom, a fresh pair of boxers on and another set for me. It's a kind gesture because I'm sorely lacking in clean undergarments, and I slip them on under the covers as he crawls back into bed.

For a while, we just lie there, a distinct few inches between us, staring up at the glass-paneled ceiling. Stars are nearly impossible to come by thanks to the city's heavy light pollution, but it's not any less stunning to be admiring the blank night sky from the warmth of this bed.

It feels different. Different than anything I've experienced before. Different because it's not perfect. It's not error-free. It's not a predictable sheet of numbers that add up to a neat sum or a flawless record that begets awards. In fact, it's a little bit criminal.

"How many forgeries have you really sold?"

Fin twitches next to me, but he doesn't look my way, and I don't look his.

"That's a pretty presumptuous question."

"Are you not going to answer it?"

He shifts again, and the sheets tug at my bare skin.

"How many times have you tricked your mom just to appease her?" he asks instead.

"Is that relevant?"

"Ballpark it."

"I can count the times on one hand."

Fin lets out a soft breath. "I can't."

I frown and roll over, propping my head up on my hand so I can gauge Fin's expression.

"Are you saying you're *that* good? You just pitch forgeries left and right?"

Fin drops his head my direction, a smirk quirking up the corner of his mouth. "Replications, and I think I just proved to you I am *that* good."

"Don't flatter yourself," I taunt back, but there's a smile I can't really help, and Fin eventually rolls all the way over too, meeting me in the middle.

"This painting takes exactly eighteen hours to complete. It requires fourteen different colors, seven brushes, and this ridiculous palette knife for one particularly tricky corner where the paint is layered four times."

"How can you possibly know that?"

"Because I'm that good."

I purse my lips disbelievingly at him, and he finally gives in.

"I've done this particular set about a hundred times, okay?"

"Why so many?"

Fin lifts a shoulder casually, glances away, and then finds my eyes again. "This artist is one of the first my grandmother ever showed me. He was her favorite."

It's difficult to see in the low light of the hanging moon, but I think a flush of red is creeping into Fin's cheeks.

"When I was young, we lived, well, modestly. She always dreamed of owning one of his works, but there was no way we could afford it, so when she taught me to paint, we practiced by making replications of this particular set. Over and over again—I must have made two dozen before I figured out the right brush strokes and the right shades. I kept starting over until I got it right."

"Then how did it ever get to the point where you wanted to sell them?"

Fin lets out a sigh and collapses back onto his pillow. He laces his fingers together and pins them behind his head, staring through the blank glass ceiling.

"Funeral expenses. Those ones I never marketed as authentic, though. Just enough to get a few bucks for a decent replica."

"Oh," I say, and I wonder if it's too imposing for me to reach out and place a hand on his bare chest. "She must have been an incredible woman."

"She was." Fin lets out another breath, almost a quiet laugh. "If it wasn't for her, I'd have been the kind of kid who went around town spray-painting penises on people's houses."

"You would not," I say on a laugh.

"Oh, I would," he reassures me, and Fin rolls toward me once more, that smile returning. "And I'd make them uncomfortably accurate. Wrinkles and veins and hairs and everything you really don't want to see. Every color too—I don't discriminate like those knuckleheads who tagged your place."

"I'm pretty sure the color was insignificant."

"I'm pretty sure you don't know kids these days."

I don't argue it because it's true and instead turn the conversation back on him.

"How's your kiddo who got picked up by the cops the other day? I know he's wrapped up in this mess too. Did you find him a lawyer?"

Fin's brows cinch together. "Kiddo?"

"You haven't told me his name, so what am I supposed to call him?"

"It's Kai."

"Fine. How's Kai? Did you find him a lawyer?"

"I did. So long as these asshole cops don't try to pin anything else on him, I think he stands a chance."

I don't take the bait because it's really not my place anymore, and I don't think Fin will appreciate finding out what Steve does for a living, especially given our current situation with Lou.

The thought of my boy held captive in some criminal hideout slogs through my mind once more—never really having gone away since the night before.

"Do you think Lou is lonely?"

Fin takes a long, slow breath, and then he surprises me by reaching out. He cups my chin and fixes his gaze on me.

"Lou is going to be okay. First thing tomorrow, as soon as this painting is dry, we'll set up the swap and get him back."

I don't reply except to close my eyes and settle into his touch. It's both firm and tender, meaningful and uncomplicated, and eventually I fall asleep, hopelessly snagged in that eerie in-between.

Twenty-Eight

I wake first the next morning.

Fin is sleeping on his stomach, head turned toward me, one arm gently resting against my side and the other tucked under his pillow. I'm tempted to reach out and push his hair off his forehead where it's clinging to his skin so I can admire this new angle of his face, softened with the paralysis of slumber, but I don't.

Instead, I ease away from his touch, climb out of bed, and tiptoe into the bathroom.

He hasn't moved by the time I come back out, and I find the flannel he stripped off me crumpled on the floor. It definitely has paint on it, smudges of yellow and purple and blue dried across the shirttail, but I put it on anyway, fixing the buttons as I cross the room.

I grab my phone off the table and aim for the sliding door, like there's any chance I'm better at sneaking around this creaky houseboat than Fin is, when I step on a paintbrush.

I slap a hand to my mouth, trying to curb the urge to wail because the bristles are still wet with paint and they squish between my toes. Behind me, Fin stirs but doesn't seem to wake, and I stoop to grab the offending tool.

Only, as I glance forward toward the side table and the easel, I notice something else on the floor. It's an inch-and-a-half thick, white canvas brushed with color, and it hits me all at once.

I'm not sure how I didn't notice it before, but the easel is empty and I know it's the forgery on the floor. I scramble to it, dropping to my hands and knees, and barely stifle another gasp.

The canvas is face-up but sitting halfway under the side table where a tipped-over bottle of purple paint—the one I tried to close the night before—is balanced on the edge, color oozing from its partially open lid. A thick, wet bead of paint drips, landing in a lilac puddle that's pooled in the corner of the canvas and sending a splatter of color across the previously finished piece.

"Fin! Oh my god, wake up!"

I snatch up the painting between shaking hands and run back to the bed, where Fin has launched up to sitting, stiff as an ironing board.

"What's wrong? What happened?"

"What did we do?"

Fin's eyes, still groggy with sleep, snap open. He curses, tears the painting from my hands, and is out of bed, crossing to the easel and propping the canvas up on the narrow ledge before I can say another word.

I don't follow him. I stand immobile, noticing every splinter of wood in the floor beneath my bare feet as Fin curses again and drags a hand through his hair.

The contentedness I saw yesterday when Fin stood in front of the easel is gone, replaced by ropes of tension winding between every muscle in his back, snaking over his shoulders and up his neck, and I feel it too. I feel the tightness twisting around my lungs and my heart, and it forces out a desperate breath.

"We ruined the painting."

"It's not ruined," Fin snaps back, but he doesn't turn around to look at me, instead running his hands over his face.

"There's an entire puddle of paint in the corner. It's purple, for crying out loud!"

"I know what color it is," Fin retorts, and it's fiery and angry and...frightened?

Fin whirls around, the sharp planes of his face suddenly drooping, the luster once brightening his features completely snuffed out. The next few words die on his tongue, but I know exactly what he wants to say, exactly what he's afraid to admit: he's sorry, and this time it's real because there is absolutely nothing he can do to fix it.

Tears spring to my eyes. "I have to get Lou back. I have to!"

"I'll make another. I'll get it done—"

"We don't have *time*. Our deadline is in five hours, Fin. I know you can't—"

"I will. I'm not going to lose that dog or you over this."

Fin crosses the room in two steps. One of his hands finds the curve of my hip and the other cups my chin, bringing me within a breath of distance.

I know I should think before I speak. I know I should pause and regroup and recenter my emotions, but I don't want to. I can't.

"You did this," I say, practically hurtling the accusation at him. "*You* scammed those people and *you* got Lou taken and *you* came up with this ridiculous plan to paint your way out of this mess when I could have just paid them off!"

"I couldn't let them take your money."

"Well, it's not up to you anymore."

I splinter from his grip and swipe away the moisture under my eyes, using the momentum to storm back to the table and snatch up my phone and keys. When I turn back around, he's different. Detached. Demoralized.

"I'm going to the bank, and when I get back you damn well better have the exchange set up."

"Millie, it's not a good idea."

I shake my head. "I'm beginning to think none of this was."

***

I make one phone call on the way to the bank, and it's teary and pleading and apologetic, but it's the only thing I know to do, the only decision I feel confident in.

"Grant, please," I cry into the phone as I take a turn far too sharply. "I made a mistake, and I need help. I don't know who else to call."

"Hey, take a breath. I've got you. I'm here. What's going on?"

"Steve is going to kill me."

"Oh, I doubt that," Grant says with a laugh. "The guy couldn't harm a fly, let alone—"

"Someone kidnapped Lou."

"Wait—what?"

It's exactly the response I expect, and I can hear Grant scrambling on the other end of the line. I don't know where he's at or what he's doing but he tells me to keep talking, so I do, detailing everything that happened since the day Lou got ahold of Seph's painting.

There are a few times when I ask him to pretend like he's not hearing me confess to a crime—or the intent to commit one—and he tactfully brushes me off. He's always been good at that, distinguishing between what his friends share with him in confidence and what they share with him as a cop. It's comforting knowing he's not as black-and-white about the law as Steve or Hannah or my mom, for that matter.

"And you know where these guys are keeping Lou?" Grant asks.

"No, but Fin's got a direct line to them, and I told him to set up a meet."

Grant breathes into the phone. "Damn, Millie. Why'd you wait so long to call me? Do you even trust this Fin guy?"

"I know he's not going to let anything bad happen to Lou," I say, and even though it's not easy to admit, I do believe it. "I just don't think I can do this alone."

"And you shouldn't. I'm glad you called. Tell you what, meet me at your place. We'll drop off your car and go together in mine. I want this guy to know who he's dealing with."

I begin to protest but take one glance down at the oversize boxers and paint-covered flannel I'm still wearing and agree. I'm at home and changed into jeans and a tee by the time Grant arrives about ten minutes later.

It takes us another half hour to get to the bank because Grant insists only the main branch would have that kind of cash on hand, but after the convincing flash of his badge and many groundless reassurances I'm not pulling the money out under duress, the bank manager finally agrees to my request.

I've never seen that kind of money in bills before—I only ever see large amounts on spreadsheets and clients' bank statements—but it's not like the movies either. There are three neat stacks, each banded with yellow tape. They're definitely too thick to fit in my pocket and make me uneasy to hold onto anyway, but Grant doesn't seem phased and stuffs each stack inside his jacket.

We drive back across town in silence, except for the few directions I give him to Fin's place. It's not hard to find as most locals know where the Mission Creek houseboats are, but I do direct him where to park so we have a clear view of Fin's house from the shoreline.

"When we get in there, I need you to let me do the talking," Grant says, shutting off the engine.

"Do you think this isn't going to go well?"

"I know guys like this, Millie. The Robin Hood types. He lures you in with this story that he's only harming the rich so he can help the poor, but what he's been doing with this fake art is a crime regardless of who he's scamming."

"He's not a bad person."

"Surely Steve taught you better than that."

I hesitate, somewhat affronted by the comment, but I remind myself I am defending a professional forger.

"I like him, okay? Even if he did a bad thing."

"It's not a big leap for people willing to commit simple crimes to progress into something more severe."

"But, Grant—"

"How well do you really know him?"

I shrug because it's all I can do, and I know it's answer enough.

"You'll see," Grant says, and he swings open his car door.

I catch a glimpse of Grant's gun as he grabs it from its holster under the steering column and then secures it in the waistband of his jeans. He and Steve always carried a personal weapon when they weren't on patrol, but I don't recognize this one, which means it's a service-duty pistol. He's walking in here as a professional—probably has cuffs in his pocket—and I'm afraid this is getting way more serious than I intended.

I follow Grant down the path and across the footbridge, but with every step closer to Fin's house, I wonder if I am in real danger. I wonder if I can trust Fin, if he will put me first, or if I've just been so fascinated by the bad-boy side of him that I've willingly blinded myself to all the red flags. I wonder if I've walked right into his con all on my own.

Grant knocks on the door with more force than necessary, and when it flies open and Grant and Fin meet face-to-face, I *know*.

I know what I've done.

I know what Fin's done.

And I know I've committed the gravest crime yet.

Twenty-Nine

For a moment, both seem frozen in place.

Fin is wedged in the doorway, one hand fisted on the doorknob, the other on the frame, his full tattoo on display. Grant is rocked up on his toes, his dominant hand stuck midair, halfway to reaching for his gun.

Then, both look at me.

"You brought a goddamn *cop* to my house?" Fin demands.

"Millie, go back to the car," Grant says.

I don't budge. I know Grant's vehicle placement was strategic, but I'm pretty sure Fin deduced Grant's occupation solely by the haircut and posture. Grant, too, clearly made his own judgments as soon as the door opened, sizing Fin up like he needs to prepare for hand-to-hand combat.

Fin takes the moment of hesitation to grab the edge of the door and he attempts to swing it closed, but Grant wedges his boot in the gap.

"Come on, man," Grant says, "don't make this any harder than it needs to be."

"Fin, please," I beg. "I just want Lou back, and Grant can help."

Fin mutters something I don't catch but lets the door swing open. He's halfway across the room, snatching up another flannel and shoving his arms into it like he detests being seen in nothing but a T-shirt, when Grant bulldozes inside.

I follow, but everything feels different this time. Unsteady. Uneasy. Unfamiliar.

It's not the room where I watched Fin re-create his most cherished painting. It's not the place where he laid me down in his bed. It's not the quaint, quiet houseboat where I realized I was falling in love with the *not*-good guy.

"Millie, what were you thinking?" Fin demands.

"Don't talk to her," Grant warns. "Talk to me."

"You're in *my* house. I'll damn well talk to whoever I please."

"Rein it in, man. She brought me here to help. This doesn't have to be a fight."

"Like hell it doesn't." Fin then rounds on me. "I don't give my address to just anyone, Millie. You can't go bringing people here."

"I didn't know what else to do!"

"How do you even know this guy?"

"He's Steve's partner, okay?" I say, almost a shriek. "Well, former partner, I guess. Steve moved on to…"

Fin stops dead, the hem of his flannel falling slack as he finishes the last button. He looks between me and Grant, and then licks his lips, tightens his jaw, and narrows in on me once more.

"Steve's a cop?"

My chest burns with the realization that I'm on the wrong side of this betrayal.

"I didn't think it was relevant."

"Not relevant? Millie, we—*damn it.*"

Fin cuts himself short again, tosses another fiery look at Grant, and then turns around, stalking across the room toward the painting we ruined. There's a faint purple splotch still visible in the corner, though it's obvious Fin tried to clean it up, tried to right our wrongs like there was any chance he'd be able to pull off this exchange with a flawed piece.

"Millie's told me everything," Grant starts in again, and he pulls his shoulders back in what I've come to know as his cop stance. "I'm not here to arrest you for the multiple crimes I know you've committed—though, don't get me wrong, I absolutely could. I'm just here to get the dog back. You help me with that, and I can consider looking the other way on your other...*indiscretions.*"

Fin runs a hand through his hair and faces us once more. He's losing an internal debate right now. I can see it in the way he's assessing Grant, like he's calculating every possible move he might make, every potential outcome.

But then, he looks back at me, his face somehow rosier even though his eyes remain ice cold. He glances at the painting once more, flawless in the daylight except for that corner.

"Did you get the money?" Fin asks me.

"Grant has it."

Fin visibly bristles but doesn't look Grant's direction when he speaks again.

"We're meeting on their turf."

I start to repeat the statement, to question it, when the realization hits me. I don't want to say it out loud because I don't want to incriminate Fin anymore than I already have, but I'm fairly certain we're about to head right back to wherever he was working his side gig with these henchmen, the place where he scammed them—almost successfully.

"I need an address," Grant steps in again.

He's moved in front of me, almost like he's concerned Fin's about to do something unpredictable. But I know better. In fact, I know what Fin's going to say before he even says it.

"It's the pier."

Grant lets out a curt laugh. "Great. Which one?"

"Man, if I have to tell you, you can't be that good of a cop."

"You know, I was kind of hoping you weren't that kind of criminal."

"Okay," I jump in, "no one here is that kind of criminal. It's the people who took Lou who are the bad guys. Can we please just go now?"

"*We* can go," Grant says.

"*You're* staying here," Fin adds.

"Aren't you two just adorable?" I snap back, thoroughly annoyed that the only thing these two can agree on is my obedience. "There's no world in which I don't go."

"It's dangerous," Fin argues.

"Steve would never forgive me," Grant pipes up.

"And sometimes cows fall asleep standing up."

"What?" Fin and Grant reply at the same time.

"None of those are reason enough for me not to rescue Lou. Understand?"

They exchange a glance before looking at me again, unease still evident, but they're at least wise enough not to voice it again.

"For the record," I say, stepping toward Grant and prodding him in the chest, "I don't belong to Steve. And also for the record," I go on, swinging around to face Fin, "I call shotgun."

"For what? Aren't you driving?"

"We're taking my ride," Grant interjects smugly, dangling his keys in the air. "Which means you get the back seat. Where you belong."

I'm between the two of them before either can sling another insult, and I've got a hand on Fin's chest.

"Let's keep it civil, please."

Fin doesn't reply but I can tell it's not for lack of want. I'm certain the guy has a whole string of unsavory words for the cop I just dropped on his doorstep, and I'd be willing to bet Grant isn't done either. It's the downside of Grant being a little more liberal with the law: he's also a little more liberal with the lawbreakers.

He seems to enjoy himself pulling open the back door for Fin when we get to the patrol car, and I try not to let the guilt distract me. Yes, I definitely breached some unspoken code of trust with Fin by sharing his home address, but I'd also do just about anything to get Lou back.

"It works like every other seatbelt, Millie," Grant says as he settles into the driver's seat.

I try jamming the buckle into its slot unsuccessfully, realizing it's at least my third attempt, and give up. Grant lets out an amused sigh and then leans over me. His chest brushes mine as he reaches for the belt and tugs.

"Hey," Fin says from the backseat, "why don't you hurry it up? We're on a deadline here."

"Is that what your buddies said?" Grant cuts back, and I think he drops his chest even closer to mine as he cocks a grin at Fin and snaps the buckle into place.

Freaking men. Badge boys or bad guys—they're all a bunch of delicate flowers.

Fin huffs and falls back into the seat, stretching his arm across the backrest. I watch him in the rearview mirror, the prisoner partition between the seats a checkerboard across his reflection, and it suddenly feels more believable—the idea of him being a so-called criminal.

Maybe it should have hit me when he told me about his past. Or when Lou was taken. Or when I realized he had a direct line to the men responsible. It just didn't quite sink in until now. The Robin Hoods of the world are still thieves and tricksters and technically *wrong*.

We ride in silence the rest of the way to the pier. It's a familiar drive, but Grant doesn't park near the dressed-up gallery or the dock where the night market is held. Instead, he takes a side entrance between rows of still-abandoned warehouses. The gate he passes through, strangely unlocked, has a single rusted sign clinging to the chain-link fence. In bold, red font it says No Trespassing and beneath that, a familiar moniker: Pecora Industries.

"You're not gonna want to park anywhere they can see this thing," Fin pipes up again, grabbing the cage as he pulls himself forward.

"Not my first rodeo, Picasso," Grant cuts back.

I don't bother getting in the middle this time. Grant will go to the grave defending his honor and all the traffic stops and trespassing calls he and Steve handled in this exact neighborhood. It's another reminder of why Steve's not even here now, having been bustled away on his free trip to thank him for his service in cleaning up the docks.

This side of the strip is not nearly as glossed up as the opposite end, many of the warehouses still standing in disrepair, but it's a far cry from where it was before all the bored millionaires started demanding action.

"Millie, you need to stay in the car," Grant says as he shifts the gear into Park.

"No way. I'm going in there to get Lou. I'm—"

"This isn't a debate," he interrupts, a tightness in his voice I haven't heard in years.

"He's right," Fin adds from the back seat, and I finally whirl around to face him, to remind him exactly whose side he's supposed to be on, but I'm not sure I deserve that loyalty anymore, and more frighteningly, he doesn't look willing to give it.

The man staring back at me through the black wire cage isn't the one I grew to love on that beach in Capitola or on the deck at his houseboat. This is the man I met on that bench in the museum two weeks ago. This is the stubborn, angry, and uncompromising person who was just in it for the money. This is someone *I* scammed. The bad guy *I* robbed of his privacy and his safety, all in the name of making good on a bad call.

When I don't say anything else, Grant exits the car and lets Fin out of the back. They lock me in and silently cross the deserted lot in which we've parked, stepping over weeds sprouting from cracks and skirting around the corner of a nondescript warehouse.

I lean back against the headrest and practice my breathing. I had no idea it would be so easy to become the bad guy too.

Thirty

It's not exactly how I imagined it, this being-the-bad-guy thing on a covert hostage exchange in some abandoned warehouse district—*if* I can even call it a hostage exchange. I mean, I know it's technically a dog we're dealing with here, but it's Lou. *My* Lou.

I glance out the window again. There's been no sign of Grant or Fin since they rounded the corner, but there's also no criminals lurking behind broken windows or hooded hostages held at gunpoint. It's just strangely silent. A little boring if I'm being honest.

I consider checking my work email. Dismiss the idea of catching up on my podcast. Start and stop a game on my phone three times. And finally realize the only sensible thing to do to relieve at least an ounce of guilt-ridden anxiety is email my realtor.

I check the empty lot once more before dipping my head to open up a new message.

It turns out it's surprisingly difficult to explain to a consummate professional that in two weeks' time I've solicited an art forger, lost my ex-boyfriend's dog, and offered up my life's savings for a ransom payment all without explicitly incriminating myself. Ultimately, I land on "financial hardship" and "many regrets."

Although, I'm not sure the regret thing is entirely true. There's a swirl in my gut that hasn't subsided since the night before, and I have to tamp it down again before I tap the Send button.

The message closes, but nothing else happens.

I suppose it stands to reason that furtive meet-up locations don't have reliable cell service or free Wi-Fi, but it doesn't stop me from trying to find it. I'm fairly certain Grant and Fin—and Steve, for that matter—would all lose their damn minds if they knew I was about to exit the car, but I've been collecting red flags like souvenir coins these days, and one more isn't going to overload my coin purse, right? Right.

The car door shuts way too loudly behind me, and it startles a bird that's scouting for trash near a couple of steel barrels in the corner of the lot. I do the cliché thing and hold my phone in the air, walking around in circles, trying to find a bar of service, but that bird snags my attention again.

It flaps back to the barrels, landing on an edge and eyeing me ominously.

Now, I know for a fact it's not a witch-turned-crow, but I walk toward it anyway because what else do you do when a black-feathered fowl flaps for your attention?

"You hoarding the Wi-Fi over here?" I joke, and the bird has the audacity to crow back at me.

I'm within a foot of it, my phone still aloft, when my shoe slips and liquid splashes up on my shins. I groan in disgust, and the bird squawks once more and takes off.

I'd shamelessly curse it for luring me into a dirty puddle, but it's not water I'm standing in. Black specks dot my jeans, soaking into the fabric, dark and permanent like oil. I reach down to touch it, just to be sure, but then I hear it: a dog barking.

I'm no expert on canine vocals, but it's certainly not an eager or excited sound. It's tense and distressed and coming from a warehouse on the right where there's a door stuck ajar, the hinges rusting. Steve's old rules briefly come to mind again as I look back toward the car I've already fled, but I don't remember any explicitly prohibiting the exploration of dilapidated warehouses wrongfully imprisoning dogs. So, I put my phone away and sneak inside.

The door creaks behind me, returning to its partially ajar position, which allows a sliver of light to illuminate the dark hallway, and I follow it until the golden stripe fades into black. I reach a corner, take the turn, and find rows of shipping containers but stop cold just as I catch a glimpse of the scene around the edge.

There's another bark, followed by an anxious whine and the distinct scrape of nails clawing at the concrete floor, and this time, I know it's Lou because I can see him.

I don't have a completely clear line of sight, but he is visible tugging back on a makeshift rope-turned-leash, pacing and scratching and whining as he bows down to the floor. He's tied to a post in the middle of the room and next to him is Fin.

I hold my breath and risk another inch to see better. Fin is sitting against the post, uncharacteristically dejected, his hands in his lap and his head resting against the metal pole. He shifts slightly, enough for me to see the stark white of plastic zip ties cinched around his wrists.

I catch a gasp in my throat just as two other figures move into a pool of light spilling down from a row of dusty overhead windows: one man taller with a dark beanie pulled low, nearly to his eyes, and the other man shorter, a scally cap plopped right on his thick head.

"I told you. We've got the cash," Fin says, his voice ragged.

"You said you'd have the paintings," the shorter man replies.

"Yeah, well, there was a little mishap with some purple paint."

"You think this is funny?" the other man demands.

"Not as funny as that godawful wig you're—"

I wince as Fin's comment is cut short with a thump, the taller man kicking Fin's outstretched leg, and Fin recoils, hissing another insult at them. I whip back around, leaning up against the metal wall of the shipping container and sinking to the ground as panic swells in my gut, nearly snuffing out my breath.

"It's a beanie," the man counters, presumably to Fin.

"Under the beanie, dimwit. Your hair's all messed up on one side. Don't you know how to put on a wig?"

"I told you it looked ridiculous," his partner adds.

"What was I supposed to do? The alternative is I look like you."

"You mean distinguished?"

"I mean *bald*."

"At this rate, we'll all be bald by the time this exchange is over," Fin jumps in dryly, and Lou even adds a bark to the mix.

"Okay, tough guy," the first man—the one who's apparently hiding a cueball under his beanie—speaks up. "You're the one who didn't deliver on the goods."

"I also didn't think you'd be dumb enough to turn down cash," Fin says.

"*Enough*," another voice spurs up, and I know it.

I peek around the corner, looking for Grant, but don't see him. I want to breathe a sigh of relief because he's got a gun and police skills and surely a dozen other cops on speed dial, but if Fin's tied up, then wouldn't Grant be too?

I take another breath as silently as possible and try to focus. Try to figure out what my next move is. Try to channel all the good-guy tricks I've learned from my ridiculously fair and good-natured ex-boyfriend until—*swish*.

The email stuck in my outbox sends, the coordinating sound unmistakable proof. I snatch up my phone, scrambling for the power button, but—like she knew I was out of service for the past ten minutes and finally has the chance to get ahold of me—it rattles with the familiar tinkling sound of my mom's ringtone.

"What's that?" someone asks.

"Who's there?" another growls.

"Millie," a third says, and I know it's Fin. "*Run*."

I try—I really do—but it feels like one of those dreams where you're pumping your arms as fast as you can and your feet just won't move, like they're stuck in sludge. I make maybe one step toward escape when that beanie-covered mop of fake hair whips around the corner.

The man's fingers snag my upper arms, and he yanks me close and then twists me into his chest. I let out a shriek, but his arm is around my throat before I can utter a word, and he presses his jaw against mine.

"What do we have here?" he asks, the gritty edge of his voice sending shivers down my spine.

I fight his grip uselessly as he drags me around the corner. I'm stumbling along with him, trying to stay on my feet, when he jerks us to a halt in the middle of the room.

Lou howls and yanks on his leash, and Fin lunges toward me, but apparently his feet are also zip-tied, and he topples over sideways. The man holding me tightens up, and his partner rounds on us, almost like a cartoon villain, his cheeks flushing red and his stubby finger prodding the air.

"It's *you*," he says, "the girl who's been tagging along with Van Bro here."

"You know that's not his real name, right?" I spit back because I really can't help it, but that greasy forearm around my neck flexes and I end up choking for air.

"Loosen up, Lars. She's not a threat," someone else calls.

It takes me a second to finish calibrating the scene. I just scored a name for at least one-half of the criminal pair who have been following Fin for the past two weeks, which means I can stop referring to them as the tall guy and the short guy, but it's all irrelevant because the voice who said it is the very same voice over which I thought I could breathe a sigh of relief.

It doesn't make sense until I see him, and an automatic plea for help dissipates in my throat because he doesn't look himself. He's hardly a shadow of the person I once knew, but it is Grant who steps into the pool of light. It's Grant who just called my captor by name.

"Not a threat?" Lars growls in return.

"Not if you take her phone. Why haven't you done that yet?"

"I tried to tell you they're not that smart," Fin interjects, but no one pays him any attention.

Instead, Lars tightens his hold while his partner fumbles for my cell. When Grant holds out a hand, he turns it over, but the pair clearly aren't appeased.

"She's seen our faces," Lars goes on.

"She knows who we are," the other adds.

"I think you greatly underestimate how truly forgettable you are," Fin pipes up again, giving an amused snarl as he leverages himself up to his knees. "Now, let her go before Lou tears down this whole damn warehouse trying to get to her."

Lou jerks again on the rope, his anxious barks quickly devolving into growls, and Grant gives a slight nod, apparently in agreement with Fin. Lars finally slackens his grip, drops his arm, and gives me a shove forward.

I take advantage of the momentum and stumble away, dropping to my knees and seizing Lou around the neck. He whines happily and draws his tongue across my cheek, and both of us scoot toward Fin.

"Are you okay?" he asks under his breath.

I nod, barely, before turning back around. "Grant, what is going on?"

He lets out a long sigh, pockets his hands, and shakes his head, and as I look between him and the pair staring me down, it finally clicks. The yet-to-be-named man sneers at me, puffing out his chest, and Lars, the tall guy, finally pulls off his beanie, the wig underneath apparently winning the battle.

"Oh my god, you're all...you're all working together?"

Grant huffs. "I really wish you had just stayed in the car, Millie. I didn't want you to be a part of this."

"I don't understand. What have you done?"

"What have *I* done?" Grant repeats, letting out a laugh and glancing amusedly at the two hostage-takers. "Why don't you ask your boyfriend here what he's done?"

Lou launches to his feet, as if to warn Grant, and I have to wrap my arms around his neck to keep him steady. Meanwhile, Fin edges nearer to me, that unmistakable scent a reminder of exactly how close we've been in the past few days, but I'm not sure if I should soak it in or turn up my nose.

"Go on," Grant taunts, jerking his chin toward Fin. "Why don't you come clean about the painting that landed you in trouble in the first place?"

"Yeah, Van Bro. Why don't you fess up?" the shorter man speaks up again, and all three seem to inch closer.

"Don't need your help, Murray. Besides, she already knows."

"The one you stole from them?" I ask Fin before jerking my head toward the officially named pair.

"Oh, so she doesn't know," Grant cuts in again.

"The rest has nothing to do with her," Fin says.

"It does now that you've dragged her into your little crime spree."

"Honestly, what that guy was doing with that painting was the far greater crime."

"'That guy'?" Grant mocks, letting out a sharp laugh and turning to face me. "You wanna know who 'that guy' is, Millie? You want to know who Fin actually stole that painting from? Who's been calling the shots since day one?"

I know I'm going to get the answer with or without response, so I just keep quiet, rhythmically rubbing down Lou's fur and trying not to glance back at Fin.

"I'm surprised you didn't put it together before now," Grant goes on. "I expected more from you, but hey, I guess we can't all be crime-solving superheroes like Steve, can we?"

Grant takes another step closer, and Lou growls.

"Fin has been working for a known criminal for months, Millie. He's been running black market art dealings for him and he's been doing it under his own goddamn name. You've seen that tattoo, haven't you?" Grant jerks a finger toward Fin. "Want to know what his real name is? What his signature looks like?"

"His signature?"

"You know damn well this wasn't his first crime, don't you?" Grant jeers.

I glance at Fin's forearms, pressed together due to the ties, the glistening black lines of his tattoo seemingly climbing up his skin.

"Don't listen to him, Millie," Fin says. "Grant isn't the cop you think he is. He turned on Steve. He turned on his own partner and started working for this guy too, the same guy I scammed."

I scoot another inch backward, raising a hand to my mouth and shaking my head like I can rattle all the loose pieces into the right spot.

"Grant is working with you," I say, eyeing Lars and Murray, "but you two have been going after Fin, and all of you are working under someone else. But who?"

"Guess you were right, Grant," Lars says, his fake wig shifting as he tosses his head. "Girly didn't figure it out the first time she saw us together. Musta been too busy making eyes at the boss."

Grant moves, settling in next to the others, and I finally see it—something I should have seen the second Lars pulled off his hat to reveal that mop of hair. The two men who've been chasing Fin are the same men who were at the market the day I just so happened to run into Grant. The day Hannah pointed out the oil splashed on his jeans—oil he could only have been exposed to if he was at this very warehouse before.

"Oh no," I say on a shaky breath, and I grip Lou tighter.

"He's a traitor, Millie," Fin argues. "They've all been working for the same guy. They're working for *him*."

Fin's pleading expression grows stony as his eyes flick over my shoulder. Grant whirls on his heels, the two co-hostage-takers gasp, and even

Lou's quiet whine fizzles into a whimper as someone else steps lazily out of the shadows.

"My, my, that is quite the introduction."

His voice—just that short phrase—is a soft, silky purr. One I recognize and know. One that belongs to a face I truly couldn't forget.

Thirty-One

"Vincent DeLobo."

The name ghosts over my lips without effort or thought, simply a reaction to the face I've seen so many times on the news and at the market and plastered on the biography plaques at the art gallery on the pier.

"I don't even need the introduction, do I?" he crows, moving past Grant and heading my direction. "Millie, is it?"

"I'm not here for anything other than Lou and—"

I stop myself short and DeLobo smiles, a crooked, half-cocked smile that causes the corners of his eyes to crinkle.

"Lou and...?"

All the strength I can muster still isn't enough to speak up. When I walked into this warehouse, I was looking for Lou and Grant and Fin, and now I'm not sure anyone except the dog is innocent.

"Questioning loyalties, I see. Not everyone is as they seem, are they?" DeLobo taunts, and it riles Fin up enough that he gets to his knees.

"Let her and the dog go, DeLobo. This is between us."

"I don't think I'll be doing that."

"You don't need her," he argues again, and DeLobo tsks in return.

"Oh, that's where you are wrong, my boy. You see, now I know this lovely young lady is of value to you, much like a certain painting of which I was robbed."

"Like I said, I can get you more valuable replicas. I can get you cash."

DeLobo purses his lips, amused. "No, I don't think that will do anymore."

"I won't let you hurt her."

"Hurt her?" DeLobo claps back, and he casts a strangely affectionate look toward me. "I would never harm one of your pawns. Not when she can tell me everything I need to know about *you*."

"I don't know anything," I blurt before I even know what I'm saying. "I just met him. Two weeks ago. I don't even know the guy's full name. He's basically a stranger."

"Gee, thanks," Fin grunts under his breath. Meanwhile, the two henchmen chuckle quietly and even Grant sighs.

DeLobo lifts his sharp chin. "Is that so?"

"Yep," I say, all mock confidence. "His favorite candy could be chocolate for all I know. And maybe he drinks kale smoothies. I'm not even sure if the guy likes sunsets, and I mean, what kind of person doesn't like sunsets?"

"Wow," Fin jumps in again. "That hurts, you know. I really thought you'd remember my favorite candy is—"

"Enough," DeLobo interrupts, and he tosses a deadly glare at Fin before zeroing in on me. "All I need to know is where he lives—where he's keeping the painting."

This time, I snap my jaw shut. Pretending I don't know a single one of his favorites is one thing. Pretending I don't know the location of the houseboat in which I've been hiding for the past several days and have already thoughtlessly disclosed to Grant is a whole other ball game. I keep my eyes fixed on DeLobo and hope like hell Grant isn't vindictive enough to give it away.

"Go on now," DeLobo urges. "That's all I need and then everyone can go home."

I glance left at Fin, who's restlessly tugging at his zip ties, and then turn forward again. "I—I don't know."

"She's lying."

The statement comes from Grant, and now I know Fin *wasn't* lying: Grant really did turn on Steve. Perhaps turned on the whole police department.

DeLobo glances backward, a smug grin tightening his already tense face, and then he takes another step closer to me. Behind me, Fin is fidgeting harder, and if he's trying to get out of his zip ties, he's clearly losing the battle.

"You really don't want to make this any harder than it has to be, Millie," DeLobo goes on, treating my name like a curse word.

He closes another inch between us, and Fin wrestles more forcefully with his ties. I hold steady, managing my breaths, when Fin's clasped hands graze me.

He presses something into my free hand, something small and round and smooth, and I wonder if Fin was hit over the head when he was captured because I'm pretty sure he just gave me a pill and I'm very sure we have absolutely no hope in fighting off DeLobo by lobbing tiny tablets at his face—assuming that's Fin's plan of course. Honestly, what other plan could he possibly have?

"She's not going to talk," Fin speaks up, and I wish I had half the confidence he did. "Neither of us are."

"Give it time," DeLobo coos. "Everyone talks."

"Well, it'll be six hours at least."

Fin moves quickly, raising his bound hands upward, but he flashes another small, white object, no larger than a pea, in DeLobo's face, and then, without hesitation, pops it in his mouth and swallows.

DeLobo frowns. "Is that—"

"Swallow it, Millie."

I react faster than I can think and slap my hand to my mouth. A coated pill drops on my tongue and I gulp it down, the round tablet painfully working its way down my esophagus.

"Uh, boss," Lars speaks up, "I think that was—"

"I *know* what that was," DeLobo snarls, and he reaches for Fin's jaw first, forcing it open. "Did you just swallow—"

Fin makes a gagging noise and then licks his lips. "Would have been much easier to do with water, but yeah, the pill's gone, which means we've got about five minutes before I start regurgitating useless childhood memories and nonsensical stories."

"Wait—what?" I demand, looking toward Fin.

He just grins wickedly at me and then jerks his chin toward DeLobo, who practically growls as he rips his hand from Fin and reaches toward me next.

"You didn't—"

I stick my tongue out meekly. "I did."

DeLobo snarls again and pushes back up to his feet, rounding on the other three men. "Who did this? Who gave them those pills?"

"Oh, don't worry," Fin calls back, "I found them on the ground."

"*Ugh.* Are you serious?" I cry vehemently, and I swear I can already taste dirt and dust and the bottom of DeLobo's shoes.

"Time for us to go to sleepy town."

"This isn't over," DeLobo counters, and he turns, rounding on Grant. "Take them to the storage room, and make sure it's secure."

Grant falters, his brows cinching together. "You don't mean—"

"Lock them in."

"I really don't think—"

"I don't pay you to *think*."

Grant stammers again, and I can tell the confidence he once held is gone.

"Would you rather Lars and Murray take care of them?" DeLobo snaps when Grant doesn't move.

The pair behind me shift on their feet and rub their hands together. I know it's supposed to be menacing, but I can't help but think they look more like they're eager for Girl Scout cookies and not readying to imprison their kidnap victims. Regardless, it's enough to spur Grant into action.

"Millie, get Lou," he demands, and then he hurries toward us and drops to his knees in front of Fin.

I consider my options for a moment, wondering if there's any chance Fin and I could get the upper hand on four grown men, but quickly shelve it. By the looks of it, Fin does too, as he willingly offers up his ankles.

Grant produces a pocketknife, slices the ankle zip ties, and then grabs Fin by the elbows to help him to his feet. I hurriedly untie Lou's rope from the post and then Grant grabs me by the elbow too, directing all of us between a pair of shipping containers and plunging us into darkness.

"Hurry back now, *officer*," DeLobo says, and I know it's as much a threat as anything.

"Grant, please, you can't do this," I say as soon as we're far enough out of earshot.

"I don't really have a choice," he snaps back.

"Smartass here thought it was a great idea to get tangled up with a damn drug dealer," Fin pipes up.

"Oh, and you're brilliant for scamming the guy?" Grant counters.

"Hey, I was doing just fine before you tried to blackmail me."

"You nearly ruined the biggest bust of my career."

"Wait a minute," I jump in. "I thought—aren't you—what are you guys talking about?"

Fin grunts as Grant pulls on his elbow—harder than necessary, surely—and then we round one more corner.

"In here," Grant says, jerking Fin toward a steel door.

I follow them in, Lou obliviously trotting alongside us like I've just leashed him up for his daily walk, and then Grant takes one more glance backward before shutting the door and finally cutting Fin's wrist ties.

"Damn it, you two really screwed the pooch on this one," Grant nips, though the tension in his voice suddenly shifts.

"Dog puns? Really?" Fin retorts.

"I had everything under control until you got involved."

"Oh yeah, looks real good when you've got kids doing hard time for drugs your ringleader is pushing."

"Well, if you hadn't let him snoop around the warehouse in the first place—"

"Guys!" I jump in again, accidentally tugging on Lou's leash. "What the *hell* is going on?"

Fin and Grant finally look my direction, their expressions slackening, and Grant lets out a sigh. He crosses the room toward a wall lined with wooden crates I hadn't noticed when we walked in and then slides the lid off one.

He jerks his chin toward the box. "See for yourself."

I frown at Fin before meeting Grant and peering inside. Cushioned between curly shavings of wood are tiny plastic baggies—hundreds of them—and they're all filled with small round pills. I grab one, examining the miniature black pawprint stamped on each white shell.

"Is this—"

"Puppy Love," Grant confirms, and he snatches the pouch back from me and returns it to the crate. "I've been working an undercover gig trying to bust DeLobo for pushing the stuff. As far as he knows, I'm a bad cop looking to score some extra cash in exchange for keeping the police off his trail and away from this damn warehouse."

"Oh my god," I say, still focused on the hundreds of pills. "Did I just—am I on—did I do drugs? Drugs you found on the *floor*?"

I round on Fin now, panicked tears springing to my eyes, and he holds up two hands.

"They weren't on the floor. Ding-Dong over here slipped them to me when he zip-tied my hands before you arrived. *Way* tighter than necessary, by the way."

Fin scowls at Grant.

"I had to make it look believable."

I whimper, still ten steps behind reality, and I drop Lou's leash to slap my cheeks, like I might wake myself from a nightmare.

"What's going to happen to me? Am I going to get high?"

Grant nods meekly. "A little. But you did only take half a dose."

"It's going to be fine," Fin adds.

"It's going to be fine?" I repeat and then whip my head toward Grant again. "Aren't you trying to get this off the streets?"

He waves a hand listlessly. "Well, yeah, I mean it is illegal and we certainly don't want kids getting ahold of it, but for healthy adults, it's pretty harmless."

"Harmless?"

"Well, it will still produce a high, and you may get a little fuzzy and a bit nostalgic and probably want a good cuddle, but—"

"Cuddle?"

"Listen," he says, and he grabs me by the shoulders, his eyes boring into me like a laser. "We've got about three more minutes to explain before you both go all loopy, so hear us out, will you?"

I blink several times, and suddenly it seems like my lashes are wispy feathers, moving much slower than they should be.

"We? Us? Are you implying—"

"Fin and I knew each other long before today."

I swing my head toward Fin, though his face looks a little fuzzy, and he just nods in acknowledgment.

"I started the undercover gig about six months ago when I got passed up for the promotion," Grant goes on. "I helped DeLobo pack and route shipments so I knew where all the drugs were going, and this asshole"—Grant jerks a thumb at Fin—"he was my sawdust supplier."

"Sawdust? Like sawdust from wood?" I ask Fin skeptically.

"Does it come from anywhere else?"

"But you chop it and then...you shave it?"

"Apparently one of his many talents," Grant adds, though it's definitely a little sour.

"How did you even find him?" I ask Grant, and that makes him twitch. He takes one glance at Fin, who jumps in quickly.

"Same way you found me."

"Don't tell me..."

"*SawdustOrBust* at gmail dot com."

He fires up a cheeky grin, and I pinch my lips together because I suddenly have the surprising urge to giggle, but Grant just rolls his eyes and continues.

"I needed someone who looked a little shady and this guy definitely fit the bill. Anyway, everything was going just fine until art-guy over here got the bright idea to steal from DeLobo."

Fin shrugs exaggeratedly. "The dingbat was laundering money by buying and selling priceless works on the black market."

"Wait—an art black market?" I cut in.

Fin chuckles. "I don't think these things really have specific identifiers—"

"But it's like my podcast?"

Both men frown at me.

"You know, that financial crime podcast I love. Fin, I told you about that episode on black market antiquity laundering and—"

"Yeah, okay, something like that," Fin confirms reluctantly, though his lips seem to be getting a little looser. "Anyway, DeLobo asked me to help facilitate the transactions and no way was I letting those pretty paintings get picked up by a bunch o' birdbrains who didn't know their worth."

"So you swapped in fakes?"

"How many times do I have to tell you they're replications?"

I roll my eyes—slowly, very slowly—and then Fin waves his hands around.

"Piece o' cake duping most knuckleheads on the black murket," he says, beginning to slur his words. "Not so piece-o'-cakey tricking LeDobo when he decided to keep a piece I already replicated."

This time, a giggle manages to sneak out. "That's the one Tweedledee and Tweedledumb were trying to get back from you?"

Fin grins. "They couldn't find their way out of a paper bag...no, a holey bag...no, a wet paper bag with holes."

"Yeah, well, they can certainly find their way back to this room, and you two are clearly well on your way to the funny farm," Grant says, and he snaps a finger in front of my face to redraw my attention. "I'm sorry you had to find out like this, Millie, and I'm sorry I was kind of an ass out there."

"Kind of an ass? You were Grade A donkey fresh from the market."

His lips flatten into an impossibly straight line, and I just smirk at him and turn to Fin.

"So were you, dingleberry. Why didn't you just tell me why you smell like sawdust all the time?"

"That's what you're concerned about?"

"Millie, are you getting any of this?" Grant asks.

I slap a hand to my chest in dramatized offense and stumble backward, which requires Grant to reach out and restabilize me.

"Oh, I'm getting it. I just found out my criminal boyfriend is working with my criminal friend-friend and everyone's doing all sorts of criminal crimes."

Fin snorts. "Does that mean Lou committed a canine-al crime? Wait—a crimi-nine crime?"

I gasp. "How dare you! Lou is fin-nocent. Get it? *Fin*-nocent?"

"Okay," Grant says, and this time he pats me on the shoulder. "You two are going to stay in here and ride this out. I'll lock you in, and I promise you'll be safe, but I can't have you blowing my cover out there. Also, Millie, take your phone back, will you? Who even has a ringer turned on these days?"

"It's my mom's favorite song."

"It almost blew the whole op."

"Not my fault the service is so finicky around here. Are my bars back? Can I call for help yet?"

Grant glances at the screen before plopping it in my hands. "It's spotty at best, and no. You're not allowed to send so much as a tweet before I get everything under control out there. Understand?"

I tap two fingers to my forehead in a very sloppy salute. "Yes, sir, officer, sir."

He just rolls his eyes and looks at Fin. "That goes for you too. No one makes a move until I get back."

Fin holds up two hands in surrender. "Couldn't if I wanted to."

Lou barks, as if in agreement, and I thump Grant on the shoulder this time.

"Go get 'em, tiger. I'll be cheering on my criminal friend-friend from the safety of this very dark room."

"Wait—go back just a minute," Fin interjects. "If he's the criminal friend-friend, does that make me the criminal boyfriend?"

"I'll leave you to it," Grant says, and it takes another five seconds or so for my brain to realize he's already out the door, leaving Lou, Fin, and me behind.

Thirty-Two

Lou barks, a simple *pay-attention-to-me* bark, but it rattles around entirely too aggressively in my head.

"I think I need to lie down," I mutter, slapping a hand to my forehead.

Fin is still in front of me, but he appears kind of weightless, all his edges almost squiggly, and he floats a little to the left.

"Right," he says, spinning on his heels and waving a hand, "we can lie down here"—he points at a stack of crates three tall, pauses, and redirects his aim—"or actually here"—he lobs a finger at the crate Grant left open—"or that corner looks...nice?"

He lands on a dark space between two towers of more crates. I think DeLobo referred to this place as a storage room, and it's exactly that. No couch, no chair, no flat surface except for the dusty concrete below our feet.

Lou whines next to me, and I pat his head lovingly. "We need something soft."

"Are you suggesting we use Lou as a pillow?" Fin asks.

"No, no, no," I say, but it does make me giggle a little. I totter over to the open crate and peer inside. "We can make a bed with *this*."

"More drugs won't make concrete any softer."

"Not drugs. Wood shavings."

"Huh?"

"If it's good enough for cows, it should be good enough for us."

Fin whips his head left, then right, his brow cinched. "Where are the cows?"

"Just help me, will you?"

I manage to slide the lid all the way off, and it thumps to the floor, sending another reverberating throb through my head, but I plunge my hands into the crate anyway grabbing fistfuls of sawdust. Then, with the enthusiasm of an unleashed toddler, I toss them.

"Like this!"

It's a very messy snowstorm of soft, flaky shavings as I fling them toward the corner, and Fin lets out a howl and slaps his knee.

"We're going to need a lot more of that," he says, and he does a full three-hundred-and-sixty degrees before turning another one-eighty and marching toward the crates in the opposite corner. "I got it."

I glance skeptically at Lou, who whines again, but Fin is already tugging at another crate and pushing off the lid.

"If I remember right, this one is just..."

"Sawdust!"

Fin tips the crate over, and it's an avalanche compared to my contribution, a wave of cuttings pouring out and spilling onto the floor. A plume of particles swirls in the air and that familiar scent blooms tenfold. I inhale deeply, and suddenly all the comments Fin and Grant made about Puppy Love—how it may loosen some backlogged childhood memories or induce a state of extra-cuddly euphoria—skip back into my mind.

As the last flakes flutter out, Fin drops to his knees and starts spreading the shavings around, pushing a pile together near one end and flattening the rest so it actually looks a little like a bed. I skip back to the crate and scoop out a few more armfuls.

"We still need more."

"How much more?" Fin asks.

"Enough to cradle our joints, of course! A good sawdust bed has to be at least four inches thick to successfully ease discomfort and aid in quality rest. It'd be so much better if I could get my hands on a waterbed that we can tack down to the floor first, but—"

"Wow. Who *are* you?"

I sneer at Fin and his features contort dramatically and then we dissolve into a fit of unflattering and clumsy laughter. I drop to my knees, fluff up the pillow pile a little more, and then topple sideways. Fin follows suit and then slaps a hand in the bedding, patting the space between us for Lou.

I think Lou considers his options for a moment, his head cocking to one side—and honestly, who could blame him?—but after a few more aggressive pats from Fin, he pads over and plops down, delivering a wet kiss to my chin first and Fin's second.

"I grew up on a dairy farm, okay?" I say, letting my head fall to the side and earning a clear view of Fin's cheeks, which are unusually rosy.

He props up an elbow and settles his jaw in his palm. "So that's where all the strange farm knowledge and cow idioms come from?"

"Well, it couldn't be a *cow*-incidence, could it?"

"Cow puns too?"

"If you have leverage, milk it for all it's worth."

"What have I done?"

"Unlocked a very a-*moo*-sing skill of mine," I say, raising a finger proudly.

"I thought you lived here since you were ten," Fin diverts, though he's smiling, and I roll all the way over to my side and drape a hand over Lou's back, who is panting quietly between us.

"I have. My parents split about then and I moved out here with my mom, but I still spent all my summers in Iowa."

"On a farm?"

"Of course. It was my dad's place, and you know one person can only milk, like, eight cows an hour, right?"

"You know how to milk a cow?" Fin asks, and I think his lips twitch with amusement.

"With my own two hands."

"I don't know if I should be impressed or intimidated."

"Both," I say, and I scrunch my nose up at him. My face does feel a little numb, and it's a relief to confirm all my muscles still work.

"So answer me this," Fin goes on, waving a hand in the air like he's conducting a choir, "if you grew up on a dairy farm and have no problem milking cows yourself, how the heck do you have an aversion to dairy?"

"When you're force-fed a glass of raw milk with dinner every night of your childhood, it starts to lose its appeal."

"Does that mean you don't eat cheese either?"

"Oh, heavens no! Cheese is completely different. Cooked cheese, of course—none of this cold, cardboard, charcuterie crap. But don't tell my dad. He'd be utterly appalled." I stop abruptly, slap a hand to my mouth, and squeal. "Get it? *Udderly* appalled?"

"I'm not sure what I did to deserve this."

I beam proudly and pat Lou's back more aggressively, causing him to wriggle and give me a wet-nosed nudge, then drop my head into the sawdust pillow. Fin settles in too, and both of us find either side of Lou's skull and scratch behind his ears.

For a while, we lie there in silence, staring up at the plain black ceiling of this storage room with no bovine witticisms to distract us.

My mind starts to creep backward strangely, and I don't know if it's the drugs coursing through me or the itch of dust in the air that does it, but I skip back to our date night at the gallery. Then, the day I met Fin on the bench in the museum. Then, the weekend before when I sat in Steve's house on that old couch watching the news.

I filter through every chance I had to dig into who Fin really was, to figure out what that telling image on his forearm meant, to make it known that some subconscious part of me noticed it.

I wouldn't let myself see it clearly then. In fact, I'm not sure I want to see it so clearly now, but I can't ignore it any longer and this high-induced curiosity of mine finally wins out.

"I have one rude question left, don't I?"

Fin glances at me and then resettles his gaze on the blank ceiling. "You do. You planning on using it?"

"I think I have to. Rules of the game and all."

"Make it a good one, then."

"Grant didn't really find you through some sawdust email, did he?"

Fin doesn't respond right away, so I roll over to face him. I reach over Lou's back and, without hesitation, I snag Fin by the wrist, gently twisting his forearm so his tattoo shows in full.

I hadn't seen it—his tattoo—on the day we met, but it was impossible not to notice every time he took his coat off. I inspect the lines again, each contour somehow coming to life, almost as if the creature stamped there were inhaling its first breath.

I know I've seen this image before. Just smaller, slighter, less distinguishable.

"Your real name is Griffin, isn't it? You're the infamous art dealer who's been all over the news. The one with the famous signature who no one's been able to catch."

Fin lifts his gaze to me, and I drop his arm.

"How long have you known?" he asks.

"I know I came up with a lot of good nicknames, but Fin really can't be short for much else."

"You never said anything."

"Neither did you. Not even when you showed me that replica. The one with your signature on the back."

"You recognized it?"

"It's a griffin. Just like your tattoo. How couldn't I?"

Fin rolls toward me, his brows furrowing as his eyes flick back and forth between mine. "Millie, I couldn't tell you."

"But Grant lied to me just now. He lied to *me* for *you*."

"He was protecting the case. It's why I pretended I didn't know him when you brought him to my place. It's why we put on the whole show out there with DeLobo's guys."

"No, that's not it," I say, though I'm not sure why.

Grant may not be the most perceptible guy, but I wasn't at all ambiguous when I told him exactly how I felt about Fin. Even after knowing what Fin did.

"How did you really meet?"

Fin heaves another breath, his chest rising dramatically. "Grant's the one who finally caught me."

"*He* caught *you*—Griffin, the black-market art dealer?"

Fin nods heavily. "I've been doing this art replication gig for a long time, but he got the one-up on me the day Kai showed up at the swap I had scheduled with DeLobo's guys."

"Grant was there? Does that mean Kai is the same kid Steve and Grant picked up?"

"It was never supposed to happen like that, Millie. I had no idea Kai followed me into the trade, and when Grant and Steve busted us, Kai ran one direction and I went the other. Grant got to me first, and I tried every offer in the book to make sure Kai got off clean.

"Grant even wanted DeLobo bad enough he was willing to cut both of us loose if I just helped him bust the guy, but apparently that ex-boyfriend of yours is pretty damn good at his job."

"He's not that good," I say, the image of a puffy-chested, cape-wearing Steve finally cracking. "Sure, he can get the bad guys to cave, but he couldn't make an innocent person confess to a crime they never committed. And he *knew* Kai was innocent."

Fin lets out a breath that causes a few flakes of sawdust between us to flit into the air.

"I imagine Steve didn't have much of a choice when the kid was copping to a real crime."

"Steve was a wreck," I say, recalling that phone call Hannah took at the hardware store. "He had no idea how a kid could have gotten tangled up in that mess or why he'd confess in the first place, and—" I stop short as it hits me all at once. "Kai thought he was protecting you by confessing."

"He saw the drugs all over the warehouse and made some really bad assumptions."

"Assumptions that you were wrapped up in the drugs DeLobo was pushing. He confessed to the crime so you couldn't. I bet he thought he'd get a lighter punishment than you might, being underage and all."

"That's why I needed the lawyer—and a damn good one."

"But why didn't Grant just tell Steve? Why didn't he let him know what the plan was? Surely their boss could have undone everything right then."

Fin doesn't respond right away, just shakes his head.

"Oh my god," I say, a whoosh of air spilling over my lips. "Steve wasn't in on it."

"Listen, I never met Steve. Grant kept us at a distance, and even when he talked about his partner—or, former partner—I didn't realize his Steve was your Steve. You never even told me he was a cop."

"I try not to make it a habit to detail my ex's career."

"Yeah, well, Grant was pretty clear Steve's the kind of guy who doesn't operate in the gray, can do no harm, always gets the credit for closing the cases."

"Case in point with the all-expenses-paid trip to Sonoma," I fill in, but Fin winces.

"I think that one was faked."

"What do you mean?"

"Steve was getting in the way, so Grant somehow convinced DeLobo to foot the bill for a few 'appreciation' trips for the force. The whole purpose was to get Steve out of town for a few days so they could pull off their biggest shipment yet."

"And the department willingly accepted the gifts from a known criminal they were tracking?" I demand, the auditor in me urgently resurfacing again.

"Yeah, I don't think Grant's boss knew about it either."

"What?" I launch up on my elbows, eliciting an impatient huff from Lou. "The op wasn't even sanctioned by the department?"

"Grant may have gone a little rogue."

"That's a *lot* rogue, Fin. He could lose his job over this."

"Not if he busts this guy," Fin argues, and he, too, sits up a little more. "Grant was close. He was going to call in the official bust today, but the whole kidnapped-dog thing got in the way."

Both of us glance downward, and Lou lets out an exasperated sigh, like our simple act of staring at him is disrupting his sleep.

"Does that mean no one knows we're here?" I ask. "No one is actually coming to stop DeLobo?"

"Everything's going to be fine. We're going to get out of this."

"How can you be so sure?"

"We've made it this far, haven't we?"

I don't reply because I'm not convinced that's adequate reassurance, but I have to let it slide since a hundred other thoughts are clamoring for attention.

"Fin," I start again, glancing up at him, perhaps the courage of the drugs spurring me on, "I need one more possibly-rude question."

"Your first one wasn't all that bad. I suppose I can give you a freebie."

"Are you ever going to quit?"

Fin silently lifts his free hand and reaches for the back of Lou's neck, kneading his fur.

"I've never had a reason to before."

"And now?"

"Millie, the day I got that email, ever-so-politely soliciting under-the-table and off-the-books help, I was a mess. I got one of my kids arrested. I was broke. I was scamming criminals. Then, this goofy-ass dog chews up an even more ridiculous painting and suddenly I was the guy scouting pink paint and walking on the beach."

I don't respond, instead inching my fingers forward to gently scratch Lou's side.

"I don't want to be the bad guy. I don't want to be the criminal boyfriend." He pauses, pets the pup a couple more times, and then returns his gaze to me. "I don't want to go back to me before Lou."

He says it quietly, solemnly, like every word is packed with twice the meaning, and it's pure. Honest. And also...really hilarious.

"Me before Lou?" I cackle in return. "Did you come up with that all on your own?"

"What's wrong with that?"

"You're an axe-throwing, wood-chopping lumberjack, and you just punned off a romance novel. A really sad romance novel, actually. Have you read it?"

"I think that's enough," he says, grimacing, and he pets Lou a little more aggressively. "I have a sensitive side. I'm an artist. I'm from San Francisco, for crying out loud, not rural Iowa. I am comfortable enough with my masculinity that I can admit to knowing the plot of a few love stories, and some pretty damn good ones at that."

I giggle some more, throwing my head back and letting the dizzying whirr of the drugs stir fuzzy feelings in my chest.

"Also, I don't throw axes," he says. "That's thoroughly irresponsible."

"With all the random hobbies you have, I'm surprised it's not one of them."

"They're not hobbies. They're all very serious jobs."

I laugh again and roll over, the momentum sending a few wood shavings in the air as I lie back on the makeshift pillow.

"Me before Lou," I repeat, less mocking this time as I mull over the words and let my fingers trail down Lou's side and scratch beneath his rib bones. "I don't think I ever made an uncalculated move in my life before I brought this furball home."

"Why am I not surprised by that?" Fin says smugly, still rolled up on his side, watching me.

I tilt my head his direction, noticing new lines crease around his eyes, laughter lines I didn't know he had.

"What if I don't want to go back either?"

Fin purses his lips. "Why would you?"

"I've done bad things. I helped cover up an incredibly expensive ruined painting. I'm an accomplice to a very prolific art forger. I led a cop straight to your house and got all of us wrapped up in a doggie hostage exchange with drug dealers."

Lou whines at this, and Fin pats his head a little more meaningfully before looking back at me.

"Are you about to apologize?"

I open my mouth, but the words I expect to spill don't come.

"Listen," Fin says, "I can understand if you don't want to be in this anymore, if you don't want to be in this with me—"

I shake my head before he can finish the sentence. "But I do, Fin. I do want to be in this. I want to be here. I want to be the person I am with you."

"You mean, the gummy-worm-hating, kale-smoothie-drinking math nerd who hates getting roses for holidays and would rather eat out of a food truck than a five-star restaurant?"

"How do you know I don't like roses?"

Fin shrugs. "Seems like a fiscally responsible person's nightmare."

The response makes me smile and I know it's exaggerated and goofy because of the drugs, but I'm not embarrassed.

"I like the way you make me feel, Fin. I like that I don't have to pretend around you."

"To be fair, I did make you pretend once."

"To make a very sad man feel better."

Fin cocks a brow dramatically. "Is that all it takes? I mean, I could be a very sad man who needs you to make me feel better."

"You're hardly a sad man—grumpy, yes, but sad, no," I say, and I reach across Lou and cup Fin's chin just so I can feel his smile when I smirk back at him. "Will you forgive me for leading Grant back to your place?"

"Will you forgive me for not doing this right the first time?"

I frown, pulling back. "Doing what right?"

"When we sober up," Fin goes on, the slight slur of his voice reminding me we've got at least a couple hours to go, "will you go on a date with me? A real date? Nothing pretend about it."

I smile without effort, and I know that whirr in my belly has nothing to do with whatever illegal substance is surging through my veins.

"Technically, it'd be a fourth date," he tacks on. "Or maybe it's the fifth. Does this count?"

"Do numbers really matter anyway?"

Fin grins, a full, captivating, rescued-from-the-pound, dog-like grin, and then he leans over Lou, almost flattening him into the bed of wood shavings, and presses a kiss to my lips. It's soft, gentle—colorful, even—as reds and oranges and yellows swirl behind my eyes, blending into the brightest, rarest shade yet.

When he pulls away, I still see the colors, still feel them whirling around me, and I sink closer to Lou and closer to Fin, and he scoots inward enough to settle his arm around Lou's head and weave his fingers into my hair. He rests his chin atop Lou, who lets out a deep breath that causes his jowls to flutter.

"I do like this guy, but"—Fin drops his voice to a whisper—"it will be nice when he's not always between us."

"Don't worry. He'll be going back to Steve's as soon as he gets home. I mean, assuming we *do* sober up and *do* get out of this mess."

Fin frowns exaggeratedly. "I don't know about you, but I'm halfway sober already."

"No you aren't. You haven't had a straight thought since we got into this room."

"Cross my heart," he says, sloppily drawing an imaginary line over his chest. "Sober Sally."

"Nice try. I know that's not your name."

"See? You're sobering up too."

"Hardly."

"It's Griffin Hale, by the way. Still one *n*."

I smile as Fin gently combs his fingers through my hair.

"Millie Collins. Still no *n*. Well, in my first name at least."

"I beg to differ, *Millicent*."

Fin says it on a laugh, and I let one out too.

"Oh, I do like the sound of that."

Thirty-Three

"I do *not* like the sound of *that*."

"Who else did you invite to our hostage exchange?" Fin demands, sitting up straight and sending a whirl of sawdust in the air.

"Oh, like I drafted up an evite and spammed all my friends?"

"Remind me how Grant got the memo."

"Okay," I say smugly, though there's a hint of humor under my voice. "But they are calling *your* name."

Fin frowns and glances toward the back of the door like he just noticed it.

"Griffin Hale? I need you to stand down. I am armed and coming through this door in three...two..."

I'm not sure the voice on the other side actually says *one*. Between the pounding on the door and the responding howl from Lou and the confused sputtering from Fin, it's all a blur, but a gust of air screams into the storage room and overhead lights blink to life.

"Hands where I can see them!" the man yells again, and Fin scrambles to move, only it's not to comply.

He throws his left leg up and over Lou and me, landing on his knees and squaring his back to the door. Lou whimpers as I grab for his collar and Fin eventually does toss his arms in the air, but he's actively shielding us from whoever just burst into the room.

"Don't shoot," he calls. "I've got a civilian and a—"

"Lou?"

The dog yips. I grip his collar tighter and squeal. And then, I peek around Fin's side.

"Steve?"

"Millie! Thank goodness I found you."

"Steve?" Fin echoes, and he twists halfway around to face the door.

"Hands up!" Steve yells back, aiming a taser straight at Fin's chest.

Fin slaps a hand to his sternum and lets out a gusting breath. "Damn, man. I thought you said you were armed."

"I am! Now, hands up and step away from the girl and the dog."

"Steve! Steve, please," I interrupt, though I'm still pinned under Fin. I giggle unintentionally as I poke him in the waist so he bends sideways enough for me to see more clearly. "It's fine. We're fine. Please put that thing down. Lou's about to go berserk."

"Millie, I don't think you understand—"

"No, I don't think you do. Brace yourself: I'm letting Lou go."

"Millie, no—"

"Too late."

I beam as I slip my fingers free from Lou's collar and he bounds out from under Fin's legs and barrels toward Steve.

I have to give Steve credit—he's steady. He drops to one knee and snags his dog by the collar but somehow manages to keep the taser aimed at Fin even as Lou prances and slobbers and barks and generally acts like a two-year-old buzzing on Halloween candy.

"All right, my hands are up," Fin surrenders, though he's smiling at me. "I'm going to move off Millie. Don't do anything stupid."

Steve ignores the comment and calls for me instead. "Get over here and get behind me."

"Oh, Steve," I say, and I can't hide the amusement as Fin maneuvers his leg over me, dusting me in more shavings. "I'm not going anywhere. Partly because this bed we made is very comfortable, and partly because—well, no, this bed is just cozy."

Steve frowns, and it's his very serious *I'm-trying-to-be-a-big-bad-cop* look.

"A bed? Millie, what is going on? Are you...?"

"High," I say, beaming. "And I don't mean hello."

There were very few times I think I ever surprised Steve—namely, once when I tried to tell him I didn't want two dozen roses for every birthday and Valentine's Day and the only other instance when I brought Lou home.

"Man, put the taser down, and I can explain the rest," Fin starts in, but Steve just tries to point it more forcefully, still wrangling Lou with one hand.

"What did you do to her?"

"Relax, it was Grant's idea."

"Grant?"

"Yeah, your partner? Or ex-partner. Whatever you two like to call yourselves."

"Partner," Steve fills in unnecessarily. "I still consider him my partner."

"Great. Then I'm assuming he's filled you in since you're here and all."

Fin looks at me, and I look at Steve, and I don't need to be sober to catch the distinct stages of confusion, consideration, then understanding playing across their faces.

"Uh-oh," I say, pulling my knees to my chest. "You didn't identify yourself as a cop just now, which means...you're not here on official business, are you?"

"You better be glad because you know I'd have to arrest you after what you just told me."

"But how did you—*oh crap.*"

It clicks at once, and I scramble to get my phone out of my pocket. The screen blinks to life, and I realize I never quite managed to get the thing fully turned off—just silenced. There are ten missed calls, four text messages, and even a few DMs through my social account.

"Your mom called in a panic, Millie," Steve explains, taser still raised at Fin. "She said you declined her call and your location seemed off and she told me everything about this guy you've been hanging out with, and I'm here to tell you he's not who you think he is."

"She made you come home from your trip?"

"She said you were in danger."

"Danger? Why on earth would she think that?"

"Do you know who this is?" Steve demands, and he shakes the taser at Fin again.

"I know exactly who he is, and my mother does not. She doesn't even know his full name. How did you figure that out?"

Steve frowns again, and by now Lou has calmed and is blissfully leaning against Steve's leg accepting head scratches.

"After I got off the phone with your mom, I called Hannah, and, well…"

I scoff. "You used your good-cop charm on her, didn't you?"

"I was trying to look out for you. I had no choice but to ask her about it."

"And she told you?"

"Not everything," Steve says with a grunt.

"But enough?"

"Enough to convince me I needed to see for myself what was really going on."

"Oh. My. God. You didn't."

"What was I supposed to do?"

"Not go snooping through old camera footage to see what your ex-girlfriend was up to."

"The cameras are there for your safety."

"That's not what Hannah said."

Steve just tightens his look, huffing through his nose. I shake my head in disbelief.

"Did you seriously go back and look at the recordings?"

"You brought a criminal into my house, Millie. He was basically waving around his tattoo like he wanted the whole neighborhood to know who he was. It didn't take much deduction to figure out Fin was short for Griffin and then—"

"He's not a criminal—"

"The department's been tracking this guy for months—"

"And *this guy*," Fin cuts in gruffly, "can hear everything you're saying."

Steve and I look his direction, and even Lou perks up at the sound of his voice.

"Buddy, I don't know what information you're still operating off of, but I've been working with Grant since the day you picked up Kai for trespassing."

Steve frowns. "Kai?"

"Yeah, the kid you hauled down to the station and conned into confessing to distribution charges."

Steve's face contorts like one of those abstract portraits by Picasso.

"*You* were the other intruder that night. *You* were the one Grant ran after. He said he lost the guy, but does that mean—he let you go?"

"Glad to see you're not all hot air."

Steve clenches his teeth and jerks the taser, surely wishing it was something a little more threatening. "Why would Grant do that? What did you do to him?"

"I didn't do a damn thing," Fin says, and he finally lowers his hands. "Seems Grant was tired of living in your shadow. Sick of not getting credit for all his work. A little frustrated, even, that you hardly had to put a pair of cuffs on a kid before he was coughing up free tips on closing that Puppy Love case."

"He knew everything! I don't even know how—" Steve cuts himself short, and his brows cinch together as all the pieces start to fall into place. "The only reason Kai knew about the distribution ring, about how it all worked, was because he learned it from *you*."

"Pretty sure he picked it up from a TV show, but that's really not relevant. I wasn't running the drugs. Kai saw me in the exchange with DeLobo's guys, but all I was doing was rescuing a priceless work from their sticky little fingers. If I had known Kai was there..."

Steve shakes his head and glances at me again. "Millie, this man was forging art and laundering money for criminals. How the hell did you get tangled up with him?"

"It doesn't matter," I reply. "What matters is Grant is out there with DeLobo and his cronies right now, and he doesn't have any backup."

"Wait—Grant is here now? With Vincent DeLobo?" Steve asks, his entire tone shifting. "Why would DeLobo be here?"

This time, Fin laughs and he throws his arms out sideways. "Bro, we're standing in a room full of crates filled with Puppy Love. Do I really need to spell it out?"

Steve's shoulders tighten, but he doesn't reply, and Fin barrels on.

"I'm telling you Grant will vouch for everything when this is all said and done, but he's the one who figured out what DeLobo was really doing with these warehouses. He ran an undercover op to expose him. And right now, he's out there trying to bust DeLobo as we speak, and if you're not in on it yet, then we're gonna blow his cover."

Steve gulps audibly. "He's going to need my help."

Fin chuckles. "I really don't think—"

"I've got to get out there. You and you—"

"Okay, really, can you put the taser down?" I demand as he swings the device toward me.

Steve drops his eyes to the weapon as if he just realized he's still holding it and finally lowers it and secures it in his belt.

"Can you watch Lou a little longer?"

"Steve, I don't think it's a good—"

"My partner is in trouble," he interrupts again, "and if you're—well, if you're *indisposed*—I can't risk you being out there with me."

"Steve, let me help you," Fin tries, but Steve just shakes his head and nudges Lou.

"Go with Millie, buddy. I'll be back." He then looks up, swinging his gaze between us. "I'm locking you both in here. Don't do anything or go anywhere until I come back to get you."

I scrunch up my face at Steve. "What on earth would we do?"

His eyes just flick toward Fin.

"Don't worry, man," Fin says. "Sounds like the unarmed, unprepared cop has everything under control. We're not going anywhere."

***

"All right, we're definitely going out there," Fin blurts as soon as the lock clicks into place.

"We're doing what?" I demand, still on the floor running one hand through the pile of wood shavings and the other across Lou's back.

"You heard the guy. He has no idea what the hell he's walking into, and I'm not gonna be the one responsible for getting the good guy killed."

"Killed?" I shriek.

"What do you think will happen when Steve barges in on the biggest drug deal of DeLobo's career?"

"I don't know. A negotiation, I guess."

"With nothing but a taser and ten percent of the story?" Fin challenges.

I purse my lips and frown.

"Millie, he's not going to talk his way out of this one with a feelings stick and good vibes."

I grimace. "Okay, yeah, you're right. He's digging his own grave."

"Thank you," Fin replies smugly, and he stalks over to the door.

I'm just about to ask how the heck he thinks he's going to break us out of this makeshift prison when he slides his fingers across the top of the doorframe and plucks up a key.

"Wait a minute," I say, getting to my feet and brushing the shavings from my clothes. "You've had a way to get us out of here the whole time?"

Fin glances back at me and shrugs. "Did you really want to go anywhere else before now?"

I don't answer except for the smile I can't exactly hide. Lou follows as I get to my feet and keeps close when I sidle up next to Fin.

"Now, when we go out there," Fin says, lowering his voice as he slots the key in the lock, "we're going to be very slow and very quiet. We want the element of surprise here, and—Lou, *no!*"

The door pops open as Fin undoes the lock, and Lou takes the opportunity to nudge his way through the gap. He's gone before Fin even finishes his protest, barreling down the hallway surely in the direction Steve just went.

I'd scream in alarm if not for the fact that it's a little funny Fin has officially graduated to the point in his and Lou's relationship where the person cries helplessly and the dog does whatever the heck he wants.

"What is so funny?" Fin snaps, but I can't even get more than another giggle out before he's grabbing me by the hand and dragging me out of the room.

We sprint—or half run and half stumble—in the direction Lou took off, though he's no longer in sight. It takes a few turns, one entire lap around an open shipping container, and then the sound of people shouting to figure out where he went.

"Lou, stop! Stay!" Steve commands in the distance.

"How'd he get out?" someone else replies, and I think it's DeLobo.

"If you're out," a third voice jumps in, clearly Grant's, "that means—"

"Couldn't miss the party," Fin says proudly as we round the corner.

It's like a cartoon, everyone standing in a circle tossing confused looks at everyone else. DeLobo is on the far end, his cronies sidled to his right and Grant on his left. Grant has his gun raised and aimed at Steve, who's holding his hands in front of his chest, and Fin and I have just rounded out the ring with Lou in the center barking at DeLobo.

"Shut that dog up," DeLobo growls.

Everyone moves at the same time. I think DeLobo's henchmen are planning to physically grab him, but between the rest of us, there isn't a single one who'd stop at anything to keep that from happening.

Grant takes the opportunity to swing his gun at Lars and Murray as they advance while Steve dives for the dog. Meanwhile, Fin rolls into the center almost shielding Steve as he pulls Lou back to the edge of the circle.

"What do you think you're doing?" DeLobo snarls at Grant.

"Come on, man, it's a dog."

"It's the cop's dog," DeLobo adds, and he tosses a look at each of us in turn, like he's trying swiftly to string it all together. Lars and Murray threaten to move, but DeLobo whips an arm out, holding them back. "Don't go anywhere. It seems we have a traitor among us."

"The only traitor is you, DeLobo," Steve adds and he gets back to his feet, posturing at his enemy. "I thought you were the good guy. I thought you were cleaning up this city."

DeLobo sneers. "I've done just that. I've funneled millions into this town."

"By running drugs," Steve cuts back, and then Grant jumps in too.

"You only cleaned up this pier to protect your criminal empire. You didn't want people thinking it was a good place to snoop around."

"I didn't want vagrants running around," DeLobo corrects, and he tosses a look across the circle at Fin, who's stepped back only enough to reach me.

"Vagrants?" Fin replies. "You ran out people who were just trying to survive."

"You didn't have a problem joining me when I tossed a little cash your way, did you?"

Fin bristles, the muscles in his back twitching as his fists clench. "I did what I had to do."

"Once a criminal, always a criminal, right?"

Everyone looks Fin's direction, even Grant, who is still aiming his pistol at the henchmen, and no one speaks, not until DeLobo starts up again.

"How about we make a deal, Griffin Hale, famous art dealer?"

"You're not in a position to make a deal," Fin snaps back.

DeLobo chuckles and glances around the circle. "You may think you turned the bad cop, but I don't see backup. It's four on three, advantage to the guy with the gun, and no one's made a move yet."

Fin glances at Grant, who looks at Steve, and I wonder if the three have just developed their own covert language because I have no idea what any of them is thinking.

"That's what I thought," DeLobo goes on, and he lifts his chin a little higher. "I'll tell you what, I don't need the drugs anymore. They don't move the kind of money your little scam does. I'm willing to give these cops what they want—a whole warehouse full of the big, bad drug they've been trying to get off the street."

"For what?" Fin snaps back.

"For you, of course."

Fin pulls back his shoulders and laughs—a full, enthusiastic laugh. It rumbles in his chest, and I hate that I notice it, but my heightened senses haven't exactly waned yet.

"I'm not going anywhere with you, man. I'm not making art for you anymore. I'm not dealing on the black market for you."

"No?" DeLobo replies, amusement in his tone. "Then I guess I'll just have to recruit one of your protégés. Seems like you've got a whole class of up-and-coming criminals."

"Those kids aren't criminals."

"Not even the one about to do time for my crime?"

DeLobo spits out the comment like venom, and I know it burns right through Fin's skin. He never meant to get Kai in trouble, he never meant to bring any of those kids any closer to crime than they already were, but it's a short distance between where they are now and the tempting life DeLobo would surely offer them.

"I'm not in this business anymore, DeLobo," Fin finally responds, grit in every word. "I'm not coming back to work for you."

The circle seems to exhale collectively, the henchmen chuckling, Grant and Steve sighing, and me letting out a breath I can no longer hold in. DeLobo tsks.

"It's a shame, really. We could have made millions together."

"It's not worth it. You're on your own, DeLobo."

"Then, I guess now is a good a time as any to make sure you know this isn't going to end the way you want."

"It is, DeLobo," Steve tries again, "because you're going to do the right thing. You're going to turn yourself in. You're going to come with us."

"With who? You and two-faced over here?"

DeLobo tosses a look at Grant, who can't hide the shame he's feeling. His cheeks are hollow, his eyes empty, even his shoulders slump, though he still manages to keep the gun raised. Meanwhile, Steve tries to hide the hurt, tries to bottle the sting that's causing him to wince at the thought of his own partner turning on him.

"Officer," DeLobo says as he continues to eye Grant, his voice slick with contempt, "that handgun you're holding is rigged to backfire."

"What?" Grant huffs, but it's obvious there's concern in his voice.

"Standard protocol when I turn a good guy. You remember I had your piece inspected when you joined, right?"

Grant's cheeks flush. "Damn it, DeLobo. You know this is my regular pistol, right? If I fired this gun, are you saying it would have...?"

DeLobo lifts one shoulder in a listless shrug. "A necessary risk."

"I don't believe you."

"Want to take a shot and find out for sure?"

Grant doesn't reply and instead glances sideways at Steve and Fin again.

"I knew what you were from day one," DeLobo goes on. "Desperate to prove yourself. Thinking you can get the one-up on someone like me. You think I don't have contingency plans in place for every shifty cop who's ever tried to chum up to me?"

Grant swallows roughly, and though he doesn't lower his gun, I know he's feeling powerless.

"Every shipment that went out over the past few months has your name on it. I've got video of you letting the criminal who facilitated the sale of millions of dollars of fraudulent artwork get away. Proof you started working with him to crate all those drugs. You take me in and all that evidence showing your undercover op was only invented to hide your trail goes straight to the feds."

"I'm a good cop," Grant argues. "No one will ever believe that."

"I think they will when they realize Detective Steve Rogers was the one signing off as the receiving agent." DeLobo swings his head right to sneer at Steve. "Isn't it true everyone says you're the only guy who can make criminals voluntarily walk right into jail?"

Steve shakes his head, like he wants to argue it, but I know there's no use.

"I think this little conversation is over," DeLobo goes on, returning to face Grant. "You're going to drop your gun, you boys are all going to crawl back from whatever hole you came out of, and we're going to be on our way. Understand?"

"I'm not a boy," I say, though it's under my breath, and Fin reaches back and touches me gently. He thinks it's funny; he just won't admit it.

"You won't get away with this," Steve adds, like he's reciting lines from a movie, and Lou barks as if he's been trained to speak on command in support of his owner.

"Tell that dog to shut up," DeLobo snarls again, and Fin steps forward.

"I got it. You won't hear another word from him."

He relinquishes me and slips a hand in his coat pocket, and before I can even register what on earth his comment means, Fin plucks out a familiar baggie—the one he brought along with him for the road trip to Capitola Beach. He grabs it by the bottom and with a quick flick of his wrist, jerks it backward.

Dog treats scatter everywhere, some of them dinging me in the knees before dropping to the floor, and Lou does exactly what any reasonable human who has ever spent five minutes in his presence would expect him to do: he goes for the goods.

Apparently, it's enough to distract DeLobo and his henchmen as Grant, Fin, and Steve all take the brief moment of confusion to pounce. Grant shoves his gun back in his belt and goes for DeLobo, on whom Fin clearly has his sights set also. Meanwhile, Steve lunges for the pair of cronies, clotheslining both and whirling around to prepare for a hand-to-hand battle.

I crouch to the floor, scooping up as many treats as I can and luring Lou away from the commotion just as Fin lands a fist in DeLobo's gut. Grant follows it up with one to the cheek, and Steve is still alternating swings between Lars and Murray.

"Griffin—on your left!" Steve yells, just as one sidekick slips away.

Fin ducks a swing from Lars and kicks out a foot that brings the towering criminal to the ground, then scowls at Steve. "Bro, it's just Fin."

"Can we do introductions later?" Grant says with a grunt, landing a blow that causes DeLobo to double over and then trading spots with Fin.

Fin takes the opportunity to slip an arm under DeLobo's pit and secures it behind his neck, effectively immobilizing him.

"You know the guy's been over to my house already, right?" Steve says, ducking the second sidekick and finally getting a grip on his wrist. He pulls his arm up tight and then nudges him in the back of the knees until he collapses.

"Oh yeah," Grant says and thumps down on Lars's back, just as he tries to stand again. "Millie told me about that."

"She told you?" Steve asks, and by now his opponent is handcuffed.

"You're not the only one who's easy to talk to," Grant says with a smirk, and he tightens handcuffs around Lars too.

"I really hope you guys aren't fighting over my girlfriend," Fin jumps in, and he simultaneously firms up his grip on DeLobo, who drops to his knees.

"Girlfriend?" Steve says.

"They are kind of cute together, aren't they?" Grant adds.

"Cute? We're goddamn adorable," Fin finishes, and then all three look at me.

I'm speechless. Clearly. Have been for, like, five minutes while these three bunglers casually clinched a win over each opponent in the midst of an entire conversation. I open my palm, letting the last of the treats tumble out as Lou snatches up each piece and then greedily licks for crumbs.

Then, I glance up at Fin, who's beaming over a grunting DeLobo, and say the first thing that comes to mind: "Oh my god. I'm dating an insane person."

Thirty-Four

"You three bozos ready for a ride in the back of a cop car?" Steve asks, jerking Murray back to his feet. Grant follows suit with Lars, and Fin definitely takes pleasure in tightening his grip on DeLobo.

"It's really not as bad as I thought it'd be," Fin adds.

"How about you join us, then?" DeLobo snarls in return, his lip bleeding from where someone landed a fist.

Fin scoffs, but neither Steve nor Grant says anything else. I simply grab Lou's rope-leash, which is trailing behind him as he sniffs at my feet for more errant treats, and hope I can find my way back out of this maze of a warehouse.

I know Grant's car can fit at least two of them, and assuming Steve came straight here in his Charger, one criminal will ride low-security. As for Fin and me, I suppose that means we get the passenger seat in either vehicle.

Lou, on the other hand, might have to ride on the roof. It's one thing to haul him up on my lap in my SUV but a whole other challenge to do that in a sedan outfitted with a laptop, radio kit, and half a dozen other—

"Cap! You found her!" a voice shrieks, and it's one that definitely shouldn't be here.

I whip my head up, apparently having crossed the entire warehouse and opened the door outside while debating seating arrangements, only to find both Hannah and my mom zipping out from behind another officer. Or, another *wall* of officers.

"Cap?" Grant echoes.

"Cap," Steve repeats.

And I know it has nothing to do with Steve's nickname.

A man steps forward, crisp navy blues and two gold bars across his chest, and he's got a gun raised.

"On your knees, hands behind your head—all of you."

Lou whines as I drop to the asphalt automatically, still grasping his leash while I weave my fingers together.

I think about arguing. I think about telling this man—who I know to be Steve and Grant's boss—or any other cop who will listen exactly what happened because there are a lot of criminals here, and I don't think I'm one of them, but the protest doesn't even make it to the tip of my tongue.

As DeLobo, Lars, and Murray comply, the captain trains his gun on Fin.

"You too, Hale."

I think Fin looks at me. It's quick, hardly a flash in my direction, but I feel it in my bones. I feel the shame and the regret and the sorrow, and I think I finally understand the urge to break the rules. I understand the need for chaos, the compulsion for thievery, because I want to spring to my feet, grab him by the hand, and run.

I'd break every law not to watch those cops slap cuffs on his wrists, drag him up by the elbows, and shove him in the back of a cruiser, blue and red lights whirring incessantly. I'd do it for him, but he shakes his head.

I'm not sure how long it takes or if people are talking because I don't hear a thing. I don't *feel* anything until someone is pulling me back to my feet, taking Lou's leash from my hands, and wrapping an arm around me.

"I'm sorry, Millie," Steve says, and it's right in my ear.

"Do something! Make them stop. He helped you! He can't go—he can't—" But the words falter on a muffled sob as Steve pulls me in harder. "You—you did this, didn't you? This is *your* fault."

I push back against Steve's chest as he frowns down at me.

"Millie, I had no choice—"

"You turned him in! You led the cops straight to him. You—"

"No, Millie, *you* did."

The accusation rattles the air, and Steve finally lets go, finally takes a full step back. Hannah, who's been fidgeting with Lou's leash, gently touches my shoulder, and even Grant and my mom look on speechless.

I take one last glance as the back door of the police car slams shut, one last look as the past two weeks seem to whisk away.

Fin doesn't bother looking up.

***

The rest of the night is a blur.

My mom drives Hannah, me, and Lou back to her house. I can only assume Hannah agreed to take Lou for a few more hours, but I don't care enough to ask. My mom serves up her lasagna, I pick at my salad, and the news plays on a seemingly endless loop in the background.

I catch bits and pieces about what they're dubbing one of the biggest raids in department history and how one of their newest detectives so bravely called for backup on a rogue-bust-gone-wrong. There's a report of ransom money tied up in evidence and real estate on the pier being seized by the authorities.

I don't catch anything on recovered art or that infamous half lion-half eagle signature, but I try not to listen for it either. All week, I ignore updates from my podcast and phone calls from Steve and Grant, and I even send my realtor to voicemail three times. The only person who manages to get through is Hannah and it's only because she agrees to play hooky with me on Friday and have a movie marathon, with *Trader* being the first play of course.

"Did you know this couch is horrible?" Hannah asks, kicking a leg up on the armrest and sinking between two nearly flat cushions.

I keep my eyes trained on the Saturday morning news, which is really just a talk show at this point. "It was *supposed* to be temporary."

"And now?"

"I'm going to die in this apartment."

"Oh, come on, you don't really think your offer's going to fall through on the new house, do you?"

I swing my head her direction, though I don't make much other effort to move from my stretched-out position on the couch. "I *guarantee* my offer is going to fall through."

"Just because you don't have a down payment anymore?"

"*Precisely* because I don't have a down payment anymore. Do I need to explain how mortgage loans work?"

"Please spare me," Hannah says with an exaggerated gag, and she tosses the blanket she's been under onto the coffee table. "Come on, we need to get out of this place."

I try to sink a little deeper into the wafer-thin cushions. "I'm not going anywhere."

"It's Saturday. Won't your insides turn to mush if you don't have that gross green smoothie you love?"

"My insides are just fine."

"Your insides have been neglected for a week. Plied with pizza and ramen and"—she swipes up a torn-open bag that's fallen under the coffee table—"gummy worms, of all things. When did you start eating these, by the way?"

I snatch the bag from her grip and shove it between the couch cushions. "It's not relevant."

Hannah just hums in exaggerated disappointment, springs up from the couch, and swipes up my blanket next. "I watched *Trader* three times in one day without complaining. You can get your butt off the couch and take me to the smoothie cart."

"Oh, so it's about you now?"

"If that gets you up, then yes."

"Hardly," I groan in return, though I do drop my feet to the floor.

My apartment looks like an entire classroom of twelve-year-olds had a weeklong sleepover. Candy wrappers dot the floor, half-drunk soda is abandoned on the TV stand, chocolate chips are smooshed into the carpet—though that was at least Hannah's doing. She made it through about fifteen minutes of the documentary before volunteering to bake cookies again. They didn't turn out black this time, but I'm not convinced they weren't compromised in some other manner. I didn't try them to find out for sure.

"You know, we could go see Fin if you want," Hannah offers, too candidly.

"Where? In *prison*?"

She shrugs. "They have visiting hours."

I shove my hair back and tug on the oversize T-shirt I've been swimming in for the past several days. "Hannah, I ruined his life. He was just fine before me, and I—"

"Well..." Hannah mumbles, grimacing, "he was scamming a drug dealer."

"And that's all anyone will ever see now."

"Is that why you haven't gone yet? You're scared of what it will look like?"

"No," I say, surprisingly easily, but I disappear into my room to change into something halfway acceptable for a smoothie run. I've got patterned leggings and a sweater on when I come back out to the living room, where Hannah is pulling on jeans and a jacket.

"I can call Grant," she offers, grabbing our purses from the counter. "I'm sure he'll tell us what's going on, help us get in to see him."

"You think he really wants to see me? After I led the cops straight to his doorstep? And then let my ex-boyfriend turn him in?"

"I'm sure that's not how he sees it."

"I have ruined every relationship I've been in, Hannah. You've said it yourself."

She opens her mouth, though nothing but a long sigh spills out.

"It was fun while it lasted, okay?" I say, finally heading toward the door and grabbing the handle. "But I just don't see how we could ever get past—"

"Oh, hi," someone says as I swing the door open wide.

He's taller than me by at least a foot, but he can't be any older than eighteen, still with round cheeks and long-lashed eyes.

"I was just about to knock. Are you...Millicent?"

My hand falls to my side and I'm pretty sure my heart sinks all the way to the floor.

Hannah sidles up next to me, eyeing the kid. "Who's asking?"

"You don't know me, but I'm—"

"Kai."

The name practically jumps out of my mouth, and I think it surprises me more than him. He just smiles sweetly, a single dimple puckering one cheek.

"You know each other?" Hannah asks, waving a finger between us before shielding her mouth and mumbling at me. "Girl, if you wanted to commit a crime, this really isn't the one. He doesn't even look legal."

She whispers the last sentence, and I have to brush her off. "He's not. Seventeen, right?"

Kai nods when I look at him.

"How much did he tell you about me?" he asks.

"Probably more than you want."

Kai just nods again and then lifts up something in his hands. It's a couple feet wide, not quite as tall, and a few inches deep, wrapped in brown craft paper.

"I was asked to bring this to you," he says. "It's a housewarming gift."

I let out a short laugh. "I really don't think—"

"Fin insisted."

The name seems to skip through my brain, causing a few nerves to fire, and I try to keep them from spilling into tears or protests or pleas of insanity and instead hurry to take the gift from Kai's hands.

"Fin sent you?" Hannah jumps in again, and I see the confusion practically carving wrinkles into her pale skin. "Are you...? Is he...?"

Hannah swings her attention back to me, and I nod. At my mom's on Sunday, I did manage to spill the whole story about how Kai confessed to a crime he thought Fin committed, how Fin was working for DeLobo to raise the funds to pay for Kai's lawyer and a new art space, and how all of it seemed so anti-criminal to me. Mercifully, neither challenged my opinion, but it didn't matter anyway. I told them whatever happened—whatever was going to become of Fin—it didn't involve any version of *us*.

"I would have brought this over sooner, but it wasn't quite done," Kai goes on.

I glance down at the package again. "Sooner?"

"I picked it up Sunday night," Kai explains, "before the cops could get to his place. I'm pretty sure they took just about every piece of art in there since it's almost impossible to tell what's real and what's not. But this one—"

"This one's an original," I guess, though I don't dare peel back the paper. "Why are you really here, Kai? There's no way you're just running errands for—"

"That's exactly what I'm doing," he interrupts and he shoves his hands in his black jeans. "My lawyer called me on Monday and said I was cleared of all charges. They knew my confession was fake. They had the guy responsible."

My throat constricts, wrung like a wet towel.

"Anyway, a couple of us took the liberty to finish the piece for you. It didn't seem right giving you something for a new house that was only half done. Is this the new place, by the way?"

"No," I say quickly, still gripping the package uneasily. "I'm not sure there will be a new place. How did you even get this address?"

He shrugs and finds a spot on the floor to stare at. "I had a couple guys who owed me a favor."

"A couple guys?" Hannah repeats.

"They gave you my *home address*?" I demand.

"Yeah, okay, I see how that's a little sketchy now."

"It was Steve, wasn't it?" Hannah says, and she crosses her arms like playing hardball is her favorite game.

"Uh, yeah, I can't give up my sources."

"I'm going to kill him," I spit through gritted teeth, and Kai takes a short step back and raises his hands as I swing my attention toward Hannah. "We're going to his house first."

"I don't think that'll be necessary," Hannah says, and her terse look quickly morphs to a sheepish grin.

"Hannah, what did you do?"

"You were so sad."

"And you think Steve is going to make that better? How many times do I have to tell you—"

"Not Steve," she jumps in. "Lou."

"Lou?"

"Come on. It's Saturday. Smoothies and dog park day. And we all know it's not nearly as much fun without an actual dog to take to the dog park."

"Hannah, you *have* to stop volunteering to dogsit."

"I didn't! We're just meeting them there."

I growl a long, pained *whhhyyy* and jerk my head between Hannah and Kai, expecting at least one of them to say something that makes sense, but neither does. Instead, Kai just says his goodbyes and Hannah shoos me out of the apartment.

I consider driving us the opposite direction, hitting the freeway and heading as far east as I can go, but chewing out Steve for trading my address to repay a debt is just a little more tempting. In fact, I've got a whole week of rage ready to unbottle all over his perfect life with Seph—who apparently came back from Sonoma with another three-figure sale and trophy to match—and I almost make it.

I complain all the way to the cart, the entire wait in line, drop an extra five-dollar tip in the Superman side of the tip jar, and don't even stop to breathe until that gate clicks behind us at the park.

I see Lou before I see anyone else—or rather, he sees me. His tail wags so hard his butt sways to both sides, and then he takes off at a gallop. Hannah swoops in to grab my drink just before Lou plants his muddy paws all over my leggings.

I wish I could be mad—and not at Lou. I want to be mad because I want everyone to understand just how unfair it is to have something you didn't know you wanted robbed right from your hands. I want them to know I'm not here to appease them, but the anger seems to evaporate with every lick and whine and eager, drool-filled nudge.

I knead my fingers behind Lou's ears, give him an air-kiss, and plan to wrangle him in for a full-bodied hug, when he does a complete one-eighty and bolts back the direction he came from.

I spot Steve then, standing next to Seph and Grant, and I climb back to my feet and stomp my hardest in their direction. Finger in the air, face screwed up in anger, I formulate the most scathing accusation, letting it tumble to the tip of my tongue before it completely and utterly fizzles.

"Remind me never to get on your bad side."

"Fin?" I say on a gasp.

I don't know how I didn't see him before, how I missed that familiar backwoods-dairy-farmer-meets-solitary-city-boy look, but he moves out from behind Steve and settles his hands in his Carhartt pockets, fixing a smirk on his face I think I've only seen once before.

"What are you doing here?"

"Currently?" Fin says, crouching to the ground. "I'm being put to work petting this pup."

Lou pounces for Fin as I struggle to get a dozen other questions out, and he rubs up against Fin's knees. Fin gives him a pat on the head and then looks toward Steve.

"I'm sorry, Millie, for how everything went down last weekend," Steve says, and then Grant steps forward.

"We worked out a deal. Sprung this guy from the clink last night."

"You did what?" I demand, and by now Hannah's returned to my side, and I train my glare on her. "Just this morning you said—"

"I didn't want to spoil the surprise," she jumps in, grinning giddily at me. "Figured a dog park meetup was as good a place as any for a little reunion, huh?"

Her words don't seem to land, and I have to look back at Fin to make sure he's still there, make sure he hasn't just evaporated on thin air, a vision I only imagined was real.

"Millie," Fin speaks up again, getting back to his feet. "I understand if you don't want to see me, if you don't want to have anything to do with me, but I couldn't not try."

"Not try?" I say, huffing out a despondent breath. "Not try? Fin, oh my god, I left you in jail all week!"

"Yeah, I guess I wasn't sure why you didn't try to bail me out."

"I thought you hated me!"

"How could I possibly—"

"I got you *imprisoned.*"

"Can we keep our voices down?" he says, raising two hands and casting an awkward glance at a couple who skirts the long way around our group. "So this is an incredibly awkward conversation to be having in front of all of your friends, but—"

"*Friends*?" I cut in again, and I'm pretty sure I won't be able to utter another sentence without dramatic emphasis, but I try anyway. "Have you people been in on this all week? And you didn't tell me? What is *wrong* with you?"

"Whoa, whoa," Steve starts.

"That's not exactly how it happened," Hannah says.

"It was an accidental deal?" Grant adds, more a question than anything.

"Oh, for crying out loud," Seph jumps in, and I finally fix my attention on her. Her ashy-brown hair glides along her shoulders as she shakes her head. "These boys thought they were doing the right thing by keeping you out of it. I tried telling them it was a horrible idea, but no, they wouldn't listen to me."

"Seph, you suggested we bring Millie down to the station as soon as we arrested Fin," Steve says.

"You should have!" I cry, and Seph just tosses Steve an *I-told-you-so* look. "Was this the plan all along? Did you already have a deal set?"

"Okay, it wasn't a deal so much as a last-ditch effort," Steve admits.

Meanwhile, Grant claps a hand to his shoulder. "You wouldn't believe it, but this guy marched right into the captain's office and outright *lied*."

"What?" I glance between Fin, Steve, Seph, and Grant. No one seems to argue the point.

Steve sighs heavily and glances down at Lou, who is making the rounds, begging for attention from everyone. "Millie, it was my fault half the department showed up in the first place. I thought you were in trouble, so I called in backup as soon as I figured out where you were. I had no idea what was really going on."

"I tried telling you," Fin says under his breath, but Steve ignores it and continues.

"I didn't *lie* to the captain so much as backed up my partner, okay?"

"I see how much I matter to you," Grant says with a sarcastic huff, and Steve smirks at him.

"I told the captain I knew about Grant's undercover op, that he had enlisted Fin for help, and without him"—Steve jerks his chin toward Fin—"we never would have busted DeLobo and his guys."

"Oh my god, you did lie."

"I really don't like that word," Steve goes on.

"If it helps, you can just call it an alternate portrayal," Fin offers. "An anti-replication, if you will."

"What have all of you done?"

"To be fair," Grant says, "your guy didn't get off totally free."

"Yeah, I do owe restitution in the form of several thousand dollars."

"What?" I demand, but he just shrugs.

"I did bend a few rules."

"But you—you're here."

"Ain't that something?" he says with a laugh.

For what feels like the tenth time, I look around the circle, eyeing Steve and Seph, Grant and Hannah, Lou—who's now moping at Fin's feet—and Fin again.

"I don't understand," I say. "What does this mean?"

"Well, as I mentioned earlier, this is incredibly awkward having this whole conversation in front of your friends," Fin says, and he pauses deliberately to toss another glance around the circle. When no one moves, he jerks. "Can I have a minute alone with her or what?"

"Oh, right, yeah," Steve mumbles.

"Of course," Grant adds.

"Come on, Lou," Hannah calls, and he trots off with her after the others as they meander down one of the well-worn paths.

Fin turns back to me and then nods toward a nearby bench. "Will you take a seat for a minute?"

I do so silently because I'm still not sure this entire encounter is real, let alone the person standing in front of me, but he takes a seat on the bench too, and when his hand brushes my knee, I know. I *know* it's real.

"I messed up, Millie—I know that—and I honestly deserve to be locked up in a cell right next to DeLobo himself. I'll even walk myself right back to the station if that's what you want, but—"

"Fin," I say, his name hardly a whisper, but he just shakes his head and continues.

"You asked me the night we lost Lou if this was a scam, if I somehow tricked you, and I need you to know without a shadow of a doubt that all of this has been real. Very real. I don't think I knew it right away, but I know it now. I like you, Millie. I want to be with you. I want to take you on a real goddamn date every night for the rest of—"

He stops abruptly, and I can feel my breath spill out of my lungs.

"For the rest of what?" I ask.

"Well, I mean—how long does it take for you to forgive a criminal?"

"Fin, I ruined you," I counter, the admission nearly splitting open that wound again. "I got you arrested. I was selfish and impatient and messed up a perfectly good thing."

The words stumble on the way out as Fin frowns, shakes his head fervently, and moves closer.

"Are you kidding? You *saved* me. If it weren't for you, I never would have quit. I never would have had a reason to. And if that's not the most selfless thing you could have done, I don't know what is.

"Millie, I know you think you're the guilty one here—it's been all over your face since the day I met you—but I'm telling you right now, you're ten times the superhero Steve wishes he could be, and I'm going to take you on a date so I can tell you that every damn day until you believe it."

I do nothing but blink, and Fin cocks his head.

"And then, probably a few more dates for good measure because lord only knows how long it'll take you to forget I was once a prolific art forger."

"Replicator," I say automatically, and Fin grins.

"I'm cashing in my favor, by the way," he says, and he scoots even closer, his knee brushing up against mine.

"Who said you had a favor to cash in?"

"You did when I faked that painting for you."

"That was clearly an exchange of services. I paid you for that."

"No, that was definitely a favor."

"I think you're gravely mistak—"

"How many days are in two-and-half weeks?" Fin cuts in, and he reaches for my hand.

It's warm and surprisingly soft, and I wonder how quickly he's going to rough them up again by chopping wood or slinging paint or doing whatever it is he plans to do to pay back the mountain of debt he apparently owes.

"Seventeen-and-a-half," I reply skeptically. "But I think you know that."

"Just giving you the opportunity to demonstrate your math skills."

I roll my eyes. "What's at the end of seventeen-and-a-half days?"

"That's when my houseboat will finally be released from evidence."

"They seized the whole boat?"

"Real, live caution tape and all," he says, squeezing my hand. "They're offloading evidence or whatever they're looking for, so I am technically homeless until then."

"Wait just a minute. Are you asking to stay with me? Is *that* the favor?"

"It doesn't have to mean anything. We've slept together without sleeping together."

"And that's what you want?"

Fin scoffs dramatically. "Of course not, but I think I'd be kind of an ass if I expected that."

"You would."

"Come on, I think I'm pretty entertaining to have around," Fin says, a tempting smile turning up the corners of his lips. "Besides, I heard you're going to have a pretty nice house here in another week."

"Ha!" I toss my head back. "You want to know what else is tied up in evidence? My down payment."

"I wouldn't be so sure about that, but I'm getting ahead of myself here," Fin says, and he finally lets me go and slaps his hands to his knees. "Millie, I may have been a *little* inebriated and, you know, tied up in some questionable circumstances last time we talked, but I'm telling you I'm stone-cold sober now, and I mean every word I said. I like you. Hell, I'd tell you I love you, but something makes me think you'd like that about as much as a dozen roses."

"I don't hate it," I admit before I can stop myself.

"Progress," Fin hums. "Now, I'll ask you one more time: Can I move in with you-slash-take you on a date-slash-try to keep you out of jail for the foreseeable future?"

Another laugh tumbles from my lips. "Do you really think you're that good?"

"Oh, Millie, we both know I'm that good."

And he is.

He's got me wrapped up in a kiss before I can utter another word, and it's everything I didn't know I needed. It feels like the day on the beach, the night in that hotel, the morning I woke up next to Fin, the water rocking underneath us and his arm stretched across my stomach.

"I was beginning to think you'd never come around," Fin says, nuzzling into my neck, his breath stirring my hair. "Millie, I'm so sor—"

"We don't like that word, remember?" I hurriedly cut in, leaning back just enough to press a finger to his lips.

"Only when it's used to apologize for who you are."

"Which was definitely what you were going to apologize for, right? Being a criminal and all?" I press a quick kiss to his lips before pulling back. "By the way, if you're supposedly homeless, where did you stay last night after you got bailed out?"

"It's funny," he says, though his laugh is a little forced. "Didn't have a whole lot of options, so I slept on Steve's couch."

"You didn't."

"He offered. Besides, it's pretty damn comfortable."

"Yeah, I know that, but—"

"Can we just not talk about him right now? Not exactly over the whole getting-arrested bit yet."

Another laugh spills from my lungs, but Fin silences it, crushing his lips to mine again. I don't know where Steve or Seph are, if Hannah and Grant still have Lou, and whether we're officially *those people* in the dog park that everyone else comes here to stare at, but I don't care either.

I know what I want, and this is it.

Thirty-Five

A Few Weeks Later

"So, did DeLobo ever get all the evidence to the feds?" Hannah asks, stabbing her fork into the mound of lasagna my mom served up.

"You mean the security tapes and shipment manifests?" Grant confirms, waving his fork in the air. "It made it to the feds all right. Apparently DeLobo had a failsafe in place, and they were calling me up about two seconds after we slapped those cuffs on him."

"So they believed it?" she goes on.

"It made for a long afternoon where I had to do a whole lot of explaining, but no, they didn't."

"Not even with Steve's name signed to it?"

"Not you too?" he claps back, and she sneers playfully at him as he nudges her under the table.

"The captain cleared up any misconceptions," Steve adds in, scraping up the last bits of pasta on his plate. Grant makes a tsking noise, but Steve doesn't notice. "He also helped clear Kai's name—you know, the kid I picked up."

"The one you were distraught about because Dingus over here was too busy making deals with a criminal to vouch for the kid?" Hannah elaborates, and I swear Grant doesn't even flinch at the insult. In fact, he's smiling at her.

"Everything worked out," Grant says.

"How do you figure?" Fin demands, feigning amusement, and everyone swivels his direction.

He finished his lasagna in about two bites but has been waiting patiently, watching the rest of us. I tap my fingers to his knee under the table now because he's here and he's mine and that's what good girlfriends do, right?

"I still had to pay bail," Fin goes on. "Lost the retainer I coughed up for his lawyer. And my kid's now seen the inside of a jail cell."

"He did confess all on his own," Steve points out.

"To protect you," Grant adds.

"That doesn't make it any better."

"It doesn't," Grant agrees, "but he's also got a free ride to the academy now. Him and every one of your kids in that little class of yours."

"That on your dime?"

"We all know the money you spent wasn't even yours to begin with so—"

"Not the point."

"Fine," Grant says with a huff, leaning back in his seat and gripping the armrests. "I was going to wait to tell you this but given you're not the most patient person in the world, here it is: the department seized all of DeLobo's old warehouses and is donating one back to the community as a shared art space. It opens next month."

Fin shakes his head and glances at me before eyeing Grant again. "You're screwing with me."

"Wish I were," Grant says dryly, though he can't hide the smile turning up his lips.

"Shit. That's pretty damn cool," Fin says.

"You're welcome."

"I wasn't thanking you."

"How about some more lasagna, boys?" my mom offers up too enthusiastically, and she pushes the glass dish across the table we're all crammed around. "Grant, take seconds. Fin, you too. And Steven, I know you'll need to get your energy back up after such a heroic rescue."

Everyone at the table—except Steve—rolls their eyes. Even Seph, who is seated next to me.

Our casual friendship sort of just happened after the meetup at the dog park. As we all watched Lou pounce around with a lady bulldog, Seph casually let slip that she'd been sitting outside in Steve's car the entire time the drug bust went down. She was so thrilled to have been a "part" of the action, she went home and made coordinating T-shirts in various shades of pink for herself, Hannah, and me.

Believe it or not, there's a glitter-clad image of a wineglass filled with tiny white pills on the front, and under the image, pinot-red font that says, "Rosé or Bust."

She was wearing the tee when the news crews showed up at her and Steve's house shortly after the arrests were made, and she felt rightfully snuffed when she didn't get a feature. Steve, on the other hand, got a solid ten minutes of airtime.

He insists he gave credit to Grant, but somehow their captain and any news reporter who would listen seemed to think Steve stormed the entire operation in a valiant attempt to free Grant from a quickly deteriorating bust.

"You know it's all in a day's work, Goldie," Steve goes on, helping himself to the lasagna and beaming proudly, and that's when Lou finally perks up.

He's been under the table the whole time but lets out a pitiful whine to remind everyone of his presence.

"That's right, boy," Steve coos, more to the table at large. "I've said it all along: we couldn't have done it without Grant."

"Save it," Grant growls in return, smacking Steve's fork with his and taking the newly cut portion for himself. "I know that's not what the dog said. He's been sleeping at Fin's feet all afternoon."

Fin glances under the table as if he hasn't noticed, but I know he has. He's been sneaking a hand under the tablecloth slipping the dog scraps of bread the entire meal.

"Couldn't tell ya why," Fin lies, and Grant just shakes his head.

"Steve, if you didn't come home when you did, that pup of yours probably would have moved into the houseboat."

"Would have sunk the houseboat, more like," Steve jokes.

"You know, it's sturdier than you think," Fin argues. "Millie and I just got back into the place and took several days to stress-test the whole—"

"All righty then," I blurt, slapping a hand down on Fin's. "No one needs the details."

Hannah chuckles. "You were stress-testing it for all the renovations, right?"

"Of course," Fin says, frowning at her like there couldn't possibly be any other explanation. "The place hasn't been updated since the sixties, and Millie wanted a little space that wasn't her house or her office or her office in her house."

"Anyway," Grant goes on, "all I'm saying, Steve, is that you should probably be thanking Fin too for helping with *your* little drug bust."

"Right. Fin," Steve says, clearing his throat. "Now that everything's settled, I should apologize for the way I, uh, treated you."

"You mean when you busted down the door of that storage room and threatened me with a taser?" Fin asks, and he leans back in his chair, draping a hand over the back of mine.

"I was acting on the information I had at the moment."

"Which was wholly inaccurate."

"Well, you are technically a crimin—"

"*Steve*," Seph scolds, and I'm pretty sure she pinches his leg under the table. "Fin, here, seems like an incredibly loyal and trustworthy person. I think a few bad calls can be forgiven."

Steve drops his fork to whip his gaze around the table before turning back to her. "A few bad calls? You do know what happened while we were gone, right? He came over to the house to—*ouch.*"

Hannah sits up, a stern glare on her face, clearly having just kicked Steve under the table. "Weren't you going to tell us about the rest of your trip to Sonoma? Surely you and Seph had a wonderful time researching rosé grapes."

Steve frowns and falls silent, crossing his hands on his lap.

Next to me Fin sighs. "Thanks, Hannah, but Steve's right about this one."

"I don't care how right he is," she counters, turning that mulish look up to ten. "If rosé grapes are involved, there's only one expert at the table. Let's just hear from Seph, okay?"

Seph perks up, pulling back her shoulders. "You really want to hear about wine?"

"Of course we do," Hannah fibs, and there's a general murmur of assent around the table.

"I can't believe I'm going to be the first one to tell all of you this, but"—she leans forward, pressing her hands together giddily—"there's no such thing as rosé grapes."

"You don't say!" Hannah gasps.

"How about that?" Grant adds, slapping his thigh.

"News to us all!" I pitch in, and then my mom gently dabs her lips with the napkin and sets it down.

"Oh, Seph, honey, don't tell me you thought—"

"She *is* the expert," Steve interrupts, and he tosses a polite, though unmistakable warning glance at my mom.

Next to me, Fin shakes his head, and he finally sits forward so he has a clearer view around me. "Seph, I don't know why everyone at this table is being so damn phony, but I'm not in the con business anymore. I need to tell you something about your painting—the one with the rosé grapes."

"Again, Fin," she says, raising a hand delicately, "they really are just pink grapes, and I sold it anyway."

"Wait—what?" I blurt.

"You sold it?" Hannah clarifies.

"My masterpiece?" Fin demands, though I think Seph totally misses it.

"I spent a pretty penny on that," Steve adds sullenly.

"Honey," she says, patting him on the chest soothingly, "it's just a painting, and honestly, I got a fortune for it."

"You sold it for money?" Grant demands, sitting forward in his chair. "Like to a real person?"

"Oh, don't be silly. I sold it to an art gallery. They paid double what Steve originally bought it for. Said it was the best Jean-Luc Pompo work they'd ever seen."

"Oh my god," Fin mutters, and everyone else except for my mom mumbles something similar.

In the week following the bust, Grant debriefed Steve on the entire unsanctioned operation, including everything I had told him about how I met Fin in the first place. I filled my mom in on all of the non-illegal details and Hannah managed to get up-to-speed on the parts she didn't know herself, apparently having met up with Grant at some point and forcing the entire story out of him.

So the only people at this table who have no idea Seph committed a crime are Seph herself and my mother—the one who is now pushing more salad across the table and urging Seph to detail every single moment of the extremely pricey deal.

It goes on for about fifteen minutes as Seph turns out to be a very thorough storyteller, and not a second goes by that someone isn't cringing or trying to drown their unease with a cough or otherwise withering under the realization we're all accomplices to art forgery.

"So, uh, Millie," Grant steps in as soon as there's a lull in the dialogue, "how about those penises on the side of the house?"

I set my fork down and smile. "You noticed them, huh?"

"Hard to miss," he says with a laugh.

It turns out the two-and-half weeks Fin supposedly needed to stay with me was just enough time for my funds to get released from evidence and redeposited into my bank account. In the interim, he managed to track down the sellers of my dream house, convince my lender the newly deposited cash wasn't at all shady, stolen, or otherwise, and simultaneously explain to my realtor that—*oops!*—I mistyped that email and meant to say I'd *found* my fortune, not lost it.

I didn't discover what he was doing until my realtor called me up asking if I'd changed my email to *SillyMillieFindsAFortune* at gmail dot com.

"You know, there's a reason I asked all of you to do Sunday night dinner at my new house instead of my mom's place this week," I go on.

"I figured my place was just getting a little cramped," my mom adds innocently.

"Didn't you want to show us the new office space?" Seph guesses.

"We all know we're just here so you can brag about that painting Kai delivered," Hannah says.

"It is amazing," I agree, and I glance toward the sliding glass door at the back of my house.

I can't see it from here, but it's on the wall, just above my desk. I didn't open it until closing day, though I wish I had done it sooner. It was the painting of Capitola Beach that Kai had taken from Fin's place, and he and some of the other kids who were mentored by Fin finished it with their own flair.

Instead of one almost impossible-to-replicate color, there are dozens. Shades of ice blue and soft pink I've never seen, vibrant greens that seem to scream violet, reds that feel more like deep, dark copper. It's Capitola in a kaleidoscope of color.

"The full house tour happens when the sun goes down," I confirm, "but we've got one thing that has to happen before then. Fin, we've got all we need, right?"

He pushes back from his chair and pops a kiss on my lips before rounding the table and disappearing behind the other side of the house, the one that wasn't carelessly vandalized. There's a distinct clank of metal on wood and the rustle of goods shifting in a paper bag and then he reappears, paint can in one hand, rollers in the other, and a bag of brushes, sponges, and more caution tape than we could ever have use for tucked under an arm.

"No way," Grant protests.

"You can't be serious," Steve adds.

"I did not sign up for this," Hannah says.

Lou scrambles out from under the table and gives a loud, encouraging bark. Fin winks at him, then smiles at me, before turning back to the rest of the crew.

"It's high time I teach all you city folk how to paint."

Epilogue

A Few Months Later

"Where did you get that?" I ask as I shut the car door and round the back.

Fin is closing the trunk and shaking out a dark-blue quilted coat. He frowns at me and shoves his tattooed arm in its sleeve first, then the other. It's tasteful—the coat—neatly stitched and short-collared with something that looks a lot like sheepskin inside.

"The store. Where else?" he says, shaking his shoulders until it settles over the flannel underneath.

I hitch a brow, putting on my best skeptical look.

"What?" he says with a huff. "I never did get my peacoat back from that rather unpleasant woman who was working the coat check at the gallery. I needed a replacement."

"What's wrong with your Carhartt?"

"To meet your dad for the first time? Please. I'm not gonna show up in my workwear."

"Oh, did you think you'd get out of working on this trip?"

"Aren't we only here for a day?" Fin asks, and his cheeks flush.

I'm sure it's a teensy bit to do with feeling nervous, but I'm also guessing the handsome, frigid-weather coat he's sporting in the balmy heat of late May in Iowa isn't helping much either.

"Come on," I say, lacing my fingers in his before he can ruffle the hair he spent twenty minutes fixing at our last rest stop. "I bet he's already in the barn."

We parked in front of the main residence, a quaint, three-bedroom farmhouse painted white on the outside and surely still a confusing shade of blue-green-yellow on the inside—in my old room at least. I think my dad insisted on leaving it that way so one day I'd grow up and learn a valuable lesson in sensibility. Which maybe I did, or maybe I didn't. It's hard to tell these days.

"Lou! Not the chickens! The chickens are *not* toys!" I yell just as he bounds across the lawn and toward a flock of grazing birds.

They squabble—a horrible, cackling sound—and loose feathers swirl in the air in their flightless attempts to dodge him. I'm pretty sure Lou gets a taste of at least one scaly foot before it's Kai who finally catches up to him.

"My bad, Millie," he calls back to me, lunging for the dog and hauling him back a foot so the birds can scamper across the yard. "I turn my back on this monster one second..."

"One second is far too long," I mumble, though I can't exactly blame him.

I hadn't even noticed Kai let Lou out of the car since I was busy harassing Fin over his outfit choice. I should have known he would: the kid's spent three days sharing the backseat with the beast as we drove literally halfway across the country, so they've grown pretty close.

Together, the three of us and Lou cross the yard and head toward the milking parlor. It's an isolated barn, smaller than the neighboring two, but it's everything I remember from my summers here—busy, loud, and smelly—and damn, does it feel like home.

"There she is," my dad calls just as we step foot inside.

He scoots off a stool he's got propped under a cow, grabs a towel from the milking rack, and wipes his hands, all before wrapping me in a hug.

Then, it's a quick, firm handshake with Fin and Kai, and finally a very strange look for Lou.

"I'll be damned. You weren't kidding," my dad says, turning that look on me.

"Why would I kid?" I tease back.

My dad just shakes his head, then returns to the cow he abandoned in the stanchion and drops back onto the stool.

"Is that it?" Fin asks, barely a whisper in my ear.

I glance up at him. "What else were you expecting?"

"I don't know," he says, dropping his voice even lower. "I know I've talked with your dad over the phone and all, but this is the first time in person. No grilling? No shotgun threats? No *you touch my daughter and I'll turn you into a scarecrow?*"

"Where do you get this very misguided perception of Midwest farm life?" I tease back, wedging an elbow in his ribs.

Fin's expression just flattens, and I pat him lovingly before skipping to the next stall over and grabbing a stool under another cow who's already secured in her stanchion.

"Hey, city boy," my dad calls over his shoulder. "Your cow's on the end. Get to it, will ya?"

"Wait, Millie," Fin tries, but I'm already shooing him toward his animal.

"Kai," my dad goes on, not even looking his direction as he scoots closer to his cow, "there's a couple guys I want you to meet. They're wrangling cows at the other end of the barn. You can't miss 'em."

"Yes, sir," Kai says, his single dimple puckering.

"And leave the dog, will ya?"

"Yes, sir," Kai repeats, and then he's off, jogging across the barn.

"Dad, Lou's kind of a handful," I warn, but my dad just shakes his head and reaches for his cow's udder, wrapping his thumb and forefinger first.

"Nonsense. Lou, lay down."

I start to laugh at the completely absurd idea this eighty-pound, painting-eating, dognap-surviving dog will even *think* about obeying a near-stranger when he does exactly that. Lou whines a little as Kai disappears but then licks his chops and slumps down on his belly.

"How did you—"

"I don't hear a lot of milking," my dad says, and he tosses me a sideways glance.

I just smirk back at him, grab a rag to clean my cow's udder, place my bucket, and then start squeezing. I'm pretty sure I hear Fin practically whimper next to me as he shrugs off his very nice, brand-new coat and delicately places it on the rack, but he plays along. He grabs his own stool, crouches down, and then promptly exhales loud enough to blow his cow over.

"Better," my dad mutters, working into a rhythm. "Now, why don't you two explain all of this to me again."

"Explain what?" I say, and my dad only squeezes his fists harder.

"Start with the reason you're hauling your ex-boyfriend's dog across the entire country."

"Oh, that," I say sheepishly, glancing toward Fin.

He might as well be on another planet. The poor guy is hunched over in front of his cow, a wet rag in one hand and silver pail in the other.

"Fin, the rag's to clean her, the bucket's to catch the milk."

"I get that, but..."

"But what?"

"I mean, this is kind of *personal*," he says, grimacing. "I feel like the least I can do is get her name first before I go tugging on all...*that*."

"Oh, is that right?" I say with a laugh.

"Hey, I'm trying to be a better person here."

"Check her tag," I concede, nodding toward the yellow plastic clipped to her ear.

Fin flips it up, then eyes me, horrified.

"She doesn't even have a real name?"

"Ninety-eight is a real name," my dad huffs from the next stall over. "Now grab the girl's teats and start squeezing."

"Oh god, Dad—"

"Um, sir—"

"She's gonna dry up at this rate," my dad bellows, and by now his bucket is about two-thirds full.

"Start with two fingers," I finally say, half on a laugh, as I peer around the stall to watch Fin. "Thumb and forefinger at the very top of the teat. You want to almost pinch it."

"And then what?" Fin huffs back, rubbing his hands up and down his jeans like he's terrified touching his cow will make her keel over.

"Then squeeze with the rest of your hand."

Fin eyes me again sideways but makes an attempt, rubbing his hands down his jeans one more time before finally grabbing the udder. He flexes his hand tentatively, pulling slightly.

"Squeeze, son," my dad bemoans. "Don't tug."

"This is mortifying," Fin says, mostly under his breath as his cheeks begin to flame.

I can't help but giggle and quickly scoot over to his stall to show him the proper technique. I wrap my fingers around his, pinching at the top and then squeezing firmly until a stream of milk sprays into the bucket.

"Gentle but firm," I say.

"I'm never going to live this down, will I?"

"You wanted some sort of initiation. Here it is."

Fin sighs again but manages a few successful pumps on his own, and I return to my cow.

"Now, Millicent," my dad goes on, emptying his pail into a larger bucket lined with straining mesh, "why in god's name do you still have this dog?"

"I don't *still* have him," I clarify. "We just picked him up a couple days ago."

"For what?"

"I volunteered to help out Steve, okay? Is that so bad?"

"Why?" my dad probes, and I glance sideways at Fin.

He's engrossed in his task, gently squirting short streams of milk into the bucket. I'm not sure I've ever seen him concentrate so hard.

"Steve's getting an award in D.C.," I explain.

"Another one?" my dad asks.

"Yes, another one. It's hosted by some National Law Enforcement Officers group. I guess they have a hand in a few academies out there and asked if he'd stay to teach a class on criminal conversion or something. And you know Steve—he couldn't say no, but he didn't want to spend the whole summer away from Lou either."

"So he asked you to bring him his dog?"

"He didn't ask outright," I admit. "It was more of a very long and awkward phone call where he posed the thought and then walked it back about a dozen times."

My dad breathes heavily through his nose, and I know it's because he's holding his tongue. Of all the people who adored Steve, my dad was not among them.

"Why couldn't his new girlfriend bring the dog?" he asks instead.

"We don't want to get into that."

It wasn't long post-drug bust that Seph discovered she was miraculously cured of her "allergy" to short-haired, large-breed dogs, but Steve still makes every effort to keep the peace between them. She's come a long way, to be fair, and has even ventured to take Lou to the dog park a few times, though Hannah and I always seem to get a last-minute invite on those days.

We don't mind that much.

"Besides, she's already in D.C. with him, schmoozing some canned-wine company," I finish.

"Canned wine?" my dad repeats, and he goes so far as to stop milking his cow so he can swing his head my direction and grimace at me.

"Hey, this looks pretty good, doesn't it?" Fin speaks up suddenly, squeezing his cow's udder one more time.

I peer into his bucket, where an inch of milk is puddled in the bottom, and then glance at mine, which is half-full, and my dad's, who is two-thirds through his second bucket.

"You're doing a great job," I say, beaming at him. "Maybe you want to stay here and work with Kai for a bit?"

"Wait. I mean, I'm not that good," Fin says, a silent, terrified plea.

"You've got nothing to worry about, son," my dad says, spinning forward on his stool once more and emptying his cow's udder.

I just roll my eyes and resume my work.

"Anyway, since we were already planning to bring Kai out here for the summer, it just made sense we bring Lou along with us."

Lou perks up at the sound of his name but doesn't make an effort to bolt. My dad gives him a quick look, one that seems to praise him for being a good boy, and Lou proudly huffs and lays his chin back down on the straw-covered barn floor.

"Kai seems like a good kid," my dad says.

"He is. I wish he could have found a job back home, but even with an expunged record, he was having a hard time. Fin thought it'd be good to get him out of the city for a bit, get him into something stable so he can come back with a clear head."

"We'll keep him busy for the summer."

"I appreciate it, Dad. I know it's a lot to ask, but—"

"Are you kidding?" He turns to face me. "I can't milk all these cows by myself."

"Still only managing eight an hour?" I tease.

"It looks like you're down to about four."

"I'm out of practice here."

"I see that," he says, though his smile is there, barely visible under his days-old stubble. He pushes up from his stool and grabs the pails he's filled. "I'm gonna go check on the kid. And, hey, your guy's not doing half bad...for a painter."

"Told you he'd come through."

"You best get him out of here before he chaps those hands."

"Dad, we're fine. He's fine. We're here to help. Right, Fin?"

I turn to look at Fin, who's frowning intently as he counts each squeeze. He doesn't seem to hear a word we're saying.

"Get out of here for a bit. It'll take a couple of hours at least to show the kid around."

"Dad, honestly—"

"And leave Lou."

"What are we supposed to do without Lou?" I ask, retrieving my full bucket and rising to my feet.

My dad tosses me one of his famously skeptical looks. "I think you'll figure it out."

He lets out a short whistle, to which Lou responds immediately. He bounds to his feet and trots to my dad's side just as my dad rounds the stanchions and heads deeper into the barn, sparing neither me nor Fin another look.

"Fin, did you see that?"

"I did it!" he exclaims proudly, leaning back on his stool and slapping his hands to his knees. "Did you see this? I did it. I milked a cow."

I step into his stall, peer into the bucket, which has a foamy layer of cream atop about four inches of milk, and then smile at Fin. I don't show him my bucket, and I'm glad my dad took both of his. I stoop down, grab the pail, and set his next to mine before swiping up Fin's coat.

"Lou's gone."

"What?" Fin blurts, and suddenly he's back on planet Earth. "What do you mean? Where is he? What happened?"

I toss Fin his coat, a short laugh slipping out. "Relax. He went with my dad. I just never thought I'd see the day he'd so easily abandon us."

"He really abandoned us?"

"Walked away without a peep."

Fin shakes his head and gets to his feet, tucking his coat under his arm. "I guess he never really was ours to begin with, was he?"

I shrug. "It was kind of nice while it lasted, though."

In another second, Fin has his arms wrapped around me, pulling me into a hug I didn't know I needed. It's not like I won't see Lou in a few hours at dinnertime or miss him on the remaining sixteen hours of our very long road trip, but it is strange knowing there's an official ending to our time together.

"Come on," Fin says into my ear, and then he drops a hand and laces his fingers with mine. "I've got something I want to show you."

I stumble over a few tangled-up replies as he tugs me out of the milking parlor and back toward the car before I finally manage something halfway coherent.

"How? What could you possibly show me in *my* hometown?"

"I've never had a problem coming up with new places to show you before now."

I scrunch up my nose at him as he looks back at me with a smirk.

"Well, I do think you'll be hard-pressed to find a place I haven't been before."

"I'll take my chances."

"Just tell me where we're going."

"Just humor me, will you?"

I consider doing the exact opposite, even going so far as to cross my arms in protest, but he takes the dissent as invitation and smacks me with a kiss instead. It's short, sweet, a hint of that sawdust smell on his skin, and I might as well be putty in his hands.

When he opens the door, I slide in, sitting on a couple empty gummy worm packages and crumpling up a few peanut butter cup wrappers. Meanwhile, Fin starts the engine, cranks one of my The Cure-inspired playlists we've been listening to, and then steers us down my dad's driveway and toward town.

It's about a ten-minute drive to the main drag, which boasts hardly four stoplights—one of which is really just a blinking red light that's only moderately successful in encouraging drivers to yield.

It's nothing like Capitola Beach, certainly incomparable to San Francisco, but it's not an unhewn or desolate place either. In fact, it's a little like that lone painting Fin and I admired in the Pecora gallery: antiquated buildings with paint that seems to crackle under incessant sunlight, austere residents loitering in doorways that are almost fluid in their arches, birds hopping between trash cans like dainty fingers playing connect-the-dots.

It's authentic, however raw and unpolished.

That painting—the one that depicted the pier in its original state—isn't there anymore. The whole gallery was shut down amid the DeLobo scandal, but we did rediscover the piece a few weeks later posted up in the nearby Museum of Modern Art.

It shares a space with work completed by local artists—people who grew up in and around the boardwalk, Bay-area natives who knew what the city looked like in another life, even someone who managed to reimagine a recognizable dim sum restaurant, giving its black-door-on-a-blacker-wall look a refreshing pop of color.

"Have you been here before?" Fin asks suddenly.

He's parked in an old lot with hardly a handful of spaces, most of them overrun with weeds.

"Have I been where?"

"Here," Fin repeats, nodding toward a nearby brick building.

It takes only a second for me to recognize the sun-faded sign on the wall.

"How did you—"

"The internet," Fins says dryly. "Again, there's a whole lot more to it than you think."

I ignore the jab. "What are we doing here? We can't go in there."

"Why not?"

I stutter, blinking a few times as I whip my head between the building and Fin's just-as-stony face.

"If we go into that place, we're not coming out just us."

"Isn't that the point?"

"Fin, I don't think you understand. This is what happened before—" I stop short. "I don't know if I can do this."

"You've done things much harder than this. I mean, you scrutinize spreadsheets all day long and do all your math on the oldest calculator in existence."

"It's hardly *old*."

"It's got a damn spool and prints exclusively in that ridiculous typewriter font."

"Well, I don't think—"

"Come on," he says, and that smile finally crests. It's enough to send a tingle deep into my belly, and I have to swallow another breath to still it.

Fin exits the car, rounds to my side, and then practically drags me out, his fingers laced in mine again as he brings me well within his control. I'd love it, if not for the fact that I know he's leading me into a deed I'm not sure I'll ever be able to undo.

"It's okay to make an uncalculated decision every once in a while," Fin says somberly.

"This isn't just uncalculated. This is a commitment. This is a lifelong thing."

"Are you saying you don't want to do it?"

I let out a short breath as I glance toward the front door of the building. I can't see anything inside, though I don't need to. I know what's behind those doors. I know why we're here.

I turn back toward Fin. That smile is still there, still teasing the corners of his lips, and I have to catch my breath like I'm still that girl on the beach watching him watch the sunset. I knew from the first time I saw that look, I wanted to see it over and over again. I wanted to be the reason for it. And I still do.

"I'm all in," Fin goes on. "I'm all in if you are."

"Fin..."

"You know, it's going to be a really awkward drive home if you say no and we've got nothing but your podcasts and fairy music to keep us company."

"I told you we can listen to your punk rock playlist," I say with a bite, but Fin just smirks.

His arms are around me now, and he's somehow pulled me closer.

"Tell me you're all in."

I consider it, weave my arms around his waist to eliminate that last inch of distance between us, and then beam up at him.

"I'm all *Fin*."

The loudest, longest groan rumbles from his throat, and he practically suffocates me in his grip. I think it's equal parts exasperation and consuming affection, and it's strangely similar to the pounce of an eager puppy. After a sloppy kiss—one that'd rival even Lou's smooch—Fin pulls away and strides toward the building.

I read the sign one last time as I follow Fin inside and know we'll never be the same again. We'll never be the same *after* this.

"Welcome to The Humane Society," a woman says as we enter. "What brings you in?"

THE END

A Note of Thanks

Dear Reader,

A heartfelt thank you for being a crucial part of my debut as an author. Your early support and valuable feedback has made the release of *Me Before Lou* unforgettable. I wouldn't be here without you!

Reviews and recommendations are the lifeblood of independent publishing and the best way for readers like you to find my stories. If you're able, please consider leaving a review on Amazon, Goodreads, or the retailer where you found Lou and share what you think. You can also tag @RenditionPublishing or @JessWritesAtRendition on social media; we love to see and share your posts!

Cheers to our shared love for stories, and can't wait to share what's next!

Gratefully,
Jess Torres

About the Author

Jess Torres is one-half of Rendition Publishing, writing the stories you see here and handling the marketing side of the business. She works alongside her husband, Drew, who helps develop the plotlines, names half the characters, and writes music for all the heroes.

The couple live with their daughter and a whole furry crew in the beautiful Pacific Northwest, where they spend rainy days plotting elaborate connections between the overlapping universes of their romantic comedies and dramedies.

Keep up with the author at
jesstorres.carrd.co

Join the Readers Club for exclusive news, updates, and freebies at
rendition.eo.page/readersclub

Follow @RenditionPublishing and @JessWritesAtRendition on
TikTok and Instagram

Also By

A Standalone Romantic Comedy
Coming Soon by Jess Torres

Movie, She Wrote

A Spinoff Romantic-Drama Series
Coming Soon by Alter-Ego Morgan Towers

Times We Had
Vows We Made
Rules We Kept
Truths We Told

Visit jesstorres.carrd.co for more!

Made in the USA
Columbia, SC
04 June 2024